I0788565

VAMPIRO TRILOGY
VOLUME III
BROTHERHOOD OF THE BAT

Don W. Hill, M.D. and Tom Cavaretta

ISBN 978-1-969268-07-6 (paperback)
ISBN 978-1-969268-08-3 (hardcover)
ISBN 978-1-969268-06-9 (digital)

This is a work of fiction. All of the characters, names, incidents, organizations, and dialogue in this novel are either the product of the author's imagination or are used fictitiously.

Scriptures marked KJV are taken from the KING JAMES VERSION (KJV): KING JAMES VERSION, public domain.

Printed in the United States of America

To My Late Co-Author

THOMAS CAVARETTA (June 24, 1960-March 23, 2020). Well, Tom, you sure had a hell of a lot of nerve to kick the bucket before we completed the VAMPIRO TRILOGY! At least I'm grateful that you were able to get some of the research finished before your untimely demise. Thanks for looking down upon me and giving me the spiritual inspiration I needed to complete this crazy-ass work of fiction. I promise you that on behalf of your widow, Marcy, and your two boys, Nick the Shiv, and Joey the Bull, I'll honor my contract with you. After all, we shook hands on it, and a man's word is a man's bond. Enjoy your eternal reward, Tom. You'll truly be missed down here.

—DWH

To the Actress, Tashia Gates

With this dedication, the title of "The World's Best Surrogate Daughter" has been officially bestowed upon you. A million thanks for lending your considerable talent to convert my entire catalog of crazy fiction into a most enjoyable audio format!

—DWH

CONTENTS

INTRODUCTION

Writing a novel is a difficult task. Writing a trilogy, even with extensive creative input from a co-author, is actually a more daunting challenge as great care must be taken to maintain fidelity to the story line and its complex subplots. However, writing a trilogy when the co-author on the project actually dies before the third volume has been initiated is a scenario that could have potentially crashed an entire planned endeavor directly into a brick wall.

As for many, the year 2020 will not be missed. As a consequence to the COVID-19 pandemic, the United States in many ways has been left broke as well as broken. Yes, 2020 was indeed a bad year, and one that I'd like to permanently erase from my memory.

While working in my backyard at my home in Arizona this past January, I was wearing an old pair of work shoes about as supple as splintered plywood. I developed a nasty blister on the dorsum of my left foot over the metatarsal-phalangeal joint of the second toe after being impaled by a rather nasty, sharp barb from a Mexican fan palm frond that pierced the top of my shoe. Within three days, I was in the hospital fighting for my life.

I had acquired a flesh eating staph infection, and the blister on my left foot had rotted down to the bone. When bacteria had entered my bloodstream, I developed septic hypotension in conjunction with acute renal failure and hepatic insufficiency. I even had a transient episode of blindness that I found to be particularly annoying.

I was not surprised when my doctors told me that I was looking at a 50% chance of mortality on that specific hospital admission.

After the second toe of my left foot ended up in a jar of formalin (in conjunction with weeks of antibiotic therapy), I had finally rallied.

A major disappointment to me was that the pathology department refused to return my amputated body part. You see, I had ultimate designs to utilize the toe as bait on a deep-sea fishing trip, but I digress...

At the time of my illness, I received a telephone call from my co-author, Tom Cavaretta, who told me in no uncertain terms that I did *not* have his permission to die until we had completed the third volume of the Vampiro trilogy. That was a tall order indeed, but I complied nonetheless.

Life is filled with irony. Although I recovered from my illness, a month later, Tom suffered from a sudden death event just when we began to work in earnest on Volume III of this project. It was tough to get back on track after Tom had passed away, but it was a job that had to get done.

After wallowing about for the better part of half a year, I finally put my nose to the proverbial grindstone and completed the trilogy on December 7, 2020. I'd like to think that I received celestial inspiration from my late co-author, as some of the outlandish events portrayed in this zany work of fiction surely could not have come from my own addled intellect! Therefore, I'd like to thank my late co-author for his inspiration in finishing this trilogy once and for all.

At this juncture before any individual tackles this tome of horror, humor, and science fiction, I'd like to simply reiterate what Tom Cavaretta would often say to our readers: "Enjoy the bite!"

—DWH

1

AN URN OF EARTHLY REMAINS

"Tell me, Dr. Marshall," Parker Coxswain asked as he passed a cup of hot coffee to the young woman who was sitting directly across from him at the research conference table, "What exactly do you know about, well-human vampirism?"

"Vampires? No doubt an interesting subject matter, I suppose," Dr. Marshall casually commented with feigned indifference.

"Your late brother, Booker, and his entire research team for that matter, were actually deeply entrenched in the subject matter before his premature demise from an acute sickle cell crisis," Parker elaborated.

"Is it safe to assume that you were a member of his research team?"

"I was, indeed," Parker answered with a nod.

"Who else did Booker work with here at this university?"

"The only other permanent member of the core unit was the hematology/oncology fellow, Dr. J.D. Brewster, whom I believe you had briefly spoken to on the telephone before your trip out here to Santa Fe. However, only Book and yours truly had a dual MD/ PhD degree. Needless to say, there was a bevy of other research associates that had rendered assistance to help us sort out a most peculiar clinical problem that we encountered which concerned a specific hospitalized individual here. The list of experts covered a venerable cornucopia of medical specialties." Parker said.

"Such as?"

"We're talking pathologists, an infectious disease specialist, an entire internal medicine team headed up by a tenured professor named Dr. Horatio Cloud, multiple diagnostic radiologists, a nephrologist, a mammalian research physiologist, and the like," Parker Coxswain further elaborated.

"Impressive credentials one and all, no doubt," the visitor correctly noted.

"I must admit however, that we even got some invaluable technical intervention from the nuclear medicine department, which frankly is comprised of a group of abrasive individuals not known to be particularly cooperative with others," Dr. Coxswain expounded with a wry smile.

"Sounds like you were engaged in some pretty serious business before Booker died," the woman opined. "Is there anybody currently hospitalized with a presumed case of human vampirism at this facility? If that's the case, I'll humbly request an opportunity to carefully evaluate an actual living specimen, uh—I mean a living patient afflicted with this reportedly rare disease process."

"Not here, nor anywhere else for the time being as far as I know. It would certainly be helpful for our future research endeavors if we stumbled upon another case sooner than later, however. Tell me something," Parker Coxswain asked, "Did the dearly departed Brother Booker ever have a chance to tell you in any details about what we encountered out here before he passed away, Dr. Marshall?"

"You don't have to call me Dr. Marshall. Please feel free to call me Birdy," the visitor interjected after a moment of diversionary hesitation. "The first name given to me by my parents when I was born was actually 'Bertha', but I hated my name so much that I actually had it legally changed when I turned twenty-one years of age about a decade ago."

"Do tell."

"Well, I was tormented when I was a youngster. The kids that I went to school with called me 'Big Bertha', as if I was a corpulent, peg-legged, junkie hooker from Oakland, or maybe a gargantuan World War I artillery siege weapon," she explained with a sardonic grin. "When I was an adolescent, I developed anorexia and I lost a ton of adipose weight, but that actually didn't matter one lick to my group of so-called peers. I obviously had issues of perpetual low self-esteem as a consequence to my tortured circumstances. To my brutally cruel and insensitive classmates, I would always be known as 'Big Bertha', no matter what I did, or how I looked, or how much weight I had lost. I suspect a bit of permanent psychological trauma was inflicted upon me along the way. Nice, eh?"

"Terrible!" Dr. Coxswain exclaimed as he stifled a rather unsympathetic chuckle.

"However, when I was at the end of my high school career, I donned a new persona. I insisted on being called, Birdy," the woman answered in a rather obvious attempt to skirt Dr. Coxswain's original and rather pertinent questions.

"What's the matter with the name, Bertha?" Dr. Coxswain pressed. "When you left home for college, I'm a bit surprised you weren't able to leave all of that adolescent angst and teenage distemper in the rear view mirror."

"One would think," Birdy answered with a sigh, "but that was simply not the case."

"Frankly, I like the moniker that was originally bestowed upon you," Dr. Coxswain said with what turned out to be a rather ineffectual attempt at re-assurance. "It's a name that sounds, I don't know—*substantial* somehow, I suppose."

"Well, Dr. Coxswain, you hit the nail on the head," Birdy answered. "A girl's name should *not* be 'substantial', as you have just professed. A girl's name should be light and airy, much like an ascending arpeggio in a comedic operetta."

"Formality is superfluous," the research scientist stated. "Call me Parker. How on earth did you find your way here? J.D. Brewster and I knew that Book had a sister as he had shown us your picture once before. Now, maybe at one time in the remote past, your brother had told us your name during some light-hearted banter over a cold beer and a platter of nachos at a local watering hole. If that was the case however, Brewster nor I could remember that specific detail at the time that Booker had passed away. When your brother died, we were literally in shock. The collective members of the research department were actually at a loss as to how to get in touch with any of Booker's kin to let them know what calamity had befallen him."

"Did you not bother to check with the medical staff office?" Birdy asked. "They surely must have known something, anything."

"Went down that road," Parker answered defensively. "The only thing that the administration at this university had on file about your brother was that he was a black male, he was unmarried, and that his parents were deceased. No 'contact number' was listed in his personnel file in the case Booker had developed a medical emergency. In my opinion, that was a pretty lousy job that the Santa Fe College of Medicine had done regarding data management."

"You won't get any argument from me about that," Birdy said with a tinge of anger in her voice. "It shouldn't have taken weeks to have let me know that Booker had passed away. We both had busy lives and didn't talk to each other very frequently, so it wasn't uncommon for us to go a few months between chats on the phone."

"All the blame can't be cast upon the shoulders of the university. You see, by the same token, I must confess in a full and embarrassing self-disclosure that it was a pretty lousy job that Booker's alleged friends had done by not knowing a whole lot more about his personal life and who he truly was as a human being. Damn! For that, I'm terribly sorry."

"Ah, don't beat yourself up about it," Birdy said as she dismissively flipped her wrist towards Parker. "J.D. Brewster called the Gulf Coast College of Medicine in Houston where you three boys received your initial medical training. It took the Gulf Coast a while to dig up any meaningful information, but fortunately, they found a considerable amount of dope about my brother within an old file cabinet in a warehouse that contained the details of all the former students who had previously graduated from the program. In the end, that's how Brewster was able to get in touch with me to explain that Booker was,–was gone. I'm just sorry I found out that he had passed away long *after* his cremation."

"Can't blame you if you're steamed about the whole ordeal," Parker added.

"By the way, where's his urn of earthly remains?" Birdy asked. "I'll venture Booker would have planned to have his ashes dispersed somewhere back home in the Lone Star State."

"I certainly hope you don't find this to be, well,–macabre, but after the memorial service that the university held in Booker's honor, J.D. Brewster and I flipped a coin as to who would function in the capacity of a collegial curator with the expressed purpose of keeping tabs of his funerary urn," Parker explained. "Brewster won. To my knowledge, he's got the urn at his apartment where it's guarded day and night by Brewster's pet skunk, Monsieur Pepe."

"Is it safe there?" Birdy asked.

"Brewster's been known to smoke an occasional cigar, but he's recently assured me that he's been *very* careful in his fiduciary responsibility concerning said urn's welfare and of its sacred contents. He insists that it's rather unlikely that he's accidently flicked any cigar ash into Booker's urn. I believe that's indeed the case, at least up until now, assuming of course that Brewster has maintained a comportment of sobriety ever since Brother Booker was welcomed with open arms into a glorious afterlife, complete with angelic beings strumming upon harps of pure gold while singing Led Zeppelin's 'Stairway to Heaven'. If not however, all bets are off!"

Throwing her head back and laughing out loud, Birdy said, "I can see now why Booker viewed you two gentleman to be his best friends. Tell me something, Parker, were you there when Booker died? Tell me what happened."

"Yeah, I was there," Parker reluctantly answered. "In fact, the entire research team was present when Booker passed away. As I had intimated, before Booker had his terminal event, we were providing care for a gentleman who had been infected with human vampirism. I believed at the time that our team was on the threshold of some very important scientific discoveries. Our research had indicated that this peculiar disease is caused by a virus that in an odd way is somewhat similar to the feline leukemia virus. Be that as it may, there were just a few things that we needed to sort out about the nature of the illness before we could write up a report for a peer-reviewed journal. Sadly, that's when things got out of control. If we had just a bit more time, it's possible that we would have filled in the blanks. It appeared that the patient infected with this disease had a renal gradient where iron was lost right through the urinary tract and wasted in the urine."

"What help did my brother provide in sorting out this peculiar finding?" Birdy pressed.

"Booker had the idea that this peculiar virus has the ability to infect multiple organs in a synchronous fashion. Our clinical observations suggested the infection seems to cause some of the marrow stem cells to de-differentiate into pluripotent stem cells, and that would account for an extraordinary ability for tissue regeneration in patients harboring the virus. J.D. Brewster actually found electron microscopic evidence of virus infection in the bone marrow, and the last bit of evidence that we needed was proving a direct viral infection in the renal parenchyma. The other thing that Booker had an idea about was that individuals infected with the virus that causes human vampirism would be physically repulsed by people afflicted with sickle cell disease," Parker added.

"Is that important in any way?" Birdy asked.

"Well, perhaps it could act as a systemic defensive mechanism for an individual afflicted with sickle cell in the unlikely event that he or she ever encountered a human vampire," Parker speculated. "Regarding the particular unpleasant topic of disorders of human hemoglobin, Booker had full-blown sickle cell disease. I assume that you've been screened for the same inherited illness somewhere along the way?"

"As you might gather, sickle cell disease is the curse of being black, I suppose. I have one genetic allele. That means, as you probably already understand, that I have the *trait*, but not the full-blown *disease*," Birdy explained.

"Be that as it may," Parker continued, "we never got to the finish line with our clinical research because that's when a security breech occurred at the University Hospital and everything went to hell in a hand basket."

"Please fill me in," Birdy petitioned. "I certainly witnessed the effective amount of security that was on hand when I first entered this facility."

"Frankly," Parker explained, "the current upgraded security is a direct consequence to what happened that triggered Booker's terminal sickle cell crisis."

"It makes no sense to me that this would ever be an unsafe environment at any time or under any circumstance," Birdy observed.

"It would be unethical for me to tell you the name of the patient who had been infected with the virus responsible for human vampirism, and I am not exactly clear on all of the parties that were involved with the catastrophe that occurred on that fateful day, but the patient was clearly targeted to be kidnapped by what was presumably a secret bioweapon division of the United States government. A research team from the CDC was also on hand, as they had their own designs on the patient in question," Parker stated.

"What are you telling me?" Birdy asked. "Did a confrontation ensue?"

"That, my dear lady, is an understatement. To be frank, it was a shit storm rated at a 'category five' on the hurricane scale, and your brother, Booker, was caught in the middle of it. In addition, there were other nefarious characters appearing on the scene who inexplicably, for one reason or another, apparently had a personal score to settle with the patient in question. At one point, Booker was actually held as a captive by one of the combatants."

"At the point of a gun?"

"No!" Parker exclaimed. "It was more like at the point of a *fang*! When the dust settled, the patient's room was a disaster zone complete with empty shell casings on the ground, a blown out hospital window, a missing patient, and your brother supine on the floor and gasping for air as a consequence to an acute exacerbation of his underlying sickle cell disease. It was is if a ton of bricks had fallen upon him as a result of all of the violence that had occurred in the patient's room."

"Did you provide medical care for Booker when he got sick?"

"No," Parker answered, "Booker was admitted to the intensive care unit, and his case was managed by the internal medicine and hematology/oncology service. As I had mentioned, J.D. Brewster is a hematology/oncology fellow here, and I know that he was directly involved with your brother's case at the time that he had passed away. When you pick up the urn from Brewster later on today, you can ask him for specific details about what went down from his perspective. I've already given Brewster a call and he was excited to have an opportunity to meet with you face-to-face. Let's keep track of the time so you do not miss the opportunity to meet with Brewster and have an in-depth conversation with him when you go to pick up your brother's urn."

"I plan on doing just that," Birdy noted. "I see why my brother got *sick* but can you tell me why he *died*?"

"The stress from what Booker went through caused his red cells to sickle like mad. This blocked blood supply to his brain, heart, eyes, and kidneys. Despite oxygen therapy, aggressive intravenous hydration, and even subsequent exchange transfusion attempts, Booker died from multi-organ failure within just a few days. I was hoping that Booker would slip into a peaceful coma at the time that he had passed away, but that certainly was not the case. He was awake, lucid, and knew exactly what was going on during the entire process of his prolonged demise."

"He was awake at the time that he died?" Birdy asked. "Oh, my God! Square up with me, Parker. I need you to tell me something, and please be honest with me. Did my brother suffer?"

"Don't do this to me, Birdy," Parker replied. "Don't do this to yourself. What difference does that make at this time? Booker's gone. Why do you want to know this?"

"Because I don't *want* to know this, I *need* to know this, damn it! There's a difference!" Birdy was insistent. "Tell me. Did he have a painful death?"

Parker Coxswain paused for moment to collect his thoughts. If Parker was the only person that Birdy was going to talk to that day, he would have lied through his teeth. It would have been a perfect opportunity for him to sugar coat the events surrounding the death of her brother. Unfortunately, Parker knew all too well that Birdy would not conclude her visit to the St. Francis College of Medicine, or depart from the city of Santa Fe for that matter, without first picking up her brother's urn and having a frank conversation with Dr. J.D. Brewster.

Brewster was a man with a reputation for being brutally honest with his patients. Was that characterization an attribute or was it a flaw in his innate constitution? Parker knew that particular bivalent critique was entirely contingent upon the circumstances which readily varied from time to time and from patient to patient.

Nonetheless, when it came to patient care, Brewster was honest to a fault. If at this particular moment Parker tried to lie to Birdy Marshall, an ingenuous declaration would no doubt come back to bite him on the ankle, or perhaps his ass!

"It was fucking horrible," Parker blurted out. "Booker died in agony. To this day I'm still haunted by what I had witnessed. There. Is that what you wanted to hear?"

After weeping inconsolably for several moments, Birdy composed herself and dabbed at her eyes with a tissue that she had taken from her purse. Thank you for your honesty, Parker. I know I would have found out the details one way or another if you hadn't told me the truth just now."

Once Birdy had composed herself, Parker thought the best course of action would be to segue to a lighter topic. "Forgive my manners, Birdy, but I never asked if you specifically followed Booker's path at the Gulf Coast. What field of medicine do you practice?"

"What?" Birdy asked before coming quickly to the realization that Dr. Parker Coxswain really had no idea as to who she was or what she did for a living. "I'm not *that* kind of doctor, Parker. I have a PhD in a non-medical discipline, not an MD degree. In fact, I'm an associate professor at the Prairie Baptist University in Houston."

"What's your discipline?"

"I'm an archaeologist!" Birdy crowed with considerable pride. "I dig around in the dirt and look for dead bones. I couldn't imagine being the kind of doctor that actually took care of living and breathing human beings. I'm more comfortable amongst the remains of the dead. *Long* dead, in fact. I hope you don't find that too weird. I'm just being honest with you."

"Honesty is the best policy," Parker said decisively.

"Maybe not always," Birdy noted after she learned the devastating truth that Parker had just spewed forth about her brother's ghastly demise. "Nonetheless, I need you to be honest with me one more time. A while back, my brother told me that one of his research colleagues had seen my picture and wanted to go out on a date with me specifically because I was a *black* woman. Would that person happen to be you?"

"Guilty as charged!" Parker blushed. "Well, I wouldn't have wanted to go on a date with you if you were, well,–a black *man*. I can assure you that!"

Birdy laughed as she squeezed Parker's shoulder. "You're crazy!"

"Well, maybe I am," Parker said. "Nonetheless, I'd be honored if you had dinner with me before you head back to Texas. I assume you'll be leaving New Mexico as soon as you have a chance to meet Dr. J.D. Brewster and pick up the urn that contains your brother's earthly remains."

"Well, if the truth be told, I'm actually going to be staying out here in New Mexico for just a bit longer," Birdy clarified. "I'm incorporating an expeditionary field trip on my current foray into this peculiar 'Land of Enchantment', which as best I can tell, is an over-hyped misnomer."

"Business to attend to?"

"Precisely. There's an archaeologist from Northern New Mexico Tech that I'll be meeting here tomorrow afternoon. As a courtesy to me, he'll be driving down here to pick me up from Taos. He's a member of the Navajo tribe, and his name is Dr. Zachary Hawk. From Santa Fe, we'll be heading out to the Four Corners area to visit Chaco Canyon in the Northwest part of the state. While up there, we'll try and get some legitimate work done during the short time that has been allotted to me before I head back to Houston. I'm happy to report that Dr. Hawk already has in his possession a dig permit from the state that's worth its weight in gold!"

"Research project of some sort?"

"You could say that. I have a theory about human predation and human sacrifices that occurred out there in the desert during pre-Columbian times," Birdy explained.

"Sounds terrifying," Parker conjectured. "I assume you're referring to human cannibalism. Are you implying structured ritualistic ceremonial events, or cannibalism committed with the explicit intent to ingest a readily available and adjacent food source, such as a fellow human being? An act of *depredation* during a time of *deprivation*, perhaps?"

"Both! You appear to be a rather clever architect within the realm of the English language, Parker."

"Thanks!" Parker replied. "I have my moments."

"Well," Birdy elaborated, "as it turns out, Dr. Hawk took rather harsh exception with my recent publication about what I believe is evidence of that very distasteful subject matter. You see, I found corroborating items that gave substantial credence to the plausibility of my theory amongst artifacts harvested on a prior dig in the Four Corners from last year."

"Such as?"

"Come on the dig with us, Parker, and you can see any new evidence that we find with your own eyes!" Birdy suggested. "I'll officially declare that you're now my new medical/anatomical liaison officer. Besides, you could be a good buffer in light of the sparks that will most likely fly between yours truly and Dr. Zachary Hawk."

"I'm not sure if I meet the criteria to be a good body guard on your behalf."

"Trust me. You'll fit the bill rather nicely. Hawk refuses to believe that his ancestors could have been capable of such brutish behavior," Birdy said. "He wrote me a hostile letter stating that my theory was racially prejudicial. Dr. Hawk said he would expect nothing less from, and I quote, 'a woman of European ancestry who obviously has a hostile agenda to purposefully portray the Native Americans in such a degrading and uncomplimentary light.' Ha! Can you believe that?"

"Wait till he gets a load of attitude from you!" Parker laughed.

"As he's never met me before, allow him to behold in awe this feisty black woman who now stands before you! I'm fired up, I tell you!" Birdy extended an index finger and playfully poked Parker Coxswain on the tip of his nose. "You best take me out to a nice place for dinner tonight, dear sir. I want to be wined and dined! I'll get all shined up like a new penny for the occasion. Get the picture?"

"You're on!" Parker promised.

"My offer for you to go out on an archaeological dig with me was on the square, Parker," Birdy reiterated with a tinge of hope in her voice.

"I'll give it serious consideration," Parker said. "Let's see if you'll still feel the same about that field trip invitation you've offered me after our dinner date. Perhaps you'll find me to be little more than an unsophisticated bumpkin!"

"That I doubt," Birdy replied with a flirtatious laugh.

"If the truth be told," Parker said, "I don't want to rub Dr. Hawk the wrong way when I meet him. I guess what I don't get is why this archaeology professor got all worked up about your theory concerning the remote possibility of human predation and religious sacrifices that may have occurred in the desert centuries ago, especially since he's never even met you face to face."

"It must be more than just professional jealousy, I suppose," Birdy said with a shrug. "You should know as well as I do by now that human beings are tribal by nature. Except for wealthy, white, self-loathing, anti-American, leftist progressives, most people are rightfully proud of their own race and ethnic heritage. It would seem to me that Dr. Hawk had a visceral reactionary response to my scientific treatise for that reason, and likely that reason alone."

"Barking up the wrong tree if you ask me," Parker responded. "How could your theory, if indeed it turns out to be true, possibly reflect badly on his tribal nation of the Navajo in this modern day and age? After all, we've *all* come from a long line of savages as best I can tell. Have we not?"

"If you find plausibility in the evolutionary theory, our human ancestors climbed down from trees and out from caves as best I know. Nothing to be ashamed of. Just how it is."

"You'll get no argument from me," Parker said.

"Well, my published theory about ancient human predation in the deserts of the Southwest is perhaps a tiny bit more complex than what I've told you thus far," Birdy confessed.

"Could you elaborate?"

"First, allow me to amend my last proclamation. To be frank, my published theory about ancient human predation in the deserts of the Southwest is actually a *whole* lot more complex than what I've told you thus far."

"You have a captive audience before you, Dr. Marshall," Parker said with considerable intrigue. "You have my undivided attention!"

"You asked me a question when I first walked into this conference room, Dr. Coxswain, and it's time for me to give you an honest answer," Birdy Marshall said as she pulled closer to the man who was about to take her out on a romantic dinner date. As she took one last swallow from her cup of coffee, she opened the proverbial poke and a black cat jumped out of the mysterious bag of secrets.

"You've confided in me, so I'm obligated to respond in kind. Quid pro quo, if you will. It's only fair. My turn, Parker! Let's postpone my scheduled meeting with J.D. Brewster for now. High time for me tell *you* what *I* know about human vampirism..."

⁕

Before Colonel Augustus Placard became a prisoner of war at the hands of a rather angry *bandito*, he was the successful team leader of a small group of commando killers. Commissioned by "Uncle Sam," Placard's heavily armed team would launch off on clandestine raids to wage lethal warfare amongst the shadows that encroached the seedy back streets found across the border in old Mexico. The ire of his commando team was aimed directly at the illicit drug and narcotics trade that flourished along the Rio Bravo. His four man team included two vampires who had been recruited into what was actually a top secret United States bioweapon military program.

After all, the United States was a shamefully flaccid, impotent, and effete nation that was totally incapable of weaning a rather large percentage of the American population away from a variety of vora-cious drug addictions. The accompanied consumption of copious amounts of illegal recreational substances flooding across the border could not be logistically curtailed by fiat. If that was indeed to be the case, the only apparent recourse was a direct interdiction against the financially endowed yet profoundly dangerous demonic source of this evil.

Perhaps that was the only option left at the time to stem the flow of these dangerous products that were destined to invariably fall into the welcoming arms, and then subsequently injected into the chronically phlebitic veins, of the addled *Americanos*. Unfortunately, the government had no idea at the time that it was waging a futile and interminable conflict that could never be won by *any* conceiv-able strategic method.

Nonetheless, Placard's unit of soldiers was vicious and without mercy. The colonel's team was able to effectively wipe out no less than two different drug cartels to nearly the last man in a sequen-tial fashion. The enemy included the Routa Gang who had previ-ously occupied the border territory in Mexico known as La Frontera, and also a notorious nation-wide cartel known as the Calle Vampiro organization.

Unfortunately, Placard was captured before his team pressed on with the final brutal battle that was to occur against the Calle Vampiro clan at their fortified compound on the outskirts of Guadalajara. It would turn out to be a bloody altercation that ultimately resulted in the literal extermination of nearly all of the members of the cartel, and also their family members including women and small children.

As the colonel was now kept chained to the floor inside a cage within a non-descript concrete block building in Durango, he was totally unaware of how things were going in the war on drugs that had been unofficially declared by the United States upon its Southern neighbors.

Placard had company however in his make-shift prison. His cell-mate was a rather stout Russian-born emergency room doctor named Ilya Putinov who everybody knew as "Russian Bear". While doing charitable work at a volunteer clinic in Mexico at the Gulf Coast town of Playa Caliente, the big man had been captured by the cartel with the expressed intent of forcing upon the doctor indentured servitude. Russian Bear was now a commodity who was expected to provide medical care for injured or sick cartel members.

The only way Colonel Placard or the Russian Bear hoped to learn anything about what was going on outside the confines of their holding cell was contingent upon whether or not Russian Bear would ever be brought out of the cage for the intended purpose of rendering medical services on behalf of a wounded or physically ill cartel member. There was a problem, however. Bear had been chained up for weeks and no patients were ever brought to him for medical management! Why was that the case? In light of these unexpected circumstances, Russian Bear and Colonel Placard were never allowed to leave their jail cell. As predicted, they were therefore deprived of fresh air, exercise, or even exposure to any sunshine for that matter.

Something rather peculiar indeed must have been going on at that time. Colonel Placard and the Russian Bear whispered amongst themselves about the oddity that no Calle Vampiro cartel members had ever been brought to the block house for the dispensation of the Russian doctor's medical care. This boredom and isolation afflicting the two prisoners was going on for what seemed to be an eternity.

Naturally, the reason why the Russian Bear's medical practice was no longer thriving was that almost the entire contingency of Calle Vampiro cartel members was now dead, save the block house guards named Llaves and his younger stooge known as, "The Cat Fucker."

The colonel and the doctor would have been elated if they had ever learned that the American bioweapon commando squad was successful in its last battle against the cartel. It turned out to be a definite win for Placard's team, but sadly it was a pyrrhic victory at best. Unbeknownst to Colonel Placard, one of the vampires on his team was killed in the line of duty. To add salt to that wound, the federal government ultimately pulled the plug on the bioweapon program purely on the grounds of political posturing and gamesmanship in Washington, D.C.

The block house guard, Llaves, eventually learned from a postal communiqué that his colleagues from the Calle Vampiro cartel were now dead, and he was sadly a man who was little more than a sole survivor on a desert island. It was a very precarious situation for him to be in, because the enormous void that had been left behind after the extermination of the Routa Gang and the Calle Vampiro cartel would no doubt be filled sooner than later.

It was only a matter of time before some other cartel entity, or perhaps an alternate iteration of an "import/export" narco-terrorist consortium would be knocking upon his door, more than eager to take advantage of a geo-political situation that was obviously in disarray. What was Llaves to do?

"Well, here we are again! It seems that this will be another fine day at the 'Chateau Block House' without any visitors," Bear said to his jail keeper. "El Tor said he'd keep me alive and I'd be busy as a physician when I was dragged away from the Calle Vampiro compound and dumped into this nasty shit hole. I know for certain that the compound was under attack when you brought me here in chains. As fate would have it, I'm growing old here and haven't seen one patient yet. What in hell happened back at the compound, Llaves? Did everybody from the Calle Vampiro cartel get killed off, or what?"

"Shut up, 'Dancing' Bear," Llaves said. "You *gringos* need to let me think for *un momento*."

"I know for a fact that we're running out of provisions," Bear added. "That slimy little cat humper that you sent into the city on a bicycle was supposedly on a mission to pick up some groceries for us. Well, he seems to have disappeared, has he not? Do you think he ran away? Maybe he got greased. No, wait–I'm wrong! I'll bet he's out there greasing up *un gato grande* for a little feline lovin'. What do you think, *cabrito*? In any event, I think it's highly unlikely that we'll ever see that punk-ass, demented low-life ever again."

"Shut up, Bear! I'm not going to tell you again. *El cojo gato* will eventually return. You won't starve." This time Llaves grabbed an aluminum baseball bat that was in the corner of the block house and he slammed it hard against the bars of the cage.

"Something's wrong, Llaves, and you know it! I can see it on your face," Placard added. Look–I've seen you try to make phone calls and you can never get anybody on the line. I've also seen you fire up the short wave without any success, either. We're all alone out here. That's a fact that's now painfully obvious. I also think that you know something must have happened to the cartel members back at your compound."

"*Verdad.* Something very bad did occur, Colonel," Llaves finally confessed. "Your team of killers was no doubt responsible for what must have happened out there."

"¿Qué pasa, amigo?"

"I'm not your friend, asshole. Don't ever make that mistake again," Llaves replied. "I received a letter this morning from the madam who ran our notorious Brothel *de los Niños.* Her name is Lucia Aragon. She told me a terrible story that several armed gunman showed up at the compound with automatic weapons and simply killed everybody there, including women and children. You wouldn't know anything about that, now would you, Colonel?"

Placard looked down and simply shrugged without offering a verbal reply.

"After that, the assassins burned the compound down to the ground! Madam Lucia Aragon is now hiding out with the Chihuahua cartel in Ciudad Camargo, but she's afraid that she'll be hunted down and killed sooner than later."

"How sad," Russian Bear said while he bit his lower lip. "I remember Madam Aragon from the time when I was a prisoner at the Calle Vampiro compound. She was always nice to me."

"What?!" Llaves asked. "Don't tell me that you're the kind of man who enjoys sexual favors from little children, now are you? If so, I'm just going to take my scatter gun and blow balls to kingdom come. That shouldn't reduce your value on the open market very much, I would guess. Hey! We could come up with a new name for your sorry ass. We could start calling you the 'Castrated Bear.' Like it?"

"You're a sick bastard, Llaves," Russian Bear answered. "How dare you accuse me of pedophilia?"

"Relax, Bear," Llaves said. "I just wanted to watch you dance around the prison cell like the circus animal that you truly are."

"What happened to the madam? How could she have possibly survived the assault on your cartel when everybody else was killed?" the Russian doctor asked.

"Apparently the only reason Lucia Aragon survived the attack on the compound was that she was captured by some hillbilly vampiro from Arkansas who took pity upon her."

"Joe Cephas Smoot!" The Colonel exclaimed. "He's a good lad. Sounds like something he would do."

"In any event, the hillbilly simply chased her away instead of putting a bullet in her head like his colleagues had done to everybody else who was there," Llaves explained as he buried his face in his hands in fear. "God! Everybody's dead…"

"So sad," Colonel Placard opined as he gave the Russian Bear an enthusiastic yet discreet "high-five," all the while Llaves was wallowing in a greasy stew of grief and guilt.

"Your sympathetic wishes are most appreciated," Llaves said in all sincerity, not recognizing sarcasm when it was right under his nose.

"Well, I guess there's only one thing left for you to do right about now," Placard said. "You should open up this cage and just let the Russian Bear and me escape from here. You don't have to worry about any pesky transportation issues, as I'm certain the Bear and I can find our own way back to the United States without any major difficulties. No hard feelings, buddy boy."

"Nice knowing you, Llaves. Wish you the best of luck," the Bear added with a caustic smirk. "Maybe I can drop you a postcard sometime. Don't forget to leave me your forwarding address once you get to Hell."

"Nobody's going anywhere," Llaves concluded as he was finally able to regain his composure. "As you're a physician, you'd still be a valuable commodity to another cartel, Dancing Bear. As for you Colonel Placard, you're obviously a brilliant military tactician. When the Calle Vampiro cartel first captured you, I told El Tor that he should've used you to help formulate a battle plan to annihilate our other surrounding competitors, but he sure as shit wouldn't listen to me, now would he? Well, if our compound fell to the gringo commandos, then so be it. I'm glad El Tor is dead and gone. He might have been my boss, but he was nonetheless *un idioto.*"

"So, what are you going to do with us?" Russian Bear asked. "Are you going to sell us off like a couple of slaves?"

"Rest assured, it'll be to the highest bidder."

"Bad idea," Placard said. "In fact, that's a downright terrible idea."

"If that's the case," Llaves said, "I'll just shoot the both of you now and be done with it."

⚜

"I can't tell you what a pleasure it was for me to have had an opportunity to meet with you, Dr. Brewster. Thank you for looking after the urn that contains my brother's ashes," Birdy Marshall said. "This trip has been cathartic for me in so many ways and on so many levels."

"I'm just glad it provided you with some emotional closure, I suppose," J.D. Brewster replied. "I find it rather astonishing however that you've invited Parker Coxswain on a field trip up to Chaco Canyon today to dig around for some old bones. I guess you guys must have really hit it off on your big dinner date last night, despite the fact that he's little more than an industrial-strength turd when you get down to the brass tacks. Any salacious romantic revelations? After all, I'm a voyeur at heart."

"Dr. Brewster?!" Birdy exclaimed with a blush. "A proper young lady would never kiss and tell. The same would hold true for a proper gentleman, I'll have you know."

"Who ever said that I was a proper gentleman? What's wrong, Birdy?" Brewster asked with a most mischievous grin. "Did I make you squirm just a bit?"

"Why, you most certainly did!"

"Good," Brewster said. "I can't help myself, I guess. I'm a prank prowler. I'm always on the look-out to tweak somebody just a bit. It must be an innate character flaw or perhaps a character attribute. I can't decide."

"Maybe both! Booker told me all about you," Birdy revealed. "He said of all the people that he had ever met in his entire life, that you were the one man who absolutely had the most perfectly suited surname."

"What—the name 'Brewster'? Well, maybe so if I'm purposefully going out of my way to brew up trouble amidst every conceivable situation that I find myself."

"Be that as it may," Birdy declared, "I had a most enjoyable time with Parker last night if you must know the truth. I had never been on a date before with somebody who was so, well—"

"What? *White*?!"

"Well, I was going to say the word 'crazy'," Birdy answered mildly annoyed, "However the word 'white' would also be an appropriate adjective at this juncture in the course of my life's events. I know that you and Booker were alumni from the Gulf Coast College of Medicine, but I don't suppose that you had any real chance to interact with him at all when you were both in Houston at around the same time."

"Quite true."

"How did it come to pass then that you ever met my brother or had a chance to work with him?"

"I met Booker when I came out here to New Mexico to work on an internal medicine externship during my senior year in medical school. Your brother was the one who most directly influenced my decision to take this current post in Santa Fe. You see, it was a tough time in my life."

"How so?"

"Sadly, my fiancée back in Houston died from an acute medical illness when I was doing that particular elective rotation out here in the Land of Enchantment. I can never forgive myself that I wasn't back home when she passed away, as she died alone. I guess in the end, what difference does it make now? After all, doesn't everybody die alone? Nevertheless, I should have never, well—" Brewster's voice broke and he couldn't finish the sentence.

"I'm sorry! I didn't know."

"Not many people do. What's in the past is in the past," Brewster said in a near whisper.

"Maybe you'll find somebody else in the future," Birdy said. "Our existence on this planet is hard enough as it is. Are you starting to date again?"

"Been busy."

"Humans are social creatures and we're hard-wired to pair-bond. Having a mate is what makes us complete as spiritual beings. Life is short."

"So I've heard. Let's wrap things up so we can get you back to see Dr. Coxswain," Brewster said. "After all, he seems to be rather fond of you."

"I need your opinion," Birdy pleaded. "I'm going to take Booker's remains back to Texas. Where do you think he would most enjoy having his ashes dispersed?"

"That's easy," Brewster replied. "Right on the beach in Galveston. Hands down. That's the *only* place you should ever consider as a location to cast his ashes to the four winds."

"I have one last question to ask you before I get out of your hair," Birdy said. "Booker was rather adamant that he must have emanated some type of unpleasant aura that was repulsive to individuals infected with the virus that causes human vampirism. Now, Booker had full-blown sickle cell disease. As for me, I only have the sickle cell trait. Do you think that somebody who has the sickle cell trait would also be physically repulsive to somebody who is a vampiro?"

"That's a very good question for which I have no answer," Brewster replied. "Why do you ask?"

"I don't know," Birdy said. "Perhaps if I was ever in a dangerous situation–oh, never mind. It was a silly question after all."

"Getting late. It's time to say *adios*," Brewster said, "but I've got a feeling I'll see you again someday."

After a brief moment of awkward silence, Birdy extended her hand and said, "I don't think I'll ever forget you, J.D. Brewster."

Brewster smiled, warmly took Birdy's hand, and offered a reply in kind. As he gently and most graciously kissed the dorsum of Birdy's right hand, he sweetly said, "I don't think I'll ever forget you either, Dr. Marshall."

He turned his head slightly to face the urn that Birdy held closely to her chest. Brewster closed his eyes and uttered a heavy sigh as he patted the metal container on the top lid. "I don't think I'll ever forget you either, Dr. Marshall."

⚬⚬⚬

Blake Barker was a vampire, and he had nobody to blame but himself. He had committed an egregious error when he consumed an egg that was previously utilized in the Huevo Limpia spiritual cleansing ceremony. Blake simply refused to believe the advice offered by his domestic, Lorena Pastore, who had warned him that certain eggs from chicken, duck, and water fowl were a reservoir for the infection that caused human vampirism.

When the transformation was complete, Lorena had absconded with Blake's only son, Nathan, and had taken him deep into the heart of Mexico to escape the seething vampiro rage that Blake became afflicted with. Blake happened to be at the Calle Vampiro drug cartel compound when Colonel Placard's hit squad arrived and burned the facility to the ground after killing everybody there. Although wounded by the cartel member named Llaves, Blake Barker survived the military assault upon the compound.

Blake was now determined to find his son, and if possible, to seek revenge upon Lorena for having the audacity to kidnap the child in the first place. Blake was able to commandeer a heavily armed and also heavily armored urban assault vehicle that had been abandoned at the burned-out compound by Colonel Placard's hit squad once their mission was successfully completed.

The first order of business for Blake Barker was to head to Rancho Feliz in Western Mexico, as that was the last confirmed location that Lorena had taken young Nathan.

There were two problems that Blake had to contend with. The first issue was that he was not feeling well. Although he had recently dined on the blood and iron rich internal organs of a stray pig, the meal did not resolve his symptoms that consisted of a pounding headache, palpitations in his chest, cyclic fevers, shortness of breath, and the appearance of bruises and small purple spots on his integument and inside the lining of his mouth. The second obvious issue was that he didn't exactly have a low-profile vehicle to ferry him about. If he encountered any *Federale* or banditos who had coveted the military vehicle with lust while he was on his quest, he could only surmise that he'd have to fight his way through such a predicament. Problems aside, he was compelled to soldier on toward Rancho Feliz outside the town of Santa Sangre, west of Guadalajara to find his son…

⸺◦⣿◦⣿◦⸻

"I sent out an invitation to no less than three different drug cartels to see if there was any interest in buying you boys at a big discount. I'm happy to report that I received a reply from a heavy hitter. It happened to be from the *Madera* cartel!" Llaves boasted.

"Who are these jokers?" Colonel Placard asked. "Never heard of them. Besides, what kind of silly label did they choose to name their cartel? The translation of the Spanish word 'madera' into English is 'wood.' Does their name reflect the material that one can expect to find deeply implanted between their ears?"

"You can be an impudent fool sometimes, Colonel Placard. The formal name of this cartel happens to be, *'Astilladora de Madera.'* Feel free to offer them disrespect at your own peril," Llaves warned.

"Well, what in hell does that mean? I'm sorry to say that my command of the Mexican language is a little rusty and the word 'Astilladora' is not in my vocabulary. I guess I need to brush up on my skill at speaking in the Latino tongue. In the meantime, I would be most appreciative if you could just tell me what that word means in English. Is it somebody's name?"

"No dice," Llaves answered. You're going to have to figure that out on your own accord. You're such a smart ass, that I know you won't be able to keep your mouth shut. I'd pay good money just to see you piss them off. If and when you do, I hope you'll get subjected to the full 'Astilladora Attitude Adjustment' Program.' A fun time to be had by all."

"Sounds interesting," Russian Bear said. "Is it anything like the 12-step program offered through Alcoholics Anonymous?"

"Keep it up," Llaves warned. "If the Madera gang comes out here to inspect the merchandise and you shoot your mouth off like that, you'll wish that you had never been born."

"Movie cliché," Placard mumbled as he stifled a disrespectful yawn. "Sounds like you've been watching too many old James Cagney gangster flicks, if you ask me."

The hostile banter was suddenly interrupted by somebody banging on the front door of the block house. "Well, that's probably our amigo, El Cojo Gato, who has returned, albeit late, with a supply of groceries for us after all," Llaves thought out loud.

"Are you talking about 'The Cat Fucker'? Well, hell! Nobody ever told me his name in the Mexican language before!" Bear said with a sarcastic smirk.

"You know, he might be little more than a dim-witted, sexually frustrated slimy midget that you gringos despise, but I've worked with him for years. Incidentally, despite his most peculiar name, I've never seen him take sexual pleasure with un gato. Not once. Not ever. Now, if you're talking about *un perro*, I guess, that would be a different matter altogether."

"If you ask me, he needs to get his name straight then," the colonel said. "From my humble perspective, as it's now 1986, the modern, post-androgynous, emasculated, metro-sexual man should be sensitive and all-inclusive in the use of the English language, especially in its application to nomenclature. God forbid if anybody should ever accuse me of harsh or discriminatory verbiage. Therefore, from now on, I'll refer to our beloved little feline fucker with a more ubiquitous and diversified label. I know! How about if I just call him the 'Animal Fucker'? Like it? That way, all bets are covered."

"I've actually just discovered at this moment that you're quite, I don't know-*sensitive*, Colonel! You possess an undeniable urban and progressive panache!" the Russian doctor reported with pithy sarcasm. "I find that most alluring!"

"Thanks, Bear! Frankly, at this moment, I don't care if the midget has a feline fetish, or if he diddles with donkeys, humps hamsters, or even if he's horny for hippos. Open the door, Llaves! Let the nasty little pervert in already, *hombre*. I'm hungry."

Llaves peaked out the front door, but saw not a living soul in the vicinity. On the front porch however, there was an old, olive green, army foot locker. On the top lid of the foot locker, somebody had taped a handwritten memo. Llaves looked around with suspicion to make sure he was not about to get ambushed. When he confirmed that the proverbial coast was clear, he grabbed the handle on the end of the foot locker and dragged the bulky luggage into the block house to give it a closer inspection.

"Well, what did you get?" Russian Bear asked. "Fan mail from some flounder?"

"Nothing so romantic," Llaves answered.

"Well, don't leave us in the dark," the colonel demanded. "How much are the big bear and I going to be worth to the Madera cartel if they want to buy us in a straight-up, cash-and-carry transaction?"

"The note attached to the top of the trunk says that the buyer wants to know if my terms are open for negotiation. It says that the trunk contains a down payment in the form of a non-refundable, earnest deposit to indicate their good faith. What does that mean, Colonel?" Llaves asked.

"This is turning out to be a good, old-fashioned, horse trade," the colonel answered with a grin.

"Or perhaps *slave* trade," Bear added as an amendment to emphasize the gravity of the situation. After all, the peril that the two prisoners were facing was considerable.

"It sounds like they want to roll up their sleeves, sit down with you over a bottle of nasty, turpentine-laced mescal, and bargain big time, Llaves. ¡Mano-a-mano!" Colonel Placard added, "This could be good for you, but bad for us. Well, hombre, don't just stand there with your thumb up your ass. Open up the damned trunk and see how much we're worth! To be honest, it would be downright decent of you to give us the right of first refusal on any deal that's going down."

"Shut up, Colonel," Llaves said. "You'll have no say-so in this matter."

"Well, we damn well should," Russian Bear added. "After all, the colonel and I are the ones who are going to be sold. Suppose we won't be comfortable with our new living accommodations? Suppose they feed us crappy food? What then?"

"*¡Silencio!*"

When Llaves opened the trunk, he recoiled in horror. "*¡Va chingar mi abuela!*" He picked up the baseball bat and gently sifted through the old trunk, which was essentially utilized as a make-shift urn. Some human remains including long bones, pelvis, and skull could be easily recognized. In addition, a prominent silver front tooth somehow escaped being melted down in what must have been a crude funeral pyre.

"¡Dios mío! No, no, no!" Llaves cried out as he repeatedly crossed himself.

"What in the hell is in the trunk, Llaves?" Placard was now alarmed. He demanded to know what was going on. "Are we in trouble here? Is it a bomb?"

"Es el *cuerpo* de Cat Fucker!" Llaves cried out. "They must have burned him alive!"

2

CHACO CANYON

By the time Zachary Hawk turned due west on N.M. State Highway 64 at the village of Chama, he realized that he knew absolutely nothing about the interloper who was sitting in the back seat of his four-wheel drive Bronco.

"Marshall told me that she had invited you along on this trip, she explained to me that you were a research scientist. I just naturally assumed that you had a doctorate in the field of anthropology or archaeology." Hawk snapped his head back to briefly scrutinize his unexpected passenger before a much-belated question and answer vetting session was undertaken. "Just a moment ago, I heard Dr. Marshall ask you when you had to return to work at the St. Francis College of Medicine back in Santa Fe. So, let me get this straight. You're what—a *medical* doctor of some sort?"

"I am indeed," Dr. Parker Coxswain placidly answered.

"That's just perfect," Hawk said in exasperation. "Who exactly are you and what can you bring to the table on this expedition? No offense, but this is a working trip. Don't expect me to be your tour guide, pal."

"Well, *you* are a research scientist, Dr. Hawk," Birdy Marshall said from the front passenger seat of Professor Hawk's Bronco as she readily came to the defense of her newfound boyfriend. "Well, at least you *claim* to be a research scientist at Northern New Mexico Tech. If you indeed consider yourself to be a dyed-in-the-wool research scientist, then you're a man who certainly seems to make a lot of assumptions. Frankly, making assumptions without keeping an open mind is antithetical to the scientific method. It allows personal bias to enter the equation of research which can unarguably thwart one's perception and subsequent reception to any new scientific discoveries. Am I not correct?"

"Hold on," Hawk said. "I take umbrage with that characterization."

"Do you, now?"

"In fact, I categorically refute those allegations."

"Do you, now?" Birdy repeated. "Empiric observations suggest otherwise. As a case in point, when you picked Dr. Coxswain and me up in Santa Fe to go on this trip, you were clearly surprised to see that I was not of the Caucasian ethnic persuasion as you had expected. Was that not an ill-founded assumption on your part?"

"Yes," Dr. Hawk sheepishly answered. "I guess it was."

"Now, you don't think that Dr. Parker Coxswain can add anything to this trip," Birdy added. "Parker, why don't you tell Dr. Hawk about your background?"

"Be happy to," Parker replied. "I have an MD/PhD degree. My PhD degree is in the field of Anatomy and Physiology. My thesis was on the effects of chronic lower-tract gastrointestinal physical trauma induced upon murine subjects and the possible co-relation to what at the time was known as the GRID Syndrome."

"What?" Hawk asked.

"My research team, Rip Ford and I, analyzed the histopathological appearance of the traumatized lower gastrointestinal tract of these animals once they were sacrificed to see if chronic changes within the mucosal lining of the large bowel could be readily recognized that would theoretically place the test subjects at an increased lifetime risk of acquiring the GRID Syndrome by, shall we say, a direct cause and effect."

"Who provided funding for this research?" Hawk asked.

"Why, it was your Uncle Sam!"

"Not *my* uncle," Dr. Hawk replied. "Not now. Not ever."

"I most assuredly wouldn't think so!" Parker said. "Nonetheless, we couldn't discount the prospects that we were dealing with an infectious agent however all along, and perhaps the trauma to the gastrointestinal mucosa only provided a conduit for the transmission of what would eventually be recognized as an RNA virus that causes the disease now known as AIDS."

"Sounds like the government funded the project in an attempt to prove that the disease now known as AIDS was a consequence to a 'lifestyle issue.' Am I correct?" Hawk asked. "Seems like a waste of time and effort to me."

"To the contrary, although we didn't discover the virus that caused AIDS per se, my research group confirmed that the disease was not a lifestyle issue after all. Be that as it may, with a strong background in anatomy, I'm certainly able to recognize human bones amongst any rubble that you and the good Dr. Marshall might be sifting through," Dr. Coxswain conjectured.

"Do you need any additional evidence that you are the type of man afflicted with bias as a direct consequence to a propensity to make assumptions, Dr. Hawk?" Birdy asked with a grin.

"Touché! I've thrown in the towel," Dr. Hawk said as he raised his hands to surrender.

"I just want to help if I can, Professor," Parker diplomatically added to smooth out Hawk's ruffled feathers. "I appreciate that the great scientific mystery that we're dealing with in this situation is to try and find an answer to the question as to what might have happened to the pre-Colombian society known as the Anasazi."

"Precisely," Dr. Hawk said. "Was there some type of catastrophe or cataclysmic happenstance that had befallen the Anasazi and forced them to flee their well-established nation in the Four Corners area?"

"You've read my published theory, Dr. Hawk," Birdy Marshall said. "I attribute the fall of the Anasazi nation to a pre-historic dangerous infestation of individuals into the community who were infected with the disease of human vampirism! The human long bones found out here on the dig that occurred a year ago indicated tooth marks from creatures possessing an impressive complement of upper maxillary canine incisors, but normal human-like canine dentition in the lower mandible."

"The bite marks found on those relic bones must have been made by a recognized natural contemporary carnivore that sadly was afflicted with some type of a severe genetic mutation, Dr. Marshall." Hawk postulated.

"Your 100% correct." Birdy said. "I believe they were humans who had been mutated into *los vampiros* as a consequence to a virus infection."

"I know it has just been leaked by the news media that there was one case of human vampirism that occurred along the Rio Grande Valley near Las Cruces, but that individual disappeared. There've been no reported additional cases," Dr. Hawk said.

"Hold you horses, Dr. Hawk," Parker said. "There was definitely more than one case in New Mexico this year. I was on the research team with Birdy Marshall's late brother, Booker. We took care of one individual down there at the St. Francis College of Medicine in Santa Fe. By electron microscopic evaluation, we had confirmed that the disease is indeed caused by a virus."

"You were involved in a case of vampirism?!"

"Why do you think I was invited to come along on this expedition?" Parker Coxswain asked. "I can assure you it was not based upon my innate charms and boyish good looks."

"There are some in this vehicle who might express an alternative opinion regarding that proclamation," Birdy said as she looked back to flirt with Dr. Coxswain.

"I can't tell you what happened," Parker explained. "As I don't know all of the facts about the peculiar circumstances at the time, but the patient in question also disappeared."

"Wait a moment!" Hawk petitioned. "Did you happen to know a doctor on the internal medicine service at your facility named Dr. Horatio Cloud? I need to know. Not only was he a member of my tribe, but he was my cousin."

"Of course I knew who he was," Parker answered. "He was a captain of one of the four inpatient internal medicine teams at the University Hospital. However, I never knew his first name up until the moment you spoke it just now. He always insisted on simply being called, 'Cloud'."

"He disappeared," Dr. Hawk said with a tinge of remorse. "Do you have any idea what might have happened to him?"

"Cloud professed to be in love with the sister of the human vampire. On the day Cloud vanished, he said he was going down to Mexico to find her. He left the hospital and that was the last anybody has seen of him."

"I need to know the whole story," Hawk pleaded.

"Little else to say, except for a few minor details," Parker said. "I can fill you in later."

"That's the first solid lead that my tribe has learned about his disappearance," Dr. Hawk said." Can you tell me the name of the woman he was involved with?"

"Frankly, I don't recall," Parker answered.

"Well, surely you can at the very least tell me the name of the patient in question. Perhaps I can figure out who the woman was with that information alone."

"No dice. That would be tantamount to an unauthorized release of confidential patient information. Most assuredly, I'd get my ass in a sling if that happened," Parker replied defensively, "As for now, my lips are sealed."

"Well, we'll see about that," Dr. Hawk replied with a thinly veiled threat. "Let's get back to the subject matter at hand, shall we? Does human vampirism exist? That may be the case, but there's no evidence at this time that this is some type of ancient disease, despite current romantic curandera folk lore to the contrary. If human vampirism occurs now as a natural event, so be it. However, I've seen no evidence as of yet that this was some type of remote illness that caused a plague in pre-Colombian times."

"An assay performed through the courtesy of the comparative anatomy department at Texas A&M stated that the canine marks found on the ancient bones discovered last year could not have been made by any known dog, wolf, or bear. No recognized carnivorous animal in the weasel family like the skunk, badger, or wolverine was likely responsible, either. Nor could the bite marks be attributed to any cataloged feline species, wild or otherwise. To be perfectly clear, I'm not just talking about animals that are recognized to be indigenous to the Western Hemisphere," Birdy interjected.

"My understanding is that the descendants of the Anasazi are thought to be the Pueblo natives that currently reside in this state in addition to Arizona, and may be as far north as Southern Utah. That doesn't answer the question however as to why a flourishing and successful society simply disappeared," Parker added. "I guess the same could be asked about the Maya and the Aztec down south in Old Mexico."

"With all due respect to Dr. Birdy Marshall's unconventional theories, let me fill you in on what we *think* we know," Hawk explained. "We believe the last inhabitants of Chaco Canyon abandoned the site approximately 1200 A.D. It appears that the Anasazi civilization had existed at that site for more than a thousand years. Up through the 11th century, there is indisputable evidence that the Chaco Canyon region was the cultural hub of the Anasazi homeland."

"Although I've never been there, I've seen the Chaco Canyon on a map," Parker confessed. "It doesn't appear to be particularly big as a geological phenomenon, as best I can tell. If a small tribe lived there at one time and decided to pack up their tents and move on, what difference does it make at this point?"

"You can't imagine how big the size of the nation was at one time," Birdy replied. "It's quite astonishing. The nation extended well beyond the confines of the Chaco Canyon. It appears at one time to have covered a 50,000-square-kilometer area with tens of thousands of residence!"

"Well, that's a horse of a different color then," Parker admitted.

"Indeed!" Birdy exclaimed. "It's actually rather amazing to think that the Anasazi had an intricate highway system which consisted of hundreds of miles of roadway that connected the various settlements throughout the Empire. In addition to complex multilevel dwellings constructed within the walls of the cliffs and hill sides, the Anasazi appeared to be intrigued with the movement of the heavenly bodies within our own solar system and the vast array of stars embedded within the Milky Way Galaxy. We've found structures that we believe can be nothing else then celestial observatories!"

"Okay, Dr. Hawk," Parker asked, "I've heard Dr. Birdy Marshall's opinion about what happened to the Anasazi. Whether true or not, you must have at this time your own theories as to what transpired. Would you care to enlighten me?"

"Well, here it goes," Dr. Hawk started. "From my perspective, it was a multifactorial set of unfortunate circumstances. For all of its natural beauty, the Land of Enchantment is a harsh environment. That statement is as true now as it was a thousand years ago. Analysis from tree ring specimens confirms that there was a prolonged and horrific drought in the late 13th Century that likely lasted for many decades. In addition, the Anasazi were probably poor stewards of the land upon which they lived. One may speculate that trees were over-harvested as a source of fuel and also for building material."

"Building material?" Parker asked. "I don't understand. They lived in adobe dwellings built into a cliff side."

"These multi-story dwelling's used logs as the roof for the lower apartments and the same wooden structure became the floor for the attached upper dwelling. See?" Hawk explained. "Although there currently is no evidence that the Anasazi were victims of violent attacks from other outside warring tribes, there certainly is evidence of fraternal warfare that occurred amongst the Anasazi people themselves."

"What would incite intramural friction to spiral out of control like that?" Parker asked.

"Human nature, I suppose," Dr. Hawk answered "After all, how many Americans killed each other during the Civil War? This country was coming apart at the seams during the violent resistance that occurred against government institutions during the Vietnam conflict. Incidentally, I ended up getting drafted and I was an unwilling participant in what I now forever refer to as the South East Asian War Games. At the time I was a humble desert rat that got dropped off in the jungle. I can tell you, I was not a happy native. Do you remember the race riots of the 1960s? I certainly do. Those are simply three examples of what has happened in *our* country in relatively modern times. Do you think human nature has changed that much over the last few eons or so, Parker?"

"Honestly, I don't know."

"Well, I don't think so," Hawk answered what was most assuredly *not* a rhetorical question.

"In summary, I'll venture that a lot of bad things happened a thousand years ago that culminated in the collapse of the Anasazi culture. Nonetheless, I take strong exception to the claim that Dr. Marshall has made that the Anasazi actively engaged in cannibalism or human vampirism for that matter."

"I've merely expounded upon theories that have been shuffling about since the late 1800s," Dr. Marshall said. "However, I'm not surprised that my current theory has engendered a great deal of controversy. I suspect you're rejecting the evidence to the contrary, as you're suspicious that *white* archaeologists and anthropologists are casting aspersions against the Native Americans. From my standpoint, nothing could be further from the truth. Last time I looked in the mirror, as a case in point, I didn't look like an Anglo."

"I won't buy that idea for a minute, Sister Birdy" Hawk said. "In fact, not for a second."

"Why not? Do you deny that the Hopi pueblo of the Awatovi was attacked by other Hopi villages around 300 years ago or so?" Birdy said. "That's a confirmed historical fact, as it occurred during the period of Spanish colonization. That, Dr. Hawk, was in a relatively modern time of recent recorded history, not something that occurred eons ago. The entire village was burned down to the ground and the victims were *cannibalized*!"

"Yes, it happened. No bearing on this particular discourse as far as I can tell. Who cares? No sweat off my nose," Dr. Hawk replied. "Those people were *Hopi*. I'm a member of the *Navajo* tribe. Have you forgotten? In any event, I'd like to believe that my people are a bit more, well-refined I guess is the adjective that I'm looking for."

"What in the world are you talking about?" Birdy Marshall asked. "The Hopi, the Navajo, and a host of other tribes are believed to be the direct descendants of the Anasazi!"

"So what?"

"Are you going to sit there and tell me that the cannibalism amongst the Hopi was a *de novo*, one-off the assembly line, isolated event and not something that was learned from their forefathers who were the now-extinct Anasazi? Spare my life!"

"Sounds like you are getting a bit testy there, Dr. Marshall," Dr. Hawk observed. "Or perhaps, in light of your boyfriend who's sitting there in the backseat, you're getting a bit *testes*!"

"No need for vulgarity," Birdy replied. "If you disagree with me, just say so. An *ad hominem* affront coming from you seems to be a bit juvenile, if you ask me."

Dr. Zachary Hawk was growing weary of his verbal sparring match with Dr. Marshall, so he gave a quick glance to Dr. Coxswain who was sitting in the back seat of the Bronco. "In order for me to accept the theories proposed by Dr. Marshall, we're going to need to find certain specific á la carte items on the Chinese menu."

"What might they be?" Parker asked while Dr. Marshall was on a slow simmer in the front seat.

"I'm talking about finding at least one of three items from column 'A' and/or one item from column 'B'!"

"What are the elements that comprise column 'A'?" Parker asked.

"1.) Evidence that any discovered human bones have indisputable signs of human bite marks or cuts caused by hand crafted tools. Now, I'm not talking about the controversial long bones that were previously found at the dig site a year ago, as whatever animal that inflicted the damage to those human bones has, as of yet, not been conventionally agreed upon. 2.) Evidence that any discovered human bones had been cooked in a fire or otherwise have a glossy shine as a consequence to being boiled in water. 3.) Evidence that any discovered human bones had been broken with a rock or similar tool in an effort to obtain the nutritious marrow inside."

"I'm downstream to all of that," Parker replied. "Tell me though what is the item that can be found in column 'B'?"

"The indisputable skeletal remains of a human vampire," Dr. Hawk answered with a grin. "In my opinion, that trumps everything else!"

When the unmistakable sound of several motor vehicles had pulled up to the block house in Durango, Llaves peeked out the front door to ascertain if the visitors were friends, foes, or dispassionate individuals who only wanted to conduct a business transaction. Despite finding that his associate, the slimy little cat fucker, had previously been incinerated while he was still likely very much alive, Llaves was fearful that any type of violent confrontation would be futile. After all, his visitors were likely armed to the teeth with a venerable smorgasbord of large caliber automatic weapons.

"What in the blue fire do you think you are doing, Llaves?" Colonel Placard asked. "You can't negotiate with these people! Close that damned door. Even if you give up Bear and me to them directly without asking for any type of monetary compensation, they're going to kill you anyhow. They've already shown you what cards they're going to play the minute they immolated *El Cojo Gato*!"

"Shut up, Placard," Llaves said. "I know what I'm doing. I'll earn enough on this transaction to make a little nest egg for myself and you two gringos will be out of my hair once and for all."

"Unlock the cage, give us a couple of guns and some ammo, and let's shoot it out with these nasty bastards!" Bear pleaded.

"This is not going to end well for you no matter how you slice it, Llaves!" Placard exclaimed.

"Well, maybe so." The two prisoners were right, and Llaves intuitively knew it! After he collected his thoughts for a moment, it was time for Llaves to let his visitors know that their arrival had not gone unnoticed. "Who's out there, and what do you want?" Llaves shouted out through the crack in the door.

"My name is *Lobo Grande*," a voice shouted back at the doorway. "I'm here on behalf of the Madera Import/Export Corporation. You know what we want. We've already made a down payment, and

I'm certainly hopeful that you've had an opportunity to carefully review the contents of the foot locker that we left on your doorstep. Now, to my way of thinking, our payment to you has been made in full. If you'd only release the two gringos to our custody, we'll simply be on our way. I suspect you're indeed a reasonable man and my men and I are here to conclude this business transaction in a reasonable fashion."

"I'll be out in a minute," Llaves said as he closed and bolted the door from the inside. "I count six men and they're all armed with what appears to be 7.62 millimeter FAL long arms," the jail keeper said to his two prisoners. "A few also have holstered pistols of various caliber. None of them appear to have any body armor, however."

"What are you packing?" Placard asked.

"I've got this AK, two banana magazines with 30 rounds apiece, and a .38 back up on my ankle. That's all that I have."

"What are you waiting for? Unlock the cage and give me your pistol," Placard requested. "We'll all go down swinging at the plate."

"Here's the pistol," Llaves said as he passed the handgun to Placard and Bear who were still locked up in the cage, "but I won't let you out."

"Why not, Llaves? I'm begging you!" Bear pleaded. "Why won't you just let us go? What in hell is the matter with you?"

"Hide the gun somewhere on your person," Llaves said to Placard. "You boys stay out of this fight and you just might live to see another day. The clock however has run out for me. I have no illusions now. Whatever I do, I won't come out of this alive. It was nice to have made your acquaintance. Good luck, muchachos!"

Llaves threw the bolt open on the door and rushed forth, hosing down the opponents that were misfortunate enough to be standing in front of his blazing Kalishnikov assault rifle. Lobo Grande had fallen to the side to escape the spray of lead the moment he saw the barrel of the AK pop across the threshold of the block house, but two of his henchmen were not as fortunate. Multiple slugs from the AK ripped through their vital organs and they were instantaneously killed before they could even comprehend what had occurred.

Llaves collapsed when he was brutally gut shot by one of Lobo's men. Two additional rounds subsequently slammed into his left arm that had been holding the extended fore stock of his automatic weapon. As Llaves fell to his knees in agony, his left wrist exploded, and all of the muscle and tendons between his ulnar and radius bone on his left mid-forearm had been violently excavated and reduced to non-viable bloody chutney.

Lobo Grande gave the signal to his team to cease fire. He briefly attended to his fallen comrades and confirmed that they were both dead. He signaled his three surviving *soldados* to follow him carefully into the block house while Lobo bravely took point. As he stepped over the critically injured man named Llaves, Lobo cleared his throat and spat a thick wad of nicotine-impregnated phlegm upon the man who was writhing upon the ground directly beneath his feet in obvious agony.

"My men and I are coming in," Lobo shouted through the open doorway. "If anybody moves, we'll kill you on the spot!" Fortunately, Placard and Russian Bear had the wherewithal to take a prone position and cover their heads with their hands when the shooting had started. In retrospect, when Llaves had kept them out of the fire fight, he had indeed saved their lives.

"Which one of you is Colonel Placard?" Lobo wanted to know.

"I am," Placard answered boldly without raising his head.

Lobo then scrutinized the large man with coarse black hair and simian-like "uni-brow" who was in the prone position beside the colonel. "Is it safe then for me to assume that this other big, hairy beast is the one that they call, Russian Bear?" Lobo asked with a smirk as he poked the doctor in his rib cage with the barrel from his FAL long rifle.

"That would be me," Bear answered.

"Good! It looks like everybody's here for the *fiesta*. My name is Lobo Grande, and you two people now work for me. I'm glad you didn't put up a fight, or else I would have subjected you to the extreme punishment that *Señor* Llaves is about to receive."

Placard briefly raised his head to survey the situation. Through the doorway, he saw Llaves lying on his right side in the fetal position, rocking slowly back-and-forth, uttering an intermittent low-frequency moan.

"Llaves is finished," Placard said. "Why don't you let him simply die in peace?"

"That's not going to happen after he killed two of my best men," Lobo said. "If he had simply conveyed the ownership of you two gringos directly to me, I would have let him live."

With that overtly fallacious comment made by Lobo Grande, the three other surviving members of the Madera crew began to laugh out loud. Apparently, his own joke was funny enough that Lobo uttered a resonant snort as he pinched the bridge of his nose in an effort to stifle an additional embarrassing chortle.

"Nah–that's complete and utter bullshit!" Lobo boasted. "Even if Llaves had surrendered directly to us without putting up any kind of fight, we had direct orders from my boss, *El Martillo Grande,* to subject this *cabron* to the Astilladora Attitude Adjustment Program."

"What might that be?" Bear asked.

"You'll learn about it soon enough," Lobo said. "In fact, it's part of our induction ritual that any slaves that are acquired to do our bidding should be baptized during the culmination of the sacred Attitude Adjustment Program. That way, they will understand how important it is to be a member of the Madera family. More importantly, it would strongly discourage any slave from ever contemplating trying to escape from our gracious hospitality."

"Is that so?" Placard asked with a less than polite timbre.

"Once you've gone through the sacred baptismal ceremony, I want you to tell me how you think about things and specifically if you've had an adjustment in your own attitude! I have no doubt that you'll be a team player when it is all said and done."

Lobo Grande turned to one of his soldiers who also happened to be his personal driver and asked, "Villanueva, why don't you free these gentleman from their rather unpleasant incarceration and bring them to the table so I can have a chat with them in a proper and more dignified manner?"

The man named Villanueva found a large key ring hanging from a nail on the opposite wall of the block house. He took the key and unlocked the cage, and then guided the two prisoners to meet their new warden who was sitting at a small table in the cramped room.

"We have very simple rules set forth by the Madera cartel. If you cooperate with us and follow our orders, your physical beatings and torture will be kept to a minimum. You will be fed, given clothing, and you'll be given a cot to sleep on if and when the opportunity arises. Frankly, it will be as good as life will ever get for you, but I'm certain that you'll be able to make the best of the situation."

"I can't wait," Placard responded.

"I must say, Colonel Placard, I certainly admire the work that you've done on behalf of the United States government. Your team of assassins completely neutralized the Routa Gang and also the entire Calle Vampiro cartel. Strong work! As best as I can tell, you did it with the snap of the finger!"

"I'd been on two search and destroy interdiction missions down here to Mexico before," Placard said. "Why haven't I previously heard of the Madera cartel? Where did you people come from?"

"We came straight from Hades to pay you a visit, Colonel. The Mexican cartels are like the magical Hydra with many heads. The Hydra guarded the entrance to the underworld at the Lake of Lerna in ancient times. On one fateful occasion, the powerful Hydra had battled Heracles and his nephew Iolaus to the death. These two champions of ancient Greek mythology soon learned that if one of the heads of the Hydra had been decapitated with a sword, a new head would simply regenerate to take its place. Well, here we are!"

"Well," Placard spoke with extreme confidence, "if you know anything about my hit squad, you'll know that they'll stop at nothing to rescue me. Once they do, they'll dispense with your organization as they have with all the others we've encountered thus far."

"Could it be that you've not been keeping up with current events?" Lobo asked with a chuckle. "It would seem so. Your team no longer exists, Colonel Placard! The Hispanic vampiro in your organization, Morales, died in battle."

"What?!"

"I'm not lying," Lobo said. "His arms and legs were hacked off with a machete before the head of the Calle Vampiro cartel, El Tor, crushed his skull with a baseball bat."

"No!"

"Wait! There's more," Lobo continued. "Your very own government decided to liquidate the bioweapon program previously under the direction of General Sibley in San Antonio. It's come to our attention that your right hand man, Dr. Ron Shiftless, also betrayed you as he commercialized the hillbilly vampiro named, Smoot."

"I don't believe a word that you're saying!"

"Just as Llaves sold you and Russian Bear to me, Dr. Ron Shiftless sold Smoot to the highest bidder. It happened to be the Leben Kur pharmaceutical company out of Germany."

"How do you know this?" Placard asked.

"When we saw the work that you had accomplished with two or three *vampiro* soldiers on your hit team, we just had to have one. We were planning on kidnapping Joe Smoot, but that bastard named Shiftless foiled our plans," Lobo explained.

"If you know the location of Smoot, give me his number," Placard said. "I'll give him a call and invite him to come on down with some of his well-armed friends."

"Not necessary now, Colonel. We have a much more powerful vampire to capture. We believe you had previously hired an additional vampiro mercenary in your crew named Blake Barker. He reportedly wiped out the entire Azteca gang in La Frontera," Lobo said. "At one time, he was a prisoner at the Calle Vampiro compound, but Barker apparently escaped the cartel when your team showed up to cause a bit of trouble. Not to worry–we'll find him."

"I know the man, but he wasn't a member of my crew," Placard said. "A free-lancer, no doubt. How many of those Azteca fuckers did you say that he killed?"

"All of them."

"Nice!" Placard said with a grin. "When I get out of here, I'm *definitely* going to hire that son of a bitch after all!"

"You just need to sit back, relax, and plan on spending the rest of your life with us, Colonel Placard."

"Why don't you just shoot me and get it over with?" Placard asked. "I don't know what good I can possibly do for your organization of cut throats."

"I'm going to depend on you for military strategy when we take on our competitors which might range from the Mexican Federales to other cartel members."

"What in hell you expect out of me?" Russian Bear interrupted.

"Did you ever provide any medical care for members of the Calle Vampiro cartel?" Lobo asked.

"Of course, but that was at their compound. Since they shipped me out here to this block house in what now seems to be a century or so ago, I've not had an opportunity to display any of my considerable medical skills on any patient," Bear boasted to irritate Lobo. "No cartel members were ever brought in here to be evaluated or treated by me."

"Well, the members of the Madera cartel certainly have no intention of allowing you to suffer from a diminution of your medical skills," Lobo said. "In fact, we plan to put you to work right away."

"Doing what?"

"Mostly attending to trauma cases," Lobo explained. "I think it's highly unlikely any of our cartel members will live long enough to get problems of advanced age or degenerative diseases. I don't think you'll have to worry about patients afflicted with hypertension, diabetes, cancer, arthritis, heart disease, or strokes."

"I suppose not," Bear said.

"The medical problems you will most likely encounter will be from beatings, fractured bones, gunshot wounds, knife wounds, concussion from explosions, burn injuries, amputations of various extremities, and the like."

"Sign me up!" Bear insisted with sarcasm. "Shall I expect any compensation for the medical services that I shall render upon the cartel's behalf?"

El Lobo Grande and his three thugs exploded in ribald laughter. "Oh, yeah!" Lobo explained. "Every time you manage to keep one of our cartel members alive, you'll definitely be compensated."

"In what way?" Bear asked.

"Why, you'll get to stay alive for another day!" Lobo answered with a sinister grin. *El jefe* turned to a hairy soldado named Mono and asked, "Is the astilladora de madera ready now?"

"Señor, everything is *listo*." Mono answered. "La astilladora has enough petrol to run for at least twenty minutes. We're in good shape even if you elect to drag out this unholy ordeal for longer than the usual time it takes for the standard slave baptismal initiation ceremony."

"Good!" Lobo exclaimed. "It's now *la hora* for the congregation to gather in front of the block house. It is time for the baptismal ceremony!"

⸻ ❦ ⸻

The Catholic Church at one time in the recent past had the hubris to actually believe that it was the moral compass for the world at large. The Vatican and its clergy were self-assured that the Church was indeed worthy of the title of *"La Novia de Cristo."* Sadly, as the human inhabitants of the planet Earth collectively moved closer toward a value system focused upon temporal secular materialism and further away from spirituality and the likely unobtainable goal of either redemption or eternal salvation, it was perhaps no great surprise that the attendance to Sunday Mass, even in the remote rural community of Santa Sangre, was on the wane.

Perhaps *El Diablo* was on the loose and Christianity was yet again in his unholy crosshairs. After all, if the Catholic Church could take a torpedo and subsequently sink into the deep and turbulent waters of moral decay, would that not constitute a great victory (albeit sacrilegious) for the evil forces dwelling amongst the shadows of depravity?

Then again, that might not be the case after all. There's an old military adage that if a nation has two different enemies who happen to be waging a bloody war against each other, then without a doubt, the best course of strategic action would be to simply keep a low profile, sit on the side lines, and then do absolutely nothing until the dust settles.

One might conjecture that El Diablo was simply lounging in the bleachers and smoking a 52 ring Cuban cigar while sipping on a shot of *tequila viejo con lima* and patiently watching the events unfold before him. After all, as best the devil could readily discern, the Catholic Church was apparently hell-bent on a path of self-destruction as it was saddled with the likes of a certain dreadful pedophilic parish priest named Father Garrapa. A.K.A., "Garrapa the Groper."

A wretched demon in his own right, this ordained man of the cloth could specifically be found in the tiny township of Santa Sangre in *Estado de Jalisco,* Mexico. As the evil Father Garrapa was little more than a hellish curse foisted upon the beleaguered parishioners of Santa Sangre, then rest assured, very little exertional labor on the part of El Diablo would actually need to be undertaken.

⚬⟶⫚⟵⚬

Jesus and Isaac were two 12-year-old boys in the sixth grade at *La Escuela de la Publica* in Santa Sangre. Puberty can be an extraordinarily difficult time for young males as a consequence to the physiologic spike in testosterone that invariably causes not only profound bodily alterations, but also rather dramatic emotional and psychological discord from time to time. Young adolescent boys are sadly prone to getting into trouble during these challenging times in life because of the aforementioned biological changes. However, it cannot be argued that the propensity for delinquent behavior is dramatically amplified if the adolescent in question does not have an adult male figure at the homestead to offer spiritual guidance and moral temperance.

Unfortunately, Jesus and Isaac were not only poor, but they were also without a father figure at home. Neither young man had any idea as to which *hombre* may have sired either of them. Predictably, their mothers were certainly of no help in discerning this matter, either. Allegedly, there was a litany of individuals who may have been the contributor to each of the young boy's specific genomic profile amongst the spermatozoa writhing about within a random and otherwise inconsequential recreational seminal discharge.

Many in the community believed that Jesus and Isaac were sired by the same individual, and if that was indeed the case, it would have meant that the two boys were actually half-brothers. Perhaps this coffee-clutch gossip was little more than salacious rumors disseminated by the wagging tongues of mean-spirited and bored house wives condemned to a purgatory of rural squalor. Well, then again, perhaps not.

Be that as it may, Jesus and Isaac were developing a mean streak and were becoming nothing less than schoolyard bullies and barrio thugs. Oftentimes, the two boys would wait in ambush to accost a younger child with the explicit intent to steal a lunch bag, or perhaps to simply rough-up a weaker or younger child a bit, just for the undeniable pleasure of inflicting pain upon a fellow human being. At this juncture, the two boys were likely destined to become ideal drug mules, or even worse, torpedoes for one of the Mexican cartels in the most despicable yet lucrative illicit local drug trade.

In fact, their miscreant behavior did not escape the notice of El Lobo Grande who was a captain in the Astilladora de Madera cartel. All the young boys needed, to the warped thinking of El Lobo Grande, was a bit more muscular definition in addition to a few more centimeters in height. Lobo knew that these desired physical attributes would eventually come to these future recruits with additional maturity over time, or as the case would be, further immaturity…

One day, Jesus and Isaac had taken upon themselves the task of taking a baseball bat and crushing the mail box at the convent. Their malicious endeavors were witnessed by none other than a no–nonsense, half-Irish nun named Sister Mary *Cabeza de la Bala* who knew the two troublemakers all too well. The nun crept up behind the two boys. After rolling her eyes to the top of her head and rapidly snapping her jaws like an alligator gar, she proceeded to unload a proverbial truck load of grief upon the hoodlums by way of an iron-fisted and merciless beat down.

As Jesus had a few remaining moral fibers left, he refused to strike back at a woman, much less a nun. He was quickly neutralized with a haymaker that left him dazed and crumpled into a fugue state in the fetal position by the road side.

Isaac, on the other hand, had no qualms about exchanging vicious blows with Sister Bala. He threw a right hook at the nun's face, but she easily blocked the thrust as Sister Bala was a renowned and well-seasoned street fighter. After rolling up her sleeves that revealed massive, hirsute biceps, she was poised to physically annihilate her adversary. She head-butted the boy, and this inadvertently knocked the habit off of her dome which uncloaked a dramatic and terrifying tattoo on her bald scalp that said, "Jesus Loves You!" She immediately recovered and pounced on the delinquent when he collapsed to his knees. A mighty jab to his face knocked Isaac back, and then the furious nun straddled the adolescent and continued to pummel him until his mouth and nose were bloodied.

Once the riot was quelled, Sister Bala harshly rubbed her knuckles into Isaac's sternum which caused the boy to utter a low pitched moan. "Wake up, Isaac! Jesus loves you," Sister Bala cheerfully proclaimed with evangelical fervor. "As for me? Not so much…"

Sister Bala grabbed each boy by the ears and dragged them across the street to the church where Father Garrapa was offering the sacrament of confession for the forgiveness of sins. Once in the church, the nun opened the door to the cubicle where Father Garrapa was secluded. She proceeded to tell him about the altercation that had taken place in front of the convent, and she did so in great and glorious detail. Before the angry nun stormed off to rattle her rosary beads, Sister Mary Cabeza de Bala pulled Isaac by the arm and heaved him into an open cubicle adjacent to Father Garrapa. Sadly, what was about to transpire would turn out an ultimately futile attempt to salvage the boy's immortal soul that was no doubt already teetering upon the threshold of eternal damnation.

As soon as Father Garrapa pulled back the paneled barrier that covered the mesh screen separating the priest from the parishioner, Isaac began his rote prayer to petition for Divine mercy. "Bless me, Father, for I have sinned. My last confession was about a year ago. I'm not sure what's happening to me, Father Garrapa, but I'm angry all the time. I think I hate other people. In fact, I hate *all* people. I even hate myself. Jesus and I destroyed the mailbox at the convent with a baseball bat. We did it because we're bad boys. That is the only explanation that I have for what we've done. Is there any way that you can help me?"

"Isaac," the priest answered, "what you need right now is love."

"God's love would be good right about now."

"No," the priest replied. "God's busy right now. What you need is *my* love!"

With that, father Garrapa opened the door to his cubicle. He looked around and saw that Jesus was in a pew and taking a nap, and there were no other parishioners in the church. The priest opened the door to the cubicle where Isaac was sitting and entered the tiny room.

"What are you doing, Father?" Isaac asked. "There's not very much room in here for the both of us."

"I know that," the priest answered. "That's why I want you to sit on my lap so I can snuggle with you."

Isaac pushed the priest aside and bolted out of the confessional booth in terror. As he passed the pew where Jesus was taking a nap, he grabbed his friend by the collar and they both sped out of the church as fast as they could run.

"What in hell happened in there?" Jesus asked in a panic.

"Hell!" Isaac screamed. "Hell happened and there!"

⸻∽ↄ🙴ↄ∼⸻

When the Bronco arrived at the southern gate of Chaco Canyon, the security guard at the entryway examined the dig permit documents and he indicated to the occupants of the vehicle that all appeared to be in order. With a circular motion of his hand however, the guard requested the driver, Dr. Hawk, to roll his window all the way down to engage in unencumbered chit-chat.

"Zachary Hawk, I presume? Been expecting you. Dig site 'G' that you worked at last year has been closed per the request of the Tribal Council in accordance with a new directive from the Department of the Interior," the security guard said. "Additional human remains were found near a kiva out there and the plug got pulled on any further exploratory excavations in that specific sector. As best as it's been explained to me, site 'G', as for now, will be on the back burner for an indeterminate period of time."

"Wait just a minute!" It was clear to even a casual observer that Dr. Hawk was about to blow an intracerebral gasket. "We've been traveling all the damned day, and now you're telling us that our dig's been cancelled?! The whole purpose of this trip *is* to excavate human remains."

"New guidelines. Human remains are now sacrosanct. Bunch of panty sniffin', tree-huggin', goat fuckin' progressives who made that decision if you ask me. Your dig permit has not cancelled, per se. It was just moved to a new location," the guard elaborated. "The tribe is making a demand at this time that your permit is only valid north of the canyon at a new spot which is designated as area 'K' on your map."

"Area 'K'?! Well, hell's bells!" Hawk exclaimed. "That's on the short plateau outside of the damned canyon! There were no known Anasazi settlements in that sector up there."

"Well, that's quite true, but who knows? Maybe you'll stumble upon an arrow head, a shard of glazed clay from an old piss pot, or even a souvenir shot glass from the 'Lucky Injun Tomahawk Casino.' In any event, the tribe wanted me to express their apology for any inconvenience this will likely place upon your expedition."

"What in hell are you talking about?" Hawk asked. "The whole point of this archaeological dig was to look for *human* remains in effort to try and discern the ultimate fate of the ancient ones who disappeared long ago. What idiotic tribe pulled the string on this ridiculous decision?"

"The Navajo." The guard replied. "Elder Joseph to be specific. Got a beef? Best take it up with him. You know how the Navajo are, right?"

"For shit's sake!" Hawk declared. "I *am* Navajo!"

"Can't prove it by me." The guard's bigotry was now on full display. "Hopi, Zuni, Apache, or whatever. Injun squaw in buffalo hide with a feather in her hair, or an Injun chick in saffron robes with a red dot in the middle of her damned forehead. Don't matter. You all look the same to me. If you are what you say, there's half a dozen members of your tribe including a buff old codger on the plateau. I suspect you know him. He's playing around in the dirt up there as we speak."

"What?" Hawk asked. "This dig permit was supposed to be exclusive to our team. I demand to be alone up there."

"Oh, yeah? People in hell would like a cold beer. Maybe those folks up there on the mesa are friends of yours and they're waiting for you and your team to show up. By the way, did you read the warning sign under the front window of the security station?" The guard asked as he pointed to a white poster board with red letters tacked up on the front of security post.

"Yeah," Hawk said. "I saw it."

"Let me be perfectly clear," the guard said. "*All* injuries that break the skin need to be reported here on an incident report form. No exceptions! In addition, it's absolutely forbidden under federal law for any persons to leave with *any* historical artifacts unless they have a notarized permission letter from both the Tribal Council *and* the United States Department of the Interior. You must verbally affirm that you've read the warning sign before you're allowed to go up to the designated dig site."

"Asked and answered already, damn it!" Hawk had more questions as the guard stepped away from the Bronco. "Did that other team tell you what they were looking for on the plateau?"

The guard ignored the question and motioned the Bronco to pull through.

"Have a great day, Chief!" the guard concluded as he ambled back to his post.

"Did that bastard just call me 'Chief'?!" Hawk asked his colleagues.

"Why, he most certainly did," Birdy replied rather nonchalantly.

"On our way out, I'm going to pay that pale face one final visit," Hawk threatened. "After all, I haven't scalped anybody in quite a while."

"What?" Parker asked. "You've actually scalped somebody before?"

Irritated, Hawk and Birdy glared at Parker who was sitting in the back seat. In unison, Hawk and Birdy replied in exasperation, "Shut up, Parker!"

⚕

"It's time for the baptismal ceremony!" El Lobo proclaimed to Colonel Placard and the Russian doctor. "Upon the conclusion of today's festivities, you both will be officially declared life-long slaves of our glorious cartel. The first order of business is to introduce you to our baptismal font. *Esclavas*, behold the glorious, forty horse power, four stroke, twin 'V', overhead valve, tow-from-behind, deluxe wood chipper made right here in Mexico by the Rio Bravo Power Tool Company. It happens to be the Deluxe Zip and Strip model. It can accommodate a log up to thirty centimeters in diameter and reduce it into sawdust in seconds! I apologize in advance for not bringing either of you a pair of ear plugs, as the machine is very loud, just as the screams emanating from the unfortunate individual being run through the chipper."

Lobo's men unhitched the wood chipper from the back of the pickup which had it in tow and wheeled the ungainly machine to the front of the isolated block house. They then began to prep the indus-trial-strength power shredder for the grisly task at hand.

"So, are you planning on sending Placard and me through the wood chipper?" Bear asked in terror.

"Oh, may Hell forbid," Lobo answered. "This is for your jailer, Llaves. He's needs to be severely punished for his transgressions. Not only did he elect to engage the Madera cartel in a fire fight, but he killed two of my best men."

"Look at him, Lobo!" Placard protested. "What's the point? Llaves is lying on the ground and barely breathing now. Please don't do this. He was no friend of ours, but no living being should ever be run through a wood chipper! He'll be dead in the next few minutes."

"You're absolutely right, Colonel," Lobo said with a nod and a malicious grin. "He will indeed be dead in the next few minutes. For now, Colonel, I need you and Bear to stand in front of the exit chute of the chipper for your baptism."

At the point of a gun, Lobo's men forced the two prisoners to stand a mere six feet away from the discharge port of the chipper. "Let us bow our heads and pray." Lobo started, "In the name of El Diablo, Lord Camazotz, and the Unholy Roach." Lobo said as he crossed himself in reverse order of the conventional Roman Catholic method. "Hellish demons, we beseech thee to cast your curses of damnation upon this wicked gathering. May we always abide by the demands of the evil edicts that emanate from the dark Cave of Camazotz and from the fires of hell. Strengthen the resolve of your humble servants to always delight in your will and to follow you in the path of your unholy cloven hoof prints. Amen. Okay, boys-fire up the chipper. Let the baptism begin!"

Once one of the henchmen turned the starter key to the on position, the wood chipper started immediately. Although Llaves was barely breathing when he was jammed feet first into the wood chipper, his high-pitched screams of agony were readily heard above the mechanical hum of the gas powered engine and the din of the spinning chipper blades. As Placard and Russian Bear were subjected to a shower of the bloody dismembered body parts of their former jail keeper, the baptismal ceremony was concluded with a happy cheer by the cartel members who were present.

"It's forbidden for you neophytes to bathe for the next 24 hours," Lobo commanded. "It's necessary for you to stew in the consequences of what any transgression against the cartel will bring upon you. As for now, help my men hook up the chipper to the back of the pickup and then climb in the bed of the truck. It's time for you boys to meet the other members of the cartel."

As the two prisoners clamored into the back of the truck, the big Bear whispered a question to the Colonel. "Placard, do you still have the gun that Llaves gave you?"

"I do indeed. It's nestled in my crotch. The ol' bratwurst is keeping the trigger warm."

"What do you plan on doing?"

"Don't worry, Bear," Placard whispered. "We're going to kill every one of these mother fuckers."

"What are you waiting for?" Bear pleaded. "Do it now before we get hauled out of here!"

"We're out-gunned right now. Patience is a virtue, Oso Grande," Placard answered. "It's not the right time. First thing that you'll need to do in order for us to escape from this cartel is to learn how to operate that damned wood chipper!"

⚮

The Bronco and its three occupants approached the short mesa at the outskirts of Chaco Canyon and Dr. Zachary Hawk parked the vehicle adjacent to a trail head where other cars and trucks were aligned.

"Looks like we have about a seventy foot hike or so to get to the table top," Hawk estimated as he and his colleagues bailed out of the vehicle. Birdy Marshall and Dr. Hawk strapped on backpacks recovered from the luggage compartment of the Bronco, in additional to a pair of shovels and a prospector's rock pick hammer. For his part, Dr. Coxswain lugged a gallon jug of water to be shared.

"This should be fun," Birdy said.

"Your cheerful optimism is frankly making me rather annoyed, Birdy," Hawk complained. "This is *not* going to be fun. I can assure you, this will only turn out to be a huge waste of time. The single reason why I'm pressing on at this point is to see what interloper from my tribe is acting like a pale-face claim jumper who's already broken ground on what is supposed to be *our* designated dig site."

"That was the second time that you made a racial slur about Caucasians, Dr. Hawk," Parker protested. "The first time I let it slide, but not this time. How about if I start referring to you as a 'redskin'?"

"Fine by me," Hawk answered. "It would be a point of pride, as a matter of fact. After all, haven't you heard of the football team in the NFL with the same moniker?"

"Are you serious?" Birdy asked. "I can tell you straight up that I wouldn't feel the same way if some misguided or perverted societal pressure forced a new name upon the Redskins that reflected the specific ethnicity that actually represented the majority of players that might be found on that particular team."

"What are you babbling on about, Birdy?" Hawk asked.

"I'm just sayin' that I'd go on the war path if that team was known as the 'Washington Darkies' instead!"

"If the shoe fits," Hawk said with a chuckle. "Perhaps I meant to say, 'if the foo' shits.' Get it? I just crack myself up sometimes!"

"Do I have to remind you that this prospector's hand pick technically makes me armed and dangerous?" Birdy said with an edge in her voice and a weapon in her hand.

A booming voice shouted down from the mesa to greet the three explorers. "About time you got here, Dr. Hawk. We've been up here for three days already. We've got something to show you."

"Who's that?" Parker whispered.

Instead of answering Parker's question, Hawk spoke directly to the grizzled yet physically imposing figure on the hill above him. "Elder Joseph? What in tarnation are you doing here?"

"Poker and Clover Lackey's seventeen year old son named Domino came up to this mesa hunting for specimens of raw turquoise two weeks ago at my request, and he found something very scary and rather disturbing. If you'd ever answer your damned phone at the university, you'd have known about it already. Come on up the trail and introduce me to your colleagues."

"Swell," Hawk said in disgust. "If not yours truly, then who organized the dig on behalf of the tribe?"

"Barksdale. He's part of a six man team that came out here from Flag," the elder replied.

"Barksdale?! Jesus!" Hawk exclaimed. That guy's a toad!"

"Be nice, now!" Elder Joseph reprimanded the young scientist. "Nonetheless, unlike you, he was readily available. Besides, we worked with him on the prior successful dig out in Tres Piedras a few years ago and we know he's a stickler for details. Unlike some unscrupulous archaeologists we've been associated with in the past, he's *never* tried to pocket any artifacts."

"Like me?"

"If the moccasin fits and the goat shits," Elder Joseph answered with a wry grin. "We knew you were coming up here today, but what Domino found was just too important to wait for your brand of expertise. To be honest, it was a rather time-sensitive matter we had to consider."

"Well, what is it?" Hawk asked. "How could the discovery of an ancient artifact be declared an archaeological emergency?"

"We found a burial pit," the elder answered. "For your enlightenment, what Domino Lackey found happens to be a *medical* emergency, not an *archaeological* one!"

"What on earth are you talking about?"

"I'll explain it to you as best I can when you make it to the top of the mesa," the elder stated.

"Forgive my manners," Hawk said apologetically. "The woman with me on this expedition is Dr. Birdy Marshall. She was the archaeologist who wrote an article that got published this past year proclaiming that the Anasazi civilization disappeared as a consequence to predation from human vampires."

"Perfect!" Joseph said. "You're just the kind of scientist we need on this excavation! Who's the other fellow beside her?"

"Dr. Coxswain from the medical school in Santa Fe. He's not an anthropologist or forensic pathologist, but he nonetheless comes pretty close to filling the bill. He has a PhD in anatomy and physiology."

"Can you identify human remains when you encounter them?" Joseph asked Parker.

"Naturally," Parker answered. "Tell me, sir—what other kind of bones have you stumbled upon?"

Joseph pursed his lips and answered with a cryptic shrug.

"Enough with the introductions," Hawk complained impatiently. "You said what you encountered up here was some type of a *medical* emergency. Now I can't speak on behalf of Dr. Coxswain, but as for me, I'm all ears, Elder Joseph," Hawk petitioned with a pant. "Just keep talking."

"We found eleven skulls, but no other skeletal remains."

"Strange. Before we get into all of that," Cloud asked as he and his companions finally made it to the top of the mesa, "why did the tribe pull the plug on dig site 'G' back in the canyon that I worked on last year?"

"A new edict was passed by the council of elders in collaboration with the feds. From now on, any human remains that are discovered will not be disturbed."

"Well, dust me with flour and call me fry bread!" Hawk protested. "What in hell am I missing here? If there's a new proscription against digging up physical human remains at site 'G', how can you justify the excavation of nearly a dozen skulls, and God knows what else, here at the new dig site designated 'K'?

"Come up and have a chat with Dr. Barksdale," the elder said to try and defuse Dr. Hawk's obvious agitation. "The professor will spell it all out for you."

"Bullshit! He's not a member of the tribe, damn it! You are, Elder Joseph. I insist *you* explain it to me! There's a double standard going on here that doesn't make any sense."

"Time to come clean, I suppose," the elder answered with a brief hesitant sigh. "Recently, we ordered a moratorium on further bone recovery at dig site 'G'.

"So I've heard," Dr. Hawk answered with exasperation. "I get it. What are you not telling me?"

"After all, what we found adjacent to the kiva back at Chaco Canyon were clearly *human* remains."

"And?"

"Listen carefully to what I'm about to tell you, Dr. Hawk," the elder said as he leaned forward to emphasize an important revelation. "The same cannot be said about the skulls we just excavated from the top of this mesa…"

3

SKULDUGGERY

"All right, Joe Cephas," Dr. Ron Shiftless said as he untied the bandanna that held the vampire's eyes tightly shut. "I want to be the first person to wish you a most happy birthday! It's time for you to behold the special present that I bought for you. You deserve it! After all, you're the re-incarnation of Elvis Presley to my Colonel Tom Parker."

"My gracious!" Joe Cephas said as he rubbed each eye with the knuckles of his index fingers. Once his vision adjusted to the bright sun light, the palm of his left hand lightly brushed the hood of the gun-metal gray, new, two door sports coupe that was in front of him. "It looks awful fancy! Is it one of them there hot-rod, Italian numbers?"

"It is indeed, Joe! It's the Maserati Biturbo S model. When you're tooling around Dallas in this little baby, even a country bung-hole like you will likely stumble across some young sweet thing that would be willing to ride you hard and put you away wet! By the way, I slammed my foot into it when I drove it over here from the dealership. Rest assured, it's faster than God!"

Joe Cephas Smoot took on a rather uncharacteristic somber tone when he replied, "Don't be a blasphemer!"

"Sorry about that, Holy Joe."

"I guess I should have had a car like this before I became a vampire," Joe Cephas muttered. "After all, Ron, my manhood is all shrunk up now and I don't think it works good and proper anymore."

"If that's indeed the case, I don't suppose that you'd mind me borrowing your new car tonight," Dr. Ron Shiftless added in a rather callous and abrasive manner. "I guess I'll just have to get laid on your behalf. We'll call it scoring 'virtual nookie'. Tell me now if you like white girls, Mexicans, or black chicks. I'll do them one and all in your honor, and I'll let you watch me from the broom closet. In fact, I'll even film it on my VHS recorder. That way you can replay it at your convenience at any time that you feel sexually frustrated. After all, what are friends for?"

"You make me sick," Joe said. "I can't tell you how many times I thought about ripping your throat out and draining you dry."

"Perish the thought!" Ron replied. "After all, you should look upon me as a father figure."

"A father wouldn't have kidnapped his own son and sold him to the highest bidder."

"Spare my life, Joe," Dr. Shiftless said. "You can't tell me that you miss working at the poultry plant in Butt Fuck, Arkansas."

"I do. Truly, I do. When I worked there, they let me consume as much chicken and turkey blood that I ever wanted. I had a nice boss and he treated me real good. I miss my sister, Rawlene. Hell's bells, Ron," Joe Cephas complained, "nobody even knows what happened to me. Next to being a mission specialist on the United States vampire bioweapon team with Colonel Placard, working at the poultry plant was the best job that I have ever had."

"No time for bitching, my fanged friend," Ron said as he brushed off the disappointment proffered by Joe Cephas. "After all, you're making gobs of money now, you're living in a luxury, high-rise condominium in beautiful downtown Dallas, you have fancy clothes that would look completely appropriate in any upscale discotheque, and now you have a fancy new sports coupe."

"I guess I should be grateful."

"Why, yes you should," Ron concurred. "By the way, I ditched all of your old overalls. I took them to the Salvation Army Central Donation Center, but they rejected the entire lot. They said your stuff smelled like shit, so I just gave all of your old clothes to some pathetic wino who was pushing a grocery cart that he had apparently stolen from a local Woolworth store. Oddly enough, the shopping cart was filled to the brim with empty aluminum cans and one emaciated, yet rather angry appearing stray cat."

"You did what?!"

"I found the toothless and cirrhotic old bastard down by Texas Stadium," Ron expounded. "He must've been a useless progressive Democrat on the county dole, living out the American dream as a blood-sucking societal vampire. Nonetheless, he seemed to be happy as a clam with the donation that I gave him. Even got a hand-signed receipt that I can use for a tax write-off. I guess I did my good deed for the day. After all, since you're a holy roller, you should be very proud of me. By the way, how much do you think your shit-stained, moth-eaten, old wardrobe was probably worth? Give me a range, and I'll push it toward the upper end of the estimated proclaimed value. Uncle Sam is too stupid to know otherwise. My accountant said a ball-park figure will more or less do for next year's tax return."

"You did what?!"

"Last time I checked, your refrigerator was stocked with bags of beef and pig blood. As far as it goes, I've never heard you complain when I occasionally bring over a delectable heart or liver from some poor creature like a skunk or a possum that got flattened like a pancake on the highway as road-kill. I'll have you know that the hard-working boys who procure these epicurean delights on your behalf from time to time have assured me that none of the dead critters that they scrape up from the asphalt with a shovel are more than a day old or so."

"Road kill?!" Joe Cephas asked with considerable dismay.

"Straight from the State of Texas Highway Sanitation Department," Ron explained. "I cut a great deal with them."

"Frankly," Joe replied," that's disgusting."

"Well, you're the one eating it."

"Just how much money are you making as my 'talent agent'?" Joe Cephas asked. "I wonder sometimes if you're not taking advantage of me."

"What?!" Dr. Shiftless proclaimed with a mock of shock. "I'm only getting a 49% commission as per our contract, and for you, that's a bargain. Hell, son—those big buckaroos who are shooting hoops in the NBA would relish such a generous contract with their own sports agents. I'm telling you that right here and right now."

"If you say so."

"Yes, I do say so," Ron added. "Besides, look at all the good that we're doing for the world. The Leben Kur, AG pharmaceutical company out of Germany is absolutely thrilled with the quality of the anti-wrinkle facial cream and other beauty products that they're able to mass produce after harvesting the virus-infected red blood cells found in your circulation. Allegedly, the Leben Kur Beauty Cream is able to completely eliminate age-related skin wrinkles for weeks on end once it's applied to the hideous mugs of those wealthy octogenarians from New York City and San Francisco. It would seem that Leben Kur is going to make a fortune from this product. In return, we're also going to make a ton of money, as I was able to negotiate a 10% profit-sharing plan for the both of us. You can thank me later."

"I just don't know if utilizing the gift, or perhaps curse, that I'm burdened with is simply being squandered upon the narcissistic vanity of rich, old people," Joe Cephas Smoot pondered. "If that's the case, do you think God will be disappointed in me? It would seem to me that I'm not living up to my potential as a vampire. I feel that I should be doing so much more. Maybe I can get some inspiration if I once again open up and read the Good Book on occasion. What do you think?"

"Well, well, well!" Dr. Shiftless said sarcastically. "Look at the big words that our country bum-fuck is now using! It's time for me to get you out of the sun before you start to blister. Let's get you back upstairs and get you into some clean duds. Don't forget that Leben Kur is going to do a photo shoot on you at noon for the advertisement campaign to launch their new line of beauty products. I forgot to tell you that we're also going to get some royalty for the advertisements slogan that I came up with."

"Can't wait to hear it," Joe Cephas Smoot said in resignation.

"Well, here it goes: 'Leben Kur Beauty Cream—it will make your skin soft and Smoot!' Do you like it?"

"I'm driving my new Maserati to the commercial shoot," Joe Cephas replied as he rolled his eyes, "and I'm sure as hell not going to give you a ride!"

Although Nathan Barker missed his father Blake, and never had any clear idea as to what exactly had ever happened to him, he had now settled into a routine life at *Rancho Feliz* in old Mexico on the out skirts of Santa Sangre, west of Guadalajara. He had been brought to Mexico by Lorena Pastore, but she abandoned the boy to the custodial care to the individuals who lived at the ranch. One of the people who had arrived at *Rancho Feliz* was Lorena's brother, Miguel. Although Miguel was infected with the *vampiro* virus, he was able to quell his lust for human blood by dining upon the domesticated animals that lived at the ranch. Miguel had become a foster father for young Nathan and cared for him deeply. Needless to say, the boy's affection for Miguel was mutual.

Sadly, the tranquility at the ranch was about to be fractured one fateful day when Nathan was given a specific school assignment to bring something to the classroom from the ranch for show-and-tell to enlighten the other children.

On several occasions, Nathan had been warned never to handle any of the bright yellow eggs that could be found in the chicken coop from time to time. The curandera (Latina folk healer) of the local community was a frail and haggard woman known as *La Bruja de la Desierta*. She was well aware that the bright yellow eggs would often harbor the infection that caused human vampirism. Although the virus that caused this disease was carried by a variety of different avian vertebrates, these birds were completely impervious to the effect of the infection. It would seem that birds were only a biological reservoir for the virus per se.

On the day of show-and-tell, Nathan had secretly harvested a bright yellow egg from the chicken coop without Miguel's permission, put it into a brown paper sack, and took it to school with him. While on his way, Nathan was harassed by the two miscreant troublemakers who were in the sixth grade named, Isaac and Jesus. The two older boys enjoyed tormenting Nathan simply because he was an Anglo.

"What do you have in the bag, little girl?" The delinquent named Jesus asked. "Did you bring me a nice treat for my *desayuno?*"

"I'm *not* a girl," Nathan replied. "Go away and leave me alone. Why do you guys always bother me? No matter how nice I try to be to you boys, you're always picking on me!"

With that, the tough one named Isaac snatched the bag out of Nathan's hand and held it high up in the air. "The bag belongs to me, now," the older boy said. Try as he might, Nathan couldn't recover the paper sack that had been confiscated from his possession. "That's mine! I have to take that to school for show-and-tell!"

"Not anymore," Isaac replied before he and his accomplice pushed Nathan to the ground and ran away with the yellow and extraordinarily dangerous *huevo* that was still safely nestled inside the sack.

Isaac and Jesus elected to ditch school that morning. "Let's go to my house," Jesus said. "After all, my mother's out whoring around and we can have a nice day off."

"First, we should go back and find that little brat, Nathan," Isaac said. "I hate that little gringo. We should take this yellow egg and jam it into his face and then beat the crap out of him before we dump him head first into the sewer."

"I hate him, too," Jesus said. "Whenever he talks to Father Garrapa or the evil Sister Mary Cabeza de Bala, he always says stuff like, 'Yes, Sir', and 'Yes, Miss'. He's always acting all polite and stuff."

"I'll bet that Nathan's not even old enough yet to see Father Garrapa to get a blessing in the sacrament of confession," Isaac opined. "Nathan would definitely *not* be polite to that horny old freak if Father Garrapa ever got that boy alone in the confessional booth!"

"*Verdad,*" Jesus concurred, "but I don't care about any of that. If Nathan ever gets diddled by the old priest, that *bambino* would be getting what he deserves. Nathan must think that he's better than us. I know he's only in first grade, but he can read real good, and do math, and other shit like that. He acts like he's smarter than we are. Who's he trying to be, Isaac?"

"I dunno'–white?" The two roughnecks had a good laugh about that. "Let's go find him and slap him around a bit," Isaac added. "Before I beat him up, I want him to get on his knobby little knees and pray to me as if I was the mighty Lord Camazotz!" Isaac proclaimed.

"Who in hell is that?" Jesus asked.

"You're statement is correct and you don't even know it. Camazotz *is* in hell, alright! He's the Ancient Maya god of the bats!" Isaac explained.

"How do you know about that?" Jesus asked with a tinge of alarm in his voice.

"My nasty sister, Amelia, is in high school. She made a shrine to him in our basement," Isaac answered. "She prays to Camazotz when she goes down into the darkness with her two boyfriends to smoke marijuana! After she's down there for a while, I hear her praying. She yells out, 'Dios mio-sí, sí, sí!' while she moans. She has to be talking to Camazotz, no?"

"You better let that bat stuff go this *minuto*, Isaac," Jesus warned as he crossed himself. "Do it now. Otherwise, you'll just be asking for serious trouble."

"How so?" Isaac asked.

"Abuelo said that los vampiros once lived at Rancho Feliz, and there still might be one out there to this very day! If you even *talk* about the bat god, maybe los vampiros will hear you and they'll come to pay you and me a visit in the night."

"Yeah," Isaac said. "I heard the same story. Enough about all that, already. I have a better idea–let's cook this huevo, put it in a torta with some queso, and split it for breakfast!"

"You're on!" Jesus agreed. It appeared from that moment, a plan (and perhaps the contents of un huevo) was hatched.

As for Nathan, he was forced to retreat back home to find another item to bring to show-and-tell. He elected to keep it a secret that two older boys had stolen the yellow egg from him. If he had told Miguel or anybody else at the ranch, especially the ranch manager, *Señor* Bosque, Nathan would definitely be in trouble.

⸻ ◈ ⸻

Blake Barker was sweating profusely when he turned the urban assault vehicle onto Calle Hidalgo and headed south toward Highway 15. If he was able to get through the township of La Venta del Astillero, it would be a straight shot to Santa Sangre, west of Magdalena. As the decapitated head of the vampiro named Romero Lopes was firmly impaled upon the hood ornament of Colonel Placard's military wagon, there was still a very good chance that Blake's son, Nathan, was still alive. If Nathan had somehow escaped the clutches of the vicious Lopes during the military assault upon the Calle Vampiro cartel compound on the outskirts of Guadalajara, then his son was likely now under the custodial care of Blake's friend, Miguel Pastore, at Rancho Feliz near Santa Sangre.

With his high fever and shaking chills however, just getting to the ranch would be a major challenge. "What in hell is wrong with me?" Blake asked himself as he turned his face into the crook of his left arm. He attempted to clear the droplets of sweat from his field of vision which was now becoming somewhat narrow. "I'm a vampire, damn it! I am supposed to be impervious to infections and medical problems."

Blake saw a coyote feasting upon the remains of a dead snake by the side of the road, and he thought that he should take advantage of the situation. "Maybe I just need to get some blood into me. Yeah, that's it. That's the ticket. What else could it be?"

Although the coyote was a fast runner, it couldn't gain any distance from its assailant once Blake charged out of the vehicle on a dead sprint. Biting viciously and tearing at Blake's face with its claws, the coyote's defensive measures turned out to be an exercise in futility. Once the coyote was in Blake's grasp, the febrile vampiro stuck the middle and index finger of his right hand into the feral canid's mouth and pulled back sharply on his head until the report of a sharp snap indicated that the unfortunate creature's neck had been broken. After sinking his canine teeth into the neck of the canine, Blake quickly evacuated the intravascular contents of the dead animal. He pitched the carcass of the coyote into a ditch by the side of the road and then he slowly ambled back to the urban assault vehicle.

Unfortunately, his impromptu meal had no bearing on his sense of wellbeing. Blake rested his head briefly against the steering wheel. After only a moment or so, he erroneously conjured up the notion that going back out to finish off the carcass of the coyote would perhaps get him back on the road to recovery.

Blake crawled back out of the front seat of the vehicle and recovered the carcass of the coyote from the ditch. At that point, Blake ripped open the dead animal's abdominal wall and thoracic cage to harvest the liver and heart. Once these visceral organs were consumed, Blake stumbled back to the driver seat of his vehicle, even slower than before.

A passing vehicle coming from the opposite direction stopped to give Blake Barker fair warning. "You better be careful when you reach La Venta del Astillero. The new Madera cartel has set up a roadblock and they're on the look-out to kill any former members of the Calle Vampiro cartel. Since you're coming from the direction of the Calle compound, and not to mention the fact that you're driving what appears to be an atomic bomb proof tank on wheels, I suspect that you're the kind of man that the Madera cartel would want to run through their wood chipper."

"Appreciate the heads-up," Blake weakly replied.

"Buena suerte," the other driver said before he sped away to the North.

"The Madera cartel?" Blake wondered aloud. "Who in hell are these shit birds? These Mexican cartels must be like the mythical Hydra from ancient Greek mythology. If you cut off one head, another one will immediately pop up to take its place. God almighty, I hate this fucking country!"

Since Blake had been on this odyssey south of the Rio Bravo for quite some time now in an attempt to find his missing son, Nathan, he had encountered more than one previous roadblock in the recent past. By huff, or by bluff, he had always gotten through them relatively unscathed. He truly believed that he could do it yet again. The only problem this time was that Blake was sick as a dog with a high fever and shaking chills. Somehow, he had to maintain the resolve to get over another hurdle just one more time. Blake was driving an urban assault vehicle that was heavily armored and also heavily armed. If anybody from a drug cartel was going to harass him or threaten him in any way, there would be hell to pay…

⸺⟆⟅⸺

Birdy Marshall and Parker Coxswain followed Dr. Hawk to the top of the plateau north of Chaco Canyon to meet with Professor Todd Barksdale from the High Desert State College in Flagstaff, Arizona. A well-respected archaeologist in his own right, Dr. Barksdale was brought in on an emergency basis to direct the investigation of the new and disturbing findings found buried on top of the small mesa known as dig site, 'K.'

As Dr. Hawk was a member of the Navajo tribe, he would have been at least the first (although not the best) choice to continue the archaeological explorations that had long been undertaken near Chaco Canyon in an irregular on-again-off again fashion for several years now. However, because of scheduling conflicts and Dr. Hawk's recalcitrance to answer multiple correspondence attempts from the tribe's Council of Elders in a timely fashion, Dr. Barksdale from Flagstaff was, by necessity, drafted into doing the job at hand.

"Hello there, Toad, uh–I meant Todd," Hawk stammered as he extended his hand to greet Professor Barksdale. "Good to see you again."

"Is it now?" Dr. Barksdale asked, "If you have an axe to grind, you can take the matter up with the members of the Council of Elders. In the meantime, perhaps we should act in a civil fashion towards each other if there's any possibility that we could intellectually collaborate on the problem at hand."

"I promise to keep my savage predilections on a short harness," Hawk said as he momentarily blushed with embarrassment. "What's all the fuss about up here? Aerial photos were previously taken of this entire area and there was never any evidence that the ancient Anasazi people ever had a settlement out here on this short, open plateau. It was *not* their style. In fact, if they had a settlement here, it very well would have exposed them to hostile elements, not to mention hostile marauders."

"Well, Zack, you are certainly right about all of that," Professor Barksdale explained, "but we certainly don't think that this was a settlement site per se in any way shape or form."

"What then?"

"Hold onto your skivvies, Dr. Hawk!" Barksdale exclaimed. "It certainly looks like the teenager from your tribe named Domino Lackey stumbled upon a pit where multiple executions took place. It would seem that the victims were brutally beheaded, and done so for a very particular reason."

"Sacrificial?"

"No," Barksdale answered as he pursed his lips and shook his head.

"Cannibalism?" Dr. Hawk asked. "After all, the dietary consumption of other human beings as a source of nutrition is as old as, well-human beings."

"Don't think so in this situation."

"What then?" Hawk pressed his peer.

"Punitive or pre-emptive," Barksdale answered. He turned to the young woman who was standing behind Dr. Hawk. She had remained completely silent the entire time, although it was clear that she was intellectually engaged in what was going on. "You must be Dr. Bertha Marshall from Prairie Baptist University in Houston. I believe I read a journal article that you published regarding your controversial theory that the Anasazi likely disappeared as a consequence to predation from human vampirism. Do you still believe that's a distinct possibility?"

"I do indeed," she answered. "Please call me Birdy."

"Frankly, I believe you're hitting the nail on the head. Elder Joseph told me that you'd be coming with Zachary Hawk on this expedition, but who's this gentleman with you? Is he the forensic specialist that I heard was coming up to see us from the medical school down south?" Barksdale asked as he pointed to Parker who was standing quietly in the background beside the elder.

"I have an MD/PhD degree, and I'm a research scientist at the St. Francis College of Medicine in Santa Fe. I am pleased to meet you, Professor Barksdale. My name is Parker Coxswain."

"What might I ask is your scientific background? I'm hoping you can shed some light on the peculiar skulls that were dug up from that big hole in the ground behind the tent. We've found nearly a dozen thus far, but we think that might be all that're down there for the time being."

"Perhaps I can," Parker hopefully added. "I'll have you know that I'm not a forensic pathologist, however my PhD is in anatomy and physiology. More importantly, I assisted the internal medicine team under the direction of Dr. Horatio Cloud with the clinical management of a reported case of human vampirism that sadly afflicted an unfortunate individual admitted to our facility. He'd come up from the Las Cruces area."

"That's fantastic news," Barksdale said. "There was very scant information about this matter as reported by the mainstream media. What happened to this patient? Are you at liberty to tell me?"

"The only thing that I can tell you is that Dr. Seth Blanks from the Center for Disease Control appeared on our doorstep and demanded that the patient needed to be relinquished to their facility in Atlanta for further medical evaluation. However, at the same time, a contingency of hostile goons showed up from the federal government with the apparent intent of hauling the patient off to San Antonio, Texas, to be presumably enrolled into some type of a secret bioweapon program," Parker explained. "A violent melee erupted and the patient disappeared. His whereabouts are unknown, at least to me and the St. Francis College of Medicine."

"Wait!" Elder Joseph exclaimed. "You actually knew Horatio Cloud? He's a member of the Navajo tribe!"

"Yeah," Parker added. "I know he disappeared. Dr. Cloud actually professed that he was in love with the sister of the patient that we were taking care of who was infected with the vampire virus. Dr. Cloud got a wild hare up his ass and he abandoned his post at the university. He went on a wild goose chase to find her down at a place called Rancho Feliz outside of the town of Santa Sangre in Mexico, which I understand is somewhere west of Guadalajara. We've not heard a peep from him ever since. Don't even know if he is still alive. Not much else I can tell you. As for now, let me have an opportunity to evaluate these ancient skulls that have been excavated from the earth."

"As you wish," Professor Barksdale said. "Walk this way and I'll show you the most peculiar and disturbing artifacts that I've ever found on an archaeological dig."

Elder Joseph and the team of scientists followed Dr. Barksdale into a large tent that had been pitched near the dig site. In the right rear corner of the tent, there was a four foot long plastic table that held a display of no less than eleven intact humanoid skulls. The moment that the team of scientists entered the tent, an astonishing anomaly was immediately noted. Embedded in the maxillary bone of each skull were impressive canine incisors ranging in length from 1 inch to 1.5 inches.

"I knew it!" Birdy exclaimed. "The teeth marks that were found on the femur bone excavated from dig site 'G' last year were not caused by a wolf, a bear, or a large predatory cat. These skulls on display only have enlarged canines in the upper maxillary bone, and not in the mandible. Well, Zack, there it is. In your own words, you said that you'd have to find an item from 'Column B' before you would consider that human vampirism was a problem that afflicted the Anasazi. The only item that you conjectured that would necessarily be found on the ledger in 'Column B' was the skeletal remains of a human vampire."

"Did I say that?"

"Your words, not mine," Birdy continued. "There's nothing else that we can possibly be looking at here! I suspect that these monsters were feeding upon the members of the Anasazi tribe. I would venture that these vampires were rounded up at the point of the spear and then brutally decapitated to spare the community from being slaughtered. It didn't work in the end, however."

"Why not?" Parker asked.

"I postulate that over time, there were finally a lot more vampires running around than uninfected individuals. This is why the Anasazi civilization eventually disappeared."

"So it would seem," the elder said.

"I'm not buying it just yet," Dr. Hawk said. "Remember, the Maya used to file their teeth into sharp points. I think that's what we are looking at here."

"Why would they do such a thing like that?" Dr. Barksdale asked. When no response was forthcoming, he answered his own question. "I'll tell you why. The Maya filed their teeth to honor Lord Camazotz, the god of the bat. There is rather conclusive evidence that the Maya civilization also disappeared as a consequence to predation from human vampirism. At this time, I believe Birdy Marshall's theory is correct, and what happened to the Maya civilization also happened here to the Anasazi. Let me show you something."

Dr. Barksdale walked over to a small wooden box that was on a chair in the opposite corner. "I found something just as important as these skulls. Take a look at this!" The professor passed around a small amulet that clearly was a humanoid figure with the wings of a bat. "Here it is, ladies and gentlemen. This is an amulet of Lord Camazotz. This has never been found before outside of the Yucatan!"

"Goodness gracious," Dr. Marshall said. "This can't be a coincidence."

"This doesn't prove a thing," Zachary Hawk protested. "These could be ceremonial skulls with animal canine teeth embedded into the maxillary bones as a postmortem artifact. I'll bet a box of donuts that what we are looking at here may even be an ancient forgery."

Parker Coxswain walked up to the table where the skulls were located and looked up to Elder Joseph. As he donned a pair of rubber gloves, he asked, "May I?"

"Of course," Joseph said. "You're a man with a lot of letters that follow the end of your last name. I believe everybody in here would like to know your opinion regarding this matter."

Parker picked up one skull after another and tried to wiggle the enlarged canines to see if they could be loosened from their socket. They could not. "I won't know for sure without running these skulls through a series of x-rays, but as best I can tell, we're looking at the real McCoy here."

"Getting x-rays on these skulls? Is that what you're now suggesting? Frankly, I don't think that there'd be a dog's chance in hell you'd be given permission from the government to get that done," Joseph protested.

"Well, why not?" Parker asked.

"Something really strange is going on here," Joseph said. "I can tell you right now that we're under a great deal of scrutiny. We turned up a small pictogram on a slab embedded at the base of this short mesa upon which we now stand. It was the image of a humanoid figure with the wings of a bat, displaying impressive canine teeth. We submitted a requisition to the Department of the Interior to have this artifact shipped off to Dr. Barksdale's university, but we were flatly denied. In fact, some rather intimidating individuals wearing military garb immediately showed up and confiscated the artifact."

"That doesn't sound right," Birdy said.

"That's not the half of it," Joseph continued. "Some guy in a suit showed up on a helicopter that landed right here on the top of this plateau. He wouldn't tell us his name, nor would he tell us what branch of the government that he was with. Nonetheless, he told us in no uncertain terms that we were *all* being carefully watched. If we discovered any artifacts concerning human vampires, then we're supposed to notify the agent at the entry site. As of yet, we've not informed the security detail about these eleven skulls that we just now excavated from this pit. I suppose at some point that we will, but for the time being, we have them displayed on this table to allow the scholars visiting us today to take a look at what we've turned up."

"On behalf of my friends," Birdy said, "I thank you for this opportunity. Well, if the Department of the Interior, the DOD, or the military is not going to allow any hands-on research to be done upon these skulls, then we should at least take some pictures for posterity. We could still use that information for future peer-reviewed articles to be published in scientific journals."

"No!" Joseph objected. "The suit told us that we wouldn't even be allowed to take any photographs of anything that we discover here.

All of our film will be evaluated for that purpose upon our departure. We *will* be carefully searched to make certain that no unauthorized material leaves with anybody associated with these excavation teams. Are you listening to what I'm saying, Dr. Hawk?"

"Bull shit!" Dr. Hawk exclaimed. "Let me see one of those damned skulls."

"First, let me get you a pair of latex gloves," Parker said. "It would be much safer to handle these artifacts that way."

"I don't need any gloves," Hawk said as he manhandled one of the ancient skulls. "I'll be careful."

Famous last words...

"Tell me something," Dr. Coxswain asked Elder Joseph. "You mentioned to Dr. Hawk that this situation was not an *archaeological* emergency when these skulls were excavated. Instead, you said it was a *medical* emergency. What did you mean by that?"

"Before I explain it to you," Joseph said, "let me pick your brain regarding some medical and biological questions that are important to a certain member of my tribe."

"Fire away," Parker said. This open invitation initiated a bevy of scientific questions that were hurled in the physician's general direction.

"Do you think that human vampirism is caused by a virus?"

"Yes, Joseph," Parker replied. "My team at the St. Francis College of Medicine confirmed that very fact."

"Is a virus particle a living entity?"

"That's a loaded question," Parker answered. "Although a virus may contain RNA or DNA material, it cannot reproduce on its own accord. It also naturally lacks the ability to create cellular energy as other bona fide organisms can readily do via the intracellular power plant known as the mitochondria. A virus particle does not have any mitochondria. In fact, virus particles are even smaller in size than intracellular mitochondria. You see, a virus is strictly an intracellular parasite and it needs more complex cellular organisms to act as a host."

"Get to it!" Joseph pleaded. "Is it alive or not?"

"So, to reiterate your complex question," Parker continued, "is a virus a living entity? I suppose that since you can 'kill' a virus in an ex-vivo environment with detergents and chemicals, it's 'alive.' There has also been a long recognition that the host immune system can destroy a viral particle. I guess then one could make a strong argument that a virus is 'alive,' at least at some level. See what I mean?"

"I do indeed," Joseph answered. "So, how long can a virus exist in the environment before it naturally degrades and is no longer infectious to other living entities?"

"Good question. Hard to say," Parker answered. "Do you know what a 'water bear' is?"

Neither Joseph nor Dr. Barksdale knew the answer. Zachary Hawk was too busy examining one of the skulls to offer any kind of reply, but Birdy Marshall knew the answer. "It is a tiny, near-microscopic bug with eight legs. Excuse the pun, but it's as cute as a, well—a bug!"

"You win the brass ring," Parker said. "Scientifically, the organism is known as a Tardigrade, and these adorable little harmless bugs were first discovered in the late 1700s. These tiny creatures can live in the most extreme conditions. They can survive temperatures as high as 300 degrees Fahrenheit, and it has also been reported that they can be re-animated after being frozen for decades at temperatures lower than minus 300 degrees. Think about that for a moment! That's an astonishing range of a 600 degree spread."

"How can that be possible?" Joseph asked.

"Beats me," Parker answered with a shrug. "There's more! They're impervious to ionizing radiation up to 5,000 rads. Check this out—that's five to ten times the amount of juice that a human being can tolerate in a single fraction of whole body radiation exposure! It appears that they can avoid death from desiccation by a scientific phenomenon known as 'crypto-biosis.' These miniature bugs are able to curl up into a dehydrated ball, and their tiny internal organs are subsequently protected by something called a trehelose gel coat."

"I guess this tiny bug might be able to survive an end of the world catastrophe!" Birdy mused.

"So it would seem," Parker agreed. "The go-to guy at the St. Francis College of Medicine for electron microscopy work is my colleague, J.D. Brewster. Now, to examine an object underneath an electron microscope, it has to be placed in a vacuum chamber first. Brewster told me that the tiny water bear can actually survive being placed in a vacuum chamber for a prolonged period of time. I shit you not! If that's indeed the case, that means that this tiny bug could theoretically live in outer space!"

"In light of these observations, what applications can be made to the virus that's thought to be the cause of cause human vampirism?" Dr. Barksdale asked.

"The point I'm trying to make," Parker said in conclusion, "is that if a multi-cellular miniature organism commonly known as the water bear bug can somehow survive in such harsh conditions, then it stands to reason that certain viral particles could likely do the same."

"That's terrifying!" Birdy opined.

"I agree," Parker replied, "but my question to you still stands, Elder Joseph. Why did the members of the Council of Elders consider this situation to be a medical emergency of some sort?"

"Listen to what I'm about to tell you and I think you'll readily agree."

"What member of your tribe does this information have any bearing upon?" Parker pressed for details.

"This concerns Domino Lackey," Joseph sadly explained. "He's the young teenager from my tribe who first found the skull of a vampire on top of this plateau. Domino accidently cut the index finger of his left hand upon a sharp canine tooth embedded in the skull that he had discovered. Within a week, he had transformed into a vampiro."

"Good God!" Birdy exclaimed. "Where is he now?"

"He's hospitalized under guard in a private room up in Farmington," Joseph elaborated. "Perhaps you and your colleagues at the Santa Fe College of Medicine could help give us some direction in this situation, Dr. Coxswain."

"I'd be happy to make some calls," Parker replied. "Well, it's none of my business. After all, he *is* a member of *your* tribe…"

"It feels like the word 'but' is about to be interjected somewhere along here," Joseph interrupted.

"In my humble opinion," Parker continued, "if you are out in the desert hunting for rocks, or doing anything else for that matter, you should probably have somebody come with you. After all, this is a rather unforgiving landscape. People have been known to disappear out here without a trace."

"If anyone should take the blame for what happened to Domino Lackey, then the finger should be pointed right at me," Elder Joseph confessed. "If the truth be told, I was the one who sent the boy up here to begin with."

"What were you thinking?" Dr. Barksdale asked. "I've known you for a long time, Joseph. Was this just a lapse in judgment on your part?"

"Stop right there, Todd. You know darn well that my people make jewelry from turquoise and raw silver. How on earth do you think we find it? It doesn't come down from the sky like bread from heaven."

"Sorry," Barksdale replied. "I was out of order."

"Our tribe would be most honored by any help that you can render upon the behalf of the young lad," Joseph said as he turned back toward Parker Coxswain.

"I'll go the extra mile," Parker said. "I'll even make a point of doing a courtesy consult."

Joseph smiled and nodded in appreciation.

"So, if this virus can be re-animated after existing in a dormant state for many centuries, you best be careful over there while you're examining those skulls, Dr. Hawk," Joseph warned. "I don't want you to get injured or sustain a cut on one of those nasty, sharp teeth and then get infected with the vampiro virus like Domino Lackey did."

The skull in question slipped out of Dr. Hawk's grasp, but he was able to snag it with his right hand before it shattered upon the ground. "Goddammit!" Dr. Hawk exclaimed before he slid the ancient skeletal artifact safely onto the tabletop.

With a trembling left hand, he quickly pulled out a bandanna from the front pocket of his trousers in an attempt to stem the bleeding from a fresh puncture wound on the palm of his contralateral right hand. "Sorry, Elder Joseph. It looks like it's too late for that..."

"That yellow egg that we ate two weeks ago has given us a special power now," Isaac explained to his friend after school. "It's a gift, I tell you."

"I finished eating my mother last night," Jesus said. "She was the last member of my family that I consumed. The fear that I could see in her eyes when I disemboweled her was so exciting to me! I had no idea that a person could scream so loud. What about your family?"

"Except for my nasty, older teenage sister, Amelia, they're all gone now, also," Isaac indicated.

"What are you talking about?" Jesus asked. "I'm absolutely certain that you told me that your sister was the first one that you had attacked when you first went through the transformation."

"That's correct," Isaac said, "but I had not yet honed my skills as a *vampiro nuevo*. I had only managed to bite her, but not to kill her. When she went through the transformation, we both thought that it would be a good idea if we ate her two boyfriends the next time they came down into our basement to pay her a visit."

"Perfecto," Jesus said with approval. "Tell me what happened."

"Amelia took off all of her clothing and she laid down upon a towel on the floor in the basement. She told her boyfriends to take off their clothes at the same time. It was disgusting! One of her boyfriends started to kiss her on her private parts and the other boyfriend started to kiss her on her chest," Isaac explained.

"Yes!" Jesus said as he started to pant with excitement, "that does indeed sound disgusting! Hurry up and tell me more. What happened next?"

"As per usual," Isaac continued, "Amelia began to cry out to Lord Camazotz, the Maya god of the bat. When she yelled, 'Dios mio-sí, sí, sí!' that was her signal to me to rush down the stairs into the basement and to help her finish off the boyfriends. It was so easy! Those two boys never knew what hit them."

"Did you make them suffer?" Jesus asked.

"They wished that they had never been born," Isaac smugly replied. "What should we do next with our new gift of magic from Lord Camazotz?"

"Tell me something," Jesus asked his school mate. "Is your sister a bad girl?"

"Absolutely," Isaac answered without the slightest hesitation. "She's *very* bad. What do you have in mind?"

⸻◦⸎◦⸻

"You'd better let Dr. Coxswain and Dr. Marshall take you down to the St. Francis College of Medicine to get that puncture wound in your hand attended to properly," Elder Joseph said.

Parker thoroughly cleaned the puncture site on the right palm of his colleague's hand with rubbing alcohol and then dressed the wound with supplies harvested from the first aid kit that had been brought along on the expedition. Even after Parker had wrapped an extra strip of gauze around the palm of Dr. Hawk, blood started to immediately ooze through the fresh new dressing.

"I'll take that under advisement, Elder Joseph," Dr. Hawk answered after a pregnant pause to begrudgingly pay lip service to the tribal council member.

"Famous last words of a fool," Joseph responded as he shook his head.

"Honest Injun!" Dr. Hawk said. "Look, everybody–I'm sorry I was an idiot. I should have been more careful."

"Accidents happen, Zack," Dr. Barksdale said. "I imagine that my team from Flagstaff and Elder Joseph and his crew are going to stay up here on the mesa for just another day. As best we can tell, there are no further bones or other artifacts that we're going to find in that burial pit. Don't forget to stop at the guard station and sign out upon your departure. By government regulations, you'll need to complete an injury incident report."

"Why do you think that would be?" Hawk asked.

"Liability issues. However, you know as well as I do, the government might have other concerns about what's going on out here. They may very well try to search your car before you depart the premises. As long as you and your colleagues are not trying to pilfer any artifacts from this dig site, they'll simply give you a quick once over and then send you on your merry way." Barksdale concluded as he turned and walked back toward the dig site.

"Keep me posted as to what's going on with you, Zack," Barksdale shouted from over his shoulder.

Elder Joseph was interrupted by a member of his crew who popped his head into the tent and asked for directions on the precise methodology to neatly refill the burial pit in an ecologically appropriate manner.

"Time to get back to work, ladies and gentlemen," Joseph said. "Look, Dr. Coxswain, you have my number. The tribe would be most appreciative if you could look in on Domino Lackey who's hospitalized up in Farmington after his acute transformation into becoming a human vampire. If you have a chance to see him, take that blood specialist from your college of medicine named Dr. Turk Masters with you."

"The Turk is on sabbatical until next month," Parker said, "but I know that his fellow, Dr. J.D. Brewster, would be more than happy to throw his hat into the ring. In addition to fat chicks, he digs really weird shit."

"Get it done," Joseph said, "and I'll bequeath upon you boys some righteous peyote."

"Wait!" Parker exclaimed. "I didn't think that the Navajo utilized peyote anymore as part of their religious ceremonies!"

After an abbreviated chortle followed by an eruption of ribald laughter, Elder Joseph replied as he departed the tent, "Who in hell said anything about you consuming it in a religious ceremony, white man?"

"It's already late in the afternoon," Dr. Hawk said, "and as we've got a long drive ahead of us back to Santa Fe, we need to pack up all of our gear and get the heck out of here. Let me attend to sorting out the first aid kit, and you guys spruce this place up a bit. Remember, boys and girls–it's pack it in and pack it back out."

While Birdy Marshall and Parker Coxswain quickly policed the area, Hawk made certain they were both pre-occupied before he grabbed the skull upon which he had sustained the puncture wound. He stuffed it into the large tackle box used as the first aid kit, and then secured the latches on the top lid of the box.

"Looks like we've got everything," Birdy said. "Let's roll."

At the bottom of the trail that led away from the top of the plateau, Birdy Marshall took the wheel of Dr. Zachary Hawk's Bronco while Parker kept a hawk's eye on Dr. Hawk's saturated dressing.

As the Bronco approached the guard post, Parker said, "We better keep moving. I don't think it would be a smart idea for us to file a formal open-wound injury report at the guard station."

"Why not?" Birdy asked. "Rules are rules."

"That would just give the security guard an excuse to delay an expeditious departure. Frankly, I believe our friend, Dr. Hawk, may have been infected with something a lot more serious than some common bacteria. Time is of the essence. Now, if this guard figures out that Zack sustained a cut from what we believe to be is the skull of an ancient human vampire, none of us are likely to see the light of day for a very long time."

"What on earth are you babbling about?" Hawk asked.

"Let me tell you about something lurking in the shadows that you don't know about," Parker explained. "The Governor's office has initiated something that is called the 'Night Crawler Public Safety Protocol,' and to my knowledge the program is still active as we speak."

"What in heck is that?" Hawk asked yet again. "I've lived here in New Mexico all of my life and I've never heard of such a thing."

"It's a program authorized by the state government, although the feds at the CDC have an oversight responsibility concerning the medical aspects of the project," Parker answered. "It's a secret that the public's not supposed to be aware of."

"If that's the case, how would you know about such a thing?" Birdy asked.

"Dr. Seth Blanks, who's the head of the vampire research program at the CDC, told me all about it. In fact, he allowed me to actually read the protocol. To be honest, there's some pretty creepy shit in that document."

"Well," Dr. Hawk said, "if you don't work for the government and if you are not affiliated with the CDC, why would this Dr. Blanks character ever share this kind of sensitive information with a university level research scientist?"

Parker Coxswain refused to answer the question…

When the Bronco finally pulled up to the security station at the exit, Birdy Marshall handed the temporary archaeological dig permit back to the guard before her team departed Chaco Canyon. As the guard looked though the vehicle's window to scrutinize the three passengers he asked, "Did everything go okay up there?"

"Why, fine and dandy," Birdy answered. "Thanks for asking."

"Any cameras, camera film, or artifacts that you care to report?" The guard asked.

"No," Hawk said as he leaned over from his position in the back passenger seat to address the guard. "We're clean as a whistle."

The guard wondered why both Dr. Hawk and Dr. Parker were both sitting in the backseat of the Bronco before he noticed that Dr. Hawk had a bloody bandage covering the palm of his right hand. The guard appeared to be superficially indifferent to what he had witnessed, and he simply asked, "Do you mind if I look in the luggage area of your vehicle. Remember, no artifacts are allowed to leave the premises without explicit permission from the Tribal Council or the Department of the Interior."

"That will be fine," Dr. Hawk nervously answered from the back seat.

"Will you folks be back anytime soon?"

"No," Birdy answered without looking up at the security agent. "I believe our work here is done."

"O.K. then," the guard said as he moved to the back of the vehicle. He dropped the tailgate to the Bronco and started to rummage through the odds and ends behind the backseat. One of the items that caught his eye was a large plastic tackle box with the words "FIRST AID KIT" written upon the top of the contraption with a felt-tip pen. What was peculiar was that bandages, a pair of bandage scissors, a bottle of rubbing alcohol, and other sundry medical supplies were scattered about the floor of the storage area.

Why were these items not safely stowed away in this large, makeshift, first aid kit? It was a circumstance that warranted further investigation. The guard flipped open the lid of the tackle box and was shocked to see a human skull with enormous canine incisors in the upper maxillary position. In addition, the tooth on the left side of the skull was actually coated with fresh human blood. Obviously, it was blood from Dr. Hawk when he impaled the palm of his hand on the dangerous, sharp, canine tooth.

The guard put the skull back into the tackle box, closed the latches, but failed to remove the kit from the rear luggage compartment. He then walked to the front window of the Bronco while his right hand clutched the pistol grip of his still-holstered service revolver.

"Stop right there, everybody," the guard said. "I want everybody to slowly exit the vehicle, turn and face the Bronco, and then put their hands on the hood with their feet spread to shoulder's width. Do it now!"

"Well, to hell with that!" Birdy said aloud. She ducked her head and floored the accelerator pedal and sped like a demon down the road. The security guard drew his pistol and fired three rounds into the air, but at that point, the Bronco was not stopping for Hades or high water.

Although the exit to Chaco Canyon was indeed a great distance from the dig site on the short plateau, the report of the three fired shots was nonetheless readily recognized from the men who were standing atop the open mesa.

"Oh, no!" Elder Joseph cried. "Something must have gone wrong at the exit gate."

After a moment or two, several members of the excavation team realized that something was awry and quickly got the attention of the professor from Flagstaff. "One of the skulls is missing from the specimen table," Dr. Barksdale observed. "I count only ten now!"

"Damn that Zackary Hawk!" Joseph proclaimed in furious anger. "This is not the first time he's pulled a stunt like this."

"I know!" Barksdale replied. "Last year at dig site 'G,' he tried to pocket a turquoise pendant before I caught him. Pack up your grit, boys and girls," Barksdale barked to both the Navajo and university excavation teams. We only have an hour or so before we'll be facing some very unwelcome and heavily armed visitors!"

"No, Todd! You're wrong! We only have a few minutes to bail out of here before Uncle Sam is breathing down our necks and we're all taken into custody!" Joseph exclaimed.

"There's only one way out of here and that's back to the exit south of here at Chaco Canyon. We're going to get caught no matter what we do," Dr. Barksdale said in distress. "The government is going to conclude that we conspired somehow with Dr. Hawk and his team in trying to sneak that skull out of here. They're probably going to throw the damned book at us!"

"They'll throw the book at us all right, but that doesn't mean that there's not more than one way out of here," Joseph said.

"Are you sure?" Barksdale asked.

"Don't be an idiot, Todd!" Elder Joseph said. "Have you forgotten that I'm Navajo? Our excavation team members need to abandon all of their equipment and follow me out of here right now if they want to save their own hides! Come on, let's move it, people!"

Although he was no longer a young man, Elder Joseph was still fleet of foot. He ripped down the north side of the Mesa where there weren't even any foot trails. He was unaware at that moment that Dr. Barksdale, and everybody else for that matter, failed to follow him. The tribal elder rapidly disappeared into the chaparral. From his hidden post in the brush, Elder Joseph watched in horror as to what happened next.

Todd Barksdale and the various members of the excavation team attempted in vain to rapidly break down their equipment from atop the mesa. A Herculean effort was made to beat a hasty retreat before the arrival of military personnel, but when a helicopter swarmed in from the South, it was already too late. Joseph watched in fear as the soldiers handcuffed everybody and took them into custody.

As best Joseph could discern, Dr. Barksdale must have made an offensive comment to one or more members of the military contingency.

"Who are you people, and what in hell do you want with me?" Dr. Barksdale asked a military officer who appeared to be in charge.

"I'm Captain Ray Noche. I'm the military leader of the Vampiro Containment Unit. I'll be the one asking questions around here. You must be Professor Barksdale from Flagstaff."

"That's correct, and that happens to make me an American citizen on American soil," Barksdale said in his own defense. "I have rights, I'll have you know! At this time, you people need to allow me and my excavation team go about the business at hand. As a matter of fact, you need to leave us the fuck alone! We've done nothing wrong. I'm not talking to you people unless I have an attorney on hand to represent me and my young colleagues."

"I have an attorney for you, Professor," Captain Noche said sarcastically.

"Where?"

"He's right about here in your transverse colon, dip shit! I'll invite him out of your ass and allow you the courtesy to take council in his sage legal advice. Are you in there, Mr. Lawyer? Why don't you come out for a consultation?"

The inflammatory statements the professor of archaeology had made apparently warranted the butt end of an M-16 automatic rifle to be forcefully jammed into the upper abdomen of the doomed scientist.

A member of the Navajo excavation team known as Big Boy pulled away from his captors in an attempt to render aid to the injured scientist. Unfortunately, Elder Joseph witnessed that this young man was also quickly and violently physically subdued.

When Barksdale appeared to be unresponsive after he fell to the ground, two other soldiers who had accompanied Captain Noche proceeded to kick the helpless scientist repeatedly in the gut before they dragged him into the back of an olive green military truck that had just arrived on the scene. A team of individuals donned in protective hazmat suits swarmed onto the top of the plateau from the helicopter. These men broke down the tent, gathered up all of the stray equipment, and then quickly departed. It was all over in just a matter of moments.

When Joseph saw that additional soldiers were starting to fan out from the base of the mesa to investigate the surrounding brush and brambles, it was time for the Navajo elder to simply disappear…

4

PRENUPTIAL DISAGREEMENT

"At this time, there are no less than four people that escaped the drag net that we cast out at Chaco, and we only know the names of three of the four suspects who are on the run," the D.O.D. administrator told the dozen or so individuals who were circled around the oblong conference table. "One person is known to be a Navajo official called Elder Joseph. He was apparently on the mesa moments before the helicopter and ground crew arrived to secure the site, but he simply disappeared into thin air."

"What else can you tell us?" a female attendee asked.

"We have absolutely no doubt that another person on the run was a professor of archaeology from Northern New Mexico Tech named Zachary Hawk," the administrator answered. "When Hawk entered and later left the canyon, he had another man and woman who were with him. We believe the woman with Hawk was Dr. Bertha Marshall who is an archaeologist from Houston, but we simply don't know who the man was."

One of the attendees was a liaison from the executive branch. He was twitching in his chair while he tapped the conference table with the eraser-end of a pencil. His restless behavior did not go unnoticed by the D.O.D. administrator. "Do you have a question, Mr. Jackson?"

"Well, Dr. Hawk obviously must have filed a formal application to initiate a new archaeological dig. What were the other names on the application file besides Zachary Hawk?"

"Dr. Bertha Marshall was the only other person listed. The fellow who came in with Hawk must have been some last-minute, impromptu tag-along."

"Doesn't matter. Hawk must have certainly written down any additional names on the entrance gate ledger when he pulled up to the security post at the canyon," Jackson said. "That's standard protocol."

"He did—'Hot Black Chick' and 'Pale Face Pencil Dick'. I'll let you consider which name was consigned to the woman and which name was attributed to the man on your own accord. Let me know when you figure it all out," the administrator sarcastically added. "The address that he had listed for both individuals on the entrance sign-in ledger was 'the planet Mars.' I shit you not."

"Sloppy work. We need to clobber those yahoos in New Mexico for hiring a complete idiot working at the entrance gate on our behalf," Jackson said as his voice increased in volume.

"Sorry, Mr. Jackson," the administrator said. "The security guard in question was actually hand-picked by the H.R. Department right here at the D.O.D."

"What?! That's nice. This just keeps getting better all the time. There were two excavation teams up there. One was the Navajo nation gang and the other was the university crew from the High Desert State College from Flagstaff, Arizona. Did you put the squeeze on any of those boys to see what they knew?"

"Every single one of them said that they were never introduced to the two people that had accompanied Dr. Hawk to the top of the plateau," the administrator answered.

"I assume that they were all telling the truth," Mr. Jackson said, "but exactly how hard did you push them?"

"One of the big brutes from the Navajo tribe took 240 volts before he seized-up and quit breathing on us. I'm fairly confident at this juncture that everybody on both the Anglo and Native excavation crews were all purposefully kept in the dark," the administrator assuredly answered. "You know—plausible deniability and all that jazz."

"Well," Mr. Jackson said, "that only leaves Professor Barksdale. He must have known the name of the other man that had accompanied Dr. Hawk to the top of the plateau."

"Maybe so," the administrator said, but he's certainly not talking to us about it."

"Did you hit him with the electrodes?"

"Wouldn't do a damn bit of good even if we did," the administrator said.

"Pray tell," Mr. Jackson asked, "why not? You boys aren't getting soft around the edges now, are you?"

"It would appear that Professor Barksdale is having an up close and personal conversation with Jesus right about now," the administrator answered with a smirk. "Somewhere along the way, Dr. Barksdale managed to rupture his spleen. Can't imagine how it happened. He died from an acute and catastrophic intraperitoneal hemorrhage on his way to get interrogated. So sad."

"No doubt," Jackson concluded impassively. "It appears that the High Desert State College in Flagstaff will be looking for a new director for their archaeology department, and it will most likely be much sooner than later by what you've just told me. Be that as it may, you better mobilize a few field investigators to nail down Elder Joseph, Zachary Hawk, and Dr. Bertha Marshall. Once done, we will be able to figure out once and for all who the other man was that had accompanied Dr. Hawk into the Canyon."

"On it."

"In addition, we better recover that damned skull that Hawk pilfered. If that artifact falls under the scrutiny of a medical doctor for a formal forensic evaluation, the cat will be out of the sack. By then, everybody will know that human vampirism is a *real* disease process and not just some rural myth," Jackson added.

"Why the angst?" the woman attendee at the conference table asked.

"If John Q. Public has any inkling of just how fucked up things truly are regarding our lame-ass attempt to contain this current vampiro outbreak, there would be a societal meltdown the likes of which hasn't been seen since Captain Kirk planted a wet one upon the lips of Lieutenant Uhura on the old Star Trek series!" Jackson explained.

"I believe you're exaggerating the situation," the woman countered.

"Madam, I don't believe so," Jackson replied. "The egg-heads in the think tank predict we'll see unbridled rioting, looting, and the burning down of stores and businesses, destruction of public property, the tearing down of statues, and the defacement of national monuments."

"That would be terrifying!"

"This will happen even *before* the lawless, opportunistic, urban thugs launch a well-organized and well-funded assault upon the white middle class. It's predicted that violent communists and anarchists will show up in the streets in droves in an attempt to overthrow the federal government," Jackson emphasized. "We anticipate a civil war will hit Portland, Seattle, Chicago, San Francisco, and the Twin-Cities just to name a few of the shit-hole communities that will be in the cross-hairs!"

"God forbid!" the woman said. "They better not contemplate doing any of that down in Texas. Just let them try."

"Let's just hope we have the political courage to strike back hard and crush these fucking animals when it happens. Uh-excuse my salty language," Jackson added.

"Relax, everybody. We're on it," the administrator said. "As far as the four individuals we need to reign in, Elder Joseph is smart and well connected. Unfortunately, he'll probably be a really hard guy to root out. In regards to Bertha Marshall, we've notified Prairie Baptist University to give us a heads up when she returns to Houston. By all indications, Zachary Hawk is a loner by nature. Nonetheless, we've already staked out his usual haunts. If we apprehend any of those three people, then certainly we will learn the name of the fourth mystery man who is also out there."

When the D.O.D. administrator left the conference room, he stopped at the desk of his executive secretary and handed her a legal yellow tablet of handwritten notes. "Mrs. Johns, I hope you can make sense of my chicken scratch, because I need you to put these notes in a memo format. Once done, let me proof it. Once it gets my blessing, mark it 'CLASSIFIED' before you stamp my name upon it and send it over to the Executive Branch."

"As you wish, sir."

"There are those out there who still have considerable misgivings about Congress defunding the bioweapon division down in San Antonio, and I promised that we would keep the boys in the Casa Blanca abreast of what's been going on with this vampire problem."

Upon his departure, Mrs. Johns quickly completed the task at hand, but she certainly held the instruction to keep the memo classified in utter disregard. Once the memo was sent by secure channels to the executive branch, it was time for Mrs. Johns to take her customary lunch break. On this particular occasion however, she decided it was time to get a breath of fresh air and stretch her legs. Once she left the D.O.D., she took a brisk walk up the street to a coffee shop where there was an operational payphone. It was time for her to make a long distance call to Santa Fe. The other end of the line rang only once before somebody promptly answered the call.

"Is he safe?" Mrs. Johns asked.

"For now." The voice at the end of the line said.

"Can I talk to him?" The secretary asked.

"Not at this time, but I can relay a message."

"Tell him that the older professor from Arizona was forced into retirement and other officials decided that it was time for him to go home."

"No! Sorry to hear about that. Is everybody else in the family doing O.K., however?"

"Well, I was surprised to learn that the big boy from Nambe was sent on a prolonged vacation. I heard that it's just out of this world!"

"What?!"

"The professor got a bad stomach ache through no fault of his own," Mrs. Johns said. "I know that his uncle wanted to have a chat with him, but the professor wasn't up to it. The weather wasn't particularly good, and it turned out to be a pretty chilly day."

"You think so?"

"I know so," Mrs. Johns confirmed. "The professor caught a cold and after that, he wasn't up to having a conversation with anybody. The big boy got all amped up over the professor's acute illness. I heard that our friend from Nambe was in such a shock about what was going on, that it literally took his breath away! Sadly, he'll never get over it."

"No! Anything about our avian friend of a feather?"

"The bird of prey can never return to the nest, nor can the little raven. There are wicked hunters afoot who'd like nothing better than to bag some fowl for trophies."

"How about the good doctor? Should he make a house call or not?"

"What doctor? Nobody up here where I'm located knows any good doctors. I must be getting careless, as I've misplaced your number, I guess I won't be calling you anymore. Stay well."

With that, it was time for Mrs. Johns to return to work.

⋘⋙

A waiter who was wearing a white apron and working at a corner restaurant on the plaza in Santa Fe casually strolled over to the Governor's Palace where a dozen or so members of the Navajo tribe had a treasure trove of items on full display to entice the tourists who were passing by. Also on full display was glorious capitalistic commerce, as greenbacks were exchanged for various and sundry valuable native collectibles ranging from Indian rugs to silver and turquoise jewelry.

The waiter found the elderly man he was looking for. The older gentleman was wearing a serape, and his face was hidden by a dark pair of aviator-style sunglasses. The gentleman was bald, and it appeared that he had recently shaved his head, as his scalp had a much lighter hue compared to his rugged facial features and the darker complexion of the nape of his neck. His bald head was covered with a bright red baseball cap, emblazoned with the ubiquitous arrowhead of the Kansas City Chiefs embroidered upon the front.

The aging gentleman was none other than the Navajo tribal council member, Elder Joseph, who was hiding in plain sight!

Although Joseph tried to remain stoic, tears of sorrow began to trickle down his cheeks once the young waiter had whispered some distressing news into the elder's ear. His tears of sorrow quickly turned into tears of anger, however. Joseph was absolutely furious that a member of his own tribe, Dr. Zachary Hawk, had betrayed a scientific expedition by having the audacity to steal the excavated artifact of an ancient vampire's skull.

This betrayal was directly responsible for the death of Dr. Todd Barksdale who was a true friend of the tribe. Zachary Hawk's impudence also resulted in the death of a young tribal member from Nambe, known as Big Boy, not to mention the brutal apprehension of nearly a dozen various archaeological explorers who were investigating a mysterious historical site north of Chaco Canyon. Who knew if and when these individuals would ever be freed from captivity?

As a member of the Council, it was the responsibility of Elder Joseph to ensure the safety of the members of his tribe. Therefore, he had a responsibility to warn Zachary Hawk, and also Dr. Birdy Marshall, that a great calamity was about to befall them. Secretly however, Elder Joseph was hoping that he would live long enough to witness Zachary Hawk get the well-deserved justice that he had coming his way...

⁕

"What in the hell is the matter with you?" Dr. Birdy Marshall asked Zachary Hawk at the Santa Fe apartment of Dr. Parker Coxswain. "It's clear to me that the reason you were not the first choice to organize the dig at the plateau north of Chaco Canyon is that Elder Joseph realized that you're an idiot, and an evil one at that. I suspect that the shenanigans you pulled are going to get all of us sent to prison! You should lose your academic rank and get kicked out of Northern New Mexico Tech. I'm sorry that I ever went on this expedition with you. My life might be ruined."

"Not to mention mine!" Dr. Parker Coxswain added. The New Mexico Board of Medicine might take exception with one of its physicians getting thrown in the can for being an accomplice to the felonious theft of a priceless historical artifact. If I lose my license over this, I'll take you outside. No, maybe I'll just take you out!"

"Perhaps my decisions were indeed a bit rash," Dr. Hawk admitted as he tried to down-play the gravity of his transgression. "However, maybe this is a situation where if there was no harm, there was no foul. Now that Dr. Parker got the MRI results back on the skull, he could enlighten us as to what we're dealing with. I'll make a deal with the both of you. If we've garnished enough information from this skull via a radiological assay, then Dr. Marshall and I will be able to submit an earth shaking scientific report in a peer-reviewed journal. At that point, I will be happy to turn myself into the authorities and return the skull that I had 'borrowed.' I'll tell the police, the FBI, the Navajo nation, and even the Department of the Interior if necessary that it was all just a big mistake."

"Well," Birdy interjected, "this should be a good story."

"I assure you, it will be a real doozy and a half. I'll just tell the authorities that I was examining the skull and had no intention of stealing it. It apparently had just been misplaced inside the first aid box by mistake after I got a puncture wound on the palm of my hand. I'll tell them the truth as I see it. After all, neither of you knew anything about my little escapade. That part of my tale of deception is indeed patently factual."

"If my ass is on the line," Parker said, "your story *better* be a doozy and a half!"

"What did the MRI study reveal about the skull that was excavated on the plateau north of Chaco Canyon?" Dr. Hawk asked.

"Well, as best I can tell, every single postulate that you had proposed about this ancient skull was absolutely incorrect," Parker said. "You professed that this skull was a fabrication, likely created by the ancient ones for some sort of religious or spiritual ceremony. You also claimed that it might have been an antique forgery. Yet again, you were wrong about that. I can tell you right now without a doubt that the skull is real. The enormous canines embedded in the maxillary bone have roots and are deeply embedded in the bone. This is not a fabrication from some wild-ass combination of a human skull and the dentition from some wild, regional predator."

"I'm stunned," Hawk admitted.

"In conclusion, this is *not* a forgery. The Anasazi did *not* file down the upper human canine teeth or use the Mesoamerican version of Elmer's Glue to attach the teeth of a bear or some other beast to the skull. No, my friend—this is the real deal. As I examined the 10 other skulls that were excavated from the plateau, they all looked similar. What you have in your position is not a 'one-off the assembly line' aberration. There were clearly more than one of these beasts running around at the time. Now, in my humble opinion, we should get some carbon dating done on the skull to confirm that it dates back to the time that the Anasazi had disappeared. The only problem, to my knowledge, is that we don't have the capability to do Carbon-14 testing at this facility. For that to be done, the skull will need to be shipped out to a tertiary university setting. Perhaps the boys at Northern New Mexico Tech can tackle the job. The only obstacle is that once you stick your head out of the ground, Dr. Hawk, you'll be thrust into a perilous game of 'whack a mole'."

"Yeah," Hawk concurred. "That could be an insurmountable hurdle."

"I stand vindicated," Birdy Marshall said smugly. "Nonetheless, I'll try to be gracious and courteous in my intellectual triumph over you, and I'll try not to rub your nose too deeply into the truth."

"This changes everything," Dr. Hawk admitted as he glumly sat down and lowered his head.

"Yes," Dr. Marshall concurred, "and not just for the Anasazi, but probably for many other distant civilizations that we do not even know about. In addition, this lends credence to the likelihood that human vampirism is a modern day problem for modern day humans to contend with also!"

"Speaking of modern day medical maladies that humans must contend with, we have a serious problem at hand, Dr. Hawk," Dr. Parker Coxswain reminded everybody. "You impelled the palm of your right hand upon one of the canine incisors extruding from the maxillary bone of the skull that you were holding. Now, according to Elder Joseph, there was a 17-year-old teenager in your tribe who developed the signs and symptoms of human vampirism after he scratched his index finger on the skull that he had found. This was an obvious similar accident that happened to you. If that's indeed the case, I'm afraid that you're at considerable risk for contracting this disease. Talk about a life-changing event! That's something you certainly don't ever want to happen to you."

"Frankly, I'm afraid about my circumstances," Dr. Hawk admitted. "From what you know about this disease process, about how long does it take to develop in an infected individual once he or she has been exposed?"

"From what I know," Parker explained, "it usually takes about a week or less. From my personal communiqué with the folks at the CDC, if a person does not show signs or symptoms by the 7-day mark post exposure, and if there's no evidence of pluripotent stem cells spilling out into the bloodstream at that point in time, a patient is generally considered to be in the clear."

"Well," Dr. Hawk said, "you better do what you need to do to get me into the clear. If I turn into a human bat however, I want you to promise me that you'll discharge a bullet into my head and put me out of my misery."

"I can't promise to do that," Parker said, "but in these very strange times that we now live in, I'm certain that I can find somebody who would be willing to do the job on your behalf!"

"Fair enough. What do I do from here?"

"Let's go up to the hospital. I'll make arrangements for you to get admitted to one of the internal medicine teams for observation, but I don't want you to leave your Bronco here at my apartment," Parker said. "If the authorities are looking for you and they spot your vehicle at my place of residence, then I'm suddenly going to be under the microscope also, if I'm not so already. The same goes for your rental car, Birdy. You should drive it up to the hospital on your own accord as I know you'll need to get back down to Albuquerque and fly out tomorrow to return to Prairie Baptist University in Houston. To be honest though, I'm going to hate to see you leave."

For her part, Birdy could only bite her lower lip as she pulled Parker Coxswain close to her and buried her face into his shoulder and sighed.

⸻ ❧ ⸻

Stereotypes exist for a reason, or so it would seem. The director of the commercial shoot flittered about the sound stage wearing a mango French barrette hat and a kiwi colored silk ascot that was neatly tucked into a guava-flavored, pleated, one piece jumper with an oversized Velcro butt flap. "Try and look sexy for this next shot, Mr. Smoot," the director said as he adjusted his monocle and twirled a pencil-thin whisper of a mustache that any high-end gigolo would have been proud to sport. "The Leben Kur Company wants their beauty cream product to sell, and if you're going to be the focal point of their advertisement campaign, you *must* look sexy!" The director turned his head toward the production crew and commanded, "Soft and Smoot Beauty Cream Commercial, take thirteen."

While the camera was rolling, the director began to bark out instructions to Joe Cephas Smoot. "Flutter your eyelashes, ducky! Act like you are getting a hum job from a big, toothless, Mediterranean brute who smells like anchovies. Now smile! Smile, damn it! Show me those big pearly whites!"

Frustrated, the director was not getting the shot he was looking for. "Cut, cut, cut! That's terrible! Well, grab my penis and yank it like I was an altar boy! Do you know how to smile, ducky?"

Embarrassed, Smoot sheepishly nodded his head to answer yes.

"Good!" The director shouted. "Now, do you know how to look sexy?"

Frankly, this question was way outside of the strike zone for Joe Cephas Smoot. He simply didn't know how to answer the question, so he just stared at the director in a bewildered state.

Dr. Ron Shiftless jogged up to the director to make a request. "Sir? I was hoping to have a brief word with Mr. Smoot. Let me see if I can give him a bit of gentle encouragement so we can maximize the productivity of our efforts here today."

"It would seem to me that Mr. Smoot has, at best, marginalized mental faculties," the director said as a matter of fact, but not as an aspersion per se. "Do what you can, but make it snappy."

Ron approached Joe Cephas and whispered something into his ear. Whatever was said to Smoot must have been extraordinarily effective, because the star of the commercial flared his nostrils in anger while he suddenly donned an explicitly terrifying countenance.

"Enough, already!" The director said in exasperation. "Bring out the nubile, semi-clad, large breasted hookers–uh, I mean models. I want them to dance around Joe Cephas and see if they can get him focused. Don't bring out the ginger broad from the back, though. I don't think we can air brush the needle tracks out of her forearms. Let's get ready to roll. Soft and Smoot Beauty Cream Commercial, take fourteen."

In this subsequent take, no less than four women dressed up as belly dancers began to seductively writhe about Joe Cephas Smoot in a most seductive manner. It was now time for the money shot. "Slowly turn your head towards the camera, Joe," the director instructed. "Now–give it to me! Give it to me hard! Let me see your teeth!"

It was not so much a smile, but rather a menacing scowl. Nonetheless, the vampiro pheromones were overwhelming and the four young women threw themselves at Joe the moment that they saw his fangs.

"That's it! We got it! Cut!" The director beamed.

The director had broken out into a heated sweat and he began to fan himself with his hands in an effort to calm down. It appeared as if he was a hummingbird circling a honeydew plant for a tiny sip of delectable nectar.

"Perfect! You're so virile, Mr. Smoot, that I want you to take me into an unholy state of matrimony and bring forth many offspring for us to rear–uh, I mean, to raise together!"

Confused, Joe asked the director for clarity as to what had just transpired. "Good Lord! If I'm not mistaken, I believe you just asked me to marry you! Now let me get something straight between us," Joe said before he paused. "Perhaps that was not the best choice of words that I could have used right about now. Let me try that again. Let's get a proper understanding here between us two men. Well, I'm relatively certain that I'm a man, but as for you, that subject matter at this time is somewhat debatable. Be that as it may, I want you to completely understand that I am *not* one of them there homo-satchels. No sir! No how! No way!"

"I'm not asking you to bat from the left side of the box *all* the time," the director said. "I just want you to broaden your skills and to learn how to become an effective switch hitter! A man like you should learn how to swing his big beefy bat from both sides of the plate!"

"Now, Mr. Director, this ain't Hope, Arkansas. If this was Arkansas, I'd bet an old whore-dog like you could become the governor of the whole damned state. In fact, if you weren't too busy chasing underaged, eleven year old school girls around the playground, and your ulcerated pecker didn't just up and rot off at the stump, I wouldn't even be surprised if you'd take a run for the President of the United States one day. However, let me reiterate: this ain't Arkansas. You best be concerned about keeping your trouser snake zipped up and tucked away high and dry! You've been given fair warning, as far as I am concerned!"

Dr. Ron Shiftless ran up and grabbed his associate by the arm to pull him away from a pending altercation. "Okay, Mr. Smoot," Ron said, "it is time to go. It is time to go *now!*"

Undeterred, the director stuffed a business card into the breast pocket of Joe's sports coat. "Here's my number, ducky, just in case you change your mind someday. After all, nobody wants to go through life with one of their hands tied behind their back, now do they?"

"What?!"

"Move it, Smoot!" Ron insisted. "I've got a couple of warm units of beef blood and a calf liver in the cooler out in your new Maserati. You should have a crack at it. Make you feel better. Once and for all, let's go. Do you want me to see if any of the horny hookers on the set-uh, I mean the models-want a ride? I want to give them a ride, by golly."

When the director blew Joe Cephas a kiss, he adjusted the Velcro butt flap on his jumper suit and slowly sauntered away after a seismic fanny shake!

❦

Jesus crossed his arms and leaned his back against the adobe wall while he impatiently waited for his friend Isaac and his older sister, Amelia, to get their fill. When the three ghouls had previously grabbed the little old lady earlier that afternoon, she was hanging her clothing out to dry on a backyard line. Once subdued, they dragged her into a back alley by her ankles to have their way with her. Their victim was surprisingly spry and she put up a fight, at least until she got a whiff of vampire pheromones that had placed her into a rather passive and tranquil state.

The problem concerning the pheromones that modern vampires emanate is that it might be seductive and alluring to their victims, but by the same token, it certainly makes it quite difficult for vampires to be around each other. Their own odor that they produce makes them angry and agitated. If one vampire is in proximity to another, both infected individuals become prone to violent altercations. This was a hard, cold, and dangerous fact that the three young parasites were about to discover amongst themselves.

Jesus had done as much work as the other two vampires in wrestling their victim down to the ground and dragging her out to a secluded and clandestine location. If that was indeed the case, why was he the last one to have an opportunity to strap on the feed bag and consume a tasty snack of blood and iron-rich organ tissues?

"Be patient, Jesus!" the teenager named Amelia ordered. "Isaac and I will soon let you dine upon some of her chewed-up, left-over, and sloppy scraps of flesh."

Well, that was it! Amelia just poked Jesus in the eye with a sharp stick, and he was not about to stand there and take it as if he was just some second-string bench warmer. After all, Jesus came up with the idea of forming a raiding party. Jesus was the one who invited Amelia in on all the fun. Jesus was the one who nominated the older Amelia to lead the trio into battle. Was this how his patronization was going to be repaid? He thought at least that his secret affection and support for the older teen would have at least warranted a peck on the cheek. Sadly, Amelia was apparently way out of his league and thus far, the only apparent emotional consideration that Amelia had for Jesus was, at best, contempt.

"Why, that's quite enough!" Jesus protested. "My turn, God damn it!" Jesus grabbed Amelia by the ponytail that was dangling from the back of her head. He yanked it hard causing her head to jerk backward, and then he slammed her down to the ground. Jesus pounced on the old lady and placed his mouth directly over the face of the victim. It momentarily appeared as if Jesus was actually trying to give his meal a French kiss, but nothing could have been further from the truth. Jesus rammed his sharp incisors deep into her posterior pharynx and he ripped out the old lady's tongue from where it had been previously tethered upon the floor of her mouth!

"What did you just do?" Isaac asked. "That's my sister that you just pushed to the ground! You help her up and you better apologize to her! Do it now!"

For his part, Jesus simply sneered at his former friend and held the forthcoming barrage of vociferous protestations in utter disregard. The elderly victim was now coughing and sputtering as she began to choke on her own blood. Jesus leaned back with a satisfied look upon his face as he slowly masticated the old woman's tongue as if he was merely working over a plug of Bazooka Joe's popular bubblegum. Sadly, for Jesus, he was not paying attention to what Amelia was doing, as she was certainly not out of the fight. When she stood up behind Jesus, she was now armed with a broken brick that she had scavenged from the dirt road that ran through the alleyway.

"Hey, Jesus?" Amelia said in a rather flirtatious, sing-song manner. "I have something for you, amigo!"

Jesus smiled as he turned his head back to look over his shoulder. That's when it happened! Amelia reared back and clocked Jesus in the face with the brick fragment that she held in her right hand. When he fell forward, Amelia and her brother Isaac dived in to punish Jesus for his prior disrespectful transgression.

Amelia kneeled beside Jesus as she continued to bash him in the face with the broken brick while Isaac stood between the legs of his former friend and repetitively kicked Jesus in the groin as hard as he could. In short order, Jesus was unresponsive, although still very much alive.

Amelia and Isaac casually returned to their meal who at that time had given up the ghost already. After the old lady was rendered to little more than bloody skeletal remains, Amelia and her brother pitched her lifeless corpse into an alley way dumpster and closed the lid. When Amelia and Isaac returned to the scene where they had physically assaulted Jesus, they found that the boy was moaning but nonetheless trying to arise to his feet. Although Jesus was seriously injured, it was now time for Amelia to add a humiliating insult to what had been done to him thus far.

With the toe of her shoe, she pushed Jesus back down into the dirt. She loosened her jeans and then squatted over Jesus and began to piss upon him. Amelia discharged a foul, black, iron fortified urine upon Jesus as if she was marking her territory.

"Let me make something completely clear to you," Amelia said while Isaac cackled. "I own you. I own every part of you. You're only alive at this moment because I decided to spare you. I think you've learned a very valuable lesson here. You're my slave now, and you'll always do as I command. In addition, you'll do whatever I command *when* so ordered. By the curse of Lord Camazotz, do you understand me?"

Jesus nodded his head slowly as he acquiesced to his new lot in life as a slave to another vampire, and it was certainly a role that he never saw coming. "I once thought that since your two lovers are now gone, that I could be your new boyfriend!" Jesus confessed his deepest feelings to Amelia. "In fact, I had hoped that one day I would ask you to marry me!"

"As if that would ever happen!" Amelia said as she laughed derisively. "You make me sick, little boy!"

Only one thing was for certain to Jesus at that juncture. Jesus had once asked Isaac if his sister, Amelia, was a bad girl. Without hesitation, Isaac had answered in the affirmative. It appeared now that what Isaac had told Jesus was a gross understatement. Isaac had also at one time described that his older sister was, well— *nasty*. That also appeared to indeed be the case, as she was truly nasty beyond measure.

⸻⫷⫸⸻

Lorena Pastore was the former caretaker for Blake Barker and his young family in Mesilla, New Mexico. Sadly, that was in another time, and obviously, in another life. When Blake Barker had become infected with the virus that causes human vampirism, Lorena at the time was a woman of righteous convictions who was filled with good intentions. When Blake became a vampire, she absconded with the man's son, Nathan, because she had rightfully feared for the boy's welfare.

Lorena escaped to Mexico with the small child and she fled to Rancho Feliz outside the township of Santa Sangre. When Rancho Feliz came under attack from vicious members of the Calle Vampiro drug cartel, something happened to Lorena and she somehow lost her moral bearings. She abandoned Nathan at the ranch and she made an arduous escape down to the Yucatan with her boyfriend at the time, Dr. Horatio Cloud, a Navajo from Santa Fe.

Dr. Cloud, who happened to be the cousin of the archaeologist, Dr. Zachary Hawk, sadly fell to his death into an open cenote pit in the Yucatan, adjacent to an ancient Maya pyramid. Oddly, Lorena Pastore could scarcely mourn for the death of this man. Despite Lorena's obvious flaws, Dr. Cloud for some reason, was deeply in love with this bizarre woman. Sadly, it was this misjudgment of character that he had paid for with his own life.

Yes, the doctor's love was unrequited. Perhaps Lorena was incapable of pair-bonding. Then again, perhaps Lorena was simply a self-absorbed, conceited, power-hungry *bruja* who lost her ability to truly care about anybody else or anything, for that matter.

Lorena was now deeply afflicted with delusional ideations of grandeur. She believed that she was the new queen of the Maya people that were scattered throughout the Yucatan, and it was her duty to resurrect the Maya into a freestanding and independent nation to recapture lost glory from a pre-Colombian era.

History has a way of repeating itself for those who are ignorant of the past. Totally unaware of the ignominious fate that had befallen her former boyfriend, Dr. Cloud, Blake Barker's brother, Cletus, was a man who was also smitten by the natural beauty of this petite yet stern Hispanic woman named, Lorena Pastore.

Upon the arrival of Cletus Barker to the Yucatan after the untimely demise of Dr. Horatio Cloud, Lorena's new suitor was completely mystified by the bizarre transformation that had overtaken the young woman. Perhaps with patience and guidance from a loving hand, Cletus somehow hoped that he could purge Lorena's misguided and warped conviction that she was the long lost heir to the throne of the remnants of the Mesoamerican jungle inhabitants.

Lorena and Cletus quickly established a resurrected community of the Mayan people, southeast of Peto, deep within the Yucatan jungle. Beside a pyramid lost in the jungle and an adjacent deep cenote shaft, the ancient Maya had constructed a military outpost out of stone that was 20 feet high and 5 feet deep with a circumference of over 1,000 feet in length.

The modern forest dwellers claimed that the outpost was once known as, Fortress Camazotz. Whether true or not, this claim could not be verified. Be that as it may, over six hundred loyal subjects lived within the confines of the fortress ruins, and there were perhaps an additional 11,000 people or so in the surrounding two square miles.

How could these modern Maya be possibly taken in by a frankly deranged interloper who had promised to return the forest dwellers to their glory lost? The natives in this region were frankly desperate. These individuals were primarily the refugees from the nearly four decade long Guatemalan Civil War that had ravaged the Maya. Sadly, it was a war of racial and ethnic attrition undertaken in an attempt to essentially exterminate the remnants of the Mayan people. Lorena's subjects were those survivors who secretly fled into Mexico to escape being slaughtered. They came with nothing except for the clothing on their backs, and they were simply looking for any sign of hope or an opportunity to live in a life with dignity and without fear. Lorena simply gave this sense of hope to them.

"Cletus," Lorena asked, "it's been nearly six weeks since I petitioned the United Nations to recognize the Maya people as an independent and sovereign nation. Surely, they must have made a decision by now. I want you to take the Jeep north up to Peto and check our P.O. Box to see if we've received some kind of correspondence that's been sent back to us indicating their decision about this matter."

"Now?" Cletus protested. "That's a long round trip, Lorena."

"450 years after the conquest by the Spaniards and subsequent European colonization, my people expect nothing less than a maximum effort on my part to put an end of this immoral subjugation of the Maya to a foreign power."

"What?!" Cletus asked. "It sounds like you mean a 'maximum effort' on my part to get to the post office and back."

"Don't be that way," Lorena said. "After all, are we not a team?"

"Speaking of subjugation, it was not all that long ago that you told me I was your *consort*, not your *partner*," Cletus said as he narrowed his gaze. "Is this not the same Lorena Pastore standing before me that I had this specific conversation with?"

"Don't get caught up in semantics," Lorena said. "After all, you're just now starting to master the Spanish language."

"Bull shit!" Cletus scoffed. "The hierarchy of the specific individuals involved in this peculiar and obviously tiered relationship was spelled out to me in the King's English, my dear. Moreover, it was explained to me explicitly, and in no uncertain terms. Let me reiterate: that royal proclamation from 'her majesty' was in English, not in Spanish."

"I'm going to restore the dignity of the native people in this region, no matter what," Lorena proclaimed. "It has been centuries since their rights were stripped away from them, and you're going to help me, Cletus Barker."

"Well, if that's the case," Cletus added, "it sounds like perhaps I'm becoming more of a *partner* to you and less of a *consort*. I like that idea. Before I go, I wanted to let you know that when I was checking on the progress of the new farmer's market in Ichmul, I found a working phone there. I got an outside line and I called the American ambassador today. Believe it or not, he took my call!"

"How exciting!" Lorena said. "What did he have to tell you?"

"In pre-Colombian times during the pinnacle of the Maya reign, there were two million or more people who lived in what was once the Mayan Empire. The problem is that the Maya people are scattered throughout many countries now. In addition to the relatively small population that you and I are living with down here in Mexico, the Mayan descendants can also be found in Guatemala, Belize, El Salvador, and Honduras. There may be literally millions of Maya out there. As a case in point, maybe up to 40% of the people that live in Belize have Mayan ancestry. Here in Mexico the greatest concentration of the Maya is found in the Yucatan as you and I well know. Most are members of the Yukatec tribe."

"Well, that's good!" Lorena said. "After all, maybe we can unite these people into one big nation."

"No," Cletus said, "that is *not* good. After all, we certainly don't have any influence on the Maya that live outside of the Yucatan region of Mexico as it now stands. At this time, the last census taken of the indigenous Maya descendants, just in Mexico alone, occurred six years ago in 1980. According to the ambassador, this remnant population in Mexico amounted to only about 250,000 or so people in this modern time. I'm only talking about the Maya right here in the Yucatan. That doesn't account for the population living outside of Mexico."

"Ouch," Lorena said wistfully. "That's less than I thought."

"Indeed. Be that as it may, you only obtained about 12,000 signatures from the local inhabitants on the circulating petition to name you the Queen of the Forest. Lorena, that's only about 5% of the population. We're going to need a lot more than 12,000 signatures just to get you elected as the local dog catcher, much less in getting any attention from the United Nations."

"Well, it's a start, is it not?" Lorena asked hopefully.

"Not so fast," Cletus said. "The thirty-seven year-long Guatemalan Civil War that just ended four years ago in 1982 involved the direct genocide of the Maya descendants. It's been estimated that there were about 200,000 people killed, half a million left homeless, and at least 100,000 women were raped.”

“I know,” Lorena said sadly. “That’s terrible and it’s hard for our people to talk about it.”

“Frankly, it was a campaign of organized state terror that was intended to exterminate the Mayan people. It was all perpetrated in the guise of a prolonged counter offensive military assault directed against ‘communist subversives’ that were allegedly infiltrating the country. In what was known as ‘Operation Sofia,’ the military initiated a brutal campaign to eliminate the Maya as an ethnic group. The military attack was so barbaric that it would have made the long reviled Union army war criminal, William T. Sherman from the American Civil War, blush in shame.

“What happened to our people?”

“Well, let’s see,” Cletus said. “Over 600 Mayan villages were burned to the ground, with the murder of up to 40% of the civilian population in some locations. Crops, livestock, historical artifacts, and historical records were completely destroyed. If that doesn’t characterize a wholesale genocide, then I don’t know what would fit the definition. Yes indeed, the Maya have been brutally treated for centuries but I don’t think that we have the wherewithal to change the situation one bit.”

“That’s exactly why I want to get the United Nations involved in their plight.”

“Wake up, Lorena!” Cletus said. “The ambassador I spoke with suggested that it’s a lost cause. In the first place, the Guatemalan army hired out a band of para-military barbarians known as, Los Carniceros, to do their dirty work. That gave the Guatemalan government plausible deniability about the atrocities that occurred. The head of Los Carniceros was a drug lord king-pin who called himself ‘General’ Carmel. That filthy animal is still at large, and as best we know, he’s still getting protection from the Guatemalan government.”

“I know all about Carmel. That doesn’t mean that the Maya people can’t find this man and bring him to justice. After all, he’s indeed an admitted war criminal, is he not?” Lorena asked.

"So it would seem," Cletus agreed, "but if the United Nations didn't give two shits about the Maya people during a nearly four decade long, state-sponsored genocide campaign that just ended in 1982, then they sure as hell aren't going to give two shits about these people now, four years later. To my way of thinking, the United Nations is about as useless as a teat on a banty rooster."

"It doesn't matter Cletus," Lorena said. "We have to try. Please drive up to Peto and check our P.O. Box. Please? Pretty please?"

"Well, since you said the magic word, 'please,' your wish is my command."

Lorena gave Cletus a hug as she tried to pull him back inside their thatched hutch within the confines of the fortress ruins. "Make love to me, gringo, before you go. I believe it's my time for ovarian ovulation, and I demand that you sire me an heir to my kingdom."

"Not this time," Cletus said.

"What's wrong now?" Lorena asked. "Is 'Mr. Winky' tired again today? Anymore, he seems to be tired all the time."

"No," Cletus said. "If you and I are going to be the parents of a child, whether or not he or she will be the eventual heir to a resurrected Mayan Empire, then I insist that you must marry me first."

"Oh, Cletus," Lorena said, "don't be silly. After all, to what benefit would a formal marriage offer a queen like me?"

⚊⚊⚕⚊⚊

At the CDC in Atlanta, the director of the human vampire research program, Dr. Seth Blanks, was flabbergasted by a television commercial that he had seen the night before. Anticipating that they would show the commercial yet again, he had his VHS recorder primed and ready to go. When the television commercial appeared once again before the night was over, Dr. Blanks captured the audio and video presentation to further scrutinize and review the findings with his colleagues. At 8:00 in the morning on the following day, it turned out to be the first order of business at the CDC that Dr. Blanks had to address.

Dr. Blanks hit the intercom and barked out an emergent order to the two assistant directors of the program. "Hoefferle? Kohl? If you boys are in the building, get over to my office right away. Chop, Chop gentleman. I need you guys, front and center, and I do mean now!"

Momentarily, both Dr. Hoefferle and Kohl had arrived. "Take a seat in front of my desk gentleman," Blanks instructed. "I saw something on the television last night that blew my mind. Before we get into that, let me ask you a few specific questions, Dr. Hoefferle."

"Fire away," the assistant director answered.

"Prior to joining the CDC, you were affiliated with the secret bioweapon division under General Sibley, Colonel Augustus Placard, and Dr. Ron Shiftless in San Antonio, were you not?"

"When Uncle Sam pulled the plug on the vampire bioweapon team, I was released from my contract, and that gave me the opportunity to jump over here to Atlanta," Hoefferle answered.

"So," Blanks asked, "you weren't technically a commissioned officer?"

"Nothing of the sort. I was just a hired gun."

"Fair enough," Blanks replied. "Give me the low down on why Congress pulled the funding on your project. Was the pilot program a failure?"

"Depends on how you look at it, I suppose," Dr. Hoefferle answered. "From a logistical standpoint, Placard's hit team was indeed a marvel to be hold. The four man team of assassins completely exterminated the Routa gang in Mexico, and their second assault upon the Calle Vampiro cartel on the outskirts of Guadalajara was a military victory the likes of which have rarely been seen outside of the atomic bomb attack upon that Japanese that brought WWII to a swift conclusion. Intelligence indicated that Placard's team completely exterminated the Vampiro cartel, including every man, woman, and child, before the compound was completely burned to the ground. It was fucking beautiful!"

"Well then," Blanks continued, "What exactly was the problem?"

"Often, there are ugly politics amongst casualties."

"What do you mean?" Blanks asked.

"Placard is now missing in action and presumed dead. Captain Morales was reportedly captured and subsequently butchered alive. When the plug got pulled on the project, I'm ashamed to say that we abandoned Dr. Ron Shiftless and Joe Cephas Smoot out in the field. As they never returned home, they are presumed KIA or MIA. That's something that I just have to live with, but in the end, it was not my call."

"Are you sure about all of that?" Blanks served up an intriguing question.

"What do you mean?" Hoefferle asked as he returned a query.

Blanks turned to ask another question to the other research scientist in the room. "Tell me, Dr. Kohl, do you remember when I told you that we had a 'Plan B' to keep the Vampiro Vaccine Research Project alive and on the front burner? Well, 'Plan B' constitutes our ability to get our hands on another living and breathing vampire."

"Yeah," Kohl said, "I figured as much. Well, tell me–do we have another vampire to work with on our vaccine project or not?"

"Maybe," Blanks replied. "Before I go any further, I want you gentleman to take a look at this television commercial that was aired last night during the evening news. I captured it on a VHS cassette. Let me play it for you."

With that, Dr. Blanks plugged in the VHS tape into the playback machine that was wired to the television set in his office. A somewhat grainy image appeared of the vampiro, Joe Cephas Smoot, surrounded by a bevy of scantily clad women oozing unbridled sexuality. Smoot was pedaling a new beauty cream product introduced by the Leben Kur AG pharmaceutical company from West Germany, and the cream was actually named in the vampiro's honor—*Soft and Smoot!* Dr. Kohl and Dr. Hoefferle simply stared at the television screen in slack-jawed amazement.

"As best I can tell, Joe Cephas Smoot doesn't appear to be dead to me, or missing in action for that matter," Dr. Blanks said. "Well, do you gentleman concur that what we're watching is essentially 'proof of life'?"

Dr. Hoefferle and Kohl were dumbfounded and could not even muster a reply.

"Well, there you have it," Dr. Blanks said. "If we can convince Smoot to come to Atlanta, I'll give you Plan B."

⸺⸙⸺

Dr. Zachary Hawk was admitted to the St. Francis University Hospital in Santa Fe on a planned seven day observation status to determine whether or not he had become infected with the nasty RNA retro-virus that was responsible for human vampirism. While he was paid a visit by Dr. Parker Coxswain and Birdy Marshall the day after his admission, the telephone in his room began to ring.

"To my knowledge, nobody even knows where I am," Dr. Hawk said. "My admission to this hospital is supposed to be a secret. Who in hell could be calling up to this room to talk to me?" Dr. Hawk picked up the receiver and asked, "Hello?"

The voice on the other end of the line was none other than Elder Joseph. "Keep your mouth shut and just listen to what I have to say."

"Elder Joseph?!" Hawk asked. "How did you find to me?"

"God damn it! Are you completely incapable of following instructions? Did you not hear what I just said?! Keep your mouth shut and just listen to what I have to say. If you find the New Mexico Sun morning newspaper, you'll find on page four of the first section that Dr. Todd Barksdale from Flagstaff and a member of the archaeological excavation team from the Navajo tribe who was known as Big Boy, were both killed in an accident at Chaco Canyon."

"What?"

"Shut up and listen!" Joseph continued. "It's a cover story. That article is nothing more than a big, fat lie. It was no accident. They were both murdered. Because you stole that ancient vampire skull, you jammed a stick into the bee hive. Their deaths are upon your head, and I'll never forgive you for that. I never should have trusted you after you tried to steal that turquoise pendant artifact a year ago. You're a university professor and you're out there acting like a teenage punk trying to pilfer a burrito from a Taco Hell fast food joint.

What's the matter with you? More importantly, what's wrong with me? I should have *never* given you a second chance!"

"I'm sorry, but--"

"Pay attention. This is where things get ugly. Some military roughnecks beat Dr. Barksdale to death. I was hiding in the brush at the time, but I nonetheless witnessed the event with my own eyes. The military outfit is called the Vampiro Containment Unit headed up by Captain Ray Noche. As I understand it from a reliable secondhand source, Big Boy from our tribe was tortured to death by electrocution. All the other men who were on the excavation teams have also completely disappeared. I doubt that we shall ever see them again. I hope you understand what I am saying."

"What?"

"You're slated to be caught and likely executed," Joseph continued. "The authorities know exactly who you are, and they're out looking for you. They've also figured out that one of your colleagues is Dr. Bertha Marshall. As I've been told, there's also a man hunt out there looking for her. As we speak, they're waiting for her to show back up at Prairie Baptist University in Houston where she'll be apprehended. After that, she'll likely disappear."

"What about Dr. Coxswain?" Hawk asked. "After all, he was up there with us, too! Is he in danger?"

"Not yet. Fortunately, the only living people who know the exact identity of Parker Coxswain are few and far between. If they capture me, I don't know how long I can hold out if I'm tortured. Neither do you. If you have any sense of decency, you and Dr. Bertha Marshall have to evaporate."

"Where should we go?" Hawk asked. "I have no idea how to get out of this jam!"

"I strongly suggest that you get down to Mexico. Go hide out at the Rancho Feliz in Santa Sangre, and see if you can find your cousin, Dr. Horatio Cloud. As of now, I'm on the lam. Only a few people in the tribe know where I'm hiding out, and it has to stay that way. Don't get caught and try and stay alive, won't you? Good-bye and good luck, Zachary. We shall never speak again." After delivering this dire warning, Elder Joseph hung up the telephone.

With that, Dr. Zachary Hawk quickly explained to Dr. Parker Coxswain and Birdy Marshall what was going on. Hawk made it clear that Captain Ray Noche and his Vampiro Containment Unit were on the prowl. Needless to say, every person in that hospital room was clearly terrified.

"For the love of God, I have to get out of here!" Zachary Hawk exclaimed. "Birdy, do you plan on coming with me, or what?"

"I don't know!" Birdy anxiously replied as she burst into tears." I just don't know what to do!"

"I'm going to Mexico, Parker," Hawk pleaded. "I need to find my cousin, Dr. Horatio Cloud. Tell me now—what was the name of the woman he fell in love with and followed down there? Don't lie to me. I'm certain you remember her name!"

"Okay, Okay!" Parker replied. "Her name was Lorena Pastore. Just pretend I never told you that."

"What difference will it ever make now, Parker?" Hawk asked. "You and I both know damned well that I'm never coming back. Let's go, Birdy! If Captain Noche and the Vampiro Containment Unit find us, then we're both dead!"

"Don't do anything yet." Parker pleaded. "I've fallen in love with you, Birdy Marshall! Marry me and I'll protect you. Stay right here. Give me five minutes and I'll be right back. I have something special that I was going to give you at dinner tonight, but I better give it to you now."

Parker sprinted to his personal locker in the research department and he grabbed a small black box that had a bow on it. He had of course suspected that the military was coming for Dr. Hawk, but just not that soon. Dr. Coxswain only hoped that he wouldn't get caught up in the drag net that was being cast out for Zachary Hawk.

He immediately returned to Dr. Hawk's hospital room to present to Birdy Marshall a diamond engagement ring. Sadly, he was just one minute too late. The room was now empty, as Zachary Hawk and Birdy Marshall were already fleeing for the border in an attempt to escape with their lives.

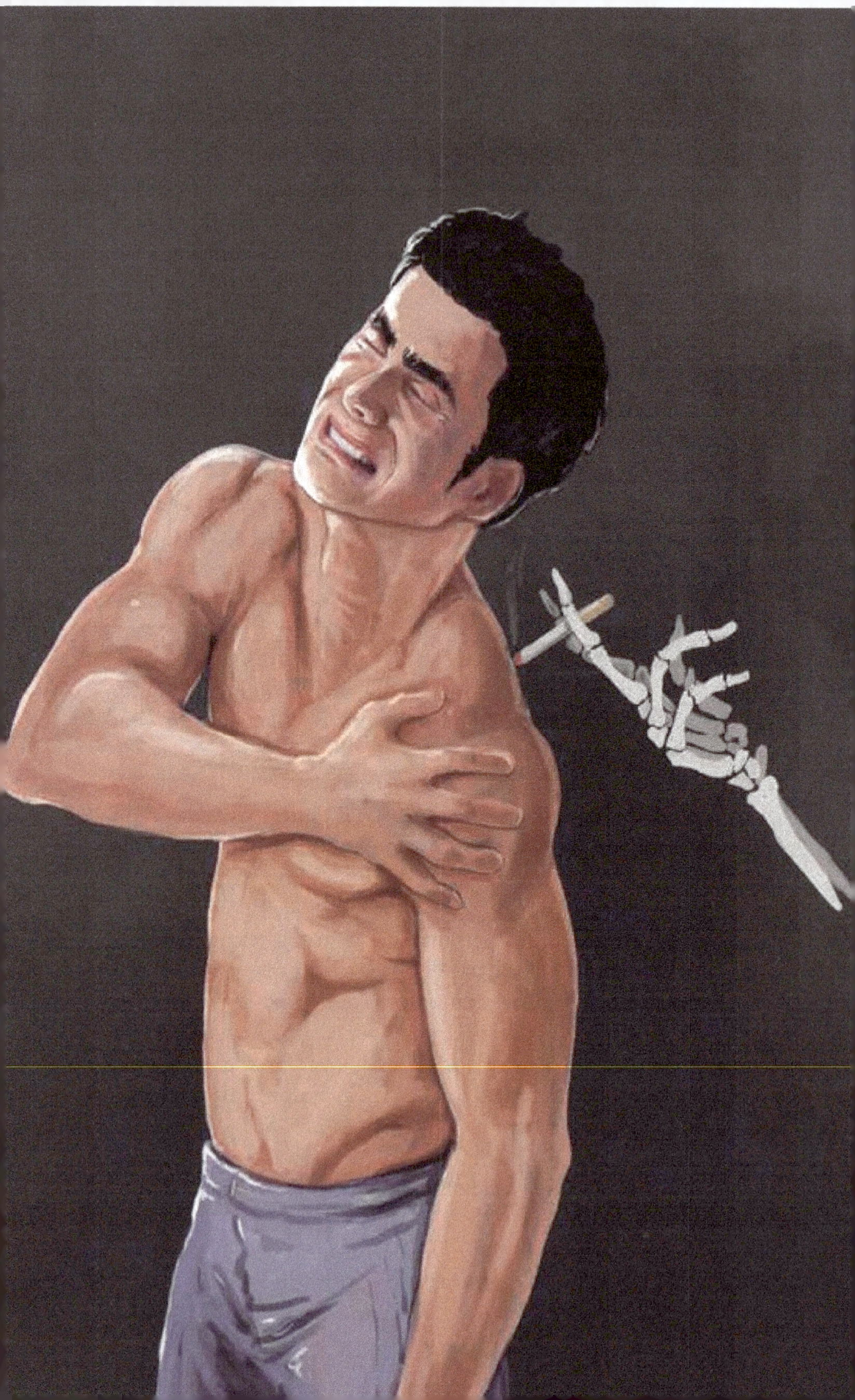

5

A LUCRATIVE BUSINESS PROPOSITION

As Blake Barker barreled toward the township of La Venta del Astillero in the militarized urban assault vehicle, another fever and shaking chill had come upon him hard. His tremor was so severe that Blake had a hard time maintaining a grip on the steering wheel of the ungainly vehicle that he had commandeered. He developed a pounding headache and his ocular acuity had tunneled to the point where he was losing his peripheral vision.

Since he had become a vampire, this was the first time Blake Barker had ever taken ill. There was no doubt that a direct temporal relationship existed between the shotgun blast to his right lateral thorax, rendered as a courtesy from the jail keeper named Llaves, and the subsequent onset of this acute febrile illness. Blake found it disconcerting that the gunshot wound in his chest was healing up nicely, however this had absolutely no bearing upon his fevers and chills which were clearly worsening.

Something was wrong, and Blake knew it, but what exactly was he supposed to do about it? After all, a man such as Blake who had undergone a dangerous viral infection induced transformation into a blood-sucking parasite would not likely be readily welcomed into a free standing urgent care clinic, or even into a hospital emergency room for that matter. The only thing now on his mind was to find his way to Rancho Feliz on the outskirts of Santa Sangre, and then get reunited with his missing son.

As his friend Miguel Pastore was also a vampire, perhaps this individual had some insight as to the nature of the acute medical malady that Blake was now afflicted with. If Lady Luck responded favorably to the plight of the parental pilgrim, Miguel Pastore would still be at the ranch when Blake got there.

Up until now, Blake Barker proudly displayed the decapitated head of the evil Romero Lopes as if it were a mere plastic trophy that had been awarded after winning the championship tournament at the Thursday Night Fat Man's Bowling League in Topeka. The lifeless skull was firmly affixed upon the factory hood ornament of the urban assault vehicle, and it was as if Blake was ready to challenge anybody who had taken umbrage with the ghastly specter. Blake's macabre automotive accoutrement was not particularly surprising concerning the circumstances. After all, Lopes had viciously murdered Blake's wife, Lynne. In addition, at the battle of Rancho Feliz, Lopes had actually crucified Blake's friend, John Stewart, upon a columnar cactus before the unfortunate individual was subsequently disemboweled. Displaying the decapitated head of Romero Lopes therefore seemed to be somehow justified.

If Blake was on top of his game at that time, he would have simply blasted through La Venta del Astillero without a second thought. If he found that there was indeed a roadblock waiting for him that had been set up by some Johnny-come-lately drug cartel, Blake would have gladly rolled up his sleeves before he proceeded to annihilate the impudent fools who had the audacity to try and stop him.

However, Blake was far from being at the top of his game. He certainly did not have the wherewithal to challenge a half dozen or more heavily armed combatants in light of his current febrile illness. Therefore, the better part of valor would be for Blake to ditch the decapitated head of Romero Lopes once and for all to assume a more discrete profile. However, in any way that Blake could possibly slice it, his urban assault military vehicle would never be able to slip through any town or past any road block under the radar. Nonetheless, he had to try.

Blake pulled his vehicle over to the side of the road and jumped out of the cab. He dislodged the decapitated head of Romero Lopes off of the factory hood ornament and proceeded to wedge the lifeless head underneath the rear wheels of the massive dually live-axle truck suspension. Once done, Blake climbed back into the cab, jammed the transmission into low gear, and then he proceeded to crush the skull of Romero Lopes into a pancake. Blake found the sound of the bones being crushed in the skull to be absolutely exhilarating. It gave Blake such a sense of emotional satisfaction that he felt compelled to back up the truck and repeat the procedure again and again while he laughed hysterically. "Take that, you filthy fuck!"

Somehow the vengeful act of desecrating the decapitated head of his longstanding nemesis was not only a cathartic experience for Blake Barker, but it was also an experience that Blake found rather invigorating. His acute fever had suddenly broken and Blake was now feeling strong enough to take on whatever his adversaries had planned for him in La Venta del Astillero.

Blake shoved the transmission into drive and proceeded to motor south, past the burg of El Campestre on the Carretera la Venta Nextpac road, directly toward the location where the Astilladora de Madera cartel had set up a cross-road barrier to shake down travelers east of La Venta del Astillero. Within about 50 yards of the road-block, the vampiro astutely ascertained that it was manned by a total of three men dressed in black jumpers, and each was toting an FAL automatic assault rifle. It was now time for Blake to go to work.

As Blake nosed toward a row of orange safety cones that were blocking the entrance lane onto Highway 15, he slowed his massive vehicle down to a crawl. One of the cartel foot soldiers who was wearing a medical face mask and protective eye wear briskly stepped out into the street and started to bang on the hood of the urban assault vehicle before Blake came to a complete stop. "Hello, sir!" Blake said to the man who had waived his truck to a stop. "Are you with the Federales?"

"No, not exactly," the thug answered. "The Federales are now working for our organization, however. We're the Astilladora de Madera Import/Export Consortium."

"Fancy that! Pleasure to meet you."

"I assure you, the pleasure's all mine."

"So, what's your relationship with the cops now?"

"The contract to control the activity of the Federales was previously owned by one of our competitors, the Calle Vampiro cartel. Since those bad boys went out of business, we had a golden opportunity to absorb this lucrative business relationship with the federal *policiá*, and all it took was just a bit of fine-tuning to their agreed-upon compensatory clause."

"Is that so?"

"Indeed, it is," the cartel thug replied with a squint.

"What's with the medical face mask?" Blake asked. "Have you caught a cold? I truly find it extraordinarily courteous and respectful toward the people that you're shaking down on this road for pesos. It would seem to me that you and your boys are trying to protect the population at large from getting infected with some type of nasty, community acquired virus of some sort. Nice! Kudos to you and your hard-working henchmen!"

"Frankly, my colleagues and I couldn't give a flying rat's ass about the public at large. We're wearing these medical masks because we expect to encounter a vampiro along this highway sometime sooner than later. As you likely know by the looks of your yellow skin and prominent canine incisors, vampiro eminate certain odors that can be surprisingly persuasive upon individuals who inadvertently inhale the mind-altering chemical scent."

"Hyperbolic rural myth, if you ask me."

"Shut up!" the thug commanded. "Enough of this happy, horseshit, chit-chat! A scientist who's working for our organization said that the chemical signal is called a 'pheromone,' whatever in hell that is. All that I've been told is that this chemical pheromone can put other people into a deep, trance-like state and they'll end up blindly following any instructions that the vampiro orders. Get the fuck out of the truck, turn around, and put your hands on the hood of the vehicle."

"Before I climb out of this cab, why don't we just test out this ridiculous theory of yours? Okay here it goes: I have a lucrative business proposition for you. Let me pass by, and I'll let you live. Now, get the hell out of my way!"

The cartel troll failed to move a single inch except to slide back the bolt on his assault rifle to chamber a round.

"See?" Blake asked. "I told you that your theory about some kind of magical vampiro, atomic powered, mind-controlling phero-mone was just a crock of cartel chicken shit. Nonetheless, I'm run-ning late as it is. So, for the last time, get the hell out of my way! Oh, my mistake–I guess I should have asked you to peel that medical mask off of your face in the first place."

Undeterred, the thug now pointed the barrel of his assault rifle through the window of the urban assault vehicle and placed it directly against the temple of Blake Barker. "So, for the last time, get the fuck out of the truck!"

A second cartel foot soldier walked up to assess what was going on. "This might be the vampiro that we are looking for. Do you hap-pen to be, Blake Barker?"

"That's me," Blake cheerfully answered. "Handsome fellow, am I not?"

"You're the mercenary that was working under contract with Colonel Augustus Placard's hit squad. You and your boys slaughtered the Calle Vampiro cartel to the point of not only financial bank-ruptcy, but also to the liquidation of their entire roster of employees except for a few stragglers that we may have picked up along the way."

"Not exactly," Blake said. "Although I actually know Colonel Placard quite well, I never really worked for him per se. I was more of a freelance assassin, I guess. That would certainly be a more accu-rate description of my rather loose association with his hit squad. In retrospect, perhaps I should have worked for him. I probably would have had a much greater opportunity to kill a lot more of you filthy mother fuckers along the way, as opposed to simply working on my own accord as a maverick."

"The Federales told us that when you were in jail in Juarez, you completely wiped out the Azteca gang with your bare hands," the first thug said with unabashed admiration.

"Well," Blake added, "that's definitely an exaggeration. It was more like with my bare *fangs*. Well, that and a straight razor I came upon that I had utilized to neutralize a rather rowdy crowd of drug dealers."

"Time for us to take possession of your military vehicle," the first foot soldier said.

"Be careful with this beast," Blake cautioned. "It happens to belong to Colonel Placard!"

"Oh, I promise you that we'll take care of it all right," the second soldier said with a sly grin as he opened up the door to the cab. "Get out of there, and I'll have Julio pull it into the shade."

The second thug motioned to the third man named Julio to take the wheel of the vehicle and park it underneath the bough of a tree by the side of the road.

When Julio stepped up on the running board, Blake got out of the truck and said, "Please treat this thing with the same deep, abiding affection that I have for it! I promised Placard that I wouldn't put so much as a scratch on this vehicle when I left the Calle compound."

"Go fuck yourself, gringo," Julio said as he climbed on board, slammed the door of the truck, and slipped the key into the ignition.

Before Blake had left the cab, he had found a hand grenade amongst the military ordnance on the heavily armed urban assault vehicle. Blake had casually pulled the pin on the grenade and set it up on the console right before he jumped out of the cab. No sooner had Julio turned over the ignition, the hand grenade exploded blowing the upper torso of the thug out the driver's side window while the lower half of his body from his pelvis to his feet remained in the driver's seat of the cab.

"For Pete's sake!" Blake Barker exclaimed as he hit the deck. "I told you guys to take care of that truck. Colonel Placard's going to have my ass on a platter when he finds out that you fellows messed up his favorite rig. I guess it is time for you boys to get that special spanking from me that you now so well deserve!"

Game on! After he jumped up from the ground, Blake slammed his forearm into the neck of *soldado primero del cartel* which immediately fractured the man's trachea. The thug clutched at his throat, barely able to inspire any ambient air across his crushed windpipe.

"Don't die just yet, amigo," Blake told his adversary. "I'll be back for you momentarily to finish you off!"

Blake recovered the FAL long rifle and shot *soldado segundo del cartel* squarely in the back between his shoulder blades as he was trying to flee the scene. Blake stomped over to the injured man who was still breathing at the time, determined to finish him off.

Although his fallen enemy had already sustained a mortal gunshot wound, Blake wanted this man to suffer. The angry vampiro dragged the FAL rifle behind him by shoulder strap attached to the butt stock. Upon inspecting his bloody handiwork, Blake proceeded to repeatedly strike the cartel member in the head with the butt of the weapon until he disassembled the man's skull. At this time, a stream of cars had stopped to witness the carnage. The travelers were ecstatic to see that the vicious members of the new cartel had just been eliminated, and they politely clapped their hands at Blake who smiled and waved back at them.

"Thanks, folks!" Blake said. "I hope you enjoyed the show. Be sure to leave a fat tip for your nice waiters and waitresses on your way out. They certainly are hard-working folks, and after all, they've been on their feet all evening. Stay sober and have a safe drive home! I hope you'll have a chance to catch my next show if and when I have the opportunity to pass through town again!"

Blake went back to the first soldier just as soon after the audience had climbed back into their cars and pulled onto Highway 15. "You know, I haven't been feeling well at all lately. I have been running fevers and chills up until this moment. I really think that there's something very wrong with me. Maybe if I dine on some fresh organ meat, that'll make me feel a bit better."

The injured thug was compelled to squeeze the lateral aspects of his trachea to maintain a partially patent airway, but his agony certainly didn't deter Blake Barker from enjoying his next meal. While his victim was struggling to catch each and every breath, Blake used his bare hands to simply rip open the man's abdomen with the expressed intent to isolate the victim's liver.

"Your *hígado* looks absolutely lovely," Blake said as he pulled a long knife out of the foot soldier's utility belt and delicately shaved off a piece of the right lobe of the man's gently pulsating liver. The vampire thoughtfully chewed upon the tasty treat before he said, "Boy, this is really scrumptious! You need to try this!"

Blake shaved off another segment of the man's liver that was about two inches long, one inch wide and about a quarter of an inch thick, much like a plank of raw blue-fin tuna that any sushi aficionado would have most likely savored.

"Have some!" Blake suggested as he impaled the piece of liver upon the tip of the man's knife and dangled it in front of his face.

The main course that comprised Blake's impromptu dinner could only look on in horror as he was actually offered a bite of his own internal organs to sample. When the man shook his head in between gasps for air, Blake Barker took this as a major affront. "Don't be rude," Blake insisted.

With that, Blake pried open the man's mouth and jammed the tip of the knife down the back of his victim's throat, eventually reaming out the man's pharynx. At the end of the entire ordeal, the tasty wedge of liver was eventually wedged in what was left of the thug's obstructed trachea.

"Man, oh man!" Blake lamented. "I've met some of the rudest sons-of-bitches in this shit-hole, shit-show country called Mexico," Blake said. "You offer man a bite to eat, and he doesn't even have the common courtesy to answer one way or another. I guess his *madre y padre* failed to teach him any social manners or dining etiquette when he was young. God, I hate this place!"

After Blake Barker had his fill, his fever, headache, and shaking chill came back with a vengeance. When he stood, he immediately stumbled and fell to his hands and knees. Although the urban assault vehicle was now a little more than a burned-out cinder, the three thugs whom he had just brutally dispatched had their own sedan parked by the roadside. Perhaps this vehicle would offer Blake the opportunity to escape the premises before any more cartel members, or God forbid, the Federales, would show up to incite more trouble.

Blake was able to crawl to the sedan, but unfortunately the keys were not in the ignition. He had to labor back toward the three men that he had just murdered. The closest was El Segundo, but his pockets were empty. The same was true for the man that he had just eaten. That only left Julio, the cartel foot soldier who had been blown in half by the hand grenade.

"I should have checked this guy out first," Blake lamented. "After all, he must have been the designated driver." Blake fumbled about in the man's incinerated jumper suit until fortunately the keys in question had been recovered. Blake tried to muster enough energy to crawl back to the sedan and get back on the road. Unfortunately, he didn't make it.

When Blake collapsed, one of the travelers who had witnessed Blake exterminate the three cartel members had come back to reassess the battle ground. When the traveler realized that his champion had collapsed after the melee, it was time to spring into action. The Good Samaritan pulled his own vehicle up to Blake Barker, opened up the back door, and dragged the vampiro into the backseat of his old, blue, Ford sedan before heading back toward Guadalajara.

"What you did today for the people in this region was rather heroic," the Samaritan said to a lethargic Blake Barker. "My name is Eduardo Gris. I'm taking you to a hospital in Guadalajara. The members of this new cartel have been known to run innocent people through an engine-powered wood chipper. As I know the cartel will be looking for you and for anyone who may have rendered you any assistance, my life will be in danger as much as yours. After I drop you off at the hospital, I hope you'll forget that we've ever met each other."

"Thanks for saving my bacon," the vampiro in the back seat mumbled before he passed out. "Barker. I'm Blake Barker. I owe you big time, amigo."

The hum of the car's engine would intermittently engender a brief state of supra-tentorial arousal during the mystery trip that Blake was now taking. When he did become briefly alert, Blake was able to realize through his feverish fog that he was being ferried about in the back of a stranger's vehicle. However, at the time, he was not able to readily ascertain as to whether or not he was amongst the company of a friend or a foe on these transient occasions of cognitive lucidity. He must have been amongst the company of a friend however, as the stranger took Blake straightaway to the University Hospital at the San Agustin College of Medicine in the Southwest corner of Guadalajara.

Afraid of retribution from the Astilladora de Madera cartel, the Good Samaritan did not want anybody to see him bring the Vampiro to the emergency room. If that had happened and if somebody had recognized the kind stranger, his life would be in peril. To make matters worse, if the word got out that the vampiro who had slaughtered no less than three cartel members ended up at the University Hospital in San Augustin, there was absolutely no doubt that heavily armed foot soldiers would have arrived on behalf of the cartel to meter out bloody vengeance against this impudent individual at any cost.

As this was indeed the case, the Good Samaritan engaged in what is known as a "dump and dash." North of the border in *Los Estados Unidos*, the technique of dropping off a patient in such a rapid fashion at the emergency room is also known as a "positive taillight sign." In any event, irrespective of the colloquial terminology utilized to describe such an emergency room patient deposit, the kind stranger pulled up to the curb in front of the emergency room, jumped out of his vehicle, opened up the back door of his sedan, and then dragged Blake Barker out by the ankles and left him there at the hospital entryway before fleeing the scene. All the while, the stranger was hoping against the likelihood that somebody had recognized him, or took note of his car and license plate for that matter.

⚕

"You're a bad, bad bear," Lobo Grande said as he buried a burning cigarette into the back of the Russian doctor. "You need to be punished. As best I can tell, you did absolutely nothing to try and save my three soldiers!"

"Save them?!" Bear said as he surveyed the carnage on Highway 15 outside of La Venta del Astillero. "What in hell are you talking about? One of your men was apparently blown in half. The top half of his body was blasted through the window of this burned out truck, and the lower half of his body was incinerated while stuck sitting in the front seat of the cab which must have been a raging inferno."

"Go on."

"One of your men was shot in the back and he then had his brains bashed out, apparently with the butt end of a rifle as best I can tell," Bear continued. "Your third man was a victim of predation. Although I'm no pathologist, by the amount of free blood that had been shed into the intraperitoneal space, it's clear to me that he was still very much alive when he was consumed."

"Well," Lobo said, "just don't stand there. Do something!"

"As you wish," Bear said. "Give me a shovel and I'll scrape up this shit and put it in the trunk of your Bimmer. That I can do for you. However, if you are planning on having me try to raise them from the dead, you're talking to the wrong guy. Last time I checked, I didn't have the stigmata of any nail marks through my wrists or feet."

"Who, or what, could have done this?" Lobo asked.

"How the hell could I possibly know? I wasn't here when it happened, and neither were you. Then again, I actually don't know about the veracity of that last statement. After all, your name is Lobo. That means wolf. That means you're a carnivore. Maybe you're more of a scavenger, like a hyena, as I know that you have a predilection to eat stuff that's been long dead and in advanced organic decay. After all, I saw that hag that you brought around the compound a while back. As best I could tell, that toothless old whore had likely been dead for years. Was she your mom? I hoped you enjoyed her company. Am I starting to piss you off yet?"

"Keep it up, 'Dancing Bear,' and someday I will personally introduce you to the wood chipper."

"I apologize. It appears that I may have digressed from the matter at hand. Be that as it may, perhaps you were here after all. I suspect that you're such a nasty fuck that you could have actually done something like this on your own accord."

"Wrong. I love my men," Lobo protested.

"That's right," Bear said with a truncated nod. "I won't contest that rather bold proclamation that you just uttered. After all, you told me when you first made me your slave that you do indeed *love* the men under your command. However, there's a lot of ways to love something or somebody. Maybe you *love* your men the way I would *love*, say, a wedge of lemon and a nice dollop of fresh *smetana* with chives upon a lovely broiled piece of salmon, which at this rate, I'll probably never again taste in the course of what should turn out for me to be a very painful and abbreviated life."

"I can assure you, your life is indeed getting shorter for you by the minute," Lobo said as he lit another cigarette. "I know that you are not a pathologist. You're an emergency room doctor. Nonetheless, you've seen a lot of trauma in the course of your medical career. I need an educated guess from you right now. In your medical opinion, just what could have done this to my men?"

"You know the answer as well as I do."

"Tell me," Lobo pressed.

"A vampire did this," Bear answered. "Nothing else is on my differential diagnosis list at this time."

"I was afraid you were going to say that," Lobo replied as he buried another burning cigarette into the back of Russian Bear.

⁎⁎⁎

"We rarely get visitors here at Rancho Feliz, Mayordomo," Miguel Pastore said to the manager of the Hacienda. Miguel finally looked up from a small stack of paperwork in his office at the ranch that had him preoccupied before he pulled off his reading glasses. "Who are they, and what in hell are they doing here?"

"They said that they're cartel members and they're looking for your friend, Blake Barker," Mayordomo answered.

"Oh, for heaven's sake!" Miguel said. "Not this again! How many times are people going to come around here looking for Blake Barker? Blake's dead as far as I know. What do they want with him, anyhow?"

"They said that they have a lucrative business proposition for him and it's one that he won't be able to refuse."

"Is that so?" Miguel asked. "What outfit sent these jokers over here? Are they from the new Astilladora de Madera cartel? I've met some of the foot soldiers from that gang and I can tell you right now, they're all top-shelf *pendejos* as best I can tell."

"No, Miguel," Mayordomo answered. "They said that they're associated with Chihuahua cartel from up North. They're dressed really nice. Silk suits with fancy ostrich cowboy boots that have a silver overlay on the tips. They even have silver belt buckles!"

"The Chihuahua gang, eh?" Miguel asked. "Those men are a bit off the beaten path, if you ask me. If they're going to try and make inroads into Jalisco, that's likely going to cause a turf war with the Astilladora de Madera cartel. I'm not sure if the good people of Santa Sangre can handle another assault from a cartel organization in light of what happened when the old Calle cartel was causing trouble around here a while ago."

"Don't worry, Miguel," Mayordomo said. "It is not like in the old 'Wild West' movies where Mexican farmers and ranchers are portrayed as helpless peons. Ever since the battle at Rancho Feliz against the Calle cartel, all of our men are now heavily armed at all times. We're not about to take shit from anybody anymore."

"Please tell me you didn't invite them into the house?" Miguel asked.

"Oh, no way!" Mayordomo answered. "If there's going to be a mess to take care of when this is all over, I want to be able to clean it up with a garden hose. That's why I have them sitting on the front porch. I hope you don't mind, but I offered them some hot coffee *con crema* with a plate of some warm raisin cookies that just came out of the oven."

"That's good thinking there, Mayordomo," Miguel said. "Tell La Ardilla and a couple of her boys to come up to the Hacienda and take care of this matter. Ask her to be so kind as to not put any more bullet holes into the front wall of the *casa*, though. The last time we had to deal with a couple of these cartel shit birds, I wasn't able to get a good match on the stucco patch work near the entryway. In the end, I had to apply a new coat of white paint to the entire front of the Hacienda. I just can't deal with that right now. I've got a lot of paperwork to do today."

"As you wish, Señor Pastore," Mayordomo said as he bowed and left the office.

Momentarily, an abbreviated burst of gunfire from several automatic weapons indicated that the unwelcomed visitors who had threatened the premises had been neutralized.

"It is all over, Miguel," Mayordomo reported. "One of the cartel members is dead and the other is bleeding out as we speak. Would you like to come out and have a snack? After all, un vampiro such as yourself doesn't have an opportunity to dine on human blood and internal organs very often."

"I suppose I could take a little break," Miguel said as he got up from his office desk and strolled toward the front porch.

"I hope you don't mind me asking," Mayordomo interjected, "but I was hoping that you might give me the permission to keep the boots and belt buckles that those men were wearing."

"Knock yourself out," Miguel answered while he buffed his canine incisors fangs with a napkin, "but if they have any money in their wallets, be sure to give it to La Ardilla and her boys. Oh—don't forget to hose off the front porch when I'm through eating, my old friend."

⚕

"Three of my men were viciously murdered, Colonel Placard," Lobo Grande stated when he asked his prisoner and slave to join him at a conference table for a formal chat. "Our friend, Russian Bear, believes that it was done at the hands of a vampiro."

"Yeah—I've heard," Placard replied.

"So, how well did you know Blake Barker?" Lobo asked. "Do you think he's capable of doing something like this?"

"Hands down," Placard answered. "The brutality that he's capable of displaying during a ruthless dispensation of his own brand of justice is truly a thing of beauty. From what he did to the Azteca gang in Juarez, I can tell you without a doubt that he's strong, fast, smart, and terrifying. Frankly, he must be running around with a sharp stick shoved of his ass because he has a mean streak that's a mile long."

"Did he fight in Indo-China with you?"

"No," Placard answered, "he was never in the military as far as I know, but by God, I should have had that man in Vietnam with me. With Dr. Ron Shiftless and me peering through a scope and somebody like Blake Barker slow-dancing with the enemy cheek to cheek, the United States should have been able to have exterminated the Viet Kong to the last man like the vermin that they were."

"So, you admire him?"

"He's a true warrior, and he probably doesn't even realize it. I would like to consider myself to be a true warrior. Yeah, I admire him. I'm going to make a point of working with him in the future after I break out from here," Placard professed.

"What are you saying, Colonel?" Lobo asked with a chuckle. "Are you not enjoying our warm hospitality?"

Placard still had the revolver that Llaves had given him and the weapon was safely nestled away in the colonel's undershorts. The only other people beside Placard in the cartel's conference room was Lobo Grande and one catastrophically obese and heavily armed henchmen who was sitting in the corner and placidly eating a bowl of roasted peanuts by the fist-full. It occurred to Placard that the guard was at the very least an extraordinarily tidy eater. As the fat man was consuming the peanuts whole without even bothering to remove any of the tough cellulose shell, there would be no bits of residual roughage or shrapnel left behind for the custodians to contend with later. It would be a real shame to be forced to shoot the docile appearing pachyderm when it got right down to the brass tacks.

It was time for Placard to make his move. "You're right, Lobo. I like it here just fine. Would you mind if I poured myself a cup of coffee?" Placard asked as he pointed to the coffee maker sitting on a countertop against the back wall.

"Well, of course! Forgive my manners, Colonel. I should have offered you a cup of coffee when you first got here. Help yourself. There's artificial sweetener back there but I'm sorry to report that we don't have any creamer."

"Thank you, Lobo, but black will be fine."

"We drink Kona coffee here," Lobo Grande said. "I've been told that it's the best in the world!"

"Do tell."

Placard stretched his arms before he got out of his chair and casually walked toward the counter on the back wall. Before he pulled the pistol out of his trousers to exterminate the two other men in the room, he glanced over his shoulder to confirm that they were completely unaware of what was about to happen. He saw Lobo lean forward to exchange superficial pleasantries with the henchman, and neither of the two men were watching him when he slowly reached down the front of his trousers with his right hand to grasp the weapon.

As the colonel slowly extracted the clandestine revolver, the door to the room suddenly burst open and six of the cartel's captains had strolled in to take seats around the conference table. The golden opportunity to escape had vanished as quickly as it had appeared. Placard exhaled a sigh before he discreetly put the pistol back down the front of his trousers. He slowly poured himself a cup of black coffee and then returned to his chair in a sullen disposition.

"Looks like you are about to have a party," Placard said, trying to hide his disappointment at a missed opportunity to escape the clutches of the drug cartel.

"In Español, we call it a fiesta," one of the captains said.

"I stand corrected," the Colonel said. "What's this all about, Lobo?"

"I have a lucrative business proposition for the captains in our cartel. We're going to try to recruit a vampiro to join our organization. We have reason to believe that your old friend, Blake Barker, is now working for the Chihuahua cartel."

"No way anything like that could ever happen. That Azteca gang was a subsidiary of the Chihuahua cartel. As Barker was solely responsible for the annihilation of the Azteca group, I seriously doubt that those fellows with the Chihuahua cartel would want to have anything to do with Barker, except for putting a bullet in his head. In light of that fact, I seriously doubt a man like Blake Barker would want to work for any of those nasty animals."

"Are you sure about that?" Lobo Grande asked. "After all, a man like you is now working for us."

"Yes, but at the point of a gun."

"You think that somehow it would be any different for Blake Barker under similar circumstances? As a matter of fact, I'd venture that once I was out of shouting range, you'd say similarly uncharitable things about my associates and me." Lobo Grande hypothesized. "Don't be naïve, Colonel Placard. After all, necessity can make strange bedfellows."

"What do you want from me?" Placard asked.

"Tactical logistics. We are going to attack the Chihuahua gang," Lobo explained. "We're going to hit them hard and take over their territory. We're going to punch them in the face and make their noses bleed. The leader of the Chihuahua cartel used to be a friend of mine. He's a mulatto known as Tigre Negro. He needs to be taken alive. I want to make an example of him. If Barker is with them, he'll come over to our team if he wants to save his own ass. What do you suggest we do first, Colonel?"

"Military intelligence in this situation is the key," Placard explained. "I'm talking about surveillance. We need to know where these people go, what they do, and when they do it. Once we have all of that ironed out, the rest of it should be a piece of cake."

"Good," Lobo Grande said. "I anticipated that answer. I'm proud to say that I was prescient enough to anticipate your needs regarding this matter. In this binder, I have the layout of the headquarters for the Chihuahua gang. We have an educated guess as to the number of foot soldiers that are now working for that cartel. We've studied the routine of Tigre Negro and we precisely know the exact number of body guards he has on hand at any given time of day. Pull up a chair and review this data that my men have accumulated on your behalf. Frankly, I think we're ready to get rolling on this hostile corporate takeover. Let's get to work!"

Later that evening when Placard and Russian Bear were able to recline upon their canvas cots in the slave quarters, the colonel whispered a question to his friend. "How bad did they beat you up today?"

"Well, it wasn't too terrible, all things considered," the Russian doctor replied. "Lobo Grande only burned me with a cigarette on my back on two occasions, but I didn't get the whip this time. Maybe our friend, Lobo, was feeling a bit tired today."

"He's a man who *never* seems to me as ever being too tired to spare a vicious beating upon a helpless prisoner, if you want my opinion."

"Perhaps," Bear finally concurred with a slow nod. "Has Lobo Grande hit you since you've been here?"

"Not yet," Placard replied. "Frankly, I think he knows better…"

━◦◦◦━

"I have a lucrative business proposition for you boys to consider. We need to expand the Brotherhood we've formed, but we still need to keep our group rather small," Amelia said. "If we add members to our Brotherhood and we get too many vampiros, or vampiras such as me as the case may be, I'd be afraid that we would simply tear each other apart at the seams! Frankly, I can barely stand being around you two boys as it is. I think another three more members added to our team will be enough. That would create a six member squad, including me as the leader. Frankly, we'll be unstoppable and Santa Sangre will be ours for the taking."

"Who do you have in mind?" Jesus asked.

"Right off the bat, pardon the pun, we need to get my friend, Celena, to join," Amelia replied.

"No way in hell we should invite her into this group!" Isaac said. "She's a deluxe bitch on wheels. In fact, she is a little snitch. If we invite her in, she'll run off and tell Sister Cabeza de Bala what we're up to. If that happens, they'll send in the Federales and we'll all most likely get burned at the stake! Think about that for just a moment."

"Bull shit! No, she most certainly would *not* snitch," Amelia said in defense of her school mate. "I trust her. What do you think about her, Jesus?"

"She's a whore," Jesus sneered. "Just like you are, as a matter of fact. The only difference as best I can tell is that Celena will charge a boy four pesos for a hand job. However, you must be a cheap, low-rent, discount whore from what I've heard. After all, Frederico told me that you only charge two pesos for the same amount of work. Tell me something, Amelia–are you starting to get warts on your palms from working overtime yet?"

This time, Jesus was ready for the vicious backslash that was coming his way. He was absolutely certain that Isaac would attack him first, so a pre-emptive strike was in order. The moment that Isaac stood up, Jesus lunged at the boy and sank his teeth into the face of the junior predator. Jesus violently shook his head back and forth, ripping out shards of facial flesh until the lateral aspect of Isaac's teeth and tongue were clearly exposed.

Enraged, Amelia sprang into action but Jesus wheeled just in time to thwart her attack. The vampira was literally parallel to the ground and just inches away from the face of Jesus when the boy clutched her by the throat and body-slammed her down into the pavement.

"Not this time!" her adversary crowed. Jesus proceeded to grab Amelia by the ankles, swinging her body overhead before crashing her down upon the pavement yet again as if he was an angry ball-player beating his bat on the ground after striking out at the plate.

"Stay still now," Jesus said. "That goes for you too, Isaac. Have you both had enough? By the way, Amelia, I'm nobody's slave!"

The pitiful moans that emanated from the brother and sister while they were both stretched out upon the ground indicated that the fight was indeed now over.

"Don't worry," Jesus said, "you'll both heal up in no time."

"Remind me to never piss you off again," Isaac said as he covered the hole in his left cheek with the palm of his hand.

"What got into you? You were like a wild animal." Amelia asked as she rubbed her shoulder which was injured in the altercation.

"Don't you get it?" Jesus asked. "We are *all* wild animals now. Well, where do we go from here? Amelia thinks that we need to expand the number of people in this Brotherhood that we've just formed. I tend to agree with her, but there's a risk that we might be fighting each other all of the time. I have an idea that we should practice something that I am going to call 'social distancing'."

"You are absolutely right," Amelia said "We should try to stay about 6 feet away from each other whenever we're in a group. That might decrease the likelihood that we'll attack each other."

"Why did you pick six feet, Amelia?" Isaac asked. "Why not three feet? Why not ten feet?"

"Well," Amelia said, "we have to start somewhere. This will be a trial and error experiment. If six feet of a distance is not big enough, we can expand it over time."

"Fair enough, I guess," Isaac said. "I can live with that."

"I can, too," Jesus said. "Let's decide who else we're going to bring into our group. I don't particularly like Celena, but as Amelia's our leader, I'll respect her choice."

"Frederico, Donatello, and Chico would be good guys to bring in," Isaac said.

"I like Enos more than I like Chico," Jesus said. "Enos has a mean streak and I admire that."

"That would make a total of seven people that we're bringing in to join us, not six. Nonetheless, I think that should be okay," Amelia said.

"How do we go about doing this?" Isaac asked. "Should we just ask them to join us?"

"Lord Camazotz, why did you burden me with an idiot for a brother?" Amelia asked as she stared down at the ground, presumably to petition the ancient Mesoamerican god of the bat who was widely believed to be dwelling in the depths of hell.

"Of course, we're not going to just ask them, you moron! We're going to attack them one by one, but not kill them. Once they go through the transformation, they'll *want* to join the Brotherhood. After all, there's strength in numbers. Besides, once they become infected, we can eat their parents and also the brothers and sisters in an ambush attack. That way, we could have food for all of us for quite some time. In the meantime, I need to come up with a formal initiation ceremony for future members. You boys can help me with the ideas, but just don't get too close to me. You guys smell like shit."

"As if you don't?" Jesus added.

"You're a genius, Amelia!" Isaac said in awe of his older sister.

"Of course I am," Amelia said proudly. "That is why *I'm* in charge!"

<hr />

"Frankly, I'm quite surprised to see that you're still alive, Dr. Shiftless," Holbert Hoefferle said. "When you apparently decided not to return to United States after your successful mission against the Calle Vampiro cartel, we just naturally assumed that you and Joe Cephas Smoot were dead."

"Wait a minute! Did you just make some seriously sick, lame-dick suggestion that Fang Boy over there and I actually *wanted* to stay lost across the Rio Bravo? To what end? Did you expect us just to wallow around in that pathetic and corrupt country known as Mexico for the rest of our miserable lives?" Dr. Shiftless was looking for answers. He then pointed toward Joe Cephas to offer him an open invitation for his much-needed perspective about the historical events that had transpired.

The former vampiro bioweapon trained by Uncle Sam had just come out of his apartment kitchen at that very moment carrying a refreshing pitcher of homemade sun tea on a tray with several red Dixie cups filled to the brim with ice cubes to offer his unexpected guests. For his part, Joe said nothing.

"Are you out of your fucking mind?" Ron continued. "I asked for an extraction after the job was done. I told General Sibley that Placard was MIA and Morales got butchered. However, I told you boys in San Antonio that Joe and I were still very much alive and well. We needed out. That's when I was told by Sibley that the plug got pulled on the vampiro bioweapon project. Tell me now, Hoefferle, were you behind any of that?"

"What are you accusing me of?" Hoefferle asked. "You can't be serious. In fact, as a man, I've never known you to *ever* be serious. You strike me as a juvenile delinquent stuck in a prison of perpetual adolescence."

"You're a pimp, Hoefferle," Shiftless continued. "You make me sick. You always wanted my job! I always knew that you were scheming some kind of a plan to eventually climb up my ass and claw your way to the top of the pyramid at bioweapon division. You boys probably want to replace me and become talent agents."

"As if I wanted your gig," Hoefferle said. "So, you're what–a 'talent agent' now? Did you remember to buff up your curriculum vitae? I thought that would be beneath even the likes of a man like you."

"Don't play dumb with me!" Shiftless continued. "I know for a fact that you were involved with some serious secret negotiations with either a big pharmaceutical company or a cosmetics firm after the government sponsored conference on human vampirism had concluded in Washington, D.C., earlier this year. You were planning on selling Joe Cephas Smoot to the highest bidder, weren't you?"

"What–like you did?"

"I should beat your ass like a kettle drum!" Shiftless snarled.

"Now, just settle down, Ron," Dr. Kohl interjected. "We did *not* come down here to Dallas just to get you and Joe Cephas Smoot all riled up. I just thought we could visit with you boys and discuss a lucrative business proposition. I was hoping that we could have a chat as gentlemen. After all, Ron, as you appear to be Mr. Smoot's business manager, we thought that we could frankly talk to you as an intermediary. However, if you're opposed to negotiating with us, we could go over to Joe Cephas and work with him directly. He clearly is the key to the resurrection of our vaccine and immunotherapy program to treat human vampirism."

"After all," Hoefferle added with a smirk, "he's only three feet away from us as we speak! If Smoot's amenable to the idea, we'll just simply cut you out of the equation. When I jumped over to the CDC from San Antonio, Dr. Blanks told me he thought that you were little more than a second-rate scientist. He never wanted to collaborate with you on *anything*. If that's indeed the case, we certainly don't need what little you can bring to the table at this time if we open up a round of negotiations with Mr. Smoot right here, right now, and right under your very nose."

Ron Shiftless stood up with the intent of boxing Dr. Hoefferle in his ears, but Joe Cephas grabbed his business manager by the back of his belt to forcefully restrain him and prevent what would have been a most unpleasant violent altercation.

"Blanks said that about me?" Dr. Shiftless stammered. "He thought, what–that I was little more than a second rate scientist? Is that true?"

"Of course," Kohl answered. "You know it's true, Ron. Sounds like you need to take a good, long look at yourself in the mirror and do a little bit of honest soul searching. From our standpoint at the CDC, we always thought that you were way out of your league as the medical director of the bioweapon team in San Antonio."

"Fuck off!" Dr. Shiftless screamed from the sharp, stabbing pain caused by a critically injured ego.

"How did you boys find me?" Smoot asked as he stood purposefully in between Dr. Shiftless and the two visitors from the CDC.

"You're all over the television now, Joe!" Dr. Kohl answered. "In fact, Fiesta Magazine announced that they were going to nominate you as the Sexist Man Alive for 1986. How about that?"

"You boys need to fill me in on something," Joe Cephas asked as he poured a glass of iced tea for everybody in the room. "Colonel Placard and I went to the University Hospital in Santa Fe earlier this year to try and recruit a patient named Miguel Pastore to join our bioweapon team. We weren't successful. He decided to join you boys down at the CDC instead."

"Yes," Kohl said. "He was on our team."

"At the time, I also met a fellow named John Stewart who had come down from Atlanta with Dr. Blanks," Smoot added. "Allegedly, that guy was immune to the vampire virus. What happened to those two fellows? Did anything pan out with the research that you were doing with them?"

"The first thing that we attempted was a trial of passive immunity by introducing immunoglobulins from John Stewart into Mr. Pastore," Kohl explained. "We were hoping that this procedure would clear the virus particles from the blood of the infected individual. Unfortunately, that didn't work worth a damn. We next wanted to take the serum from the infected patient and inject them into duck and chicken eggs to start a true vaccine program."

"How would that work?" Joe wondered.

"We know that duck and chicken eggs act as a biological reservoir for the RNA virus that causes human vampirism. If we grew out the virus in bird eggs, we could then chemically attenuate the virus and then use that antigenic bi-product as an active vaccine."

"Why bother with any of that?" Smoot asked. "When Dr. Shiftless and Colonel Placard came to visit me in Arkansas, I was told that the military had confiscated all of the infected chickens and the eggs from my Aunt Norma's coop. Why didn't the CDC just get those items from the bioweapon program to start the vampire vaccine program? After all, aren't the CDC and the military all part of the same government of the good, old, U.S. of A.?"

"Well," Hoefferle answered with some degree of obvious embarrassment, "all of those birds and eggs were inadvertently destroyed after their arrival in San Antonio. I guess that was an oversight on our part."

"Not an oversight on *our* part. It was on *your* part," Dr. Shiftless said, as he was now back on the offensive. "That was all of your doing back when we both worked for the same team, you jack ass."

"Guilty as charged," Hoefferle confessed.

"You did that behind my back," Dr. Shiftless said with a smirk. "Looks to me that you're little more than a second-rate scientist, and you probably never should have been hired by the CDC to begin with once the government shut down our bioweapon program in the end!"

"Well, despite all of that, Mr. Pastore was still working for you after the passive immunity trial in lower animals had failed, was he not?" Smoot asked. "If so, why didn't you just take his serum at that point and start on a new experimental vaccine program plan from scratch?"

"You're a lot smarter than what you generally let on, aren't you Mr. Smoot? I'm sad to say that the program never made it that far," Dr. Kohl answered. "Miguel Pastore and John Stewart left the program and they fled across the border into Mexico when Placard came back to the CDC to draft them into the expanding bioweapon team in Texas. Tell me something. When you were with Placard's hit squad in Mexico, did you ever run into Miguel Pastore or Jon Stewart down there?"

"Neither Dr. Shiftless or I had ever encountered those boys when we were across the Bravo," Smoot answered.

"Fair enough," Kohl continued. We don't exactly know what happened to Miguel Pastore down in Mexico. However, we do know that Mr. John Stewart was captured by the Calle Vampiro drug cartel. After he was viciously beaten, he was brutally crucified and then violently disemboweled, all while he was still very much alive. I understand that it was an unspeakably horrible demise. He likely died in unimaginable agony while watching his own macerated internal organs extruding out his ruptured abdominal cavity, appearing much like bloody curtain drapes that had been ripped to shreds by a chain saw on wide open throttle. It was all very sad."

Joe Cephas Smoot stopped in his tracks as his eyes grew as large as silver dollars.

"Why in hell would somebody do something like that to a fellow human being?" Smoot asked.

"Don't be naïve, Joe Cephas," Hoefferle said. "You know as well as I do that the long term goal of all the Mexican cartels is to capture and exploit human vampires to be utilized in their own, homegrown, bioweapon program. Although Stewart was captured by the cartel, he clearly wasn't the kind of guy they were looking for. I guess they just wanted to have some fun with the poor dumb bastard, so they gutted him like a fucking fish and nailed him to an enormous columnar cactus."

"Fun?! Is that what you said?"

Smoot made a surprisingly stark and expeditious decision about the "lucrative business proposition" suggested by the two research scientists from the CDC. Smoot reached out and pulled the Dixie cups of iced tea out of the hands of Dr. Kohl and Dr. Hoefferle before he succinctly concluded the meeting. "I'm sorry gentlemen to end your visit so abruptly, but it's time for you boys to leave now. Have a safe trip back to Atlanta."

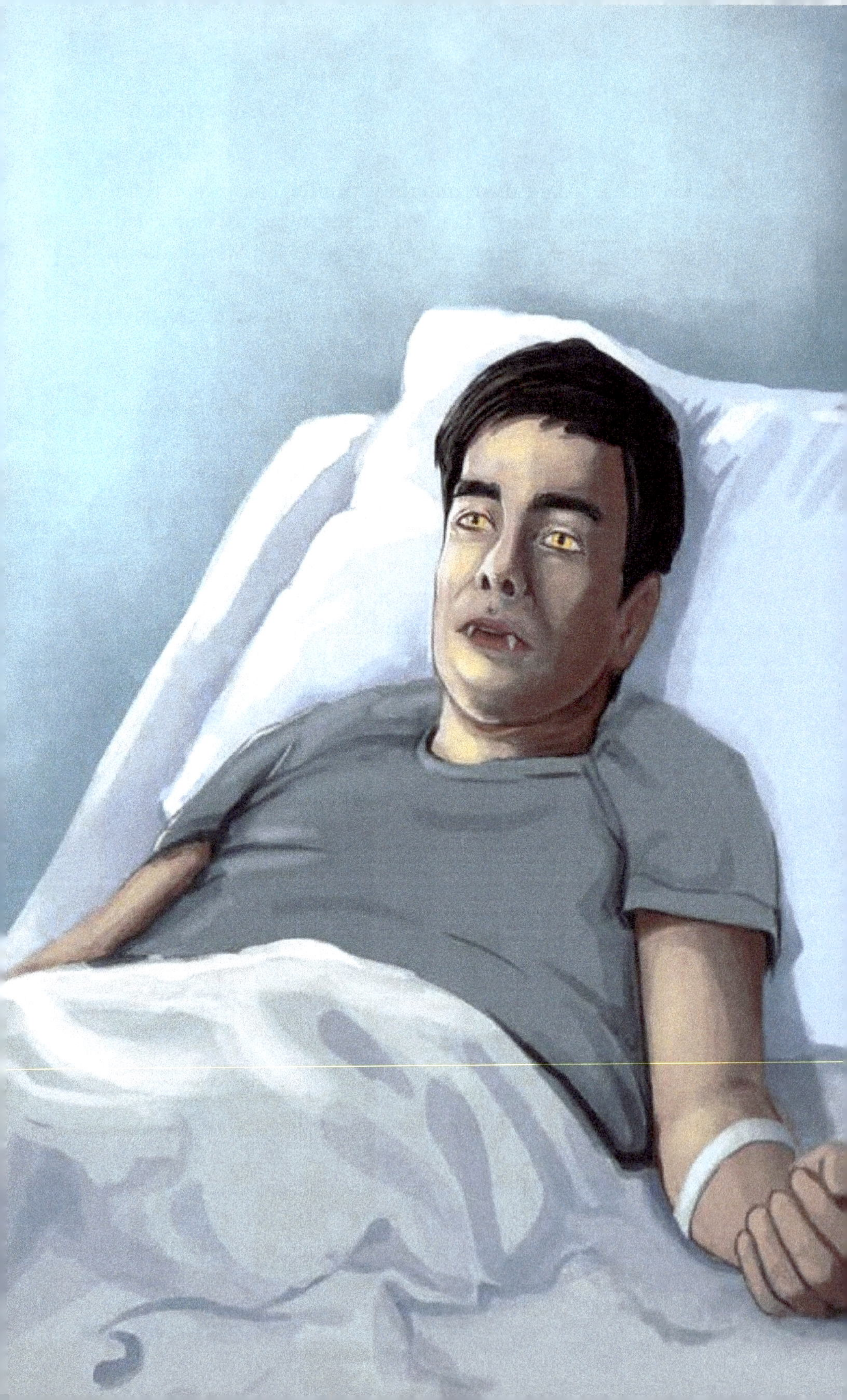

6

CONTAINMENT BREACH

"Hello, Lieutenant Noche. What brings you up to the University Hospital today," Dr. Coxswain asked when the military officer entered the consultation research department at the St. Francis College of Medicine.

"I've been promoted. I'll have you know that I'm now a captain," the soldier said.

"Congrats. Nevertheless, the question stands as stated."

"As for who or what brought me here, you did, Dr. Coxswain!"

"I don't follow you."

"That's exactly the problem," Noche said. "You've *not* been following me. More explicitly, you've not adhered to the contractual obligations concerning your state and federal agreements with Uncle Sam."

"Bull shit."

"Did you simply forget that you're serving as the medical liaison observation officer for the Night Crawler Protocol?"

"What are you implying?" Parker asked.

"Why didn't you tell me that you had a human vampire hospitalized here under the name of Zachary Hawk?"

"Stop right there!" Parker Coxswain protested. "He was *not* a vampire when he left here. Besides, he booked out of here against medical advice. When he split, he'd only been *exposed* at that juncture. He had *not* transformed into a vampire, per se. As a matter of fact, I'm not sure that he'll even do so."

"I don't care," Captain Noche said. "If somebody's been exposed, he or she might as well have the damned disease, from what I know."

"Can't prove it by me," Parker replied.

"You're a paid snitch," Noche said. "Nothing more and nothing less. Don't forget that fact. Next time you find somebody who's even just been exposed, you need to let us know."

"That's not in my contract with the Governor's office," Parker explained." The letter of the agreement is that I should only report to the military *confirmed* cases of the disease, not patients with just an exposure history. As a case in point, I have a separate contract with the CDC. It's called 'Plan B.' If I find somebody who's been exposed but not transformed, my first priority is to call the CDC, and not you boys."

"For shit's sake!" the captain exclaimed. "You mean to tell me that you're double-dipping?!"

"I got that cleared through the Governor's office. There's nothing in my contract that says I can't."

"Well, I'll see about that down the road," Noche said. "That's a conflict of interest if you ask me!"

"Nobody's asking."

"Doesn't make it ethical, though," Noche added.

"Ethical?! Is that what you just said, Captain Noche? You have the balls of a brass monkey, mi amigo. Unfortunately, I suspect that I can readily guess what the answer might be on this, but here it goes. I have no doubt that the military has the unfettered ability to simply eliminate individuals that go through the transformation and become human vampires. Be honest with me now, and tell me something, Noche," Parker pressed. "What does the military do with the folks who've just been exposed, but haven't gone through the transformation?"

"You are a smart boy," Captain Noche answered. "You should be able to figure that out on your own accord."

"Are you authorized to execute people by the guidelines found within the Night Crawler Protocol, or are you simply making up the rules on your own accord along the way?"

"What difference does it make?" Noche asked.

"Proud of that?"

"Frankly," the captain answered, "I am indeed. If I can save our country from an epidemic and maybe rescue the entire world from a vampire pandemic, then I would indeed be proud of my efforts."

"Delusions of grandeur, maybe?"

"Be nice, now. Time for me to clear up a few issues, Dr. Coxswain. You need to fill in the blanks about this Zachary Hawk situation."

"Not much for me to say."

"Does that mean you *can't* say or *won't* say? There's a difference, I'll have you know. As things stand, I'm not sure what team you play for anymore," the captain replied. "Let me ask you something, and you need to be straight with me."

"You're demonstrating paranoid ideation, Captain. Nonetheless, I'll humor you. Ask away," Parker offered as an insincere invitation. "I've got nothing to hide."

"Were you up at Chaco Canyon recently?" the officer asked. "That's where Zachary Hawk reportedly got infected."

"Never been there."

"Is that so? I'll need to look into that," Captain Noche said in a threatening manner. "During any of your interactions with Zachary Hawk before he disappeared, did he happen to tell you how he might have been exposed to the virus that causes human vampirism up at Chaco?"

"Never bothered to ask," Parker lied.

"Let me break it down for you. As it turns out, he impaled the palm of his hand on the canine incisor of an ancient skull that must have at one time or another, belonged to a living vampire. He never showed you anything like an archaeological artifact while he was here at St. Francis that would fit that particular description?"

"Of course not."

"I can tell you right now, bad things have been known to happen at Chaco Canyon," Noche added.

"Is that so? Wouldn't know," Parker lied. "Never been there."

"Yeah, so you've said. In fact, you've mentioned that twice now. Hawk had apparently gone up there with a woman and some other man. We happen to know the identity of the woman that had gone up to the canyon with him, but we just haven't found her yet. The same can't be said for the man in question, however. He remains a mystery. You wouldn't know anything about that, now would you?"

"Of course not."

"You wouldn't hold out on me, now would you?"

"I'm not even going to dignify that question with an answer. I think it's time for you to leave now, Captain Noche. There's nothing else for us to chat about today. In the future, I'll continue to participate in what you called 'double dipping,' if it's all the same to you."

"It would appear that our little 'father-to-son' fireside pep talk isn't going to have any bearing on your future behavior, now is it?" Noche asked.

"Be of good cheer, Captain. I wouldn't call our meeting of the minds to be a total waste of the ambient oxygen in this room. After all, I believe you and I have come to an understanding of the situation. As for now, if I find somebody who's just only been exposed to another vampiro, I have a *moral* obligation to call the CDC first. If I find somebody who's gone through the transformation, I have a *contractual* obligation to call you first. Those are two different circumstances, but I think that about sums it up, don't you?"

"At least we've hammered out a truce of some sort at this time."

"Now, by your leave, I'm heading up to the Memorial Hospital in Farmington to do a consult."

"You wouldn't be going up north to investigate a new case of human vampirism, now would you?" Noche asked.

"Some kind of blood disorder is all I know at this time," Parker answered. "If it's proper for me to tell you anything, rest assured, you'll be the first to know."

"That's interesting. Farmington is just north of the canyon," Captain Noche observed as he pulled at his left earlobe. "I forgot what you told me. Did you say that you've never made a trip up to Chaco?"

�⟨⟩词

"I'm glad that you agreed to come on this trip with me," Parker Coxswain said to his colleague. "I made a promise to an elder of the Navajo tribe that we'd look in on a 17-year-old teenager at the Farmington Memorial Hospital who got infected with the virus that causes human vampirism. Within one week of his exposure, he went through a full-blown transformation."

"Who's our contact up there?" Brewster asked.

"A guy named Jack Sayers," Parker answered.

"Internist?"

"Yeah," Coxswain replied, "with a subspecialty in infectious disease. He's afraid that things might be getting out of control up there in Farmington. In addition to Domino Lackey from the Navajo tribe, they apparently have two other people in the hospital that have also have been allegedly exposed."

"What in hell happened?"

"Since the kid got up there, he apparently attacked a cardiac patient in an adjacent bed," Parker explained. "The cardiac patient was apparently terminally ill. Once he received a bite from Domino Lackey, Dr. Sayers reported to me that the patient had a miraculous improvement in his cardiac function. Despite this serendipitous improvement in his cardiovascular system, he should have never been attacked in the first place."

"I'm surprised that they didn't have a guard keeping an eye on the kid."

"Well," Parker elaborated, "they apparently do now."

"A day late and a dollar short if you ask me," Brewster said. "What about the other new case that they have up there?"

"A phlebotomist from the lab got a needle stick from Domino Lackey just three days ago and although she has apparently not gone through a complete transformation as of yet, the medical staff has already noted a dramatic increase in her physical strength."

"Holy smokes!" Brewster exclaimed. "The case that we had at the University Hospital took a whole week before the transformation occurred post-exposure."

"Ain't that the shits?" Parker asked. "This is the first evidence that I know of that indicates the transformation time is likely to be a variable between individuals."

"Theories?" Brewster asked.

"Your guess is as good as mine. Maybe the interval from the time of exposure to the manifestation of symptoms is based upon the patient's own innate immune system. Perhaps it's some other variable such as the size of the viral load transmission to the new host at time of exposure."

"Do they have a 'crab-picker' on the case?' Brewster asked.

"Farmington Memorial doesn't even have a hematologist/oncologist on its entire staff," Parker answered. "That's where you come in."

"Well," J.D. Brewster said, "this isn't our first rodeo with this nasty business. I hope we can help out in some way and perhaps the outcomes on the multiple patients that are up there now will be better than what transpired with our patient, Miguel Pastore, who fled the University Hospital in terror before various, and I might add nefarious, organizations attempted to kidnap him."

"What amazed me was how fast everything got swept under the rug at the University Hospital," Parker said.

"I hope similar circumstances don't recur that would result in an adverse effect on the young fellow that we're heading up to see now. Be that as it may, how are they maintaining his nutritional status?" Brewster asked.

"The medical team exhausted the supply of packed red cells from the blood bank," Parker said. "I told them about the way we managed Miguel Pastore when he was under our care at the University Hospital earlier this year."

"You mean supplying the patient with beef and pig blood ad lib from the slaughterhouse north of Albuquerque?" Brewster asked.

"Precisely."

"How's that working out for them up in Farmington?"

"The kid is apparently consuming everything that they throw at him," Parker answered. "That's causing the medical team up there a considerable amount of concern, because the patient is now starting to exhibit dangerous and erratic behavior."

"Oh, swell," Brewster said. "If the situation is making those folks up in Farmington nervous, it's certainly making me nervous, too!"

"No doubt."

"If they have three bona fide vampire patients, is the hospital team up in Farmington willing to send them down to the University Hospital with the intention of allowing us to take over the management of this new disease?" Brewster asked.

"Absolutely not!" Parker answered emphatically. "According to the Night Crawler Public Safety Protocol, it's currently forbidden to transfer a case of human vampirism from one institution to another unless it's been specifically authorized by the CDC."

"How in hell would you know something like that?"

"I just do," Parker answered.

"What are you not telling me?"

"I'm telling you everything that you need to know for now," Parker replied. "Besides, I've never known you to be particularly enthusiastic about picking up extra work along the way."

"Although quite true, I've nonetheless been giving this vampire business a lot of thought lately. I just know that we could crank out a much better job the next time around if you and I have another crack at it. That is, of course, if we ever get a blessing from those who're royalty entrenched at CDC in the future."

"Rest assured, that will never happen," Coxswain said with a shrug.

"I suppose not, but as you know, I generally thrive when presented with a clinical challenge, Parker," Brewster explained. "After all, I dig seriously weird shit."

"As much as you seriously dig fat chicks?" Coxswain asked with a sly grin.

"Perhaps not *that* much," Brewster confessed. "In any event, if we bring this young man on board at the University Hospital, he'll need to be admitted under an alias and there has to be immediate media blackout about what's going on and what we're doing with him. If this disease is indeed caused by an RNA retrovirus like you and I now believe, we might be the first medical team to have an opportunity to offer this young man an effective antiviral treatment to try and clear this disease from his system."

"Acyclovir?" Parker asked.

"Why not?"

"I'm not sure if it would demonstrate any efficacy," Parker said, "at least in my humble opinion."

"You always have to be such a 'Negative Nancy,' don't you?" Brewster asked. "You strike me as a person who doesn't particularly like other humans."

"As if you do?" Parker asked. "As best I can tell, you don't even like yourself."

"Be that as it may, that acyclovir shit just might work in this situation!"

"Apples and oranges, amigo," Parker replied. "I don't follow you," Brewster said.

"The virus that causes human vampirism has now been given an official name: RV-1986. The name was jointly approved just recently by the CDC and the WHO," Parker explained.

"How in hell do you know that?" Brewster asked. "Do you have some inside pipeline for information that I don't know about? Besides, the WHO organization is controlled by the godless Chi-coms."

"C'mon man! The Chinese are good folks!"

"No dice. Dollars to donuts, the yellow peril on the other side of the world would try to hose us blind the first opportunity they might have. After all, they're funneling money to Democrat politicians as we speak. That filthy bastard on the intelligence subcommittee from the West Coast, Mr. E. Rod Swallowell, has already been caught chowing down on some dude's plumbing who happens to be a Chinese spy, named, Bang-Bang. Swallowell is a filthy traitor to the United States, but he'll skate through it without any ramifications because he's a fucking Democrat."

"No doubt, but in answer to your question, I *know* people who *know* people. I *hear* things. For clarity, that's not quite right. I'm actually *told* things."

"Parker," Brewster said with a mystified look upon his face, "you're a smart guy. You're a lovable goof-ball. Nonetheless, you're just a junior research scientist at a back-water institution in the middle of sheep-dip nowhere. You've only published two papers to my knowledge. How do you rate in a situation like this?"

"I just do." Parker cryptically answered.

"You are starting to scare me now. You seem to be a dark well of hidden secrets. Are you really connected?"

"Forget it. You're right. I'm nobody, I guess."

Brewster scrutinized his colleague for a moment while wondering what exactly was missing from the big picture, but he quickly got back on track with the problem at hand.

"Fine. Whatever you say. You never answered my question, however. Why did you mention that from an intellectual standpoint you wouldn't give acyclovir any consideration? I think it just might work in the virus that causes human vampirism, whether you call it RV-1986 or what would be my personal choice, the 'Booker Marshall Virus-1986.' What am I not seeing here?"

"Wake up, Brew," Parker said with a scowl. "RV-1986 is an *RNA* virus. The herpes virus, which is known to respond to the drug acyclovir, happens to be a *DNA* virus. Arguably, that's a more complex genetic entity."

"By what mechanism does acyclovir work in the setting of a DNA virus like herpes?" Brewster asked.

"Can't rightly say off the top of my noodle."

"Well, there you are. I can't, either," Brewster said. "When we get back to the university in Santa Fe, we need to make a point of paying a visit to the virologist, Dr. Joyce Lipton. Maybe the good nun can give us a clue, and then perhaps we can render a more cogent opinion."

"Not even worth trying in my opinion, damn it!" Parker exclaimed. "I am telling you, Brew—apples and oranges!"

"What's the matter with you, Parker?" Brewster asked with the look of concern on his face. "Anymore when I talk to you, you seem to have a burr up your ass. Have you heard from Birdy Marshall yet or from her new boyfriend, Dr. Zachary Hawk? Maybe they eloped together and ran off to Mexico for a little nookie in the land of *mañana*. Our maybe it's the land of bananas. I can never get that straight."

That was the apparent pecker gnat that finally bit the 'possum's penis. Parker pulled his car off the highway and slammed on his brakes bringing his vehicle to a dusty stop. He slammed the transmission into park and killed the ignition. He got out of the driver seat and circled the front of the car, opened the door to the passenger side of his vehicle, yanked Brewster out by his collar and heaved him down upon the shoulder of the road. Before Brewster could get back up to his feet, Parker took his left foot and smashed Brewster's left hand into the irregular and fractured asphalt on the shoulder of the road.

"I don't know how long it's been since somebody took you behind the wood shed, Brewster, but apparently it's been way too long."

Brewster stepped over the line, and he knew it. It was not the first time that he had pissed somebody off in his life and it would likely not be the last time, either.

"Layoff!" Brewster pleaded. "I think you broke one of the metacarpal bones in my hand!"

"You deserved it, as far as I am concerned," Parker said as he took the pressure off of Brewster's hand and stormed back over to the driver seat of the car.

"Sorry," Brewster said as he rubbed his left hand vigorously after he dusted himself off. "I'm not very good at discerning the subtle nuances of pending demonstrable emotional lability that may occur amongst discussants during human-to-human interactions from time to time."

"Understatement of the year."

"Are you—uh, are you in love with Birdy?" Brewster asked as he climbed back into the passenger side of the vehicle.

"Most definitely," Parker replied as he turned over the engine to resume the trip to Farmington.

"How do you know?" Brewster asked.

"What kind of question is that?" Parker asked. "I know for a fact that you were engaged once, and it was way back in the time when you and I were in medical school together. I even remember that the name of your fiancée was Stella. When she died, she was the head secretary for the university's Psychiatry Department."

"That's correct," Brewster said. "Enough, already. Okay?"

"From a dank fog bank that percolated out of a quagmire of confounding scuttlebutt, I heard multiple conflicting accounts about her premature demise. At alternating times, I was told that she had apparently passed away from a stroke, or a heart attack, or a pulmonary embolism, or perhaps she was even attacked and eaten alive by her pet cat."

"What?! Why are you doing this to me?" Brewster asked in a featureless monotone.

"Maybe Stella died from some other tragic, sudden-death event, akin to one thing or another. Doesn't matter now, I suppose."

"Not anymore," Brewster concurred. "Mind if I turn on the radio?"

"Leave it off, Brew. We might as well be on the planet Mars, as far as I'm concerned. Can't get decent reception out here, even on the AM dial," Parker said.

Completely oblivious that he was now torturing his colleague, Parker continued to reminisce about Brewster's dearly departed fiancée. "I met Stella a few times. Man, did she have a great sense of humor, or what? Cracked me up on more than one occasion. She was an old hippy chick, wasn't she? Always had the 60s station on in the psychiatry department, listening to those oldie-moldy tunes! I've got to say, that was a really sad shit-storm and a half that went down the chute when she up and died like she did."

"It's in the past," Brewster explained. "I travel in a straight line now. I can never look into a rearview mirror whenever I'm driving anymore, at least when I'm alone."

"Isn't that *all* the time?"

"If the truth be told," Brewster sadly concluded, "I can't even look at myself in a mirror, much less look at what all's behind me. As for now, why don't you grant me a favor and just shut the fuck up for the time being?"

Parker couldn't comprehend a direct request, much less any subtle hints from his forlorn colleague. "Did you ever come to grips with Stella's death? It must still be a very painful subject matter for you. I've been told that if a man ever loses a woman that he loves, he can't get on with life unless he has some kind of closure. Frankly, I'm not sure what that really means, but were you ever able to find any closure over what had transpired? I was always afraid to talk to you about that event. I've found that men are sometimes not able to share, well–you know..."

Brewster failed to answer, as he was just barely able to stare out at the vast horizon through the windshield without bursting into tears.

Parker continued to probe deeper into the psyche of his colleague as he finally steered his car into the parking lot of the Farmington Memorial Hospital. "If all of that story about Stella was indeed the case, then I assume that you must have been in love with somebody at least on one occasion during your miserable life. Am I right?"

"Yes," Brewster finally answered after an awkward moment of silence while Parker inched into a visitor's parking space. "No. Maybe. I'm just not sure anymore. Enough chit-chat. Let's find that Navajo kid and see what makes him tick."

"Sometimes, it seems to me that I just don't really know anything about you," Parker concluded.

"Let's keep it that way."

⚶

Cletus had just returned from the post office in the small town of Peto with a letter that was addressed to Lorena Pastore from the United Nations. Cletus could readily discern through the thin envelope that it was a one page correspondence. Any query that is answered with only a one page letter generally indicates an unfavorable response to whatever petition that might have been requested. That supposition holds true whether or not somebody is asking for a papal audience or perhaps something as mundane as statehood recognition from United Nations. To avoid any conflict with the "Queen of the Forest," Cletus elected not to open the letter and to just hand it over to Lorena and simply let events unfold.

Once he entered the ruins of Fortress Camazotz, Cletus was surrounded by no less than a dozen inhabitants of the compound who were eager to learn if Lorena's request for national recognition had been granted to the Mayan descendants. Although Cletus was not as gifted in the Spanish tongue as his younger brother Blake, the forest dwellers eagerly encircled him for some glimmer of good news.

"Un momento, por favor. Un momento. Va conmigo, amigos," Cletus petitioned the Mayan villagers.

As Lorena looked on from the doorway of her thatched hut within the confines of the compound, she saw that her consort, Cletus, was coming forward with several of her loyal subjects following in a single file line, much like how a revered teacher would guide his pupils to the office of the headmaster for a much anticipated field trip.

"I trust you knew better than trying to read a letter that was addressed to royalty," Lorena cautioned.

"I didn't open it," Cletus said. "It was addressed to you. As you are the one and only Queen of the Forest, it's your responsibility to explain to our people what has transpired in the court of worldwide public opinion."

"You are absolutely right," Lorena said. "Pomp and circumstance must be displayed during historical events important to the citizens of the jungle. Cletus, I want you to get the two obsidian blades out of the hut and stand behind me. Display each of the weapons over my shoulders. Don't forget to stand no more than three feet behind me at all times."

"Anything you say, dear."

If Lorena's self-proclaimed official title was the "Queen of the Forest", her consort's official title should have been nothing less than, "Cletus the Cucked."

"I–I love you, Lorena," Cletus meekly pined as he yet again regressed back into his accustomed and detestable subservient role.

"I know you do." Lorena answered as she opened the envelope and pulled out the reply that was sent to her from the United Nations. Crest fallen, Lorena silently read that UN had rejected her request of consideration for the Mayan remnants to be worthy of acceptance as an independent and sovereign state. The UN officially stated that a nation cannot be established solely on racial or ethnic considerations. As Cletus was standing behind Lorena, he was able to discreetly look over her shoulder and confirm the answer that the United Nations had sent to the Queen of the Forest, and sadly it was indeed the reply that he had precisely expected.

"What did the UN have to tell you, Lorena?" Cletus asked with the synthetic intonation of curious sincerity, although he was simply pretending to be ignorant of the contents of the correspondence.

For her part, Lorena was able to maintain a placid and almost content look upon her face as she ignored the question proffered by her consort. Instead, she instructed him to call out to the crowd that was milling about in front of the hut.

"Cletus, I order you to instruct my loyal subjects to lend me an ear."

"As you wish, your Highness," Cletus whispered back. He stepped forward to make an announcement to draw the attention of the forest dwellers. "Hear ye, hear ye!" Cletus shouted forth. "Your queen has an important announcement! Please give her your undivided attention."

Although she was rather short of stature, even by Mayan standards, the colorful, plumed head dress that Lorena donned had at least given her the superficial appearance of an individual, who at a cursory glance, was of average height. Before she addressed the growing throng, Lorena climbed upon a quarried block previously harvested from a fissure of limestone likely as old as the earth itself. Eons ago, the chiseled block had no doubt fallen away from the thick, defensive rampart of the ancient Mayan fortress, now being reclaimed by invasive tropical vines and thick, broad-leaf foliage.

"I bid a warm greeting to the citizens of the Fortress Camazotz, and also to the noble denizens of the rain forest. As you know, on behalf of the Mayan people, I had requested recognition of the Maya to be accepted as a freestanding, independent, and sovereign nation. I honestly had no idea how our request would eventually be received by the authorities at the UN in New York City. Today, my people, we have received a formal answer to our desperate plea! The United Nations has stated that the Mayan people will definitely be granted recognition as an independent country if we're able to exact retribution against the evil para-military soldiers who attempted to exterminate the Maya through Operation Sofia during the 37-year long Guatemalan Civil War. This war is not over, I tell you. We've only been in a short truce for the last four years, not a permanent peace. After all, we can never forget what was done to us. It's time, my people, for us to rise, resist, and repeat as necessary until we get the international recognition that we deserve!"

The crowd went wild.

"While we have no weapons at this time to engage our enemies in a guerilla war across the border into another country, I can only assure you, we soon will. As of tomorrow, I'm going to enter into negotiations with the cartel known as the *Astilladora de Madera*. We're going to offer this cartel a safe haven to grow coca plants here in our forest. In exchange, they'll give us automatic weapons and logistical support to launch out on military expeditions to hunt down our enemies and exterminate them. Tomorrow, we'll start a new program to slash and burn isolated regions of the forest before we start growing coca plants."

Alarmed, Cletus grabbed Lorena by the elbow and whispered into her ear. "Have you lost your mind? If you think the Maya were slaughtered during Operation Sofia, just wait and find out what will happen to us once the *Federales* find out what you're up to!"

"*¡Silencio, ahora!*" Lorena commanded. "The *Federales* are currently owned by the *Astilladora de Madera* cartel. The *policiá* won't give us any trouble."

Lorena called back out to the crowd to assuage some of the concerns that were being muttered amongst the Maya. "I suspect that some of you have concerns about the morality of growing coca leaves for a drug cartel, but rest assured, this is an export product that will be sent north into the United States. After all, the Anglo are part of the original European invasion of the Western Hemisphere, and if their people have an insatiable appetite for illicit recreational drugs, that's their problem, not ours. Let's gather here in the morning, and we'll start working on a division of labor to get this job done." With that, Lorena stepped down from the block of limestone and marched into the thatched hut with Cletus in tow.

Once inside the hut, Cletus went ballistic. "You're going to get us all killed! You can't just sit down and negotiate with some fucking drug cartel! It just doesn't work that way."

"Relax!" Lorena said. "That's exactly how it works."

"They'll probably slit your throat at the meeting, or worse. If you piss them off, they'll send a bunch of goons over here to Fortress Camazotz and kill everybody in this compound. I thought you cared for these people. Hell, I thought you cared for me. I must have been an absolute idiot to track you down here in the Yucatan."

"You don't understand, Cletus," Lorena said. "This drug cartel approached me, not the other way around."

"Now, why on earth would they do that?" Cletus asked.

"The cartel wants to produce a cultivated sub-type of the coca plant out here in the Yucatan. The specific species is called, *Erythroxylum Coca.*

"I thought the drug cartels grew their cocaine in Central and South America."

"If things work out for us," Lorena said, "that's about to change. The fellows I met from the cartel were very professional and they seem to be gentlemen. One was a botanist and the other was a chemist. They told me that this particular species of the coca plant can only thrive in a very acidic environment. I was told that the plant won't grow well unless the soil and water pH are below 5.5. The optimum pH value should be around 3.5 to give the greatest yields of the coca plant that can be processed into cocaine."

"Well, that's just dandy. For God's sake, Lorena," Cletus protested, "just listen to what you're saying!"

"No!" Lorena exclaimed. "*You* listen to what I'm saying! You'll be happy to know that as for now, we're spot-on with our water and soil requirements. Both the water and soil here in this part of the Yucatan have a pH of 3.6. Apparently, that's about as good as things can get without dramatically manipulating the environment."

"Well, Lorena, it would appear that you've gone from being a *curandera*, to a *gran bruja*, to *La Reina del Bosque*, and now you're graduating up to the big leagues to become of a bona fide narco-terrorist. Does that about wrap it up? Maybe there's something else out there that you want to try to add to your resume, just in case you'll ever want to go back to school and get your bachelor's degree to become a registered nurse. What in hell happened to you?"

"Don't you understand?" Lorena pleaded. "You heard the contents of that letter from the UN that I reported to our people just now. My subjects are standing at the threshold of a new era of equality for all with the redistribution of wealth to be spread amongst the masses! If we only rise up against colonial greed and force the white people of European ancestry to pay their fair share, we'll someday–"

"Stop! What are you talking about?" Cletus interrupted. "Just how much is a fair share?"

"I don't know."

"Sure you do," Cletus pressed the Queen of the Forest. "Don't hold back. I'm a *white* man, am I not? What would be my fair share? Spell it out for me so I can start saving up a few pesos in my piggy bank."

"All of it. Happy now? Everything you are, everything you own, and everything you'll ever possess. That includes everything your progeny will ever have, and it should be that way in perpetuity. There. I said it."

"You sound like a goddamned Marxist! You're a bigot. No, it's worse than that. You've degenerated into little more than a Latina supremacist who's apparently rejecting Western Civilization in its entirety. Are you a self-loathing, garden-variety racist who thinks the world owes you something? Are you ready to condemn an entire ethnic group for what you perceive to be an ancient evil that was committed in another time and another place by somebody else? Listen up!"

"Remember, Cletus, you're talking to a queen!" Lorena warned.

"Get this through your thick skull, your Highness," Cletus continued. "The sins of the father are categorically excluded from estate planning. Specifically, those sins are not bequeathed to the son as some type of trans-generational burden of ethnic or racial guilt. My Caucasian race is not a *burden* to me, but neither is it a *privilege*. Even if that was not the case, why don't you put the brakes on and take a look in a damned mirror, Lorena? *Your* ancestors came to the New World from a Western European country called *Spain*. Heard of it?"

"Don't get sarcastic with me."

"Except for the godless Moors who fucked up your country after they paddled across the Strait of Gibraltar, wasn't Spain predominantly filled with those evil *white* people that you now profess to despise at the time they sailed the ocean blue to get to the New World? By the way, that was quite a remarkable feat, if you ask me. If I were you, I'd be proud of that fact, not ashamed."

"Spare me the homily, Cletus. Spare me the history lesson."

"No, I won't. The home of your ancestors once ruled the high seas. Outside of Brazil, it colonized more than half of the Western Hemisphere. As best I can tell, they did a pretty damned good job at doing it, too! What in hell are you trying to sell to these people here, Lorena? A more pertinent question is what are you exactly trying to sell to yourself?"

"Our people don't know about my lineage, or even my ethnicity for that matter."

"Oh, the hell they don't!" Cletus corrected her. "They know that you're not *Indio.* I've heard more than one of the Mayan people refer to you as *La Reina Mexicana*! I'm telling you, they know."

"It matters not! In this modern day and age, a person can undergo a sex change operation to alter their gender, can't they? If that's the case, what's stopping a person from being able to change their race or ethnicity by a simple verbal proclamation? Therefore, *Yo soy Indio.*"

"You're not making a lick of sense to me."

"The only thing that matters is that I'm a queen."

"Likely self-ordained in your own coronation ceremony, constituting only one person who was in attendance as best I can tell!"

"It matters not!" Lorena said again. "Think about it! The reconstitution of the long lost Mayan Empire is within my grasp. Is that not worth fighting for? The people were elated to hear that they finally had a chance to once and for all throw off the yolk of oppression that has been going on for centuries. That letter from the UN offered them a glimmer of hope."

"I'm calling you out on this, Lorena!" Cletus said. "When I was standing behind you, I read the letter over your shoulder. It said nothing of the kind. Basically, the United Nations told you to go pound sand. The chances of the Maya people of ever being granted the prospects of living in their own sovereign nation are about as good as a dog's chance in hell! Why did you lie to them like that?"

Lorena was devastated. She had no idea that Cletus was aware of the contents of the rejection letter that had been sent to her from the UN.

"You—you knew what was in the letter?"

"You lied to those good people," Cletus said. "Why would you do such a thing?"

"I was just trying to sell them a bit of hope."

"Bull!" Cletus shouted in anger. "What you tried to sell them was a load of horse shit! I'm going back out there to set the record straight. Get out of my way!"

"Wait, Cletus!" Lorena pleaded. "Don't go just yet. Forgive me. I feel so vulnerable and alone right now. I need you to hold me. Hold me hard."

Lorena pulled Cletus close as she started to slowly unbutton his shirt to run her hand against his chest. As she firmly grasped his rather turgid pectoral muscles, she petitioned for a prolonged interlude of intimacy.

"Take me, Cletus," Lorena whispered as she got upon her tiptoes to nibble on his earlobe. "Take me now!"

The righteous indignation that Cletus had just professed had rapidly evaporated, much like the way an early morning ground fog enveloping the darkest recesses of the jungle will quietly remit upon the rising of the sun. Once again, Cletus Barker had regressed back into his accustomed and detestable subservient role as, "Cletus the Cuck." If it were only a title of nobility…

"I–I love you, Lorena." Cletus yet again meekly pined.

"I know you do."

<hr>

When Parker Coxswain and J.D. Brewster arrived to the third floor internal medicine unit at the Farmington Memorial Hospital, they went to the nurse's station to have their contact, Dr. Jack Sayers, paged. It was necessary for the two consultants from the University Hospital in Santa Fe to discuss the case with the local attending physician before evaluating the Navajo teenager named, Domino Lackey, who had allegedly become infected with the human vampire virus.

"Excuse me, madam," Parker interrupted a nurse working at the station. "My colleague and I have an appointment to meet Dr. Sayers at this spot at 9:00 AM today."

"Do I look like a 'Madam' to you?" The young woman replied. "I'm Nurse Raquel Abril. *Miss* Abril, I'll have you know. How may I help you?"

"I'm Dr. Parker Coxswain and this is J.D. Brewster. We came up from the University Hospital in Santa Fe. We're consultants to help out with a certain case concerning a young Navajo fellow named, Domino Lackey, who apparently is currently hospitalized on this particular floor."

"Of course!" The nurse replied. "I heard help was coming today. Frankly, I'm glad you gentlemen are here."

"Why so?" Parker asked.

"Things have been pretty crazy around here for the last few days," She continued. "Dr. Sayers told me that once you fellows got here, that you'd be willing to accept Domino Lackey as a direct transfer patient to the University Hospital. The discharge planning nurse informed me that she'd help expedite the arrangements for him to be shipped out of here in an ambulance."

"What?!" Brewster objected. "I don't like how things are shaping up."

"Something wrong?" Nurse Abril asked.

"Yeah," Brewster said as he waved his hand. "This is turning out to be a turf dump."

"If those arrangements aren't to your liking, we can readily make additional plans to have him constrained in an asylum-style straight jacket and then have him accompanied down to the St. Francis campus with an armed guard if necessary."

"Hold your horses," Brewster said. "To my knowledge, we're not authorized to accept this patient as a direct transfer. I don't believe that was ever suggested from what little I know of the case."

"Brewster is right about that," Parker said. "We're only here to do an onsite consultation and to make recommendations regarding further work-up and management."

"That just won't do!" the nurse said. "The Navajo patient is downright dangerous and he's already infected two other individuals."

"Where are those other two patients located?" Brewster asked. "Are they on the same floor here as Domino Lackey?"

"Those other two new patients are on a different ward above us on the fourth floor. Although they've not demonstrated any signs of violence, they're nonetheless kept under guard in a locked room. Dr. Sayers was actually hoping that you boys would be willing to take all three of these patients back to Santa Fe with you."

"Well," Parker stated, "we'd be obligated to take the whole batch back South, as long as Dr. Sayers notified the governor's advisory board members on the Night Crawler Public Safety Protocol. He also needs a certified blessing from the CDC to transfer the patients down to the university in Santa Fe. Of course, I would need to see the state transfer permit and the approval letter from the CDC before anything happens."

"Don't have it."

"Why not?"

"Dr. Sayers refused to let the government know what was going on here at the Farmington Memorial."

"I'll ask you once again," Parker pressed. "Why not?"

"Dr. Sayers heard the rumor that several individuals who had been exposed to the vampire virus somewhere out by Chaco Canyon had not only been apprehended and detained, but some of them may have actually been executed as there's an effort to keep a lid on top of this problem of human vampirism."

That was *not* just a rumor. That was a hard cold fact, and Parker Coxswain knew it. After all, he had been up there at Chaco Canyon when it all went down. Parker was actually a fugitive, and the government forces overseeing the Night Crawler Public Safety Protocol were actually his enemies. However, as often said, you hold your friends close and you hold your enemies even closer. Parker was forced to hide in plain sight. To do that, he needed to maintain a façade of complicity.

"What is she talking about?" Brewster asked. "You were up at Chaco Canyon just recently, Parker. Did you hear anything about government sanctioned assassinations of American citizens?"

"Not a word," Parker said with a shrug. "You know how rumors are flying around in these strange times that we now find ourselves."

"Well, I have no idea where Dr. Sayers is hiding out, but life is short and it's getting shorter by the minute," Brewster said. "I'll tell you what I'm going to do, Parker. I'm going down to the lab to evaluate the peripheral blood on the three patients at this facility that are allegedly infected with the virus that causes human vampirism. Ring me down at the hematology section when it's time to go. From my standpoint, I probably can't add anything more to the management of these three individuals that you won't be able to recommend on your own accord."

Brewster turned to the nurse. "Nurse Abril, I've already heard the low-down on the Navajo kid, but fill me in on the other two people at this facility that have gone through the vampire transformation. If you'd be so kind, I'll need a hospital face sheet print out on all of these patients, though."

"Can do." With that, Raquel Abril printed up a face sheet of all the three patients in question before Brewster headed down to the first floor main hospital clinical laboratory near the emergency room.

"Besides Domino Lackey that you already know about, another patient is a 52-year-old Hispanic gentleman named Marcus Cruz," the nurse said. "Check this out! This guy came into the hospital with end-stage hypertensive cardiomyopathy. He had been on the heart transplant waiting list for a long time, and he finally decided to give up. He was actually going to enter hospice for terminal care this week. After he got bit on the face by Lackey, a miracle occurred. Within just three days after the assault, the ejection fraction of Mr. Cruz had improved from its level on admission at 15%, all the way up to 60%!"

"Astonishing!" Parker said.

"Have either of you doctors ever heard of such a thing?"

"Supposedly, a vampire has impressive regenerative capabilities, as indeed this particular case would suggest," Brewster said with a slow nod. "Amazing, nonetheless. Give me the skinny on the third new patient."

"Penny Schaeffer. She's in her mid-20s, I suppose. She is a phlebotomist from the lab and sadly she got a needle stick from Domino Lackey before she went through the transformation."

"Sucks for her," Brewster said rather unsympathetically.

"Is that all you can say?" the nurse asked.

"That's why I always eat dessert first," Brewster answered as he turned to leave the nurse's station. "You just never know when something bad is going to happen."

"Brewster was right," Parker said upon Brewster's departure. "I don't have all day to wait for Dr. Sayers either. For some reason, he's not answering the page you sent. Please take me down to the hospital room of Domino Lackey. Maybe I can start a consultation history and physical examination upon him before Dr. Sayers shows up."

When Nurse Abril and Parker Coxswain walked passed the hallway to the lockdown room, something was wrong. The door to the room of Domino Lackey was open just a few inches, although the security key to the room was still firmly embedded into the receiver end of the outer deadbolt lock. Where was the security guard?

"Oh, no!" The nurse exclaimed. "Something bad has happened!"

"Did you eat your dessert first?" Parker asked with a smirk.

The nurse pushed open the door to see what was awry. What she and Parker Coxswain witnessed was absolutely appalling! Right past the entry way near the hospital room threshold was the security guard, reclining upon his back. Although his eyes were wide open, he was clearly dead. There was an enormous blood-filled cavity in his mid-section where his abdominal viscera had once peacefully resided.

As for Dr. Jack Sayers, he was on his knees and facing the side of the bed of Domino Lackey. The teenage vampiro was methodically, yet ever so delicately, nibbling away at the lateral aspect of the doctor's neck. Instead of putting up any type of resistance, Dr. Jack Sayers appeared to be gently and almost affectionately rubbing the hand of Domino Lackey while the lad was bleeding the doctor dry.

The physician finally fell away to his side and was gasping for his last breath when Raquel Abril emitted a blood curdling scream. It appeared just then that Domino Lackey had suddenly become aware that he had a golden opportunity to flee the premises.

"I'm sorry, Nurse Abril!" the teenager apologized. "I don't know what came over me. I've turned into an animal! God forgive me. I've got to go before I hurt anybody else. Please let me out of here!" He jumped out of his hospital bed and bolted toward the open door in a flash.

Foolishly, Nurse Abril tried to restrain the young man from departing the scene by extending her right hand to grab the teen by the sleeve of his hospital gown. Domino sharply snapped his head, and with a lightning-fast abduction of his mandible, he inflicted a puncture wound on the forearm of the unfortunate nurse to escape her grasp.

"I didn't mean to hurt you!" Domino exclaimed before he flew down the stairwell and disappeared from the hospital campus as if he were a raging desert dust devil.

"Some very angry men in military uniforms are about to show up and piss in the punch bowl. Come with me if you want to live!" Parker warned while he ripped a section of cloth from the pillowcase at the top of the bed to make an emergency bandage for the nurse's open wound. Before sprinting down the stairwell to the first floor, Parker pulled the lever on the fire alarm.

Dragging the nurse behind him, Parker plowed through the door of the hematology lab where Brewster was still looking at blood slides underneath the microscope.

"I heard the fire alarm go off," Brewster said. "What in hell happened up there?"

"I'll explain everything as soon as we get to the car," Parker said. "Before we go, I need to make two emergency phone calls. Pass me that telephone on the counter, J.D."

Brewster complied with the request of his colleague, and Parker placed his first of two long distance phone calls. "Is this the Night Crawler Protocol hotline? Good! This is Dr. Parker Coxswain. Agent number V–135. No, currently I'm *not* at the St. Francis College of Medicine at this time. I'm up in Farmington. I have a Class One containment breech at the Farmington Memorial Medical Center. Two dead. Three infected, although one escaped and is at large. Two are still hospitalized under guard on the fourth floor. Please notify Captain Noche immediately. No, I can't wait for him. I have urgent business to address, but he can call me later and I'll give him a fill-in-the-blanks update as best I can. I'll be back in Santa Fe before the end of the day. Thank you."

As soon as he hung up the phone from delivering his first message, he placed his second long distance telephone call. "Dr. Blanks? This is Dr. Coxswain. No, *Parker* Coxswain. No, not in El Paso. I'm in New Mexico, remember? That's right. No, I'm currently on a field trip at Farmington Memorial. I sure do! Actually, three active cases, one new acute exposure. It was a bite on the victim's right arm. Just about ten minutes ago. She's with me now. Are you still looking for an individual like this who's been exposed? Good. Do you still have the government-funded compensatory package that you mentioned? Good. Yes, I'm talking about 'Plan B.' Female. Latina as best I can tell. Appears to be in her mid-20s. By the way, as she's a registered nurse, I'm certain that she'll likely be on board with whatever you're planning on doing to her." Parker looked up from the phone and gave Raquel Abril a quick "thumbs-up" with a wink.

"Are you talking about me?" Raquel Abril asked with considerable alarm. "You better not be talking about me, ass-bag! I don't know who you are, or what you want to do to me, so I don't agree to do jack diddly-shit with you or anybody else, for that matter. Do you hear me?!"

Dr. Coxswain simply ignored her comments as he continued to converse on the telephone. "As far as that goes, there are three infected. One has actively transformed into a night crawler. He's a Navajo teenager named Domino Lackey. I just witnessed him murder and partially consume two people, but he escaped. The other two are apparently in transition but have *not* gone through a complete transformation as of yet. There's a fifty two year old man named Marcus Cruz and a twenty-something year old hospital phlebotomist named Penny Schaeffer. How? I was told that the older guy was assaulted and got bit by Lackey. No. No, not the woman named Penny. She reportedly got an on-the-job needle stick from the kid. As far as the nurse who took the fang? Well, I just don't know. Hang on. She's right here. I'll ask her."

Parker placed his hand over the receiver end of the telephone and looked at Raquel Abril to ask a question. "Do you people have decent workmen's comp at this gin joint?"

For her part, Raquel could only stare back at Parker Coxswain with furious anger. After a moment of awkward silence, Parker shrugged with a frown and returned to his conversation on the phone.

"You're good to go, Dr. Blanks. The nurse over here says that the accident, injury, and dismemberment clause found in their health care insurance plan is a rather generous, four-star rated policy rider."

"I said nothing of the sort!" The nurse protested. "Our health care insurance here is actually terrible."

"No dice, Dr. Blanks!" Parker said as he turned his back on Nurse Abril. "Those other two are still in guarded confinement. That's why it just won't work. You boys better get here a lot quicker than that, and then some! Why? Captain Noche and his containment team will soon be here. I'm absolutely certain that the subjects in question will be hunted down and exterminated before the day is over. Yes, that's more like it. Good. I'll be in touch as soon as the dust settles once I get Nurse Abril on a flight. Later this afternoon? Yeah. I can get her there on time, come hell or high water. No, the other two patients will be your problem. Thanks, Dr. Blanks."

Parker didn't even have time to hang up the telephone. He just threw it upon the counter and quickly guided Nurse Abril by the arm toward the exit while Dr. Brewster followed close behind. Once the party of three made it back to Parker's car, the terrified individuals jumped into the vehicle to speed back to the University Hospital in Santa Fe before Captain Noche and his containment team arrived to clean up what was certainly a God-awful mess.

"Where are you taking me?" Nurse Abril asked Parker Coxswain once the three medical personnel escaped the premises.

"I'm not *taking* you. I'm *sending* you, and it'll be far away where you'll be safe." Parker answered. "I'm sorry to say that the recent implementation of the Night Crawler Public Safety Protocol has unfortunately placed you and everybody associated with this hospital in grave danger. The local military liaison from the National Guard is a man named Captain Noche. He and his men are on their way here now. That's why we have to get out of here as soon as possible. I have a government contract that I just can't get out of. I'm a frontline medical agent for the Night Crawler Protocol, and I'm obligated to keep the state aware of any recent appearances or developments of vampire activity. That's why the captain and I know each other. At the point of a gun, I have to tell him what is going on, but I only let him know just enough to keep him out of my damned hair."

"What's he want?" the nurse asked.

"You! Once he finds out what happened here, he'll want you. That's a certainty. Either under his own accord or through a government sanctioned edict, he's taken a new 'scorched earth' policy when it comes to the government's efforts to enforce containment of this current vampire threat within the borders of New Mexico."

"What are you saying?" The nurse asked. "Am I now considered to be an enemy of the state?"

"Or worse. At first, the state had enforced a simple quarantine to those who had been exposed," Parker explained, "but it appears now that the military has taken it a step further. I'm sorry to say that the captain is starting to eliminate infected individuals, and also those who've received a bite from a vampire but who have not yet even gone through the transformation. Tell me something, Nurse Abril. Do have friends, family, a husband, boyfriends, girlfriends, or anybody else who's going to miss you once you're gone?"

"Gone for how long?" She asked. "A long time."

"I have nobody," she sadly answered.

"Good!" Parker exclaimed. "This will make it a lot easier for me to get you packaged up and sent out of here."

"What?!" the Nurse asked. "Where in hell am I going?"

"I know people at the CDC," Parker answered. "Smart people who frankly have a truckload more brains than me and who're also certainly more accomplished than I could ever be. They're in Atlanta and I think there's a good chance that they could come up with some new technology to arrest your transition into a full-blown vampire if that's destined to happen. Who knows? When it's said and done, maybe you didn't get infected when you got bit by Domino Lackey after all."

"So, there's hope for me?"

"No doubt," Parker continued. "If a post-exposure, immunological strike happens to fail, I'd still be optimistic that they could maybe come up with some ideas to keep your disease under long-term control if you go through the transformation. It won't happen overnight, however. Truthfully, it'll be necessary for you to relocate to the state of Georgia, at least for the foreseeable future. I can't make any guarantees, but there's a good chance you'll be protected from the long arm of the military that would love nothing better than to get their hands upon you."

"What would the military want with little old me?"

"They'd likely teach you how to kill," Parker explained. "The world is about to be filled with a bevy of wonderful new job opportunities for you."

"How am I getting to Atlanta?"

"Commercial flight this afternoon," Parker answered. "Once I drop off Brewster in Santa Fe, I'll take you directly down to the airport in Albuquerque. The CDC already has a ticket waiting for you at the Southwest counter."

"This is happening really fast!" Raquel said.

"Your life is going to end really fast if we don't get you the hell out of New Mexico!" Once he had finished his dissertation, Dr. Coxswain was unable to answer any more of Raquel's questions.

While on the road, J.D. Brewster could only stare at Dr. Parker Coxswain in unsettled bewilderment. Now fearful of his colleague, Brewster had to muster enough courage just to utter a simple statement.

"Sometimes, it seems to me that I just don't really know anything about you."

"Let's keep it that way."

7

A CASE OF MISTAKEN IDENTITY

Birdy Marshall looked into the rearview mirror of the old Bronco as she meticulously flossed her teeth out of either abject disgust, or sheer boredom. She would periodically scrutinize the view toward the rear of the vehicle in an effort to keep an eye out for whatever nefarious deeds Zachary Hawk was engaged. The Navajo initially appeared to be simply loitering about without any specific intent or design when a stray cat had suddenly approached the erstwhile archaeologist and started to rub against his left leg. Birdy could only shake her head and roll her eyes when Dr. Hawk grabbed the cat by the tail and body-slammed it against the asphalt.

The unfortunate feline was still very much alive when Dr. Hawk casually pitched the carnivorous quadruped upon the open tailgate of the old Bronco and began to ingest its internal organs after ripping open its abdominal cavity.

"I knew I shouldn't have come on this trip with you," Birdy complained. "Since you've become a vampire, you've acted little more than a deluxe, angry ass hole. Maybe I should have said a deluxe, angry *bat hole*. Did you even have the decency to kill that poor creature before you started eating it? I swear to God, I should have turned myself in to the authorities in New Mexico. I suspect they would have at least shown me mercy as opposed to this hell that you are putting me through right about now."

"Go ahead. Bitch and moan all you want, you ingrate," Hawk replied as he finished his snack. "I saved you a fresh cat kidney. Do you want a bite?"

"Fuck off."

"Is that the best way to talk to your only friend in the whole world on this little expedition that we're taking? If it wasn't for me, you would be dead right about now," Hawk added. "Don't you forget it either, sister."

"If it wasn't for you, I wouldn't be stuck in this God-awful shitty mess," Birdy replied. "Don't you forget it, either, mister."

"I should have eaten you when I first went through the transition," Dr. Hawk said in all sincerity as he got back into the driver seat of the car. "If I had done so, the utter silence and solitude would have no doubt been a God-send. Oh, but no. I've had to put up with your incessant chatter and whining ever since we crossed the Rio Bravo. To me, it's absolutely no mystery as to why you've remained single all of these years. If there was any poor idiot out there who was dumb enough to have married you, he would have thrown himself in front of a speeding car long ago just to put himself out of the misery that you would have caused him."

"Look who be talkin' shit right about now!" Birdy exclaimed in an exaggerated black dialect as she climbed out of her passenger seat to torture her traveling companion. As she forcefully straddled Dr. Zachary Hawk before he started the engine of the car, Birdy issued a litany of compelling demands. "Nuzzle me! Kiss me, you nasty bastard! Lick me! Eat me now, you blood thirsty savage!"

Birdy Marshall grabbed Zachary Hawk by the top of his scalp and pulled his face toward her as she started to rub her cheeks and forehead under his nose. Within moments, the desired effect had been successfully achieved when the vampire went completely ballistic! With brute strength, Hawk pitched Birdy out of his lap, mere seconds before he turned his head out through the open car window and started to engage in repetitive projectile vomiting. Once the contents of his stomach had been entirely spent, Hawk continued to rumble along with intermittent dry heaves. The cat that he had previously ingested was now completely regurgitated upon the side of the road amongst a foul admixture of florescent green mucoid secretions and caustic gastric acid.

"Don't ever do that again," Zachary Hawk pleaded. "You smell like a skunk! No, it is worse than that. You smell like funk! Pure funk, sister. No, it is worse than that. You smell like death! What on earth is wrong with you?"

"I have the sickle cell trait, you idiot," Birdy explained. "Don't you remember? I warned you of that fact once before. Just as I had predicted, my genetic quirk of having the sickle trait is a natural repellent to certain parasites like malaria. Obviously, it also appears to be an effective natural repellant against a dirt bag like you. Don't ever threaten to eat me again or I'll sit on your face and choke the life out of you. Am I clear?"

"Crystal."

"That's what I thought," Birdy smugly added. "Now, are you going to listen to me and bypass Guadalajara? You and I are not some happily married couple going on a site-seeing tour through the countryside. In fact, we're quite far from fitting that description. This is what I want you to do. I want you to turn off of Highway 23 and take a right through La Magdalena. Turn left at Santa Lucia and this will eventually get us to Highway 15.

"What are you babbling about?"

"Pay attention!" Birdy commanded. "That way, we can completely skip the entire congested metropolitan area and we'll end up a lot closer to our destination of Santa Sangre. As a matter of fact, if you had simply taken the highway toward Nayarit out of Durango, we would have been there already."

"I know where I'm going," Hawk replied.

"Yeah–straight to hell."

"I also know where I'm going amongst the land of the living," Hawk snapped.

"Clearly you don't," Birdy crowed. "You appear to be one of the rare men on this planet Earth that is directionally challenged. You just had to come the long way, didn't you? Hope you're happy with your very own primitive navigational skills. Have you ever even read a map before? Can't prove it by me. You make me sick."

"Sit back and just shut your pie hole for five minutes, will you?" Hawk asked his travelling companion. "I know exactly where we're going. On my things-to-see list in this life is the Templo Expiatorio in the heart of the city."

"I had no idea that you were interested in neo-gothic architecture," Birdy said.

"How could you possibly know," Hawk answered sarcastically, "when you never even let me get a word in edge-wise."

"Ha! Maybe they have a vampire gargoyle perched upon a church buttress that you can cuddle up with. It just might improve your foul disposition."

"Actually, I thought that this religious pilgrimage would be more for *your* benefit," Hawk answered.

"This should be interesting," Birdy said with suspicion. "How would a trip to this ancient temple possibly be for my benefit?"

"I was planning to find a priest for you," Zachary Hawk answered. "I was hoping he might be able to perform an exorcism upon you. Somehow, your evil spirits need to be driven away. It just might improve your foul disposition."

⟶⟿∫⟿⟵

Colonel Placard was still in possession of the revolver that had been given to him by the now dead jailer named, Llaves. The weapon had remained hidden within the confines of his undershorts, and as of yet, it had not been discovered by the members of the Astilladora de Madera cartel. Despite the fact that the former leader of the American bioweapon team of assassins was carefully scrutinized both day and night by the armed guards that held him prisoner, the gun was nonetheless an all-important "get out of jail card" that the colonel kept as a close-to-the-vest (or maybe close-to-the-plumbing) secret asset.

In order for the colonel to be able to utilize the revolver to trailblaze an avenue of escape, he had to be alone for a few moments with the cartel leader, Lobo Grande. Unfortunately, as the colonel was thought to be little more than a working slave, these opportunities were few and far between. Above and beyond retribution against the cartel leader, the colonel had to make certain that the Russian doctor would also have an opportunity to vie for his own freedom at the same time. If not, there was a great likelihood that Russian Bear would be brutally murdered by being dismembered with the infamous cartel's engine powered wood chipper. There was no way that the colonel could live with himself if that was ever allowed to happen.

For now, Lobo Grande was about to take Colonel Placard on a mission to exterminate a rival gang of drug dealers known as the Chihuahua cartel. When Placard was brought to the conference room, Lobo Grande was sitting on the top of his desk. Two heavily armed henchmen were standing in the corner in the background on either side of their leader. Once again, this was not a particularly fortuitous opportunity for Placard to pull out his pistol and start blasting away at his adversaries. It has often been said that patience is a virtue. Nonetheless, Placard was well aware that his patience was starting to run a bit thin.

"I believe we should test the proof of your military training, Colonel Placard. I'm hoping we can you give a passing grade on your tactical logistics," Lobo Grande said.

"My tactical logistics are only as sound as the intel that you provided me."

"My intel was sound," Lobo Grande said with more than a trace of aggravation in his voice.

"Well then, my tactical logistics will be just as sound as you profess your intel to be," the colonel quickly interjected in an effort to hold his ground.

"It better be. You'll be directly beside me when the assault occurs. These two boys that are standing in the corner will be directly behind you the entire time, amigo. If our military adventure goes sideways or if we fail to capture the leader of the Chihuahua cartel known as Tigre Negro, my boys will just kill you on the spot."

"Swell. Well, I guess I should be honored," the colonel said sarcastically. "I have no doubt that you considered running me through the wood chipper on more than one occasion."

"Yes, I suppose that's always a viable option," Lobo said with a grin. "If things go well on this military mission, I want to grant you a few privileges. If we succeed, you'll have won my trust. If we succeed you will have won the trust of the cartel. If that happens, perhaps someday I will see fit that you should be unchained from the painful shackles that bind your legs."

"Well, that's fine and dandy, I suppose," Placard said without any inference of gratitude. "What about my friend, Russian Bear? The shackles on his legs have caused a non-healing ulcer to develop on the front part of his lower left shin. If he doesn't get the shackles off his legs sooner than later, he'll have an open infected sore that will rot all the way down to the bone. Personally, I would bequeath any benefit that you plan to bestow upon me to my friend, Russian Bear. He needs to be shown a bit of compassion and consideration far more than I do at this moment."

"It remains to be seen whether or not the Russian doctor has won my confidence. For the time being, I suggest that you should be more concerned about your own affairs and your own wellbeing, Colonel Placard. I must admit however, that I do admire your altruistic and benevolent concern about your friend. To me, that confirms that you are indeed a man truly capable of loyalty."

"Will you at least give my request your consideration?" Placard asked.

"No. No I won't. If you continue to plead with me, Colonel, it will just make you look weak. Okay, boys," El Lobo said as he turned to the two thugs standing behind him. "Load the colonel on to one of the trucks with the other *soldados de pies*. It's now time to go to war against the Chihuahua gang at Ciudad Camargo."

⁓᪥᪥᪥᪥⟊᪥᪥᪥᪥⁓

As the Templo Expiatorio was located near the center of the enormous city of Guadalajara, parking spaces came at a premium. Fortunately, Zachary Hawk and Birdy Marshall were able to jump into a parking spot about a block from the religious shrine. Once the big Bronco was nestled up against the curb, the two travelers jumped out of the vehicle and began the short walk toward the tourist attraction.

"I promise. No muss, no fuss, and no trouble at all," Hawk told Birdy. "I just want to take a look around and grab some pictures. We'll be back on the road in no time. You'll thank me when this is all over."

"Famous last words," Birdy said. "Have you looked at yourself in a mirror lately? Frankly, you look hideous. Your skin has a near fluorescent jaundiced hue and you also have yellow eyes to boot. If it was not for your enormous canine fangs, you would look like a burned-up heroin junky with chronic active infectious hepatitis looking for another fix. As for now, with your nasty–ass teeth, you look like, well–you look like a damned vampire! I'm giving you a heads-up. In fact, this is a bona fide public service announcement. People are going to be staring at you. You're going to be drawing a lot of unwanted attention. If the authorities nab you because you've been careless, I'm simply going to lean back and laugh my ass off at you!"

"If the foo' shits, wear it!" Hawk answered.

"What in hell does that mean?" Birdy asked as the two pilgrims entered the temple. "You don't make any sense to me at all. Honest to God, I just can't stand being around you!"

"Is that so, Dr. Marshall?" Hawk asked. "You're truly an industrial-strength bitch on wheels. Now, I never met your brother, Booker, before he died. From everything I heard about him, he was regarded to be a top-shelf medical research scientist. Above and beyond that, Dr. Parker Coxswain emphatically told me that Booker was a true gentleman as well as a scholar. If that was indeed the case, I just don't know how your brother put up with you. I swear to Jesus, if you happened to be my sister, I'd be gnawing on my own wrists right about now!"

"Don't let me stop you," Birdy said. "Use your fangs. You should be able to make short work of it. Besides, leave my brother out of this. Are you trying to sully his memory? Better not. You remember what my skin smells like, don't you? You said it smells like death. Do you need a refresher course, red man?"

"Back off!" Dr. Hawk warned Birdy as the two archaeologists strolled the perimeter of the sanctuary, looking at everything while taking in nothing. "Tell me something. What does Parker Coxswain see in you anyhow? That pale face needs a new pair of bi-focal lenses, if you ask me."

"I'll tell you what he sees in me. A beautiful, smart, self-reliant, black woman. He sees in me what every white man should want. White men crave black women. Many are called, but few are chosen."

"I don't get it," Dr. Hawk said. "Just squaw for the buffalo soldiers. Nothing more, nothing less."

"Who's askin' you?" Birdy harshly asked. "Besides, you ain't *white* last time I checked. In fact, as best I can tell, you might not even be *human* anymore."

"Maybe I should just shut up right about now," Hawk said sheepishly.

"Maybe you should," Birdy snapped. "Parker Coxswain just happens to be smart enough to recognize me for what I am. I miss Parker Coxswain. In fact, I *dream* about him. I long for the day that I'll get to see him again. If you weren't an idiot who pilfered an ancient artifact out of Chaco Canyon, I'd be with him right now!"

With that, Birdy blew a raspberry into the face of her traveling companion, not realizing that they were being tracked by no less than two curious federal police officers who had followed them into the church.

⁕

The Good Samaritan known as Eduardo Gris was about to learn a painful lesson that no good deed goes unpunished. Soon after he had dropped off Blake Barker in front of the emergency room at the University Hospital at the San Agustin College of Medicine in the Southwest corner of Guadalajara, he returned west on Mexican Highway 15 back toward his original destination of La Venta del Astillero. Much to his astonishment, the Astilladora de Madera cartel had set up a new roadblock manned by four individuals within only a day from the time that Blake Barker had gone on a blood thirsty rampage and killed the three henchman who were shaking down the westbound travelers in the vicinity.

"Dios mio, how could this be? This new cartel must have unlimited manpower," Eduardo said to himself as he approached the roadblock. He pulled out his wallet and extracted a100 peso note to pay for the expected "toll" to get past the barricade. Unfortunately, the cartel was not engaged in a shake down at that particular moment. They were looking for somebody. Specifically, they were looking for him. Eduardo realized the peril that had befallen him as soon as he could hear two of the cartel members speaking to each other as they approached his open car window.

"Old. Ford. Four door sedan. Fits the description as best I can tell," said one wiry cartel thug called, Jirafa.

"This is it! The plates match the vehicle that was seen picking up Blake Barker on the roadside. In fact, it was right on this very spot. Time to ask this *cerdo viejo* a few questions," noted the impossibly hirsute colleague called, Mono.

Eduardo was in serious trouble and he knew it. He threw his car in reverse and backed up about 40 feet before he threw the wheel hard to the right to change directions a full 180 degrees. He rammed the transmission into drive and sped back toward the city of Guadalajara in the futile hopes of finding at least one law enforcement officer that was not on the take or was otherwise owned by the cartel. Sadly, for Eduardo, none would be found. Surely the cartel members wouldn't simply abandon their road block just to chase him down, now would they? Yes, they most certainly would. Initially, his view of the horizon behind his vehicle was obscured from the cloud of dust that his expedient departure had ejected into the atmosphere. However, as Eduardo strained to look through his rear view mirror, he soon became painfully aware that he was going to have a very bad day.

Two of the four cartel henchmen at the road block jumped into their vehicle to give pursuit. If anything at all could be said about the members of this new cartel, they were at least renowned to be well armed. To a man, they uniformly carried the Belgium made, Fusil Automatique Léger, short-stroked, gas-piston, long arm that was fully capable of spewing out the 7.62 x 51mm heavy NATO slug at an effective 650 rounds per minute. With a heavy fixed stock, the butt-end of the weapon was stout enough to crush the skull of any adversary if such a brutal tactical measure was ever warranted.

Try as he might, Eduardo was not able to escape his tormentors. Within moments, the two cartel members were directly behind him. The thug riding in the shotgun position proceeded to kneel upon the front seat of the car to get his torso through the passenger side window before he opened fire on Eduardo's vehicle. Bullets slashed through the rear of the old sedan which caused the trunk lid to disintegrate before the rear tires were finally blown out. Despite the horrific assault from flying lead projectiles, Eduardo had absolutely no intention of stopping his car come hell or high water, and surely hell was now upon him.

The high-pitched whine emitted from the rear axle of Eduardo's sedan was the unmistakable sound of a car that was now riding on a metal rim after the right rear tire was thoroughly shredded. As if Eduardo was riding an acetylene torch wielded by the very devil, sparks and flames were now pouring out of the right posterior wheel well.

Adding insult to injury, Eduardo felt a new harsh shudder also coming from the rear axle as the contralateral metal rim was unmistakably parting company with what little remained of the left rear tire. Unfortunately, the remnants of the tire quickly spooled up into the wheel well, and this acted like a differential brake that was placed on the left rear of Eduardo's car that was ignominiously coming apart at the seams.

The effective braking force on the left rear wheel caused Eduardo's car to make a sharp 90 degree turn on the highway at 105 miles an hour, and the old bomber began to flip sideways down the asphalt. The cartel thugs were amazed to witness that Eduardo remained safely buckled in his seat throughout the entire dreadful ordeal. The old land yacht barrel-rolled a total of six times before landing on the passenger's side in a concrete drainage culvert on the other side of the highway in the westbound lane. Somehow, Eduardo Gris managed to survive the single-car, catastrophic crash. The fact that Eduardo was still very much alive and uninjured at that particular juncture was not necessarily a fortuitous situation as future events would soon unfold. In light of the brutal pending calamity that Eduardo would be forced to endure, it would have been an act of mercy if the Good Samaritan had simply died in the wreckage on that fateful day.

⸻⦿⸻

"Are you Blake Barker?" The first federal police officer asked when he tapped Zachary Hawk on the shoulder. "You look like a man that we've been looking for."

"Sorry. Don't know the dude. My name happens to be Dr. Zachary Hawk. My wife and I came down from New Mexico to do some sightseeing," the vampiro lied as he pointed to Birdy Marshall, who at that time had a look upon her face akin to somebody who had just ingested a very large and angry bumblebee.

"I don't want to be too much of an imposition," the first police officer asked, "but please smile for me. I need to see your teeth."

Before Zachary Hawk could respond, the second Federale on the scene put on a medical-grade face mask and passed over another one to his colleague who was asking all the questions.

"Unless you plan on offering me a discount on dental work," Dr. Hawk answered. "I'm not inclined to show you anything."

"As you wish," the officer said as he is unsheathed his nightstick. "I'll be more than happy to give you some dental work right here and right now if you like."

"What's with the face masks that you boys are now wearing?" Hawk asked. "Are you trying to protect me from some type of infectious disease or are you guys already celebrating the Day of the Dead?"

"The only thing 'dead' around here appears to be you," the officer replied.

At that very moment, just before things got really ugly, two dozen prepubescent girls wearing white blouses and plaid skirts entered the temple. From a nearby parochial educational institution, the young ladies were on an important school field trip. As if magnetically drawn toward the powerful pheromones secreted by el vampiro, the children quickly surrounded Dr. Hawk, each vying for his undivided attention and affection.

The aggregation of school children had unwittingly become a venerable human shield that separated Birdy Marshall and Zachary Hawk from the two suspicious police officers.

"Let's work our way out of here," Hawk said to Birdy. "Keep these children close to us and let's make our way toward the front door."

"If we play this just right," Birdy said, "the kids will block these two federal agents from getting their hands upon us."

"Agreed! Let's move it."

"Stay with us, children," Birdy pleaded. "Let's all take a look at the temple together!"

For their part, the young children squealed with delight. Once Birdy and Zachary Hawk rounded past the first pew they bolted for the front door leaving the children behind in a bewildered state. The plan worked as the two federal agents were unable to get past the children before Birdy and Zachary made it back to the old Bronco.

"What in hell happened back there?" Birdy asked.

"Don't know."

"What did those federal agents want with you?" Birdy pressed.

"Don't know."

"Why on earth were those children so attracted to you?" Birdy relentlessly pushed for answers.

"Don't know."

"Why am I even talking to you?" Birdy asked in frustration. "You don't know a damn thing, now do you?"

"Apparently not."

"I don't know how you managed to get us lost," Birdy said as she studied the map once the two pilgrims were back on the road, "but stay on Avenida San Francisco. Turn left when you hit Juan Bernardino right before Colegio Guadalupe and this should get us straight to Highway 15, and then out of town."

"Sorry about all of this mess."

"No muss, no fuss, and no trouble at all," Birdy said sarcastically. "Is that what you said before we entered the temple? Why, yes you did. That was a direct quote, was it not?"

"Back off, Birdy!"

"Smell my hand, you human bat!" Birdy demanded as she waved her left hand in front of the face of Zachary Hawk. "I hope it makes you sick. I hope the odor emanating from my pores makes you want to puke."

"Back off, Birdy!" Dr. Hawk cautioned. "I'm warning you. Next time I puke, it's going to be in your lap!"

⟞⟞⟞⟞⟞⟞

The two vengeful cartel members came to a screeching halt directly parallel to Eduardo's critically wounded sedan that was now crashed into the drainage ditch. With unimaginable bravado, the two gangsters casually parked their car directly in the westbound lane of traffic with the nose of their vehicle facing directly toward *Ciudad* Guadalajara.

No sooner had the two thugs parked their car in the middle of the highway, a federal police cruiser popped over the horizon with its lights flashing and sirens blaring as if it were a streaking meteor coming directly toward the accident scene.

"Oh, shit!" The lanky Jirafa said to his colleague.

"Looks like we're in trouble now," his furry associate replied with a sly grin.

Without saying another word, the two cartel members heaved their long rifles into the back seat of their car, walked to the front of their vehicle, and dutifully put the palms of their hands upon a still rather warm engine bay hood while spreading their legs to avoid any potentially unpleasant confrontation with the two Federale officers who were now speeding toward the scene of the accident.

The federal cruiser was within 150 feet of the accident scene when the driver slammed on the brakes of his vehicle and stopped only inches away from the two cartel members who were still blocking the westbound lane of traffic. The two police officers climbed out of their cruiser and went straightaway to the cartel members. The Federale who drove the cruiser was an older individual with a receding hairline known as, Estofado, while his partner was a younger, portly fellow called, Rosquilla.

In turn, each of the thugs were quickly given a pat down by the obese officer, auspiciously to check for weapons and/or illicit contraband. Once this rote inspection was accomplished, it was time for the first federal agent to address the two criminals.

"What's the matter with you fuckers?" Estofado asked. "You boys promised me that you'd come to Nana's birthday party this past weekend. I can't tell you how disappointed she was when neither of you bothered to show up for the fiesta."

With that, the two henchmen grinned as they turned and gave each police officer a warm embrace.

"Lo siento, amigo!" Mono said. "We didn't forget! We just had to work that day to get a shipment ready for exportation. Come to the trunk of the car. I actually have a present for Nana, and I want you to give it to her on our behalf. It's all nicely wrapped with a pink bow and everything!"

"You guys are the best!" Officer Rosquilla exclaimed as he tucked the birthday present underneath his arm.

"What's in the drainage culvert?" Officer Estofado asked as he strolled over to scrutinize Eduardo Gris who was still trapped in his wrecked vehicle.

"*Basura*, more or less," the human gorilla critiqued. "I assure you, he'll be much less than that when El Lobo Grande is finished with him."

Officer Rosquilla yelled down to Eduardo. "Do think we're here to help you?"

"I would certainly hope so," Eduardo shouted upward toward the top of the culvert.

With that optimistic answer, the federal police officers and the two cartel members laughed out loud.

"If that were only the case," Jirafa added.

With that, the four men slowly worked their way down the concrete embankment to extricate Eduardo Gris from the hopelessly entangled sheet-metal and shrapnel remnants of the old Ford.

"Tell me, amigo, are you hurt?" Mono asked Eduardo. "No, no, I don't think so. I actually think I'm okay."

"Cover your face!" Eduardo was ordered just as chunky Rosquilla pulled out his nightstick to break the driver's side window that somehow remained intact throughout the traumatic and dramatic rollover accident.

Once done, the cartel henchmen and their police allies gently pulled Eduardo from the wreckage and propped him up against the side of his old vehicle to dust him off and carefully inspect him for any lacerations, broken bones, or contusions.

"Are you sure that you're not hurt?" The older officer Estofado asked yet again as he and his three other criminal conspirators escorted Eduardo out of the drainage ditch.

"It's a miracle that I'm not dead," Eduardo replied.

"At least not yet," Jirafa said with a laugh. "Let the beatings begin!"

The two cartel thugs watched with glee while the federal police officers began to mercilessly beat Eduardo Gris with their night sticks. Eduardo fell to his knees and tried to cover his head with his arms as he rolled into a defensive posture.

"Please don't kill him, gentlemen," Mono pleaded with the police officers. "El Lobo Grande wants to extract a bit of valuable information from this *bastardo*. We need to find out exactly what he knows about a certain vampiro named Blake Barker."

"Relax," Officer Rosquilla replied with a pant for air in between the dispensation of multiple sub-lethal body blows upon the victim. "We're just going to soften him up a bit for your boss. I'll have you know we have reason to believe that Blake Barker is somewhere in Guadalajara. As we speak, my associates are on the look-out for any *cerdo amarillo* with big teeth. I'll bet this hombre knows something."

Sadly, travelers driving down Mexico Highway 15 would invariably avert their eyes from the vicious beat down to which Eduardo was subjected. Every car would speed past the Good Samaritan without stopping to render assistance. Well, that is every car except a certain old Bronco driven by a particularly angry Navajo archaeologist from Los Estados Unidos, and his equally angry black female companion who was rather busy trying to wipe the vomit off of her lap with an old, mayonnaise encrusted napkin from a Taco Hell fast food joint. Both individuals were now not only on the lam from the authorities north of the border in New Mexico, but they somehow also managed to piss off the Federales in old Mexico.

"Well, well, well—what do we have here?" Zachary Hawk mused.

"Looks like they're going to beat that man to death," Birdy Marshall said with considerable alarm. "Pull over. You need to put a stop to this."

"So, you're willing to throw me to the wolves?" Hawk asked. "I thought we were friends."

"You thought wrong."

"What can I do? I'm only one man, Birdy!" Hawk exclaimed.

"You're more than that. You're not *one man*. You're *un vampiro*. You need to grow a pair, buddy boy. I don't know what that old guy did, but nobody deserves to get bludgeoned to death with night sticks. Get out there and save that man. Be a hero."

"Pray tell, what do you plan on doing once I get tossed into the breech?"

"Why, I'm going to cheer you on," Birdy said with a grin. "If anybody tries to slip away from your dispensation of justice, I'll help you mop up the left over shit with a tire iron."

"Deal!" Hawk agreed as a bargain was quickly struck. "Duck down low so they can't see you, Birdy. Keep your eyes and ears open. If I get taken down, fire up the Bronco, get the hell out of here, and try to get to Rancho Feliz near Santa Sangre as fast as possible."

Once Birdy was out of sight, Dr. Zachary Hawk pulled over and parked directly behind the big cruiser and sauntered out to confront the four men who were busy deconstructing Eduardo Gris. When Hawk walked up behind the four men, none were aware of his presence. Eduardo was in the prone position with his face turned to one side. The chunky police officer had his knee upon the neck of Eduardo who was able to weakly exclaim that he was unable to breathe. It was now time for Zachary Hawk to go to work.

"Excuse me boys, but you're blocking this west bound lane of traffic. Could you be so kind to move your cars to let me by?"

Startled, the four men reared back and glared at Dr. Hawk in stunned silence. Finally, the Officer Estofado had more than a few harsh words to say to the uninvited interloper. "I'm giving you ten seconds to get back into your car and drive around us. I strongly suggest that you get the fuck out of here right now unless you want some of the same medicine that's being dispensed to this *cerdo viejo* in front of me."

"Un momento," the furry Mono said. "Este hombre es de color amarillo. ¡Es un vampiro! It must be Blake Barker!"

"Wait! Let me see your teeth, hombre," Officer Estofado ordered.

"I'm going to start charging a peso for everybody who wants to take a look at my teeth today."

"¡Dios mio! It's Blake Barker!" Mono exclaimed.

"Who in hell is Blake Barker?" Zachary Hawk asked. "This is clearly a case of mistaken identity. This is the second time today that somebody thought I was a man named Blake Barker. Who is this fucker? Is he famous for something? Does he look like me? If he does, he must be one good-looking hombre! I can at least tell you that much."

"Get on the ground, right now!" the fat Federale said as he pulled away from the neck of Eduardo Gris who was now prone upon the ground. "I'm not going to tell you again, Señor Barker."

"Time to set the record straight on a few items," the vampiro stated. "Right off the bat, why do you think I'm some guy named Blake Barker? Well, I'm not. I'm an archaeologist down here on vacation. The next point of contention that I have with you fellows is that I'm *not* yellow. As I'm a member of the Navajo tribe, most people would actually consider to be a 'red man.' Well, to be honest, I guess I do have a bit of a yellow tinge now that I've transformed into a vampire. Nonetheless, the color red plus the color yellow equals orange. Therefore, I'm an orange man!"

"Stop with your lies! Orange man bad! Orange man bad!" Jarafa exclaimed.

"Just keep repeating that line, you bean pole!" Hawk exclaimed in an overt attempt to torment his adversaries. "Say it as many times as you like, but it doesn't make it true! Listen carefully and repeat after me. Orange man good! Orange man good! In fact, the orange man is the best that's ever been!"

Mono recovered one of the FAL long rifles out of the back of his sedan, "What's true is that I am going to blow your head off if you don't get on the ground right now. Get down on your knees and put your hands on top of your head, Señor Barker."

"Listen, boys–put your medical masks on this minute!" Officer Estofado instructed. "Otherwise, you might smell the chemicals that the vampire releases from his skin. He could trick us into doing something we don't want to do."

With that, the four criminals put on medical-grade personal protection masks upon their faces.

While Zachary Hawk complied by dropping to his knees, he was curious to know who he was dealing with at that moment. "What do you want with me? Who are you people?"

"We're members of the Astilladora de Madera cartel," Mono answered. "Our boss, El Lobo Grande, has been looking for you. You're now going to be a member of our organization. ¿Eres feliz, americano?"

"Is that so?" Hawk asked as he turned his head to address the Federales. "What about you jokers? Are you policemen, or not? Why don't you put a stop to all of this?"

"Who's the idiot now?" Officer Rosquilla asked. "We also work for the cartel, pendejo."

"Well, that's just dandy," Hawk said before he pointed to Eduardo Gris. "Why on earth are you beating that old man over there to death?"

"He knows you. We were just trying to loosen his tongue to get him to tell us how we could find you. Like bread from heaven, you just fell into our laps," the older police officer explained. "Beautiful, no?"

For the first time since the beatings had begun, Eduardo Gris had something to say. Sadly, it would be the last words that he would ever speak.

"Wait just a minute," Eduardo tried to explain. "I've met Blake Barker before, and this person here–"

"¡Silencio, saco mentiroso de caca! ¿Por qué sigues tratando de proteger a este vampiro?" Mono cursed at Eduardo Gris before he pulled the trigger on the FAL automatic weapon which cleaved away the top of the Good Samaritan's skull directly above his eyebrows.

"I should have kept you alive just to run you through the wood chipper! You would have deserved it, if you want to know my opinion. I'm just glad you're dead."

Zachary Hawk had just witnessed an innocent man executed right before his very eyes. For only a brief moment, he remained on his knees in stunned silence with his hands interlaced on the top of his head.

In the recent past, Zack had been a pacifist at heart. He had never raised his hand at another human being in anger, and in his idyllic life growing up on the Navajo reservation, he had never even been involved in so much as a minor school yard altercation. However, that was when Zachary Hawk was fully humanized. Things were different now. Very different.

"What did you just do to that old man, you hairy, monkey fucking son-of-a-bitch? Come over here!" Hawk demanded with an intimidating growl as he rose to his full measure. "Never mind, asshole. I'm coming over to you..."

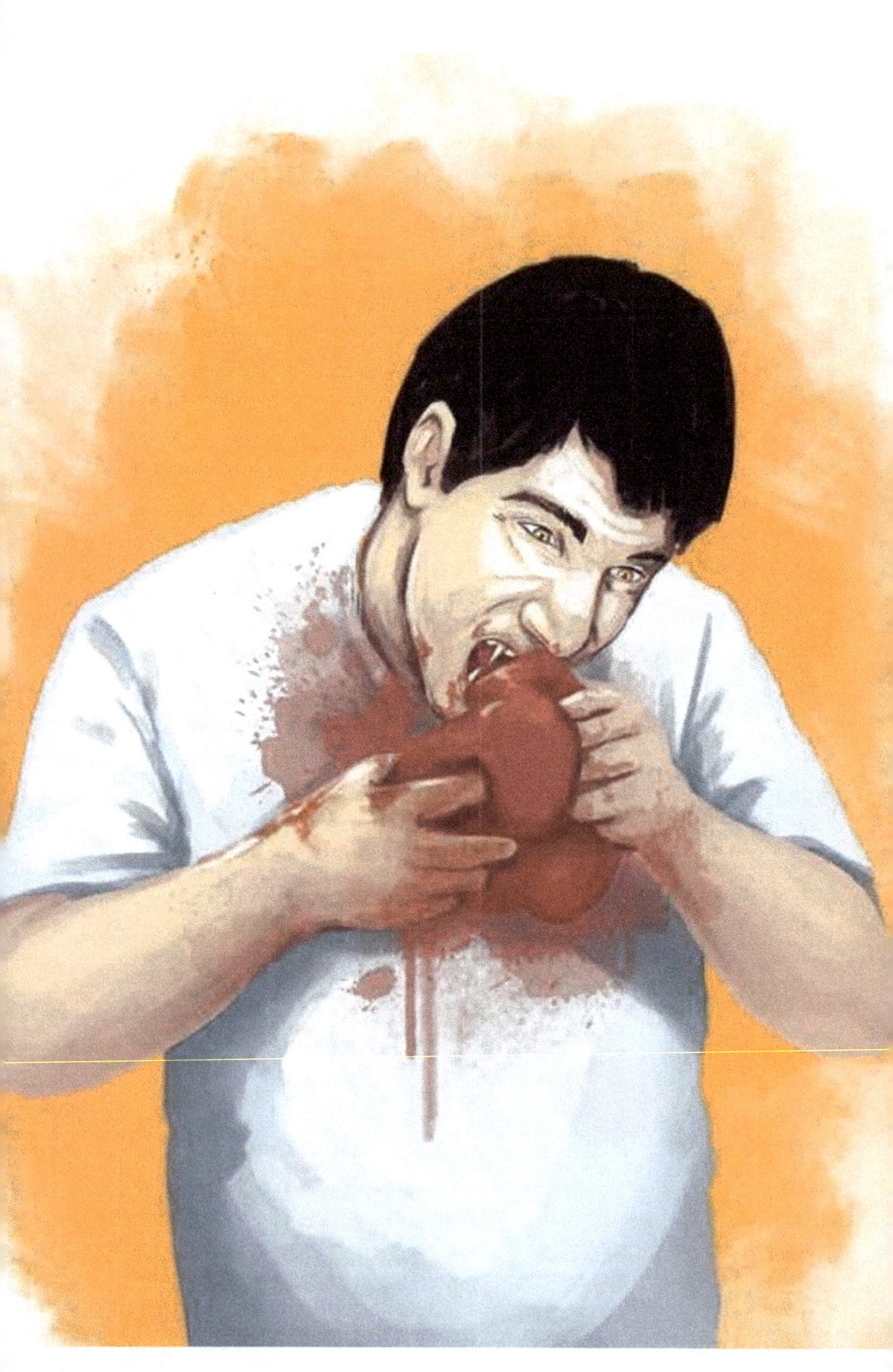

8

INTERNAL ORGANS

"Dr. Guzman!" A young medical student named Felix shouted out with excitement as he stuck his head out of the patient's hospital room to get the attention of his attending physician. "Dr. Guzman, you're not going to believe this. El vampiro has awakened from his coma!"

"I feel as if General Erwin Rommel and a division of panzers from his 'Afrika Korps' has just rolled across my skull!" Blake Barker said as he rubbed his aching head. "Where in hell am I?"

"You're at the University Hospital at the San Augustin College of Medicine," Felix answered.

"Swell," the vampiro said. "Glad to be here. You people probably saved my life. Who is El Jefe around here?"

"That would be me," the attending physician said. "My name is Dr. Roberta Guzman, and you'd be well advised not to use your real name around here. You've been hospitalized under the pseudonym of 'Señor X.' If you have any innate sense of self-preservation, you should refer to yourself with that moniker alone and never use your legal name while you're here."

"The reason being?" Blake asked.

"The new Astilladora de Madera cartel is looking for a man named Blake Barker. So are the Federales. This fellow in question apparently brutally killed three thugs that were working at a road block on behalf of the cartel, just west of Ciudad Guadalajara. Rumor has it that you're a one-man wrecking crew on a sacred mission to exterminate all of the narco-terrorist gangs in Mexico. I wouldn't suppose that you know anything about that, though."

"Not a damn thing," Blake answered with a grin. "Your name is familiar to me. Tell me something. Do have a brother who is a pharmacist up in La Frontera at Ciudad Juarez?"

"I certainly do," the doctor answered. "He called me a while back and told me he met a very interesting hombre amarillo that was possibly coming down to Jalisco to look for his missing son."

"It's a very small world."

"Indeed," the doctor opined, "and at more times than not, a very bad one."

"I can't help but think that everything in the universe is somehow connected," Blake mused.

"Of course it is!" Dr. Guzman exclaimed. "Anybody who has a pair of eyes in their head would be able to readily see that."

"How did you become a human vampire?" The medical student named Felix asked.

"I foolishly ate a bright yellow egg that was previously utilized in a huevo limpia ceremony," Blake answered.

"Oh, shit!" The student exclaimed.

"No," Blake replied. "It wasn't shit. It was a contaminated egg. What in hell is wrong with me?"

"You are un vampiro," the student replied.

"Yeah," Blake responded, "I know that, but here's the deal. I've been *injured* a lot of times since I've gone through the transformation, but I've never been *sick* before. I'll ask you once again. What is wrong with me?"

"You have developed acute myelogenous leukemia as a consequence to the underlying viral infection that causes human vampirism," the doctor answered.

"Damn! I was afraid of that. Do you have any experience with human vampirism? Do you have any experience with human vampires who've developed leukemia as a consequence to their underlying infection?"

"The answer is yes, and yes, again."

"You seem to be an intelligent and self-confident doctor, but if you don't mind me asking, what's your level of experience with this particular affliction that appears to be hell-bent on killing me sooner than later?"

"Before I was recruited to come out to the University Hospital here at the San Augustin College of Medicine to develop the bone marrow transplant service here, I was an associate professor of medicine at the Universidad Autonoma de Guadalajara," Dr. Guzman reported. "When I was at that facility, I participated in the healthcare of an elderly gentleman who was afflicted with the same disease that you have now. He was from a place called Rancho Feliz near the township of Santa Sangre."

"Oh my God!" Blake said with excitement. "Are you talking about an old rancher named Pepe Umbo? His friends knew him as El Tiempo."

"How can this be? You're from Los Estados Unidos, and somehow you've heard of Pepe Umbo? I can't help but think that everything in the universe is somehow connected." The doctor mused.

"Of course it is!" Blake exclaimed. "Anybody who has a pair of eyes in their head would be able to readily see that."

"So, do you know the ultimate fate of El Tiempo?" Dr. Guzman asked. "We never found out what happened to him after the bloody battle that occurred with the members of the now defunct Calle Vampiro cartel at Rancho Feliz."

"Sadly, the old rancher was dead when I met him," Blake explained. "The members of the cartel had crucified him to a cactus before he was brutally beheaded. They killed a friend of mine named John Stewart in a similar fashion."

"So now you clearly understand why your admission at this hospital has to be kept, how should we say, 'under the radar', No?"

"My name is, Señor X. It's a pleasure to meet you."

"Likewise. You've met Felix. The other three people in this room are also my medical students. They're all sworn to secrecy. Do you have any questions thus far?"

"Perhaps too many to count. How have you provided nutrition to me?"

"When you were in a coma, you were receiving transfusions on a daily basis. Now that you're awake, I'm hopeful that you'll be able to take in nourishment in the form of bovine or porcine blood that we can bring him from a nearby ranch."

"That would be fine," Blake stated. "So, do I have the same type of leukemia that had afflicted El Tiempo?"

"Not exactly. Pepe Umbo was battling a painful and pruritic chronic cutaneous T-cell leukemia/lymphoma that was chewing away at his hide. The skin on his body was turning into thick, tanned, red leather and was ulcerating with open and festering sores."

"Lovely," Blake said as he turned his head to look at the medical student named, Felix. "Make me a promise that you'll put a bullet in my head if that ever happens to me, young man."

"Not to worry. You have an acute myelogenous leukemia which is a type of cancer of the blood and bone marrow system that evolved out of a completely different stem cell line," Dr. Guzman explained.

"I was sick as a dog when some stranger dropped me off here at the hospital emergency room," Blake recalled. "I'm actually feeling pretty good right now except for being very weak. Have you started me on chemotherapy or some other type of cancer treatment at this time?"

"We've not tried to tackle your cancer as of yet," Dr. Guzman answered.

"Why not?"

"We thought it would be better to try and get your viral infection under control first. Since human vampirism is rare, you might be the very first person in the entire world who is being managed by receiving a trial of an antiviral regimen at this time. We're giving you a combination of two different types of drugs. One is an antiviral drug called, acyclovir. It's only been on the market for a short while now."

"Well, is it doing me any good?" Blake asked.

"You seemed to have only a partial response to this single-agent antiviral antibiotic, so we added an additional drug in an experimental fashion to see if it would add any efficacy in reducing your systemic viral load."

"So, what are you saying?" Blake asked. "Am I a human guinea pig?"

"No, Señor X. You happen to be a human bat."

"Very funny," Blake said with a smirk. "What's the name of the second drug that you're giving me?"

"It's an anti-malarial agent called, hydroxychloroquine. This is a drug that's been around for decades. By and large, it's considered to be fairly safe, however its use in this situation is rather controversial. I've been getting quite a bit of blow-back from my colleagues about using this drug on you, Señor X."

"What's the problem?" Blake asked.

"Technically it's considered to be an anti-plasmodium antibiotic and it's not actually a bona fide antiviral agent."

"It sounds like the use of that drug should be an agreed-upon private decision between the patient and his or her doctor without any bull-shit, sanctimonious interference from people who may have some type of different political agenda."

"One would think. You see, the drug hydroxychloroquine definitely works well against the intracellular parasite that causes malaria. In addition, however, there's also anecdotal evidence that it may disrupt the reproductive capability of the RNA virus that causes human vampirism."

"Frankly, I don't care about all of those details," Blake said. "Just tell me if the combination of these two drugs appear to be working or not."

"Oh, yes," the doctor added. "This combination treatment seems to be clearing the virus out of your blood and bone marrow quite nicely, although I must admit the treatment has been a bit hard on your liver."

"How so?"

"Your hepatic enzymes are now elevated and it seems that one or both of the drugs in combination are causing a chemical hepatitis in your situation," Roberta Guzman explained.

"Well, how serious is that?"

"Serious enough that we had to delay the planned initiation of chemotherapy which you'll eventually need to eradicate the malignant clone of your leukemia cells."

"I am a foreign national in your country. In fact, I'm officially a persona non grata at this time. How can I ever pay for all of this fancy treatment that you're utilizing in my situation?"

"You happen to be in luck, Señor X," the doctor explained. "When I was awarded the chair for the hematology and bone marrow transplant service at this new university, Pepe Umbo established a well-endowed foundation to engage in clinical research in the disease of human vampirism, and to also treat the patients who were afflicted with this disease and/or its complications."

"There must be a place in heaven for El Tiempo."

"If not," the doctor added, "then nobody would ever deserve to get there!"

"Amen, sister," Blake said with a dutiful nod. "Amen."

⸻

Captain Noche and his military team of soldiers from the Vampiro Containment Unit landed in two helicopters upon the roof of the Memorial Hospital in Farmington, New Mexico. Before they stormed into the facility, each of the soldiers performed a quick gear check to make sure that their hazmat suits were properly in place and their M-16 rifles were fully loaded.

"I need you boys to split into three separate six member teams," Noche ordered. "I want two teams to secure the fourth floor. There are two individuals that have been exposed and likely infected, but apparently have not gone through a complete transformation as of yet. One is a middle-aged or elderly Hispanic gentleman named, Marcus Cruz. The other is a young woman who apparently is employed here at the hospital as a phlebotomist. Her name is, Penny Schaeffer. Don't kill them here on the hospital premises. Just take them into custody and load them up on the helicopter."

"What about you, Captain?" One of the soldiers asked.

"I'll take the last team to the third floor and we're going to find an individual who has already gone through the transformation named, Domino Lackey," Noche answered. "All right, people– let's move before anybody else gets infected here!"

When Captain Noche and his team hit the third floor, the local police were already on hand to investigate the crime scene. The hallway was cordoned off with yellow tape to secure the vicinity. Upon his arrival, the military captain witnessed two dead bodies being zipped into body bags and subsequently loaded upon gurneys to be taken to a local funeral home for immediate cremation.

"It looks like my team and I are too late. We apparently missed the big fiesta that went on around here," the military officer casually stated to one of the police detectives on the scene. "I'm Captain Noche. I'm the regional military director of the Vampiro Containment Unit."

"Oh, yeah. Been expecting you. HQ said you and your team were coming. You guys got here pretty quick. It must have been a real laugh riot in this room, as best I can tell. By the way, I'm Detective Correa. There was a nasty kid in this room named Domino Lackey who had gone through the transformation into becoming a vampire."

"He was stuck in this room like, what—a normal, run-of-the-mill patient?" Noche asked. "Don't tell me that no additional precautions were taken by the hospital."

"It apparently wasn't like that," the inspector answered. "The appropriate security measures were allegedly undertaken per the published directives found within the Night Crawler Protocol. Lackey was in a locked room, and there was an armed guard stationed outside the door. Nonetheless, this warped individual managed to kill the security guard and the attending physician. The doctor was a hospital internist and infectious disease specialist named, Dr. Sayers."

"Ergo, that's the very reason our containment unit exists. That's what vampires do. They'll roll into town and trash everything. Once they start eating people, local property values turn to shit and the tax base gets eroded. Next thing you know, the local politicians are having a hissy fit about declining revenues and not having enough funds to properly sponsor touchy-feely, after-hours, adult educational classes on lesbian rights, proper adolescent masturbation techniques, the dangers of patriarchal, Anglo-colonial hegemony, and other pseudo-scientific, social justice Communist crap like that, or possibly worse."

"Rather jaded view, is it not?" The detective asked.

"Well, you're a rather young guy and as of yet, you probably haven't lived long enough to experience the perpetual punitive pleasures designed and dispensed by the dastardly, demonic, and draconian local Democratic Party members, now have you?" Noche asked.

"Well, I don't know," the detective replied. "Who are you to pass judgement? Maybe I'm the kind of guy who needs a refresher course on masturbatory manual manipulation. After all, if Uncle Sam is stupid enough to foot the bill on a late night, communal circle jerk, complete with free, glossy, full color, educational pamphlets, who am I to argue?"

"Touché."

"Be that as it may, both of the victims were partially consumed. Domino Lackey ate the liver of the security guard! As best we can tell, the poor bastard was still very much alive when the vampiro started to eat his internal organs. Can you fucking believe that? This is the first time that my men and I have ever encountered a human vampiro."

"How did this happen? My vampire containment unit was never notified that there was an infected individual here."

"Apparently, Dr. Sayers kept it a secret."

"Why in hell would he do that?" Noche asked. "That was a stupid decision on his part. It was a stupid decision that likely cost him his own life and the life of the security guard. He should have realized that this was this is an important public safety issue."

"Precisely," the police detective answered sarcastically. "After all, we heard about the rumor that your team exterminated several people who had been exposed to the vampire virus up at Chaco Canyon. So perhaps Dr. Jack Sayers was absolutely correct in his concern about this issue becoming an important public safety problem."

"You got that all wrong," Noche said.

"Do I now? In any event, I was told that Dr. Sayers simply didn't trust you people," Detective Correa added. "As that was the case, how did you folks get called into the matter to begin with if Dr. Sayers was keeping the details regarding the hospitalization of this patient completely off the records?"

"I got an emergency phone call from a physician named Parker Coxswain who came up here to do a medical consultation on this patient. Dr. Coxswain is a medical liaison agent on the Night Crawler Protocol that I work with from time to time. By the way, where is he?"

"Was he the medical scientist that came up from Santa Fe?" the inspector asked.

"He does medical research at the Saint Francis College of Medicine."

"I was told he booked out here like a scalded cat," Correa explained. "He came up to do a consultation, but when he saw Domino Lackey had killed two other people, the scientist flew out of here with the head nurse before they were attacked."

"Thanks for the information," Captain Noche said. "What was the name of the head nurse involved?"

"Didn't catch her name," the police detective said, "but you can gather all of those additional details from the ward clerk right down the hallway."

"I'll do just that," Noche said. "By the way, did anybody else get injured while the suspect was here?"

"Again, you'll need to talk to the head nurse about that when you catch up to her," Detective Correa explained. "As of yet, I just don't know about any other additional information. Obviously, I have a lot more people to interview."

"You've been a big help," the military captain concluded. "You do realize that you'll have to keep this entire matter on the QT, do you not?"

"Got it," the inspector answered. "The Governor's office has already sited chapter and verse on what the locals here in Farmington need to do."

"What's your next plan of action?" The military captain asked.

"After we get everything buttoned up here, we're going to beat the bushes until Domino Lackey gets flushed out. After that, we're going to bop him in the head with a big mallet until we knock his brains out. That's what we're going to do."

"Nice. Will you be needing any help?" Noche asked.

"Absolutely," Detective Correa answered, "as long as you boys don't accidentally shoot any innocent folks along the way."

"Sorry, but I can't promise you that," Noche said with a laugh.

"No," Detective Correa said. "I don't suppose you'd make that kind of a promise. What are you and your team going to do in the meantime?"

"I'm going to get Dr. Parker Coxswain on the phone to give me details about what transpired here right after I check on the status of the two individuals up on the fourth floor who've been exposed but have not transformed as of yet. I need to ask them a few questions before they get hauled out of here."

With that, Captain Noche gathered his men and took the flight of stairs up to the fourth floor. The military officer was absolutely exasperated to learn that neither Penny Schaeffer nor Marcus Cruz were anywhere to be found.

"What in hell happened to the two people I told you to apprehend? Did they just disappear into thin air?" Noche asked the dozen soldiers that were loitering about on the fourth floor.

"What are you talking about?" One of the soldiers asked. "We had indeed apprehended the individuals as you had instructed, and then the two doctors showed up from the CDC that you sent up here."

"What doctors from the CDC?" Noche asked. "I don't know any of the doctors at the CDC. In fact, I've never been to Atlanta. As far as I am concerned, I'm glad that General Sherman burned that damned place to the ground during the American Civil War."

"What did the doctors from the CDC want?"

"Well, Captain, they wanted the two patients and so we gave them up. After all, they had a letter in their hands that you had signed. The letter said that you relinquished the care of these two individuals to the CDC and that we were to escort the doctors and the two patients out to the parking lot where a car was waiting for them to take their entire crew to Albuquerque. They're going to be flying out to Atlanta today."

"Letter? Are you kidding me?" The military captain asked. "Show me the letter. Who has it?"

"I have it right here, Captain," another soldier said. "Maybe you forgot that you signed it, but it gave us your explicit instructions that we should cooperate with these doctors from Atlanta upon their arrival."

The military captain pulled the letter out of the hands of the soldier who had it in his possession, and it only took a cursory glance to realize that his men had been brazenly duped.

"You idiots!" Captain Noche exclaimed as he crumpled the letter and threw it upon the ground. "That's not my signature! It doesn't look anything like it. This letter is a forgery! I ought to shoot every one of you stupid sons of bitches right here on the spot. So, they told you boys that they were flying out of Albuquerque? How long ago did they leave here?"

"We escorted them out to their automobile about 20 minutes ago or so," one of the soldiers answered.

"Somebody, get me a phone. I need to call the Albuquerque International Airport and keep these people from flying out. Once they leave the confines of the state of New Mexico, we'll have no jurisdiction over them. We better catch them, and do it now as there are explicit orders in the Night Crawler Protocol that anybody that has been infected must remain in quarantine for a week to see if they undergo a transformation into a full-blown vampire. In fact, my personal orders supersede what I just said. We have the authority to exterminate them!"

"Now wait just a minute, Captain," one of the soldiers protested. Those two patients that we detained seemed to be very nice. In fact, they were polite. I can't see how they would be any threat to the general population even if they do eventually transform into full-blown vampires."

"You're not paid to think," the military captain responded. You're paid to do what you're told. We're going to join the local

P.D. on a man hunt to track down the 17-year-old Navajo boy who escaped. Let's get to work."

⚕

If the truth be told, Dr. Hoefferle and Dr. Kohl from the CDC had absolutely no intention of ever returning to Albuquerque with the two patients they had absconded with in Farmington. The team from the CDC had wisely embarked on a different course.

"Keep your foot into it, Hef," Kohl told his partner. "We're not in the clear as of yet. We just got past the town of Aztec."

"I think we're okay," Hoefferle answered. "I don't want to push it any harder. State troopers might be out on this highway slinging a radar gun from the hip in this direction. We can't allow getting pulled over by the police at this point. We're now northbound on Highway 550 and only 20 minutes or so from the border of Colorado at this rate. Once we make it to Colorado we'll be in spitting distance to Durango. Do you have the call letters on the twin engine Piper that's going to get us up to Grand Junction?"

"In my pocket. Around about way to get back home however, if you ask me. Grand Junction to Phoenix to Houston and then to Atlanta."

"Has to be that way," Hoefferle added. "Can't allow the military to sniff up our skirts."

"You didn't explain to us what would happen if we were captured by the military," the patient named Penny Schaeffer asked from the backseat of the speeding car.

"That's right! If you gentlemen work for the CDC, that means you work for the federal government," the other patient, Marcus Cruz, observed. "If that's the case, why would one branch of the government be afraid of members from another branch of the government? Makes no sense to me."

"It's not complicated, amigo," Dr. Kohl attempted to explain. "It's a turf war. Plain and simple. If the four of us are captured by the National Guard within the borders of New Mexico, we will be summarily executed. If the United States military or another branch of the federal government manages to catch us outside of New Mexico, all bets are off. Now, do you folks still want to go to Atlanta with Dr. Hoefferle and me? If not, we can drop you off at any old random gas station when we get to Durango and you're welcome to take your chances on your own."

⸎

The Brotherhood was now up to a total of six children, including Jesus, Isaac, and his sister Amelia as the original three members. Since the Brotherhood was formed, Amelia's friend, Celena, had joined the group in addition to Donatello and Chico. The original plan was to limit the group to a total of only six members, but Jesus and Isaac had petitioned Amelia to allow two more friends to join, and that included Enos and Frederico.

After Enos had gone through the transformation, it was now time for him to participate in the formal initiation ritual. The first order of business was a prayer service to honor the demon deity and patron god of the bats, Lord Camazotz. Afterward, it would be the duty and responsibility of Enos to brutally disembowel his parents and allow the other members of the Brotherhood to partake in an exquisite gourmet meal.

The parents of Enos had been previously trussed up and gagged. They were held as prisoners in the cellar of the family home while they awaited a most grizzly demise at the hands of their own son and the newly formed pre-adolescent social club known only as the Brotherhood. As the members of the Brotherhood gathered in the basement of the home where Enos lived, Amelia began the unholy ceremony with a new prayer she had just learned to the demons in the dark.

"Let us bow our heads and pray." Amelia wiped away the dust from a type-written, laminated index card that was in her possession, and she began to read a ghastly prayer that had been given to her by a total stranger who had hoped to learn more about her and her blood-thirsty group of young vampires.

"In the name of El Diablo, Lord Camazotz, and the Unholy Roach," Amelia said as she crossed herself in reverse order of the conventional Roman Catholic method. "Hellish demons, we beseech thee to cast your curses of damnation upon this wicked gathering. May we always abide by the demands of the evil edicts that emanate from the caves and the shadows. Strengthen the resolve of your humble servants to always delight in your will and to follow you in the path of your unholy cloven hoof prints, and welcome our new member, Enos, into the Brotherhood of the evil ones. Amen. Okay, boys—gut Madre y Padre and let the feast begin!"

The screams of agony from the adult parents were muffled by the gags tied around their faces as they were filleted and disemboweled while they were still very much alive.

"As Celena and I are the oldest, we get to eat the livers," Amelia proclaimed. "That leaves two hearts and four kidneys that you boys can split between you. Now, don't forget we're guests in this home. Try not to make a mess. I made a promise to Enos that we'd leave his place just as neat and tidy as we found it!"

Perhaps it was an act of mercy when Chico ripped out the heart from the mother while it was still beating and he began to devour it.

"Wait just a minute there, asshole!" Donatello protested. "I told you before we started this fiesta that I was going to eat the old lady's heart. Remember, I'm older than you."

"That's right. You *are* older than me," Chico agreed. "You're older than me by only four months, so that doesn't add up to a ripped shit as far as I'm concerned. This heart is mine. Go fuck off!"

Those fighting words uttered by Chico were only said mere inches away from the face of Donatello, and it was enough to initiate a riot. Donatello turned away as if he was willing to surrender the tasty *corazón* without so much as any further verbal protest, but his retreat from the pending altercation was merely a ruse.

On a workbench against the back wall of the basement was a pneumatic nail gun, and a simple flip of an electric switch powered up the air compressor to 120 pounds per square inch. The nail gun was loaded with 2 inch long, 15-gauge finishing nails. The tool was fully capable of firing off a nail projectile deep into a 2 x 4 inch frame as fast as the trigger could be pulled. Sadly, it would seem that Chico pissed off the wrong vampire.

While the other members of the Brotherhood were deeply engaged in a delicious meal of iron-rich visceral organs, nobody was aware that Donatello had slipped up behind Chico with a nail gun, now aimed directly at the posterior occipital skull of his epicurean adversary. The first half dozen nails that entered the back of Chico's skull had immediately blinded him, as the occipital region of the brain is the central neurological region responsible for site reception and interpretation of visual images.

"I can't see! I can't see!" Chico proclaimed as he rose to his feet and started to swing blindly away at his tormentor.

"Good!" Donatello exclaimed. "Then I guess you won't be needing your eyes anymore." With that, Donatello jammed his foot hard into the front knee of Chico which caused him to fall on his back with his arms flailing about wildly. Donatello straddled Chico's chest and pumped several nails through each eyeball. Then, in a methodical fashion, Donatello left two intersecting rows of nail holes across Chico's forehead in the shape of an upside down cross. When Donatello exhausted the projectiles that had been previously loaded up into the nail gun, Chico was no longer breathing.

Perhaps a casual observer would have been somewhat surprised to note that none of the other vampires in the Brotherhood raised so much as a finger to help poor Chico. Then again, perhaps not. It seemed that none of the members of the Brotherhood even appeared to be particularly annoyed at the brief disruption of festivities during the bloody buffet.

"Looks like we're down one man," Celena casually said to her friend, Amelia.

"Life on the Serengeti can be a bitch," Amelia answered as she attempted to stifle a yawn.

"What do you mean?" Celena asked.

"Survival of the fittest," Amelia answered. "Would you like any more of this old man's liver? It's really rather tasty!"

"Yeah, I would," Celena answered as she grabbed a lobe of the deep maroon organ harvested from the dead man and then jammed it into her maw with her bare hands. "Nevertheless, that doesn't change the equation, as we're still down one man."

"Fear not," Amelia said. "Don't forget, Frederico took a bite in the neck from us a week ago. It's time for us to check on his progress to see if he's gone through a complete transformation by now. If he has, we'll have another initiation ceremony tomorrow and we'll easily be back up to seven members in our club by tomorrow or the next day at the latest."

"Fair enough, I guess," Celena replied. "My only concern is that Santa Sangre is starting to run out of people. We're eating them all!"

"Rest assured, it's all part of the big plan I have for our Brotherhood." Amelia replied. "After all, it was necessary for us to make a bold statement if we were to be noticed."

"By the way, Amelia, the prayer that you said to Lord Camazotz was really spiritually moving. I've never felt so, well– *unholy*, if you know what I mean!"

"I do indeed."

"Well," Celena asked, "where did you learn such a corrupt prayer of damnation?"

"I'll let you in on a secret," Amelia answered, "but you can't tell a soul about any of this as of yet."

"What are you talking about?" Celena asked.

"I met a high ranking captain with the Astilladora de Madera drug cartel the other day," Amelia explained. "He was the one who gave me a copy of the prayer that I read today at the initiation ceremony."

"How exciting!"

"You have no idea!" Amelia answered. "They want our Brotherhood to work as assassins on their behalf!"

"Hired killers?!" Celena pressed.

"We'd be hot torpedoes for the cartel. They'd pay us money and give us as much human blood and internal organs that we could ever possibly want!"

"Fantastic!" Celena said. "We chose the right person when they voted you to be the head of this organization!"

On the following day, Amelia felt compelled to remind the other members of the Brotherhood that the club policy of social distancing of six feet between individuals had to be maintained, or otherwise there would be a breakdown in the political order.

"Sadly, Chico died yesterday. His death was not the fault of Donatello, but it was Chico's own fault. Let's review where things went wrong. First of all, Donatello had seniority over Chico and he made it perfectly clear that he wanted to eat the old lady's heart. By hierarchy, it was his right to make that claim. More importantly, Chico grossly violated the six foot social distancing safety rule. Chico got inches away from Donatello's face and insulted him. I'm sorry to say, Chico was an idiot."

"He was indeed," Donatello boasted. "I owned that little bastardo."

"It would really be a good time for you to shut up right about now, Donatello," Amelia warned. "If a vampiro or vampira has not learned by now about social distancing, then he or she does not deserve to be in this club. It's time for us to go to the south part of town and visit Frederico. It's been an entire week since he got bit, and it's now time to check and see if he's gone through a successful transformation. If he has, we'll ask him to join our ranks and replace Chico who had an untimely, yet perhaps well-deserved death. Let's head out before the sun gets too high in the sky. If we wait much longer, we'll all get badly sunburned."

Upon the arrival of the Brotherhood to Frederico's house, everybody was surprised to see that a transformation had not occurred.

"Well," Frederico said, "I never thought that I'd see any of you dirt bags ever again. So, you tried to turn me into un vampiro, did you? How'd that work out for you blood sucking parasites? Not so good, I'd imagine from where I'm standing. Here I am, fit as a Federale. I guess I'm immune to your weak-ass vampire mojo. My dad's here. He has a hunting shotgun. If you don't mind, I'll just go get him and he can start blasting away at you sons of bitches!"

"What?!" Amelia asked. "I don't understand why you didn't go through the transformation."

"I must be vampire-proof. I heard the story about a man who was murdered by the Calle Vampiro cartel. He was crucified on a columnar cactus at Rancho Feliz. He had previously been bitten, but he never went through the transformation before he died. If that's the case, it would seem to me that some people are just naturally immune. Some people like me."

"I've never heard of such a thing!" Amelia exclaimed.

"Well, now you have. So, if you don't mind, I have shit to do. Get the hell out of here before I get my dad, and he starts filling you nasty bastards with 12 gauge buckshot."

"Maybe we just need to bite you one more time," Celena said. "Perhaps that'll do the trick."

"I have a better idea, Celena," Frederico said. "I've got a couple of pesos in my pocket. Why don't you and Amelia give me a two minute lube job. I'll throw in an extra peso if you bitches rotate my tires and inflate my spare tube in the meantime. When it's said and done, that's about all you whores are ever good for now, is it not?"

It's a reasonable assumption that unfounded bravado killed more than one man walking about on the face on this earth at one time or another. Sadly, bravado was soon to be the death of Frederico. Amelia and Celena took Frederico down in the blink of an eye. One vampira went high, and the other went low. Celena ripped away at Frederico's neck while Amelia's face was fully immersed into the young boy's abdominal cavity where she began to gleefully feast upon his liver.

"Save me some of that liver, you bitch!" Celena screamed.

"There are two lobes to the liver," Amelia answered. "I'll eat the right lobe, and you can have the left lobe."

"Bull shit, you selfish twat rag!" Celena exclaimed. "The right lobe is the biggest lobe."

"That's right," Amelia said, "and his right lobe belongs to me! You should be thankful I'm saving any of it for a skank whore like you."

"Give me a break!" Isaac said to interrupt the feeding frenzy. "Were not going to get any new recruits into the Brotherhood if you girls eat them all!"

"Shut up!" Amelia demanded. "If Frederico's parents are here, you better get into the house and finish them off. Do it now!"

Donatello, Enos, Jesus, and Isaac stormed into the home looking for trouble. The four boys had crossed the threshold into the kitchen when a shotgun blast from Frederico's father successfully decapitated Donatello. Jesus quickly took the father down while the other two vampires were able to make short work of the additional occupants in the house which included Frederico's mother and an elderly grandmother who were trying to hide in a bedroom closet. Fortunately, the death of the two women was swift indeed.

When Amelia and Celena heard the gunshot blast, they pulled away from their meal and sprinted inside the domicile to see what was awry.

Shaken, Jesus came forth from the kitchen and pushed Amelia and Celena aside to get to the porch for a breath of fresh air.

"What went down in there, Jesus?" Amelia asked in a panic.

"I'll tell you what happened in there," Jesus answered. "Now there are only five of us."

<hr>

Although Domino Lackey received adequate sustenance in the form of bovine and porcine blood garnished from a nearby slaughterhouse when he was a hospitalized patient at the Farmington Memorial Hospital, he nonetheless had impulse control issues. He ended up killing the security guard and also Dr. Jack Sayers. If the truth be told, the young Navajo adolescent was actually rather fond of both of those individuals as they had always treated him with respect and they would even share jokes together. Dr. Sayers had promised Domino that help was on its way from the University Hospital in Santa Fe in an attempt to rescue him from the dreadful disease he was now infected with.

In light of what Domino had done however, any reasonable chance of medical intervention, experimental or otherwise, was no longer feasible. Domino Lackey was now in the crosshairs of a man hunt orchestrated by the local police and the National Guard soldiers who comprised the lethal Vampiro Containment Unit. This military outfit, activated by the Night Crawler Public Safety Protocol, now had a well-deserved reputation of "shoot first and ask questions later." It was a merciless reputation fostered by the outfit's leader, Captain Noche.

Because he couldn't control his murderous instincts that had overtaken his better nature, Domino intuitively realized that in all likelihood, his life would be over sooner than later. He had few if any delusions of redemption or salvation at that point. If and when he was ever found, he would be put down like the vile, parasitic predator that he had become. Right or wrong, Domino had even told himself that such a fate was now well deserved.

The Latin word for "guilt" is "culpa," and Domino Lackey had a straight flush of culpability in spades. Nonetheless, his self-recrimination and guilt had no bearing on his compulsive and wanton desires to consume blood and iron-rich visceral organs. If that was the case, why was he not content on simply consuming the essence that he biologically needed from lower life forms such as pigs, cows, goats, sheep, and a bevy of other domesticated quadrupeds that human beings have utilized as a food source for thousands of years?

In some vampires, the murder and consumption of other human beings is likely a consequence to an exacerbation of an underlying psychopathic or sociopathic aberrancy. After all, evil is not some abstract concept. It exists. It's real. Some people are just evil.

On the other hand, nobody who had ever met the young boy named Domino Lackey could have ever accused this polite and gracious young man from the Navajo tribe of being evil. He was far from it. He was about to enter his senior year in high school when he sustained a puncture wound on his hand from the curious skull that he had found north of Chaco Canyon. It was a dangerous skull that had prominent and sharp canine incisors. If he simply had left the damned thing alone, the rest of his life would have been gravy. Who could have possibly known however that the virus responsible for human vampirism could remain in a dormant state for centuries and could still be capable of infecting other living beings? Hindsight vision is always an after-the-fact 20/20 perception with sharp acuity. Such is the nature of life.

Domino certainly didn't want to become a vampire. He was making good grades in high school and was a middle distant runner on the track team. He also participated on the cross-country team in the fall. He was a solid "B" student, and he had plans to enter the police academy after he graduated from high school. Conservative by nature, he didn't smoke, drink, utilize illicit recreational drugs, or loiter about.

Domino had a casual girlfriend who was much more interested in him than he was in her. The young lady realized that he would be a "good catch" if perhaps she could persuade him to consider a long-term relationship. Domino however enjoyed his solitude and was not inclined to get nailed down in a bonded relationship, especially since he was only 17 years old. For all intent and purposes, he was a good kid with his head screwed on tight who just happened to get dealt a very bad hand of cards.

If that was indeed the case, how was it possible that Domino Lackey murdered and consumed two human beings once he had been infected with the RV-1986 RNA entity that causes human vampirism? Could the virus induce a subclinical encephalopathy involving the temporal lobes? After all, temporal lobe brain injuries have long been known to induce violent behavior. This was certainly a subject matter worthy of scrutiny by Dr. Blanks and his team at the CDC and also Dr. Parker Coxswain at the University Hospital in Santa Fe if the opportunity had arisen. Be that as it may, Domino Lackey was about to feed. Domino Lackey was about to commit a mortal sin yet again.

The young Navajo rang the doorbell of his English teacher, Mrs. Henrietta Rain, and the door was promptly answered.

"Why hello, Domino! I'm surprised to see you," Mrs. Rain said. "I heard that you were sick and in the hospital. Are you okay now?"

"I left the hospital today, Mrs. Rain. I am actually feeling pretty good right now although I'm getting very hungry."

"I am indeed happy to hear that you're feeling better," the teacher said. "What brings you by my house this evening?"

"I wanted to let you know that I'm going to be dropping out of school, Mrs. Rain," Domino answered.

"That's a terrible idea!" The teacher exclaimed. "Why on earth would you do that? You have your whole life ahead of you. You once told me that you had hoped to become a fireman."

"Well, I actually wanted to go to the police academy. Be that as it may, if the truth be told, I got infected with a virus. It's turned me into a living and breathing vampire. I can't help myself, but I desire human blood and human organs for sustenance. I guess I'll be going straight to hell and there's nothing I can apparently do about it. I've prayed to God in heaven about the situation, but I know He must be busy. I haven't received any answers as of yet."

"That's just terrible," the English teacher said in all sincerity. "Tell me, is there anything I can do to help you?"

As Domino was young, he had extraordinarily high levels of the vampire pheromones that were capable of overcoming a pending meal with sedation and complicity. "I need to feed now, Mrs. Rain. I would like to consume your blood and then eat your liver and heart if you don't mind."

"You'll promise not to hurt me?" Mrs. Rain asked as she was now under the direct spell of an admixture of potent aromatic chemicals that were spontaneously released from the vampire's sweat pores.

"I've always been very fond of you as a teacher," Domino answered with a warm smile. "I promise that I'll be very gentle. Now, just lay back on the couch and I'll do the rest. I'll have you know, Mrs. Rain, it was truly an honor for me to have been your student at one time. It will always be one of my most cherished memories. You were a fantastic teacher. I mean that."

"Why thank you, Domino," Mrs. Rain said just before she lost consciousness. "You were always one of my most favorite pupils..."

<hr>

On the following day, a waiter who was wearing a white apron and working at a corner restaurant on the plaza in Santa Fe casually strolled over to the Governor's Palace where a dozen or so members of the Navajo tribe had a treasure trove of items on full display to entice the tourists who were passing by.

The waiter quickly found the elderly man he was looking for. The aging gentleman was none other than the Navajo tribal council member, Elder Joseph, who was still hiding out from the military's Vampire Containment Unit, and he was successfully doing so in plain sight.

The waiter bent over to convey to the elder in a whisper about a particularly disturbing event. The waiter informed Joseph of a verified account about the murder of a security guard and a doctor at the Farmington Memorial Hospital. In addition, a gentle, popular, widowed, Navajo high-school teacher named Henrietta Rain was murdered in her very own home. All of her blood had been drained out of her body. In addition, there was evidence of predation as her liver, heart, and kidneys had sadly been extracted from her thorax and abdomen. These internal organs had apparently been consumed at the scene of the crime.

Elder Joseph buried his face in his hands and slowly shook his head. After dismissing the waiter with a solemn nod, Joseph subsequently waved an index finger to beckon a colleague who was selling silver and turquoise items under the portico. He requested that this friend assume the permanent management of the site where the elder had sold tightly woven antique Navajo rugs.

Elder Joseph quickly left the plaza. It was time for him to come out of hiding. It was time for him to go to work...

9

RETRIBUTION

"We've lost two members of the Brotherhood already," Jesus complained. "Amelia wants us to recruit more kids to join our group, but that assignment isn't going to be easy to obey since the school is now closed."

"Don't sweat it," Isaac countered. "Did you forget Amelia told us that the Astilladora de Madera cartel wants to hire us to do some of their dirty work?"

"I'll believe it when I see it," Jesus replied. "I guess when we started to eat the citizens of Santa Sangre and drink their blood, the town became frightened. Nobody comes outside anymore. Have you noticed?"

"Good!" Isaac exclaimed. "Just as Amelia planned."

"There are only five of us left after Chico and Donatello were killed, Isaac! To make matters worse, we tried to recruit Frederico into the Brotherhood, but Amelia and her whore girlfriend ate his liver right upon his front portico. We might not be big enough as a group for the cartel to be interested in hiring us anymore. What do you think?"

"We're not done yet," Isaac answered. "Not by a long shot. The Brotherhood has to do something that will shock even the members of the cartel. Something big. Something that'll get everybody's attention!"

"Like what?" Jesus asked.

"The members of the cartel have renounced God," Isaac said. "Just like Amelia, the local captain of the cartel, El Lobo, worships the Mayan bat god, Camazotz. Somehow, we have to use that to our advantage."

"Let me think about that," Jesus said. "I bet I can come up with an idea. Something brutal. Something dastardly!"

"Do that," Isaac said. "But before we present ourselves and the members of the Brotherhood to El Lobo for his consideration, we first have other priorities that we need to address."

"Such as?" Jesus asked.

"We know where Nathan Barker lives. Let's bring him into the group."

"The little gringo?" Jesus asked. "Are you shitting me? No way. I hate that little bastard."

"I do too, but he's a lot younger than us," Isaac said as he explained his reasoning. "Because of that fact alone, I think we can force that little *cucaracha* to do whatever we tell him to do."

"Fine," Jesus said, "but we have to test this theory of yours. I want to give Nathan a little homework to see if he can follow orders. After that, if Amelia gives us her blessing, then we can take a vote to see if we want to make him a new member of the Brotherhood."

"What do you have in mind?" Isaac asked.

"Let's run over to Rancho Feliz," Jesus answered. "In the mornings, I've seen Nathan tending to the chicken coop cleaning up the chicken poop."

"How do you know that?"

"I don't think Nathan's big enough to do anything else," Jesus answered. "On more than one occasion, I've gone over to Rancho Feliz to ambush little Nathan. I've tried to kill him on several occasions, but as of yet, I've not been able to get the jump on him."

"What a load of crap," Isaac replied. "The hacienda at Rancho Feliz has an adobe wall surrounding it. There's broken glass embedded into the top of the wall. It works better than barbed wire to keep people from trespassing, or otherwise breaking in and stealing shit. If you ever tried to scale it, you'd get torn to shreds. You'll no doubt heal up because you're a vampiro, but that doesn't mean it won't hurt, and I'm saying you'll hurt real bad in the meantime!"

"Not *over* the perimeter, you dumbass," Jesus explained. "*Under* it!"

"What?!"

"There's a gap of about 25 centimeters under the front gate entry way into the compound, and it's just big enough for me to squeeze into Rancho Feliz without anybody seeing me. I've actually stolen a pig and a cabrito from there in the past."

"Why didn't you share them with me, you greedy gato!"

"I gave some of the food to your sister's whore of a girlfriend, Celena," Jesus answered.

"Tell me more! Did she get nasty with you?"

"No dice!" Jesus exclaimed. "I tried to get her interested in a straight up trade. You know–physical pleasure for nutritional goods and services."

"How did that turn out for you, amigo?" Isaac asked. "I'm dying to know!"

"Not well. Celena said I'd have to get a whole lot older before she would be willing to gnaw on me," Jesus answered. "Just as well though, because something's wrong with my plumbing. It's shrinking up now, and I'd be embarrassed for anybody to see me like this."

"I'm having the same issue since I went through the transformation," Isaac sadly observed.

"Sucks for us," Jesus opined. "Be that as it may, if I'm skinny enough to get under the front gate, then you can, too."

"What if we get caught?" Isaac asked.

"Simple," Jesus answered. We're members of the Brotherhood. We're vampire royalty. We can eat our way out of any trouble that we could possibly get into."

"Well, what are we waiting for?" Isaac asked.

With that, the two juvenile vampires quickly made their way to Rancho Feliz where they successfully slipped under the front gate without being seen. They quietly made their way to the chicken coop on the left backside of the Hacienda to await their nemesis, young Nathan Barker. Momentarily, Nathan entered the chicken coop with a flat shovel, a broom, and a pale to clean up the avian droppings from the night before. Needless to say, he was certainly alarmed to find unexpected visitors waiting for him inside the chicken coop.

"Jesus! Isaac! What are you boys doing here? How did you get inside the compound?" Nathan asked.

"We have a job to do, Nathan, and you're going to help us out," Jesus said. "Do you know the priest who lives in the rectory named Padre Garrapa? He has a new nick name. He's now known as, 'Garrapa the Groper'!"

"Of course, I do," Nathan answered.

"Perfect," Isaac replied. "Has he ever taken your confession?"

"I'm not old enough yet," Nathan answered. "I've not had my first communion yet, either."

"Yeah, that's okay," Jesus said. "Nonetheless, have you ever been, well–*alone* with him?"

"No!" Nathan answered. "He scares me. Other children have told me that he's tried to touch them in their private parts."

"Yeah," Isaac replied, "that's indeed a big problem. My friends and I would like to have a private meeting with Father Garrapa. We would like to express to him in no uncertain terms that it's wrong for him to try and touch little children. I'm certain that when we're finished with him, he won't be a problem for the community any longer."

"Really?" Nathan asked. "I'll help you out if I can, as long as you boys promise not to pick on me anymore!"

"That's all in the past," Jesus said. "We want to be your friends, now!"

"Tell me what I need to do," Nathan said.

"We are going to give you instructions about how you're going to help us," Isaac said, "but first I have a question. Jesus and I are, well–different now. Our skin is yellow. Our eyes are also bright yellow. We have ugly sharp teeth now. The skin on her face looks old. I actually frighten myself when I look into a mirror and see my own reflection. You don't seem to be frightened of Jesus or me in the least. I don't understand why our appearance doesn't scare you in some way."

"Why should it?" Nathan asked. "You boys look exactly like my uncle, Miguel Pastore!"

"We do?" Jesus asked, rather surprised.

"Yeah," Nathan answered. "Uncle Miguel is un vampiro. Did you boys not know that?"

⚜

Above the banks of the Rio Conchos, Colonel Placard looked through the binoculars and was shocked to see that El Lobo Grande had completely disregarded his advice concerning the military style assault upon the Chihuahua cartel compound on the outskirts of Ciudad Camargo.

"Your men were slaughtered!" Placard protested. "What were you thinking?!"

"Quit complaining," Lobo countered. "We stormed their compound, did we not? It's all over now. My men have everything under control."

"Yes, but at what cost? Why in hell did you bring me along if you were going to do the complete opposite of what I recommended?" Placard asked El Lobo in disgust. "You could have kept your casualties to a minimum if you had only subjected the Chihuahua cartel compound to a triangulation of fire before a frontal attack. As best I can tell through these field glasses, you've suffered at least a 70% loss of your assault team. Hope you're proud of your handiwork, General Santa Anna. You just had your own, personal, Battle of the Alamo."

"A victory is a victory, no?"

"Why should I give a damn about any of you people?" Placard asked. "Every single one of you and your men are going to burn in hell someday."

"As long as we pay him homage, the gracious and unholy Lord Camazotz will look with favor upon our cartel, Colonel," Lobo replied as he spit into the dirt beside the colonel. "As for you however, I'm not particularly confident about your future status in the afterlife."

"Fuck your pagan bullshit!" Placard was now treading upon thin ice and he knew it. "If I was the head of your outfit, I'd be running *you* through a wood chipper right about now. Keep treating your foot soldiers as a disposable commodity, and what few men you'll have left will turn on you someday. I'd pay good money to see that. Same thing happened in Vietnam. If the troops encountered an incompetent platoon leader, that individual would get 'fragged.' Do you want to have somebody drop a live grenade at your feet someday? Why on earth did you disregard my strategic plans?"

"Simple, mi amigo," El Lobo replied. "Frankly I didn't really trust you. I thought you were going to try to catch me with my pants down. That's why I took matters in my own hands. Looks like you were right. You told me that a direct frontal assault would result in the heavy casualties of my men and material, and that appears to be the case. Oh, well. It was my call. I can live with it. In the future, we'll try it your way. As for now, your blasphemy against the Mayan god of the bats must be addressed, or else next time the demons in the underworld will seek retribution against all of us."

"Won't be a next time," Placard protested.

"Bold talk from a slave," El Lobo said. "Don't forget, Colonel, I own you."

Placard still had a pistol hidden in his under shorts, but he couldn't take the chance of killing El Lobo at that particular time, as two body guards that were held in reserve were standing directly behind the cartel captain.

"El Lobo to *Hormiga*, Over. Come in, Ant." Through a field radio, the cartel captain attempted to contact his henchmen who led the assault on the compound. Oddly, there was no initial response.

"El Lobo to El *Serpiente*, Over. Come in, Snake!" Yet again, Lobo Grande failed to elicit a reply.

"El Lobo to El *Tercero*. Are you there?" Lobo asked. "Where in hell is everybody?"

"Tercero here!" A response was finally returned. "I'm the only team leader left. Your plan managed to get us slaughtered, Lobo. Hope you're happy. Over."

"Did you manage to capture El Tigre Negro? Over."

"That is an affirmative, Lobo. Over." The voice of El Tercero could barely be heard over the radio amidst a crackle of annoying static.

"Excellent! Is he injured or wounded?" El Lobo asked. "Over."

"A broken jaw, and a few missing teeth," El Tercero answered over the radio, "but otherwise in good shape. Over."

"Any sign of the vampiro named Blake Barker? There was a rumor he was working for the Chihuahua cartel? Over."

"No, but we did capture a woman named, Lucia Aragon," Tercero answered. "Over."

"The name means nothing to me," Lobo stated. "Should it? Over."

"Well, it should," Tercero answered. "She's the madam who ran the notorious Brothel de los Niños for the old Calle Vampiro outfit before they got wiped off the face of the earth. Over."

"Fine," Lobo answered over the radio. "Shoot her."

"Wait, Lobo!" El Tercero protested. "She wants to work for us, now. Over."

Lobo turned to address his slaves. "Colonel Placard, I want you and Russian Bear to go down there and attend to the wounded. Make sure that El Tigre Negro receives appropriate medical care. Am I clear? I'll eventually come down to interview the whore once I'm certain the compound has been secured."

"Would you at least consider taking off the shackles around our ankles at this time?" Russian Bear asked as he pulled at the chain that was bolted to two iron rings around each of his lower extremities.

"I most certainly will not," Lobo answered. "Now, get down there and don't forget your first aid kit!"

Placard and the Russian doctor tramped through the semi-arid scrub brush to get to the wounded cartel members in an attempt to render medical aid within the confines of the Chiuhuahua cartel compound.

"We need to quickly triage these men to ascertain who might be saved and then separate them from those men who've been fatally wounded," the Russian doctor said to his colleague.

"Okay, but the first order of business would then be for us to separate the dead from the injured," Placard said.

The colonel and the Russian doctor quickly did a head count of the casualties and encountered a total of 42 men who were dead and 18 who were alive but wounded. Of those who were dead, 33 men were the loyal soldiers who had worked for El Lobo Grande, and only nine members of the Chihuahua cartel were killed in the shoot-out.

The statistics concerning the 18 soldiers who were wounded didn't look much better, as 13 remembers of the Astilladora de Madera cartel sustained bullet wounds. This meant that only five members of the Chihuahua cartel were wounded, including their leader, El Tigre Negro. No member of the Chihuahua gang managed to escape death or some type of battle injury.

Of the 80 men that El Lobo Grande had sent into battle, only 25 remained unscathed. Placard was right: a 70% casualty rate would be appalling and totally unacceptable to any military strategist.

"Now that we've got the dead separated from the wounded, Colonel, take this roll of white tape. If one of the soldiers has been mortally wounded, I'll have you put a strip of white tape across the top of his left shoe. If any wounded cartel soldier can be potentially treated, put the piece of tape across the top of his right shoe. Let's be quick about this."

Placard and Russian Bear walked amongst the wounded and the doctor would issue a simple instruction to the colonel which he immediately obeyed.

"Mark this man's left foot. The next one is also a left foot. Sitting beside him is a right foot. You've got the idea, now," Bear said as Placard quickly applied a strip of white tape to each wounded cartel soldier as instructed.

Once the tape had been administered to the shoes of the 18 injured men, Russian Bear had determined that eight of the cartel members who worked for El Lobo Grande received lethal injuries, leaving only five who could be potentially salvaged.

Russian Bear pointed out these eight critically wounded foot soldiers to the henchman known as El Tercero. "The eight injured men from your cartel with a strip of white tape on their left shoes are fatally wounded. Have your men pull them inside this first building and I'll administer morphine to keep them comfortable for what little time they have left."

Much to the horror of the Russian doctor, the eight fatally injured foot soldiers from the Madera cartel were simply hauled aside and euthanized with a bullet to the brain.

"What in hell have you done?" Russian Bear asked. "Is that what you people do if a terminally ill patient enrolls into a hospice program in this wretched country?"

A right fist propelled by El Tercero quickly quelled any further editorial comments from the Russian doctor.

The adversaries from the Chihuahua cartel had initially fared much better, as all five of those wounded individuals appeared to have a chance to survive their injuries.

While nursing his own freshly split upper lip, Russian Bear didn't pay any particular attention as to which of the cartel members received potentially life-saving medical care at that point in time. Sadly, that proved to be a lack of sound judgment on his part when El Lobo Grande soon strolled upon the scene and realized that Russian Bear was applying a dressing to the left thigh of a wounded foot soldier from the Chihuahua gang.

When he felt the hot point of a burning cigarette extinguished into the back of his neck, the Russian doctor suddenly got the notion that perhaps the dispensation of medical aid to the five alive but wounded Chihuahua cartel members was not a good idea after all.

"What in hell are you doing, you idiot?" The cartel captain asked with furious indignation. Lobo Grande had the whorehouse madam, Lucia Aragon, in tow during his inspection of the troops. "These scumbags from the Chihuahua cartel deserve only our contempt, not our help!"

"Wait! You told me to take care of the wounded," the Russian doctor said. "You didn't tell me just to take care of *your* wounded. As a doctor, I am obligated to take care of *everybody*."

"Is that so?" With that comment, El Lobo Grande motioned to his henchman, El Tercero, and immediately four of the five wounded foot soldiers from the Chihuahua cartel were executed on the spot.

The only member of the Chihuahua gang that was spared, at least initially, was El Tigre Negro.

"There. Happy now?" Lobo asked Russian Bear. "Go find El Tigre Negro and patch him up as best you can. I have a special treat for that pendejo. Escort him down to the banks of the river after you slap a bandage upon his busted jaw."

"What are you going to do with me?" Lucia Aragon asked the cartel captain. "I promise you that if you keep me alive, I'll be the best whore who's ever worked for you!"

Lobo Grande turned to El Tercero yet again with another order. "I want what's left of my men to wheel the wood chipper down to the banks of the Rio Conchos and get it prepped for a fiesta. Time for another unholy baptismal ceremony!"

"What should be done with the impudent Russian doctor and Colonel Placard?" El Tercero asked.

"Bring them along," Lobo Grande answered. "I want you to beat them to within an inch of their lives after we pray to Lord Camazotz. The Mayan bat god demands retribution for their blasphemy."

"What of El Tigre Negro?"

"When Russian Bear brings him down from the compound, bind El Tigre, but don't put a gag over his mouth. After all, he has a busted jaw and that man should be treated delicately and with respect," Lobo instructed.

"I'm calling bullshit on your last comments, Lobo," El Tercero countered with an evil grin.

"You're right!" Lobo confessed. "If the truth be told, I just want to hear him scream during the baptismal ritual!"

Once the congregation had gathered by the river, the appropriate laudatory prayers had been made to Lord Camazotz. Once done, El Tercero and three of his thugs began a merciless and vicious beat down upon Colonel Placard and the Russian doctor.

"Is this what you plan for me?" El Tigre Negro asked his former friend. "I don't deserve to get beaten to death. I always treated you and your crew with respect and I never wandered into your territory. Why did you attack us?"

"That's a lie. I know for a fact that you ventured into my territory looking for the vampiro named, Blake Barker. Is he in your custody?"

"I have no idea what you're talking about," Tigre said.

"That's also a lie. It matters not, however. Your territory is now my territory," Lobo Grande answered. "As far as what I'm about to do to you, it's nothing personal. It's just a good business decision. I have to make a statement to those who may want to oppose me in the future. Besides, you're absolutely right. You were once my friend, and it would certainly be undignified to simply bludgeon you into a lifeless pulp. I'm going to run you through the wood chipper, instead! I'll send you in by your feet. That way, I'll get to hear you scream longer!"

Once the whorehouse madam was positioned directly behind the exit chute of the wood chipper to receive her unholy baptismal blood bath, Lobo gave the signal to his men to fire up the engine that powered the terrifying device.

"Now remember, El Tigre," Lobo instructed. "I want you to scream as loud as you possibly can!"

In anticipation of an explosion of orgasmic gore, Lobo Grande jammed his right hand down the front of his trousers to violently flagellate his external plumbing while his foot soldiers gazed upon their leader with reverential admiration.

"You always were a sick bastard," El Tigre mumbled as his fractured jaw continued to swell. "I'm not even going to give you the pleasure of hearing me scream."

With that, El Tigre Negro wrestled away from his tormentors and sprinted toward the wood chipper, diving into the intake chute head first! Lucia Aragon closed her eyes and held her breath as she was showered with the aerosolized remains of what was once a fellow human being.

"Turn it off! Turn it off!" Lobo shouted in anger. Sadly, for the cartel captain, it was too late. El Tigre was already dead. "I was building up the pressure in my loins to blow a load, and now this happens! I didn't get to hear him scream. Now, everything's ruined. How's a man supposed to get his rocks off around this place?"

With that, El Tercero abruptly interrupted the additional planned beatings intended for Colonel Placard and Russian Bear. As he was a compassionate and sensitive thug, the brute expressed his sincere intent to offer his boss a measure of consolation over an obvious unfulfilled need for sexual gratification. However, a distant stranger who was standing upon the opposite bank of the Rio Conchos had immediately caught Tercero's eye.

"Lobo! Pay attention!" The henchman shouted in alarm. "Somebody's lurking on the other side of the river with a camera that has a huge telephoto lens. Whoever he is, he's taking pictures of us all as we speak."

"I wonder what he wants," Lobo asked. "Can you take some men and cross the Conchos to track him down?"

"No," El Tercero answered. "It's too deep at this bend to ford across the water while toting any of our weapons."

It mattered not. Within seconds, the voyeur wielding the high-powered photographic equipment had instantly vanished into the distant haze.

⚕

"To be frank," Cletus said, "I'm rather pleased with the proficiency that our Mayan warriors have achieved with the use of the automatic weapons that were provided to us by the Astilladora de Madera cartel. My only concern is that your new friend, Lobo Grande, promised us that he would relinquish his military advisor, Colonel Augustus Placard, to give us logistical support in our planned raid into Guatemala."

"Stop right there, Cletus," Lorena said. "Lobo Grande is our business partner. He's not my friend, exactly."

"Can't prove it by me in regards to the way you were flirting with him the last time he came down to the Yucatan to accept a shipment. You sure did take your good ol', sweet time in giving him a nice, long tour around the ruins of Fortress Camazotz."

"Will you just listen to yourself?" Lorena asked. "If a person could hear you right about now, he or she would think that you just received a nasty bite in the neck by the big, green-eyed bat of jealousy. It just so happens that Lobo Grande is a modern man who nonetheless believes in the spirit of Lord Camazotz, the Mayan bat god. Many of our own people worship Camazotz to this very day."

"Who cares?" Cletus asked. "Last I heard, the Druids still pray to trees and shit like that."

"Lobo insisted that I show him the magical cave where our Lord Camazotz is thought to still dwell amongst men."

"Oh, no!" Cletus proclaimed. "You didn't show him what dwelled inside the cave, did you? No outsiders can know about that!"

"I just whetted his appetite a bit."

"This is all starting to make sense to me, now," Cletus sneered.

"So, with my permission, I allowed him to probe the opening of the Cave of Camazotz, but I didn't allow him to enter," Lorena said with a soft, wistful sigh.

"I'll just bet you did. So, is the Cave of Camazotz now the same thing as the Twat of Camazotz?" Cletus asked with absolutely no expression upon his face. "After all, how many official titles have you now bestowed upon yourself, Your Highness?"

"Don't get impertinent with me, Cletus Barker," Lorena warned. "I'm your Queen. Don't forget that."

"Fine," Cletus said. "It's been 24 days since Lobo accepted our last shipment. He said that he would fly Colonel Placard down to the Yucatan. After that agreement, I haven't seen hide nor hair of this military advisor, if he does indeed exist. What in hell is going on?"

"There's been a bit of a setback," Lorena said. "Apparently Colonel Placard was seriously injured in some kind of incident that had occurred at Ciudad Camargo in Estado Chihuahua. I wasn't informed about the details, but apparently he sustained multiple contusions and rib fractures. Lobo informed me through the short wave that Colonel Placard will be out of commission now for a few more weeks."

"A lot of good that does us now," Cletus said. "Our intel assets from Guatemala informed me that 'General' Carmel, who was the leader of the Los Carcineros para-military outfit during Operation Sofia, is in striking distance. He's the highest ranking unindicted war criminal directly involved in the 37-year, state-sponsored genocide against the Maya people. He'll only be a viable target in the village of La Naranja for the next three days before he'll return to the safety of his protected compound in Zacapa."

"What do you propose?" Lorena asked.

"We can't afford to wait for a military advisor who may or may not ever come," Cletus said. "El Naranjo is only about fifty miles from Nuevo Coahuila, which is on our side of the Mexican border. It won't be easy, but it can be done. The hardest part of the trip would be a ten or so mile hike through the Biotopo Protegido in the Parque Nacional Laguna Del Tigre where there aren't any roads, but what the hell? Our people live in this damned jungle and have done so for thousands of years. We have friends on both sides of the border who'll be our guides. If we miss this opportunity for retribution against this butcher of human beings, we may not get another chance."

"If we're successful and we bag this beast, what do you propose that we'll do with him once we get him back to the Yucatan?"

"I'd suggest a state trial with evidentiary witnesses invited to testify about his alleged crimes against humanity," Cletus replied.

"And if he is found guilty?" Lorena asked.

"You're the self-proclaimed Queen of the Maya, are you not?" Cletus answered with a shrug. "I'll venture that you'll think up something or other to do with him. When the time comes, I would be happy to offer suggestions."

"How long would it take to put a team of our warriors together?" The Queen of the Maya asked.

"I thought that you'd never ask," Cletus replied. "They're ready now. I'll lead the team myself through the jungle to the village of El Naranjo. Carmel is there now conducting cocaine transactions. If all goes well we might not sustain any casualties at all. Our top warriors, El Dolor and Joaquin, have already made a dry run."

"If I'm the Queen of the Maya," Lorena said, "then I have the responsibility of going on this mission, also."

"I was hoping you would say that," Cletus said. "I—I love you, Lorena."

"I know you do."

After slogging through the jungle with machetes, the Mayan team of warriors finally made it past the Biotopo Protegido. With the help of a local guide, they found their way to a poorly maintained road about 40 miles north of El Naranjo. Once they made it to the road, Cletus witnessed the most curious vehicle that he had ever seen in his life. It was a school bus painted in camouflage relief, but upgraded with four-wheel drive and monster tires.

"I've never seen such a strange, mechanized conveyance as this," Cletus noted to the driver of the vehicle as he climbed aboard the giant bus with the other members of his team who clamored incessantly about a variety of musculoskeletal aches and pains as a consequence to their arduous trek through the dense rain forest. "Good to see you, Joaquin, but where in hell did you acquire this outlandish beast that you're driving?"

"Built from various salvaged rigs, Cletus," Joaquin replied. "I assure you that this has all necessary modification to get us to where we're going, but this bus is not, how would you say, a luxury item, if you will."

"Didn't think so," Cletus grinned.

"Are you in charge of the expeditionary force?" the driver asked Cletus.

"No!" The Queen of the Maya interrupted. "I am!"

"Queen Lorena!" the driver said. "I had no idea you'd be coming. My job is to get you to El Naranjo and back to this spot after you've completed your mission. I'll be able to eventually bring this very bus to Fortress Camazotz in the Yucatan at some time in the future, but it will be a long and circuitous route through Belize that will take many days."

"I can't tell you how grateful our people will be if our mission is successful," Lorena said. "Is this an act of retribution? Of course it is. More than that however, it's an act of long overdue justice for a war criminal."

"What's the set up?" Cletus asked.

"General Carmel is deeply involved in the cocaine trade south of Mexico," Joaquin replied. "Later today, he'll be inspecting an extraction laboratory in El Naranjo which assuredly is in one of the most remote places in Central America."

"Body guards?" Cletus asked.

"He only has three, but they're with him all the time," Joaquin answered.

"That doesn't sound like a particularly daunting task," Lorena said. "After all, we have a total of 30 heavily armed Maya warriors with us. Each man has an automatic weapon with several loaded magazines. We should be just fine."

"I hope that will be enough," the driver said.

"Why wouldn't be?" Cletus asked with a raised brow.

"His body guards are los vampiros," Joaquin cautioned. "I suspect that you'll take heavy casualties."

"Let's hope we can keep our casualties to a minimum," Lorena remarked, as the bus headed south. "Well, all we that we can do at this time is to be brave."

After a long and bumpy ride, the bus finally made it to El Naranjo in Guatemala. "We're here," Joaquin said as he pulled the bus over on the outskirts of the village. "I'll be waiting at this spot for you. I can't come with you as I'll need to stay here and guard the bus. You'll need to get your mission accomplished and then get the hell out. The man waiting for you outside the bus is our colleague, El Dolor. He'll take you from here."

"Anything else?" Cletus asked.

"Did you tell Queen Lorena about the sacred oath that the Maya warriors have all taken when it comes to an encounter with un vampiro?"

"I want you to explain it to her, Joaquin," Cletus replied.

"I'll have you know that it's our solemn oath that if any of our soldiers receive a bite from un vampiro in battle, we'll be forced to eliminate those individuals before they go through the transformation. I know that sounds brutal, but that's just how we do things around here."

"As I'm your Queen," Lorena said, "I countermand that oath."

"Why would you do that?" Joaquin asked.

"We do not know what percentage of individuals who get bit by a vampire will actually go through the transformation," Lorena said.

"Well, of course we do!"

"What is it then?" Lorena asked.

"Effective transmission rate is 88% to 90%," Joaquin explained. "Of those that go through the transformation, we've also noted that there's about a 3% to 5% remission rate over time where the disease eventually completely disappears in select individuals. We never knew what caused that, but now in modern times, we suspect that some patients develop antibodies to the virus that must be clinically effective in eradicating the infection."

"How on earth do you know that?"

"We've been following the course of this disease for centuries," Joaquin answered. "Prior to the development of the atomic clock, the Maya devised the most accurate calendar that the world had ever seen by watching the stars. We're very observant people, after all. If we're smart enough to do that, then figuring out the natural history of this disease process over eons was actually a piece of cake."

"Well, if the transmission rate is 88% to 90% of those who get bit by a vampire, this means that 10% to 12% of individuals who are attacked never go through the transformation. Of those that do, 3% to 5% will eventually go into a spontaneous complete remission that might be tantamount to a cure," Lorena concluded. "If that's the case, I'd like to countermand your blood oath."

"It's your right to do so as our queen," Joaquin said, "but we're all volunteers here. If you force us to rescind our oath and obligation to each other, the warriors will summarily withdraw from this mission in unison."

"Understood," Lorena answered. "Looks like the warriors have me over a barrel."

"I wish you all the best of luck," Joaquin said as he closed the door of the bus once everybody had made their exit.

Lorena turned to Cletus with a quizzical look upon her face. "Did you know about this?"

"Of course I did."

"Did you at least remember to bring one or more of the obsidian blades?" Lorena asked.

"Of course I did."

"Why didn't you tell me about these circumstances regarding the warrior oath?" Lorena pressed.

"Would it have really changed anything?"

"I suppose not," Lorena answered.

"Well, there you have it," Cletus answered before he turned toward the warrior waiting outside the bus. "Let's get to work. Okay, El Dolor, tell us about this plan of yours."

"We tried to kill General Carmel two years ago when he was inspecting his coca farm in Chisec. It was a disaster. Our six man team was simply eaten alive by his vampiro body guards. We were only armed with machetes at the time, and none of us had any other weapons of any sort. We're going to try something different this time."

"What do you have in mind?" Lorena asked.

"Chicanery at its finest," El Dolor said. "General Carmel received a telegram that a young woman from the Yucatan named Lorena Pastore was coming by for a visit. She said she grows cocaine on behalf of the Madera cartel, and she wants to meet with the general to see if they could collaborate on various projects together. Our spies are completely aware that Carmel sent a team of his men to inspect the Fortress Camazotz to investigate our grow site. He does indeed know that our tribe has a legitimate coca business."

"What do you want me to do?" Lorena asked.

"Simple," El Dolor answered. "Knock on the door and introduce yourself. Before the general will invite you inside the lab, one of his vampiros will exit the building and circle the facility to make sure that you came alone. Then, he'll stand outside the front door to keep guard. Our team will be hiding out of sight."

"What's next?" Lorena asked.

"Once you enter the extraction lab, explain to him that you only grow coca but have no refinement capabilities. You'd like to sell your raw product to him. After that, simply see how he responds. We'll neutralize the vampiro outside the building. Exactly one minute after you enter the extraction lab, there'll be another knock on the door, and it'll be our team this time. This will be your cue to tackle the general and knock him down to the ground."

"Wait!" Lorena interjected. "I'm not a very big person. How do you expect me to knock the general down?"

"The nasty animal is old and frail now, and about as big around as a pencil. You're probably twice his body weight! That's how you're going to knock him down. Once done, that's when we'll burst through the front entry with guns blazing and kill everybody who's standing. That includes human and vampiro alike. I'll put our best marksmen in front and they'll go for head shots on los vampiros. Are you capable of performing this feat, Queen Lorena?"

"I was a curandera in New Mexico in a prior life," Lorena answered. "My colleagues and I have killed more than one vampiro in the past. They didn't scare me then, and they certainly don't scare me now. Let us do this!"

"I only ask you to be careful," El Dolor said. "After all, you're the only Queen that we've got!"

While the team went into hiding on the outskirts of the extraction lab, Lorena knocked on the door and introduced herself to the vampiro who answered. Cletus watched with anxiety as the vampiro guard took a step off the portal and encircled the building while holding Lorena by her elbow. Once done, he rudely pushed the Queen of the Maya into the building to give the old general an opportunity to interrogate her.

"Hello," Lorena said. "You must be General Carmel. My name is—"

"I know who you are," the general harshly answered. "What I don't know is why you would bother to come see me. What kind of game are you playing?"

"I don't know what I have done to offend you," Lorena said, "but I just came here to discuss some business."

"Bullshit!" The general screamed at her. "I hate the Maya and they hate me. For decades, I tried to exterminate them as a race, and now the person who proclaims to be their queen has come to pay me a visit! What's wrong with this picture?"

Outside the lab, there was a crossbow manned by El Dolor that fired a bolt tipped with an obsidian blade fashioned from vampire glass. The bolt ripped through the left temple of the vampiro who was standing guard outside the laboratory, and it left a gaping exit wound in his right temple before it penetrated the trunk of a stout tree another 100 feet away. The vampiro guard was dead before he hit the ground. His body was hauled to the side by two of the Maya warriors who quickly decapitated the dead parasite just to be on the safe side. While this was being done, El Dolor knocked on the door.

"Let me in!"

"It must be the guard," the old general said to one of the other vampiros in the lab. "Stick your head out the door and tell your friend to shut up and stand at his post. It's time for me to gut this bitch!"

The second guard made a fatal mistake. He stuck his head out the door of the laboratory without first looking through the peep hole. A dozen men with automatic weapons separated this body guard's head from his shoulders before they charged through the front door with guns blazing. Lorena pounced across the table and tackled the old general and pinned him to the floor, leaving one vampiro bodyguard who was still very much alive and still very much in the fight.

The remaining vampiro bodyguard grabbed two of the Maya warriors and slammed their heads together, crushing their skulls. In the blink of an eye, he bit another person in the room before he bolted for the door.

The Maya warriors were ready for this. No less than four men sacrificed themselves by tackling the vampiro and driving him to the ground while their allies lined up in a semi-circle to aim their automatic weapons at the rolling, hand-to-hand melee. The Maya were ready to kill anybody and anything within the writhing, amorphous mass of bodies, including foe and friends if necessary.

"Shoot now!" A self-sacrificing warrior pleaded amidst the flailing dog pile as he was being viciously gnawed upon by the vampiro. "What are you waiting for? Just be brave and pull the damned trigger!"

The surrounding Maya warriors proved their indomitable mettle to the shock and dismay of the evil General Carmel who was now trussed and gagged. The Maya were clearly brave enough to pull the trigger. They continued to fire away non-stop while they methodically peeled off the dead bodies of their colleagues from the bloody mound of carnage, one after another, in an intermittent fashion, to finally expose the still breathing vampire who was at the bottom of the pile.

The jaundiced predator didn't even have a chance to plead for mercy. The ghoul was quickly reduced to an unidentifiable aggregation of miscellaneous and savagely disassembled body parts. When it was all said and done, six of the brave Maya warriors had been killed and another individual had received a vicious bite on his face. Sadly, that individual happened to be Cletus Barker.

"We rounded up seven technicians in the lab who were extracting cocaine from coca leaves, El Dolor," one warrior said to the leader. "What would you like me to do with them?"

"If they were working for General Carmel, take them out back and put a bullet in their heads," Dolor answered. "We're out of here in five minutes, men. I know damned well the Guatemalan Army will be charging in here from La Libertad. We'll all be killed if we're still here when they finally show up. Make sure all the dead vampiros are missing everything above their eye teeth. We've got six dead friends. Decapitate them and leave them here. Sadly, we can't take any of them with us. Anybody wounded?"

Initially there was no answer. El Dolor asked the question yet again. "You know the rules, gentlemen. Anybody wounded?"

This time Cletus stepped forward and raised his hand. "I got bit in the face! I got bit, damn it! I got bit!"

"Oh no, Cletus!" Lorena cried out. "Say it's not so!"

"I'm sorry, my friend, but I have to put you down." With great sorrow El Dolor whispered quietly to Cletus as he embraced a new friend and brave warrior.

"Let me say goodbye to Lorena," Cletus pleaded.

"Be quick about it."

"I–I love you, Lorena!" Cletus exclaimed as he closed his eyes tightly shut.

Once the bullet exploded the posterior brain case in the occipital region of his skull, Cletus Barker was sadly unable to hear Lorena's final words to him, or anything else for that matter.

"I–I love you too, Cletus!"

Now that Domino Lackey managed to get his mother and father salted away, it was time for him to peruse the neighborhood for another iron-rich meal. After all, Domino learned very early on that after he had gone through the transformation into becoming a human vampiro, he could only go for about three days or so without needing to consume his fill with blood or fresh, raw, visceral organs. It was time for Domino to find his next victim before all of his circulating red cells ruptured from the RV–1986 virus infection that was slowly destroying not only him, but every essential human attribute that he may have once possessed. "Hello, Mr. Blexit!" Domino said to his enormous black neighbor who lived two houses down from his parent's home. "I see that you're washing your pride and joy yet again!"

"I am, indeed," Speedy Blexit responded. "I'm just about ready to dry this baby off with some nice terrycloth towels. Why don't you give me a hand?"

"Are you going to take it to another car show this weekend?" Domino asked as he grabbed a towel and started to wipe off the water from the old muscle car.

"I am indeed," Mr. Blexit answered. "They have a MOPAR show in Albuquerque this weekend, and frankly, it would be great if I could pick up a trophy!"

"I don't know much about cars," Domino said. "All I know is that your car is loud and fast. What am I looking at here?"

"1970 Dodge Challenger T/A with a 340 small block punched out to 426 cubes that dialed in at 465 on the chassis dyno. Let me repeat that: chassis dyno, I'm talkin' now. Not measured at the fly!

Put that in your peace pipe and smoke it, son! Don't even talk to me about torque. It'll spool up on ya', that's for sure. Got enough twist in the hip to change the axis upon which Mother Earth spins upon!"

"Is that good?" Domino asked, somewhat bewildered by his neighbor's gear-head jargon.

"Way good, little buddy!" Speedy replied. "I'm running a six pack triple deuce intake, and the power plant spins the gears in a 4 speed straight into a bullet proof, limited slip, custom Dana 44 IRS with a modified 3.07 tall gear. The whole rear set up got yanked from a dead Jag XKE. Don't get no taller in the Dana series. Tall as a redwood. Hell, son! Tall as Mount Everest! I'll be the first to admit that it's a lazy dog at the get go, but dig this: I'm talkin' 160. Maybe 165 with the pedal at the metal in the one to one final drive. Got after-market discs on the front and inboards on the IRS. Cuts down on the back end sprung weight, you understand. Proud to say that I still have the original 15 inch factory Rallye wheels, though."

"Don't know what in hell you just said," Domino admitted as he dropped the towel and moved closer to Mr. Blexit, "but it sounds pretty cool nonetheless! I love the color, and haven't seen another like it."

"Medium metallic-blue. B5 paint scheme. It was a bitch to get it re-shot last year. Matte black fiberglass racing hood with front locking pins. I tell you what, Domino. If I come back with a trophy I'll take you out in the hot rod and we'll lay down some rubber if that's all okay with your mom and dad."

"I can tell this car means a lot to you," Domino said.

"First thing I bought when I got back from the 'Nam," Speedy Blexit said with a gaze upon the distant horizon. "I needed this car. It helped me feel, well–human again, I guess."

"It would be nice to feel human again, I guess," Domino said. "What happened in Vietnam?"

"Killed people. Broke things. One of the things that got broken was me. In some ways, I never came home from Vietnam. I wake up at night, and sometimes I'm still there."

"I bet a lot of people stare at you when you're driving on the highway in this thing," Domino said.

"Yeah, but sometimes not for the right reason." Speedy. said. "A while back, some toothless ridge-runner from Arkansas told me that a black man doesn't deserve to drive a car like this. He told me that I was 'appropriating' his white culture. I didn't know that there was supposed to be a white culture. Is there even such a thing a 'black culture' for that matter? I thought there was only supposed to be an 'American Culture.' I should have said something, but I simply turned my head and drove away. Last time I'll let that happen. From now on, I'm claiming that there's a black culture whether one exists or not. Now, you're Navajo, Domino. Do you feel that you're, well–an American?"

"Frankly, Mr. Blexit, I'm not even sure if I'm a human anymore, much less an American."

"I heard you were sick and in the hospital for a while," Speedy said. "Are you feeling okay now? Your color still looks a bit puny to me."

"Haven't felt better."

"What's up with Poker and Clover?" Speedy asked. "I haven't seen your parents in a spell or two."

"Well, to tell the truth, my parents have been tied up for quite a while."

"Be sure to give them my best," Speedy said. "They're sure sweet people."

"Very sweet," Domino said. "You really have no idea."

With that, Domino lunged at his neighbor and managed to bury his huge canine incisors into the lateral aspect of his neck, but Mr. Blexit was quick and backhanded Domino to thwart the attack.

"You're a damned vampire!" Speedy exclaimed. "Back off, Domino. I mean it!"

Domino lunged at his neighbor yet again, but this time Mr. Blexit was ready and he smashed Domino across the side of his head with a lug wrench. Stunned, Domino moaned and staggered away leaving Speedy to attend to his wounds.

Speedy rushed into his house and washed down the wound site with soap and hot water followed by an irrigation with alcohol before he applied a gauze dressing to the bite site. He went to the phone and reported the entire event to the local police department. Help soon arrived, but it was neither the local police nor an ambulance to render further medical care. It was a man that Speedy had known from the Vietnam War. It was Captain Noche and his squad of heavily armed men from the Night Crawler Protocol Vampiro Containment Unit.

"It's been a while, Speedy," Captain Noche said to his old friend. "I didn't see you at the last reunion."

"Didn't feel up to it last year," Speedy Blexit said. "Sometimes these reunions are, well–I just didn't make it last year. Enough small talk, Noche. I got bit by a vampiro! I got bit, damn it! It was my neighbor, Domino Lackey. He lives two doors down."

"We've been looking for him," Noche said. "Honestly, we had no idea where he lived. Couldn't get any of that information from the tribe or out of any state records. He was at the Memorial Hospital up in Farmington recently, but all the information they had on the kid had been falsified for some reason or another. Momentarily, my men and I will go over to his house and find out what kind of mess Domino left for us."

"Wait. I do *not* want to turn into a vampire," Speedy said. "Just shoot me now."

"By my own regulations, beyond the official guidelines in the Night Crawler Protocol, I certainly have the self-ordained authority to do so," Noche answered. "Perhaps there's a way out of this mess for you, however."

"What do you mean? Speedy asked. "Is there a treatment for this disease as of yet?"

"Sadly, no, but I'm familiar with an army general in Texas named Sibley who may be in a position to help you."

"How exactly?" Speedy asked.

"Rumor has it that he can pour you a tall, cool, glass of sweet lemonade made from that sour lemon that life just dropped in your lap."

"Oh yeah?" Speedy asked. "What do I have to do?"

"How would you feel about moving out to San Antonio for a while?"

⟣⟢

10

THE CURSE OF CAMAZOTZ

Celena and Amelia got into a heated argument in the alleyway behind the church.

"We shouldn't wait any longer," Celena said as she pointed to the top floor of the dormitory. "We should just storm the rectory now, find that nasty pervert, and simply eat him alive. Frankly, it'll be a fitting finale to that priest's disgusting life, and likely a better death than what he deserves!"

"Not yet," Amelia cautioned. "A week from Tuesday, the Brotherhood has a scheduled formal audition with a guy I met named Lobo Grande from the Astilladora de Madera cartel. He wants to personally witness our handiwork when we kill and consume Padre Garrapa. If he likes what he sees, he'll hire us as a group and we'll finally be able to move out of this one burro town once and for all."

"How will we know if he'll appreciate what we might be able to accomplish?" Celena asked.

"Lobo said if he 'gets off' on the priest's murder, this cartel captain will hire us on the spot," Amelia answered.

"Sounds like this Lobo character is a special kind of freak in his own league!"

"No doubt," Amelia mused, "but in the end, aren't we all?"

"Yes, but your plan is completely contingent upon whether or not that little gringo, Nathan Barker, can get his foot into the door at the spider's web. Perhaps we shouldn't take any chances and just kill the priest now."

"I disagree. Before we even think about taking down Padre Garrapa," Amelia suggested, "we first have a score to settle with that evil nun, Sister Cabeza de Bala."

"Stop right there," Celena protested. "I know that the old bullet head beat the crap out of your brother Isaac and his friend Jesus a while back, but I've never had a run-in with her. In fact, she's always treated me with kindness and respect."

"Are you that naïve?" Amelia asked. "Of course she's treated you with kindness and respect. She likes you. She likes *all* teenage girls, if you catch my meaning. Do you think your special or something? Get over yourself. The only reason anybody ever liked you at all is that you're a filthy little whore. The boys used to pay you *mucho dinero* for lessons in 'human sexuality' after school. No doubt, a considerable amount of high impact aerobic exercises was involved!"

"Slut calling the kettle black if you ask me!" Celena was not about to back down at this point. "You've had *lots* of boys. I know for a fact that a while back, you had two boys eat you at the same time before you, well–before you ate them and I do mean that literally, not figuratively!"

"What of it? I enjoyed it when they ate me, and to tell you the truth, I enjoyed it even more when I ate them. Especially their heart and livers, before Isaac and I drank their blood!" Amelia laughed.

"You disgust me," Celena said. "You ambushed those boys."

"Jealous?"

"I just never had a chance to, well–know them, I guess."

"You mean, in a *Biblical* way?" Amelia asked. "So, you're a horny whore?! That's a bad combo lunch platter that you just picked from the menstrual cycle cafeteria there, girlfriend!"

"Back off!" Celena demanded. "I know damned well that you also got paid for 'services rendered.' Did you not?"

"Well, I may have picked up a peso here or there along the way," Amelia answered. "Why not? I deserved it."

"And I didn't?"

"No! Amelia replied. "After all, you're just a whore."

"Well then, we *both* are," Celena said. "That means that you're no better than me!"

"I am in at least one way," Amelia replied. "At least I don't smell like a cross between baby cat shit and a lethal case of *pez muerto* twat rot, you filthy skank!"

"You're not abiding by the six foot social distancing rule. Get away from me!" Celena demanded. "That's why you're able to smell me. Well, maybe you're just smelling yourself. Did somebody shove a sardine up your ass? Who voted you in to be the head of the Brotherhood? You're an idiot! The social distancing orders are your own rules, not mine. You're just too stupid to obey them. Perhaps you need a refresher course on how far you need to be standing away from me!"

Celena and her friend Amelia were about to learn an important lesson on the reason why vampiro or vampira are never able to socialize in even a small gathering, much less get together and form a powerful Brotherhood of ghouls that could ever successfully conquer a miniscule town as inconsequential as Santa Sangre in the middle of nowhere.

While Celena and Amelia exchanged fierce blows with fists of iron, las vampiras were totally unaware that their nemesis, Sister Cabeza de la Bala, was swooping in for a surprise flank attack with a baseball bat!

The angry nun first took out Celena with an overhead chop against the base of her neck that staggered the teen with a bone-jarring concussion. Celena stumbled away to her left and subsequently crashed with an undignified, spread-eagle posture into the alleyway with the side of her face pinned up against an adobe wall.

It took Amelia only a moment to realize what happened. She rocked back on her right foot for leverage and then lunged at the nun with fangs bared! Despite her super-human strength, Amelia turned out to be no match for her powerful adversary. Sister Bala cocked the bat and took a lateral stance toward the incoming vampira. The nun high-stepped her front foot forward and then dispensed a mighty swing toward the face of her blood-thirsty assailant. The big-league blast dropped Amelia to the ground as if the young vampira had just been run over by a train.

After the nun had taken the proverbial starch out of the two adolescent predators, she flipped the bat before she thrust both of her fists skyward as if she had just hit an extra-inning, walk-off, grand slam.

Celena was the first to regain consciousness after Sister Bala splashed a pail of cold water into her face. Her 'frenemy,' Amelia, would also soon arouse as a consequence to the same unpleasant, chilling stimuli.

"Where am I?" Celena asked when she realized that she was in a dark place and tied to a wooden chair with thick, hemp rope.

"What are you going to do to us?" Amelia asked as her sensorium began to clear.

"One question at a time," the nun replied. "You're in the basement of the nunnery. Go ahead and scream all that you want. Nobody can hear you. As far as what I want, it's time for me to eliminate you two from the community. I know exactly what you are and what you've been up to."

"This ought to be a good laugh," Celena said, "so, don't keep us waiting. What do you think we are and what do you think we've been up to?"

"Don't try my patience, you little harlot!" Sister Bala answered. "I've seen this all before. I know what I am dealing with here. Mi madre was a curandera from Hermosillo. She and her sisters neutralized the outbreak that occurred at the Sea of Cortez back in '58. Who else is in your coven of blood sucking demons? Tell me now before things get ugly."

"As I'm looking at your face," Celena said, "things have already gotten ugly as best I can tell."

"The people in Santa Sangre are starting to disappear," the nun observed. "They closed the school because of an outbreak of some mysterious illness. Well, it looks like the disease is right here in this basement. I'm not going to ask you again," Sister Bala warned. "Tell me the names of the other children in your coven before I start to take you apart."

"Buck wong!" Celena cackled.

"What does that mean?" The nun asked.

"I thought you old nuns are supposed to be well educated," Celena said sarcastically. "Buck wong is actually a Chinese expression."

"I speak Spanish, English, and French," Sister Bala said. "I certainly don't speak the heathen tongue of the godless Chinese. I'll ask you again. What does buck wong mean?"

"It translates into English as, *'FUCK OFF!'* Dig it?" Celena replied as she spit in the nun's face.

"Fine," Sister Bala said. "You'll be the first to go undergo a soul cleansing the likes of which you've never imagined. As I'm a nun and I've sworn to uphold the Ten Commandments, it would be a sin if I simply murdered you. Frankly, I want to pummel your face with my bare fists until you are a lifeless, bloody pulp. Nonetheless, I'm going to neutralize you, one way or another. Once I'm finished with you, you'll simply starve to death in a few days. This is your last chance to save yourself. Who else is in your coven of predators?"

"Buck wong, Sister," Celena snarled. "Buck wong! Lord Camazotz will forever curse you for what you're doing here!"

Without saying another word, Sister Cabeza de la Bala pulled down a power drill from the top shelf in the basement and plugged the device into an electrical wall socket. She opened up a tool chest and momentarily fumbled about amongst its contents before she stumbled upon a very small, fine drill bit and secured it into the end of the electrically powered tool.

"This is going to hurt," the nun said. "In fact, this is going to hurt a lot!"

Sister Bala pressed the trigger on the electric drill as she grabbed Celena by her ponytail and pulled her head back to expose her enormous canine incisor fangs. At the base of the tooth where it just cleared the gum line, Sister Bala drilled a needle hole clean through one incisor and then the next. All the while, Celena was screaming in agony, but this did not deter the nun from her grisly and barbaric task at hand.

In the basement, there was a random ensemble of dusty, disorganized exercise equipment shoved into a back corner. It was quite clear that the equipment had not been used by anybody in quite some time. Celena and Amelia were rather alarmed when the nun took four 25 kg barbell weights and ran a thick shank of hemp rope through the center hole on the heavy discs, and then tied the weights to the back of Celena's ponytail. This forced the vampira's head back as it pried her mouth agape. The human parasites were even more alarmed when Sister Cabeza de la Bala stripped down to her waist, revealing that she was an extremely muscular dude!

"May Lord Camazotz preserve me!" Amelia cried out. "You—you're a damned tranny?"

"Go ahead and pray to your pagan god of the bat, if you must," the nun said. "Camazotz won't save you. You're beyond mercy or redemption. I'll have you know that I'm a *transvestite*, not a *transsexual*. Although I've always been a woman trapped inside the body of a man, it would be a sin in the eyes of God if I ever mutilated my external genitalia."

"So, tell me," Amelia boldly asked, "are you sexually attracted to Padre Garrapa?"

"Frankly, that's none of your business," Sister Bala said. "but if you must know however, I'm a lesbian tranny."

"No," Amelia answered, "you're just a sadistic freak!"

The nun pulled up a lawn chair and sat beside Celena and proceeded to run a piano wire through the hole in one incisor and then through the other. She then affixed both ends of the wire to a hand-cranked, 1,200 pound capacity, manual winch.

"Time for some dental work!" the nun sadistically laughed as she slowly turned the hand crank on the winch like the pedal on a bicycle that was out for a leisurely Sunday cruise. Momentarily, both upper incisor canine teeth were violently extracted from the maxillary bone in Celena's skull amidst copious bright red blood that poured from the empty tooth sockets and screams of unabated agony.

Celena's eyes clamped tightly shut as her body started to shake violently. After about a minute of this contrived, histrionic activity, Celena became suddenly motionless as she threw her eyes wide open and stared at the ceiling.

"Wake up, you demon!" Sister Bala demanded as she threw more water upon the face of the young vampira. When Celena did not respond, the nun was convinced that she had just witnessed the vampire suffer from a grand mal seizure event.

After untying the vampira from her chair, Sister Bala gently pulled Celena to the floor once she had removed the heavy weights that had been tied to the back of Celena's ponytail. That was the moment Celena was waiting for.

When the nun kneeled beside Celena to ascertain if she was still breathing, the young vampira reached up and clutched the cleric by the throat and pinned her to the ground. With her free hand, Celena picked up one of the heavy lead weights and proceeded to pound Sister Cabeza de la Bala in the face until her skull was flush with the concrete floor in the Nunnery basement.

Celena affixed her mouth over the open wounds in the nun's skull and took her good sweet time to take her good sweet fill of refreshing nourishment. While she fed, Celena left her colleague tied up to her chair. Amelia cursed away vociferously at her greedy friend for not wanting to share any of the impromptu gourmet meal before the two predators hastily retreated from their basement incarceration to rejoin what remained of the Brotherhood.

⚔

"It's not very often when I'm honored with a visit by an emissary from the Department of Defense," Lobo Grande said. "To what do I owe the pleasure of this visit, Colonel Esteban?"

"I assure you that I will try to be cordial with you, but this is certainly not a social calling by any means," the military officer said with a stern demeanor as he sat across the desk from Lobo Grande in an office at the cartel compound. "There are issues that I need to bring to your attention that frankly have jeopardized your prior good standing with the Mexican government."

"Before you came, I checked the payment ledgers," Lobo said. "We're certainly up-to-date on our monthly endowment to the Federales. They clearly seem to be pleased with our financial arrangement and we are certainly happy with the protection that has been provided to us. I can't imagine that there would be any issues to warrant any hostility from you, veiled or otherwise."

"It has been brought to our attention that you're now allowing the Maya in the Yucatan to grow coca on your behalf," Colonel Esteban observed.

"Is that a problem?" Lobo asked. "Shouldn't be as far as I'm concerned. I got a clearance from the Mexican Department of Native Affairs before we elected to do any business with los indios."

"The government doesn't have any problem with you hiring out the Maya for their agricultural skills. Obviously, they possess a fund of knowledge and unparalleled expertise in growing coca in the wretched jungle," the colonel said, "but we certainly take exception to their method of compensation for services rendered."

"I don't see what the problem is here," Lobo said. "We've paid a lot of our prior contract labor with weapons and ammunition in the past. At least to my knowledge, this hasn't resulted in any adverse circumstances for the government before. If that's indeed the case, why would it be an issue now?"

"Because in the past, none of your contract labor ever initiated a successful para-military invasion that crossed a border into an adjacent sovereign nation to engage in an act of lethal warfare. One of Guatemala's favored citizens was assaulted and subsequently apprehended. To make matters worse, the Maya invaders destroyed a lucrative financial operation in the coca industry," the military officer answered.

"What in hell are you talking about?" Lobo asked. "Guatemala is not within the sphere of either our concern or our influence."

"Don't play dumb with me, amigo!" The Colonel barked as he stood up and leaned over Lobo's desk. "The self-proclaimed Queen of the Maya led a raiding party of commandos into Guatemala where they captured a man known as General Carmel, killed his men, and burned his cocaine extraction lab down to the ground. Three of his body guards were vampiros, but it mattered not. You should think about that fact for a moment. The general was reportedly taken back across the border into Mexico and has been charged with war crimes against humanity by the Maya. God knows what those savages will eventually do with the general."

"This is the first that I've heard about any of this business," Lobo said. "If there was an incursion of Maya commandos into a foreign country, it certainly wasn't authorized by me."

"If that is the case," the colonel said, "then perhaps you're not keeping track of current events and you don't deserve to be a leader in this cartel."

"Who on earth is General Carmel?" Lobo asked. "Sounds like the name of a chewy candy bar that the gringos would favor north of the Bravo. I've never heard of this guy. His name means diddly shit to me. Why should I care about this hombre?"

"General Carmel was the leader of the Los Carcineros paramilitary outfit during Operation Sofia in the recent Guatemalan Civil War. His band of cut throats attempted to exterminate the Maya as a race, and now that los indios have captured him, they're going to make him suffer."

"How is that any of our concern?" Lobo asked. "The Guatemalan Civil War has been over for four or five years now."

"Although retired from active military campaigns," Colonel Esteban elaborated, "the general still has a lot of friends in the Guatemalan government. If you don't get control of this situation right now, there could be, shall we say, a rather unpleasant international incident between two otherwise fat and happy Latin American countries. That would be bad for all parties concerned. If that happens, that's on your head!"

"Fine, Colonel," Lobo said. "You've made your point. Tell El Jefe that I'll send a team of foot soldiers down to the Yucatan and we'll just simply collect their weapons. The Maya will not be happy about this course of action, but I have to think of another way to compensate them. Oddly, as an ethnic group, they don't seem to be particularly interested in el dinero, but I'll come up with some ideas on how to make it fair to them. I have to maintain a good working relationship with these people, because they've been loyal to me. Despite their primitive ways, they have excellent book-keeping skills and their mathematical calculations are precise down to the last gram of product that they produce on my behalf. Contract labor like that should be well rewarded in my opinion."

"You don't understand what I am saying, Lobo," the Colonel answered. "You're going to pick up where General Carmel left off a few years ago. I want you to send an armed team down there and exterminate the Maya, crucify Queen Pastore, destroy their crops, and then salt the earth. This will be the only way we can smooth the ruffled feathers of the Guatemalan government. Do I make myself clear?"

"That would certainly be a bad business move on my part," Lobo said. "There's another issue to consider. You told me that the Maya commandos wiped out the people that were working on behalf of General Carmel. The death toll apparently included three vampiros that were presumably the general's body guards. That's truly astonishing! I would be lying if I didn't express to you that I have considerable concern about that rather disturbing fact. How could the Maya achieve such a militaristic feat?"

"Frankly, I have no idea," the colonel answered. "I surmise that the Maya had their own team of vampires."

"Suppose I decide not to comply with your friendly suggestion, Colonel Esteban?"

"Nothing friendly about what I just said. Besides, it's not a suggestion. It's an order. You have one week to get the job done. If you refuse, my men will come in here, kill everybody, and then burn your place down to the ground with you in it," the military officer answered as he casually glanced at his wristwatch.

"My, my, my! Will you look at how el tiempo flies by? I must be leaving, Lobo. I have other serious business to attend to. I truly hope that you'll enjoy the rest of your day."

⬗∽⧓∽⬖

"Get your shirt tail tucked in," Dr. Ron Shiftless instructed Joe Cephas Smoot. "Did anyone ever tell you that you look like a refugee from the Beverly Hillbillies TV show back from the mid-1960s?"

"Must you torment me incessantly?" Joe asked his business manager. "I don't know why I need to slip on these duds. After all, I'm already under contract with the Leben Kur AG pharmaceutical firm, so they damn well know what in hell I look like. Doesn't appear to me as if I'll be re-applying for my old job at the poultry processing plant out in Hope, Arkansas, anytime soon. Therefore, if Leben Kur wants any more of my blood for some kind of an experiment, all they have to do is ask me for it."

"What you've been plugged into thus far has been the cosmetics division for the company," Shiftless explained. "It's now time to take your peculiar medical condition to a whole new level of research."

"You told me that the virus infection in my blood induced a bevy of different types of malignant disorders in a variety of laboratory test animals," Joe recalled. "I was under the distinct impression that the company was no longer interested in utilizing my essence to treat degenerative diseases, or anything else for that matter."

"Not so fast," Shiftless explained. "A Leben Kur research scientist in West Germany believes that he's successfully attenuated the virus and made it less virulent by genetic engineering. The Germans believe that they've successfully down-regulated the erythroblast receptors found on the external viral protein coat. If so, they might be able to stop the virus from infecting the bone marrow stem cells which initiates the entire vampire virus induced hemolytic cascade in human red cells from the very beginning."

"That's all good news, I suppose," Joe Cephas said, "but what I do know darn well from what you've already informed me about this disease process is that it not only infects the marrow stem cells, but it also infects the kidneys and the root of the canine incisors in the maxillary bone which causes the teeth to become so huge. From what you've just told me, or perhaps I should say from what you've *not* just told me, I wouldn't suppose that they've worked out these residual problems as of yet, now have they?"

"I'm glad you see the big picture," Dr. Shiftless said. "That's why they want to see you and throw another contract in front of your pretty face. They need more of your blood to try and work on further viral attenuation. Not only is there the issue with the kidneys and the canine incisors, there's a more important problem the research scientists are trying to contend with."

"What might that be?" Smoot asked.

"The vampire virus also attacks the temporal lobes of the brain and this causes the individual who's been infected to develop a propensity to emotionally erupt with dangerous and violent antisocial behavior."

"That's odd. I never had a problem with violent behavior when I first became infected," Joe said.

"That's because, as best I can tell," Ron hypothesized, "you don't have a brain, you dim-witted, hillbilly hayseed!"

"Maybe I was wrong about that, Ron," Joe Cephas interjected. "If the truth be told, I feel as if I'm on the threshold of a violent outburst as we speak. Let me come over there and see if I can rearrange the profile of your nose just a bit. I'll bet that if I flatten your horrific honker, it just might take the salsa caliente out of your nasty disposition for at least a day or two. Who knows? Maybe even longer if I elect to subject your sorry ass to an even more prolonged attitude adjustment program!"

The verbal sparring between Dr. Shiftless and Smoot came to an abrupt end when somebody began to vigorously knock upon the front door of the vampiro's apartment.

"Don't just sit there, Joe," Shiftless said. "Go answer the damned door."

"Well, you're closer to it than I am," Smoot protested.

"You live here," Shiftless noted. "I'm just a guest in this apartment."

"Yes, and one who's quickly wearing out his welcome," Joe said as he answered the front door.

It was a shock to see who came by for an off-the-record chat. It was none other than the former military director of the United States Army Bioweapon Division in San Antonio, Texas. It was the man named, General Sibley.

"Are you just going to stand there and stare at me, Mr. Smoot, or are you going to have the common decency to invite me in?" the general asked.

"Oh, my goodness!" Smoot exclaimed. "How on earth did you find to me?"

"You and Ron Shiftless fell off the radar a while back. Frankly, we thought you boys were killed down in Mexico. We actually didn't know that you were alive and on terra firma in the land of the free and the home of the brave until we saw you in a recent television commercial, Smoot. You were hawking some type of a beauty cream. Maybe I'm wrong. Perhaps it was an anal orifice anesthetic and lubrication jelly. I can't quite remember what product you were trying to sell on the boob tube, but nonetheless, that's how we found you," the general explained as he turned his head to give Ron Shiftless the stink-eye.

"This jackass is apparently now your business manager," the general continued, "or so it would seem."

Ron jumped up from his position on the couch and stood at attention while he stared straight ahead to purposefully avoid looking at General Sibley in the eye.

"I should have you thrown in the brig, Captain Shiftless," the general said.

"On what grounds, General Sibley?" Shiftless asked.

"Let me see. Desertion. Dereliction of duty. Insubordination. How's that for starts?" The general asked. "Give me a moment and I'm sure that I can come up with a few more allegations."

"Begging the general's pardon, but it was *you* who abandoned us on the other side of the Bravo after our last mission."

"Yes, and I take responsibility for that. It appears that Colonel Placard went out of his way to make more than a few enemies on Capitol Hill. One nasty person in particular, Congresswoman Manteen Rivers, made sure that the plug got pulled on the entire Bioweapon Division. If I knew that you boys were going to get stranded down there in Old Mexico, I would've come for you myself. As you were, Captain Shiftless. Sit down on the couch and relax. I'm not here to bust your chops," the general explained.

"Well, what's so important that you came all the way up here to Dallas from San Antonio to talk to us about, General?" Smoot asked.

"Come over here, Joe, and have a seat by Ron," General Sibley petitioned. "I have something that I want to show you boys."

General Sibley opened his briefcase, pulled out a binder, and set it upon the coffee table in front of Ron and Joe Cephas for their consideration. "Go ahead, gentlemen. Feel free to take a look. These pictures were taken with a telephoto lens by one of our assets in Estado Chihuahua on the banks of the Rio Conchos."

"Where in hell is that?" Smoot asked.

"On the outskirts of Ciudad Camargo in Mexico," the General answered.

"What are we looking at here, General?" Dr. Shiftless asked.

"The aftermath of a vicious fire fight between two competing Mexican drug cartels. This photograph shows two men in chains getting the living hell beaten out of them. The big man with black hair, simian ridge, and the bushy, uni-brow has been identified by our State Department as a naturalized American citizen who was originally born in St. Petersburg, Russia. His name is Ilya Putinov. His friends know him as, 'Russian Bear.' He was an emergency room doctor who trained at the Gulf Coast College of Medicine in Houston. He was captured by drug dealers a while back when he was doing volunteer missionary work on the Gulf Coast of Mexico in Playa Caliente. It's clear from this photograph that he's little more than a slave."

"Poor bastard," Ron said as he shook his head. "He should've never gone to Playa Caliente in the first place. It was all over the news a while ago that this particular slice of Mexico was a de facto drug cartel hot spot."

"Indeed, however that's not all," General Sibley said as he turned to the vampire. "Joe Cephas? I want you to take a good look at the image of the Russian's colleague who was also receiving a vicious beat down in the second photograph. Does that other man look somewhat familiar to you?"

"Oh my God!" Smoot exclaimed as he passed the binder back over to Dr. Shiftless. "Take a look, Ron!"

"Oh, my God! It's Colonel Placard!" Ron proclaimed. "He's–he's still alive?!"

"Maybe not for long if this photograph is any indication of Placard's current perilous circumstances south of the border," the general said. "You boys need to come back to San Antonio with me. I'm putting a new bioweapon team together, but this one is off the books."

"Search and destroy?" Joe Cephas asked.

"Not this time," General Sibley answered.

"What then?" Dr. Shiftless asked.

"Straight up hostage rescue mission. My new team will only be authorized to unleash the fire power, or perhaps 'bat' power, that will be necessary to liberate Placard, the Russian doctor, and anybody else held in captivity down there against their will by this new cartel. You'll get to meet the other members of the crew as soon as we get to the Alamo City. Pack your gear, gentlemen. I have a couple of units of blood in an ice chest waiting for you in the car downstairs, Joe Cephas. We need to be on the road in half an hour."

⸺⧼∫⧽⸺

The medical student named Felix had a big grin on his face when he entered Blake Barker's hospital room while waving a laboratory report over his head. "Hello, Señor X! I have some fantastic news that Dr. Guzman wanted me to share with you this afternoon!"

"Did you find a new source for beef or pig blood on my behalf?" Blake asked.

"Yes, we did," Felix answered, "but what I have is better news than that."

"Lay it on me, Felix!" Blake said. "I'm in need of some good news right about now."

"I am happy to report that the hydroxychloroquine and acyclovir therapy that you've been on appears to have cleared the RV–1986 virus out of your blood!" Felix exclaimed. "It looks like we're getting your infection under control."

"Are you pulling my chain?" Blake asked. "Get on the level with me."

257

"I *am* being honest with you," Felix said. "Your bilirubin has normalized. Your LDH has normalized. We currently don't find any evidence of red blood cell hemolysis!"

"Well, that would explain why my color is starting to clear up," Blake said. "However, the fangs in my mouth have shown no sign of regression."

"Dr. Guzman thinks that the transformation of your dentition is now a 'hard-wired' and permanent change that will never likely remit," Felix explained. "If that turns out to be the case, you shouldn't be particularly alarmed about that fact, however. After all, the ancient Maya used to file their teeth. I'm certain that a competent cosmetic dentist would be able to reduce your canine incisors to something that would look, well–a bit more human and less like a bat."

"Although my symptoms seem to be improving, has that had any bearing on my underlying new diagnosis of leukemia?" Blake asked.

"Sorry, but no," Felix answered. "You're still going to need systemic chemotherapy to try and get this cancer under control. Now that the virus has been cleared out of your blood, Dr. Guzman has a theory that you'll have a much greater chance of response to chemotherapy and achieving long-term survivorship that perhaps will be tantamount to a cure."

"Are–are you certain that my infection is in remission?" Blake asked.

"You have friends in high places," Felix answered. "Dr. Guzman called a doctor that she has worked with in the past at the Center for Disease Control in Atlanta. His name is Dr. Blanks. This doctor said that he knows you, and that if things don't go well for you down here in Mexico, he would be happy to have a crack at you up in Atlanta."

"Dr. Blanks? Damn! It's a small world, Felix," Blake said.

"As Dr. Guzman said, everything in the universe seems to be connected somehow," Felix replied. "Dr. Blanks was kind enough to send us a reagent kit to retest your blood. The CDC just devised the methodology to isolate the RV–1986 antigen. They also sent us an experimental antibody screen. I'm happy to report that the antigen has been cleared out of your blood and you're now demonstrating antibodies against the virus!"

"I thought Dr. Guzman was worried that the virus was starting to demonstrate genetic drift and that it would make it difficult if not impossible to eventually devise a vaccine against this damned thing."

"That is all quite true, but apparently two guys named Dr. Kohl and Dr. Hoefferle who work with Dr. Blanks at the CDC isolated a universal protein on the outer viral coat that seems to be an antigenic constant, despite the propensity for the virus to undergo genetic drift," Felix explained.

"Wow!" Blake said with enthusiasm. "Does that mean I'm cured?"

"I don't know for sure," Felix said, "but as of yet, Dr. Guzman doesn't think so. She's fearful that if you stop the antiviral treatment, the virus may show up yet again someday."

"Does that mean I might need to stay on this antiviral treatment for the rest of my life?"

"Possibly so," Felix answered. "Your case was presented at Grand Rounds this past Wednesday, and some of the infectious disease specialists that were on hand suggested that someday we may have the technology to do a quantitative viral assay to actually measure the number of viral particles left in your body, if any. As of our current technological capabilities in the latter half of 1986, we certainly don't have that type of sophisticated technology as of yet. Therefore, until that day, these other specialists thought it would be highly unwise to ever come off of antiviral treatment. They were also concerned that if you ever come off of treatment on your own accord, the infection would come right back and bite you in the butt."

"Or more likely, my bone marrow!" Blake rightly surmised. "Theoretically, if you're ever proven to have completely cleared the virus out of your bloodstream and marrow, and it could be confirmed by some future quantitative assay that as of yet does not exist, maybe then we could officially declare that you're cured!"

"Fantastic!" Blake exclaimed. "I guess that means I'm ready to start chemotherapy to treat my new underlying acute leukemia."

"Indeed," Felix said. "Dr. Guzman wants to treat you with what's called the '7+3' protocol that consists of two different chemotherapy drugs. She'll come in and tell you about it when she makes rounds. You'll need to sign a permit for us to start the treatment tomorrow morning now that you have a central venous access device placed in your chest. I can't lie to you, Señor X. This chemotherapy takes an entire week to administer, and you're likely going to get as sick as a dog. I'm obligated to let you know that there's approximately a 20% chance of upfront mortality."

"Are you telling me that this leukemia treatment might kill me?" Blake asked.

"That's exactly what I'm trying to tell you," Felix said.

"After what I have been through over the last few months, nothing scares me at this time in my life. After all, I'd like to think that I'm a brave man, Felix," Blake boasted.

"Good," Felix said. "Do you feel like you're ready to try some real food at this time instead of animal blood now that the vampiro infection is clearing out of your body?"

"Perhaps not yet," Blake answered with a laugh. "Maybe I'm not quite that brave after all!"

⚕

Miguel Pastore stood upon the front patio of the hacienda at Ranco Feliz and stared through the dusty haze at the township that was only about two kilometers away. Intuitively, Miguel knew that something was indeed amiss in the nearby settlement of Santa Sangre. The school was now closed, and Estado Jalisco issued a quarantine for the community because there was reportedly an alleged outbreak of an unspecified infectious disease in the area. Apparently the citizens of the small town were not only dying from some mysterious illness, but some individuals were actually disappearing completely!

Rancho Feliz was previously occupied by the vampiro, Pepe Umbo, who was executed in the recent past by members of the Calle Vampiro drug cartel in a most ghastly fashion. The old rancher was

260

crucified upon a columnar cactus and subsequently beheaded, so the community was no stranger to the presence of human vampirisim.

Miguel Pastore was of course a vampire, but he was predominantly able to satisfy his nutritional demands through the rotational harvesting of blood from the various stock yard and domesticated animals at the ranch. Up until recently when he started to consume transient cartel members who would occasionally appear at the hacienda, Miguel had never previously preyed upon humans since he had been infected with the RV–1986 virus. Nonetheless, whatever the nature of the mysterious illness that had afflicted Santa Sangre, it had all the ear markings of an outbreak of vampirism. For what other reason would the Federales have increased their police patrols throughout the community?

"Nathan!" Miguel called out to his young ward who lived at the ranch with him. "Are you in the chicken coop again? I told you not to play with the yellow eggs that recently reappeared. We must save those for the curandera."

When Nathan realized that yet again he was about to get another scolding from his Tio Miguel, he sprinted out of the chicken coop and circled around the backside of the hacienda. Nathan magically appeared on the patio on the opposite side from the coop in an unsuccessful attempt to obfuscate his nefarious activities.

"I'm here!" Nathan replied. "I'm sorry that I didn't hear you call my name at first, Miguel, but I was feeding the yearling a carrot."

"Is that so?" Miguel replied as he casually walked up to Nathan. At that time, the child had his hands jammed down into the front pockets of his trousers and was staring at the ground.

"I'm surprised at how big she's getting!" Nathan proceeded to confabulate a brazen ball of yarn. "Maybe it's time we give her a name. What do you think?"

"Tell me something, Nathan," Miguel softly inquired as he brushed away a few sprigs of soft, white chicken down from the young boy's shirt. "Since when did the yearling start to sprout feathers?"

"You caught me again, Tio," Nathan confessed.

"What I'm telling you is for your own good," Miguel said. "The old curandera believes that from time to time the Maya bat demon,

Camazotz, will place a curse upon the humble chicken. When that happens, the birds will lay infected eggs that are bright yellow in color. These bright yellow eggs are very dangerous to people. You must never eat them or even touch them. Do you understand?"

"I do, Tio."

"What do you know about this illness that's sweeping through Santa Sangre, Nathan?" Miguel asked his young ward.

"I've heard stories that los vampiros are on the loose," Nathan answered.

"Do you still see those older boys named Jesus and Isaac?" Miguel asked. "The town is under quarantine and those brats are up to no good. I want you to stay away from them. Am I making myself clear?"

"I haven't seen them since they shut down the school," Nathan lied.

"You're a good boy, Nathan," Miguel said. "I want you to go inside and Mayordomo will pour you a glass of milk and give you some cookies."

"Thanks, Tio," Nathan said as he skipped across the portal and entered the hacienda.

As soon as Nathan entered the house, Miguel realized a car was coming down the long drive toward the front of the hacienda. When the car stopped, a stranger with a camera and an enormous telephoto lens jumped out of the vehicle and walked to the front gate of the compound.

"May I help you?" Miguel asked the visitor.

"I hope so. My friends call me, Buen Ojo. I already know who you are, Miguel."

"I'm not certain how that's possible, as we've never met before."

"I work for the Brownwater Security Group in Texas," Buen Ojo said. "Let me get right down to the business at hand. A man you know named, Augustus Placard, is being held as a prisoner against his will by the evil gang of banditos that has arisen out of the ashes of the old Calle Vampiro cartel. Other individuals are also likely held there as slaves."

"Stop right there," Miguel said. "I know Augustus Placard quite well, but he's no friend of mine."

"I'm actually aware of that fact," Ojo said.

"Last time I saw him was at the CDC in Atlanta when he and a couple of his goons were coming by to snatch me up and force me at gunpoint to join the United States Army Bioweapon Division in San Antonio," Miguel explained. "That being said, what do you want from me?"

"The driveway that leads up to your compound is a quarter of a mile long and it's very smooth without any major ruts in the road," Ojo observed. "It could be used as a landing strip in an emergency situation."

"What are you talking about?" Miguel asked.

"Some friends of Placard would like to fly into Rancho Feliz, rescue the colonel and perhaps a few of his colleagues, and then beat a hasty retreat back to Los Estados Unidos," Ojo explained. "Besides, as you are un vampiro, perhaps you'd like to come along on a ride with us on our rescue mission. You have an undeniably powerful set of weapons embedded in your upper jaw, and a guy like you could come in rather handy if we get into a pinch."

"There's not a dog's chance in hell that will ever happen," Miguel said. "After my last run in with members from a drug cartel, I was lucky to make it out alive and with my own skin. Besides, I'm now the caretaker of a young boy named Nathan Barker whose father actually disappeared at the hands of the Calle Vampiro cartel. No thanks. I'd be most appreciative if you'd leave my premises immediately."

"That doesn't sound like the old Miguel Pastore that I heard about in the United States. I was told that he was a decent human being who actually cared about the welfare of his fellow man," Buen Ojo said. "I guess what I heard about you was wrong, though."

"So, are you going to lay a guilt trip upon me?" Miguel asked. "Do you think that's really going to work?"

"I most certainly do!" Buen Ojo said.

"I can't help you, but I know somebody who can," Miguel said. "Circle around the north end of Rancho Feliz and you'll pick up a dirt road that goes east. That road runs parallel to the highway. The next ranch that you'll run into is Rancho O'Rear. There's a nasty old bastard who lives there named Julio O'Rear. His ranch has a landing strip. If you flip him a few pesos, I'm sure that he'll let you land your plane there. Just leave me alone and don't let him know that I was the one who sent you over to visit with him."

"I've never heard of a Spanish surname the likes of 'O'Rear' before," Ojo said. "That surname sounds as if it's of Irish origin, not Spanish."

"It *is* an Irish name," Miguel answered. "Concerning the moniker of what's long been called Rancho O'Rear, there's no doubt a long and sordid tale behind its origins. Knowing Julio, he'll likely want to bore you to death with it. I suggest you humor the old guy with a bottle of Jameson. It's the only thing that he drinks."

"Thanks for the tip," Ojo said.

"There's only one thing that I need you to do for me," Miguel petitioned.

"What would that be?" The visitor asked.

"It's clear to me that your intent is to haul in a truck load of trouble and dump it in my neck of the woods," Miguel observed. "Ultimately, I can't stop you from poking a rattlesnake in the eye with a sharp stick. However, if you insist on doing so, please leave me and Nathan Barker out of the nasty shit storm that you're about to stir up."

⸻⚬⸻

Elder Joseph made certain that he was well armed with an obsidian blade hidden in the pocket of his light grey jacket before he dared to approach Domino Lackey's hiding place. Joseph carefully pulled away a loose sheet of plywood that was used to board up the long-shuttered Five and Dime store in central Farmington. Using his back as a wedge to push away an edge of the splintered plywood, Joseph found that the window glass of the old store had previously been shattered, likely by a prior marauding gang of miscreant looters.

Once inside the dust-encrusted establishment, he flipped on a flashlight to scan the premises. "Domino? Are you in here?" The elder asked. "It is me! It's Joseph!"

In the blink of an eye, Domino Lackey was standing in front of Joseph. Although unkempt and disheveled, the teen had a big grin on his face.

"Joseph! I can't tell you how happy I am to see you," Domino said. "How did you find me?"

"Did you forget that I'm a tribal elder?" Joseph asked. "An elder is supposed to know everything about everybody in the Navajo nation. A little bird whispered into my ear that you were probably hiding out in this old broken down building. I guess that little bird was right."

The teen embraced the elderly man and gave him a warm hug. "I've missed you, Elder Joseph. Have you come to help me?"

"I'm not only here to *help* you, Domino," Joseph said as he reached his hand into the pocket on his jacket to extract the obsidian knife and added, "I'm actually here to *save* you. You've done some bad things, Domino. You've killed people, including a doctor named Jack Sayers and a security guard at the Farmington Memorial Hospital."

"I have indeed."

"You've eaten your own parents!" Joseph said. "Poker and Clover were like family to me."

"Probably not a smart thing to do in retrospect," Domino said.

"Is that really all you have to say about the matter?" Joseph asked.

"You ate your high school teacher, Mrs. Rain," Joseph said as he started to raise his voice.

"She was a nice lady," Domino said with a nod.

"You've attacked others," Joseph added. "Now, it's not entirely all your fault. You didn't ask to become a vampire. Nonetheless, you're almost a full-grown man. A full-grown man takes responsibility for his own actions."

"It's as if I go loco when I need to feed."

"Bullshit," Joseph replied. "I've certainly met other vampiros in my long life, and these other individuals were able to sustain themselves with the blood and raw organs of lesser animals. You however, turned down a dark and evil path instead."

"Forgive me, Joseph," Domino lamented as he stepped back from the elder. "I really couldn't control myself."

"I forgive you, Domino," Elder Joseph said. "The tribe also forgives you."

Elder Joseph was just about to run the obsidian blade into the heart of the teenager when a considerable commotion could be heard outside of the old store.

"It's Captain Noche and the Vampiro Containment Unit! I can't shake these guys! They follow me everywhere I go. It's as if I'm cursed by Camazotz!"

"Who cursed you?"

"Camazotz. The Maya god of the bat!" Domino said.

"That's a load of superstitious crap."

"No, it's not! Eventually, Noche and his men are going to catch me. When they do, they'll exterminate me. I know that they're also looking for you, Elder Joseph. We have to break out of here," Domino said. "You better move your ass if you want to live!"

With his super human strength, Domino hoisted Elder Joseph upon his shoulder and sprinted toward the front wall of glass that had been boarded up with plywood from the outside. As Domino approached the glass, he held out his left arm like a running back giving a defensive safety a stiff straight-arm to avoid a tackle in a game of football. Domino blasted through the front wall of glass and plywood as if it were mere tissue paper, and then he sprinted off into the darkness.

Noche and his men tried to pursue the fleeing vampire, but the teen was simply too swift. Once his adversaries were out of sight, Domino set Elder Joseph upon the curb of a busy intersection.

"What should I do, Elder Joseph?" Domino asked. "Where can I hide?"

"You remember the tall grass in El Malpais south of Fort Wingate?"

"That's a long way from here," Domino protested.

"I'll find you there someday," Joseph said as he rose to his feet and started to run away in a lateral direction. "You better move your ass if you want to live!"

When Elder Joseph took one more glance over his shoulder, he realized that Domino Lackey must have been filled with despair. The Navajo teen had dropped to his knees and put his hands on top of his head. Domino was going to surrender! Momentarily, the young Navajo was surrounded by Ray Noche and the soldiers from the Vampiro Containment Unit.

Would Domino be executed? Most likely. It would be a fitting end to an irredeemable soul.

That was not the point. Domino was Navajo. If justice was to be served, it was the obligation of a Navajo Elder to function in the capacity to be the judge, jury, and well, you know the rest…

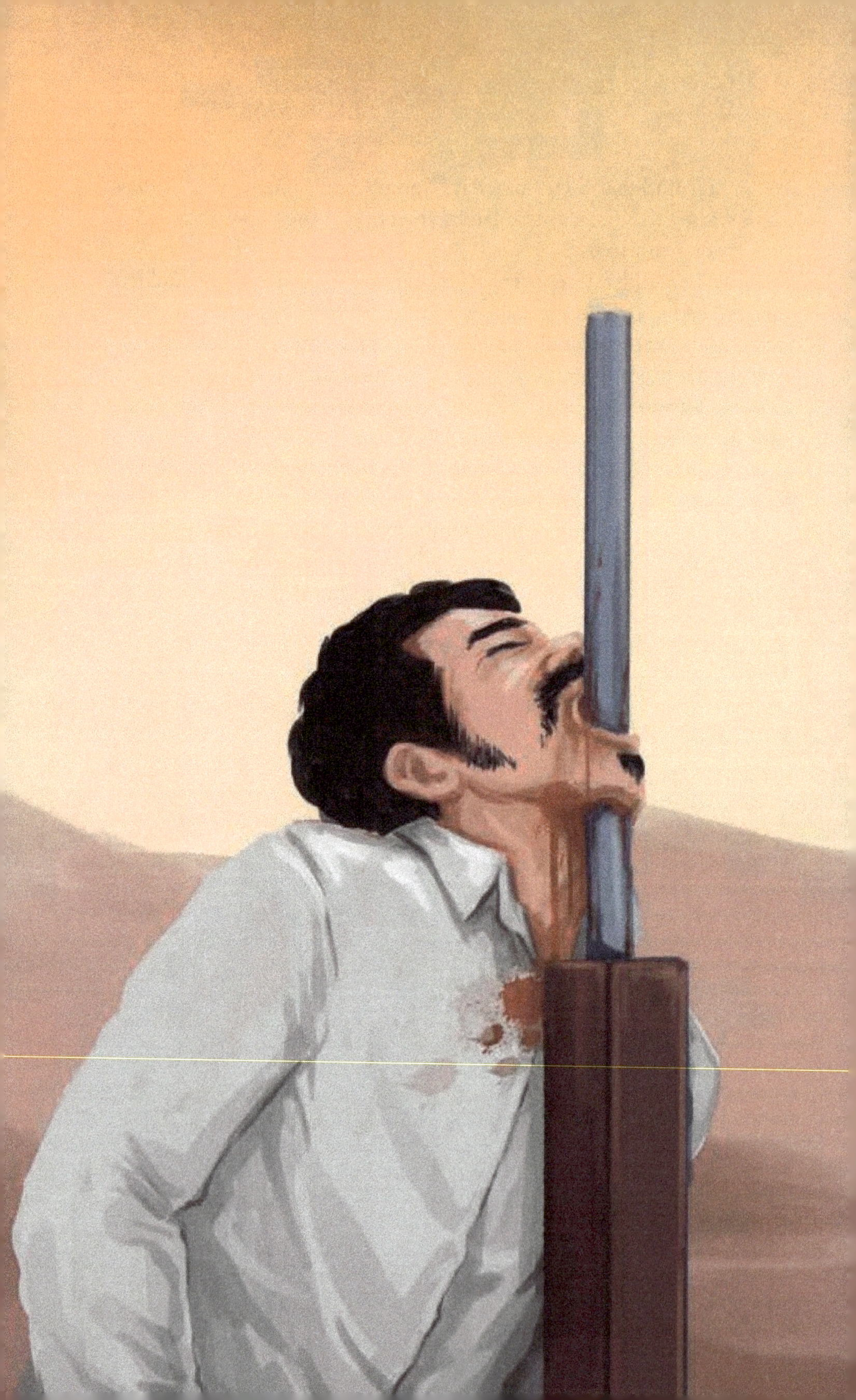

11

GREEN GROWS THE RUSHES, O!

"You know, I can't just let you walk away from murdering somebody," Dr. Zachary Hawk said to the cartel henchman named, Mono.

"This is the last time I am going to warn you," Mono said, still holding on to the mistaken belief that he was dealing with somebody named, Blake Barker. "There are four of us here. We're all heavily armed. If you're un vampiro, we now own you, Señor Barker. If you want to live, you'll work for us from now on."

Officers Rosquilla and Estofado pulled their service revolvers from their holsters and leveled the barrels of their weapons in the direction of Dr. Hawk. Meanwhile, the cartel thug known as, Jirafa, slowly extracted his FAL long rifle out from the backseat of the sedan that was still parked in the middle of the highway.

The speed of Zachary Hawk was astonishing. In the blink of an eye, he was behind Mono with his forearm around the big man's neck before any shots were even fired. Mono found his attempt to pivot away to be rather impossible at close quarters. He was ultimately unable to point the barrel of his weapon at the enraged vampiro.

"What are you waiting for?" Mono cried out to his colleagues. "You better shoot this beast before he bites me!"

Jirafa was unable to get a clear shot without hitting his friend, Mono, so he charged Dr. Hawk with the butt end of his FAL rifle in an attempt to render a disabling blow to the head of the vampiro. Jirafa's efforts turned out to be a catastrophic failure as Hawk at that time had tactical control of Mono's weapon. Hawk head-butted Mono which dropped the hairy cartel foot soldier to the ground before the vampiro rotated in time to flip the safety switch to the fire position on the long rifle and hose down Jirafa with a five round burst from the automatic weapon.

Once Mono had fallen away, the two Federale officers began to fire upon Hawk with their revolvers while retreating to the safety of the rear end of their squad car. Zachary Hawk's erratic movements were like that of a hummingbird, and none of the rounds that were shot at him managed to hit their mark.

Over the lip of the dash board from the safety of her colleague's old Bronco, Birdy Marshall watched in utter fascination as Zachary Hawk charged at the two Federale officers like a bat out of hell. Hawk took one leaping step off the bumper of the squad car and lunged over the roof of the vehicle directly toward the corrupt officers who were now out of bullets and cowering behind the trunk of the highway prowler.

The next order of business was to dispatch with the older but more physically fit Federale named, Estofado. Now that both of his enemies were on the ground, Hawk jumped up and proceeded to crush the skull of Estofado by repeatedly stomping on the man's head with the heel of his right foot. Pleased with his handiwork, Zachary Hawk now turned his attention to the corpulent officer named, Rosquilla.

As he had never tasted human flesh before, Hawk approached his next meal with unabashed enthusiasm. "Come here, lard ass!" Hawk exclaimed with unbridled fury.

"Don't kill me! Please!" The rotund Rosquilla pleaded. "I have to look after my elderly Nana at home. I'm all that she has!"

"Who's Nana? Is that your abuela?" Hawk asked, now only inches away from the face of the chunky Federale.

"No," the fat man replied. "Nana is my cat."

That was apparently the wrong answer. If there was any time in a life that was now drawing to a rapid conclusion when a boldface lie should have been proffered, it would have been at that precise moment. Unfortunately for the Federale named, Rosquilla, it was now too late!

"You can see your cat in hell!" Dr. Hawk replied as he buried his fangs into the lateral aspect of the neck of his first human meal. When Birdy Marshall realized what was going on, she jumped out of the Bronco and ran toward the vampiro. "Zack! Stop what you're doing! Once you cross the threshold of eating another human, you can't go back. You'll never be the same!"

Perhaps wiser words were never spoken, but Dr. Zachary Hawk nonetheless paid no heed to the vociferous protestations of his colleague. Within moments, it was all over when Zachary Hawk had arisen from the lifeless body of officer Rosquilla.

During the commotion, the cartel thug named Mono regained his wits and he realized that his life was in grave peril. His only chance to survive another attack from the vicious vampiro was to somehow flee the vicinity. He discreetly attempted to barrel roll on the ground toward his sedan that would perhaps afford him the opportunity to escape, but Birdy suddenly became aware that Mono was not quite yet out of the fight.

"Hawk!" Birdy Marshall exclaimed. "Look out! The hairy man is still alive!"

Before Mono could crawl into the cab of the sedan, Dr. Hawk was all over him like a bad rash. "Going somewhere, monkey boy?" Hawk asked. "I don't think so! You happen to be the guy who pulled the trigger that killed the old man by the side of the road. I have a special treat for you."

Hawk dragged the cartel thug by one arm across the highway toward the perimeter of farm field that was cordoned off by a barbed wire fence. Instead of the more commonplace wooden posts upon which one might see barbed wire strung upon, the vertical posts comprising the property line of this particular farm were 4" x 4" precast concrete vertical logs.

Extruding through the top of these concrete posts were upright, rusty prongs of exposed steel rebar. Hawk grabbed Mono by the hair and propped him into an upright position. The angry vampiro subsequently jammed Mono's head upon a prong of exposed rebar. The rusty steel shank punctured through the bottom of the man's jaw in the anatomical region known as the submental triangle, and it exited through the man's mouth that was now agape with terror.

As Zachary Hawk turned and walked away from his handiwork, he called out to Mono over his left shoulder. "Stick around for a while, you hairy bastard. Now get this straight. If I am somebody named Blake Barker, I'm one nasty son of a bitch. Now, don't you ever forget it!"

"What in God's name have you done?" Birdy called out to her colleague after she had witnessed Hawk's grotesque act of merciless barbarism.

"I'll tell you what I've done. I just nailed a living and breathing calling card upon a post as a warning to anybody else who'd ever consider trying to fuck me over in the future!" Hawk said. "Let's get out of here."

"I want nothing to do with you, Zack!" Birdy exclaimed as she jumped back into the Bronco and locked the doors. "I don't know what's become of you."

"You know darn well what's become of me." Hawk said. "Yo soy un vampiro."

"Indeed, and a very bad one from what I've seen," Birdy noted.

"You're a hypocrite!" Hawk protested. "You wanted me to prevent these four guys from killing that old man. I couldn't stop it from happening, but nonetheless, I tried to help."

"Trying to help a person is one matter," Birdy said. "Eating a person is entirely something else. Now, spiking a person's head upon a shank of rebar as if you're the re-incarnation of Vlad the Impaler? Well, that's just down right demonic! Stay away from me, Hawk!"

"Let me back in the Bronco, Dr. Marshall," Hawk said. I'm not going to warn you again!"

Zachary Hawk stood in front of his Bronco and tried to block his traveling companion from escaping the scene. "Where do you plan on going, Birdy?" Dr. Hawk demanded to know as he pounded on the hood of his own car. "Tell me! Have you already grown weary of my company? Don't tell me that our spirited and intellectually stimulating banter has somehow frightened you for some inexplicable reason!"

"No, it's not our rather confrontational discourse that perturbs me, Dr. Hawk," Birdy Marshall answered. "To be frank, I am afraid of *you*!"

"You have the sickle cell trait," Hawk said. "There's no way that I would ever dream of eating you even though I am now a vampire."

"Although you might not ever consider eating me," Birdy said, "that doesn't mean that you couldn't inflict great harm upon me."

"So," Dr. Hawk asked, "do you plan on stealing my car? I'm not going to ask you again, Birdy. Where do you plan on going?"

"I'm going back to New Mexico," Dr. Marshall shouted to her new adversary through the windshield. "I have to find Parker. It was a mistake for me to come down here with you."

"New Mexico?!" Hawk asked. "Are you out of your mind? Did you forget about Captain Noche and the Vampiro Containment Unit? They're actively looking for the both of us as we speak. Once you get back to New Mexico, you'll probably get killed."

"Will I get killed if I go back to New Mexico to find Parker Coxswain?" Dr. Marshall asked. "I'd say that there's about a 50% chance of probability that would likely happen. However, there's a bigger issue looming that I must contend with. The real question is this: Will I get killed if I stay here in old Mexico with Dr. Zachary Hawk? I'd say that there's about 100% chance of probability that would likely happen!"

With that, Birdy Marshall floored the accelerator and ran over Zachary Hawk who immediately was caught beneath the undercarriage of the old Bronco. Birdy felt a thud from underneath the vehicle when Dr. Hawk was run over by the rear wheel as she made a sharp U-turn to head back to Guadalajara and then eventually the relative safety of the United States. At that point, Birdy frankly didn't care whether or not she was still being hunted by the Vampiro Containment Unit authorized by the Night Crawler Public Safety Protocol.

After Hawk was spit out of the rear of his own car which had been stolen right before his very eyes, he was left with multiple broken bones, although none of his injuries were lethal. He would heal. After all, he was a vampire, but it would take the better part of a few days to recuperate. Should he jump into the Federale highway prowler and give chase to Birdy Marshall? No. That would not be the case. Dr. Hawk thought that the woman had caused him enough grief at that point in time.

Perhaps he could limp toward Santa Sangre and find refuge and some place where he could lick his wounds and recuperate in safety and solitude. The first order of business however, was that he had to get out of the blazing sun before his skin burned like a fat strip of bacon in a hot frying pan.

⁓⟨⟩⁓

"Welcome back to San Antonio," General Sibley said to Joe Cephas Smoot and Dr. Ron Shiftless as the three men entered the conference room to meet the other members of the rescue team. "I wish I could tell you that the United States Army Bioweapons Division has been resurrected from the grave, but that simply is not the case."

"So," Ron asked, "as I understand it, everything about this operation is unsanctioned and off the books?"

"Funded through a congressional black-ops discretionary fund," General Sibley said as he sat down at the head of the conference table. "We're good to go as long as the fucking Democrats are kept in the dark. I doubt that there's ever been a political party in the United States that actually hates the country that their members have been elected to serve."

As Ron and Joe Cephas flanked Sibley near the head of the table, the general proceeded with the formal introductions to the other people in the room. "Gentlemen, I'd like to introduce you to the other members of this hostage rescue and extraction team. At the far end of the table is our newest recruit who joined us from New Mexico. He's a Vietnam War vet named Speedy Blexit. He recently underwent the transformation after he sustained a bite from a person in the Farmington area. Unfortunately, Speedy had no viable option to survive a likely execution sanctioned by the Night Crawler Protocol, so he came out of the desert to help us on this mission."

Speedy failed to respond and simply glared at Ron and Joe Cephas with unvarnished hostility. "Mr. Blexit is currently experiencing the early antisocial and combative phase of the transformation period. Don't be put off by his hostile demeanor, as his newly found abrasive nature may be an asset for our team if a violent altercation arises."

"Hello, Mr. Blexit," Joe Cephas said. "It's a pleasure to meet you. My name is Smoot and my colleague is Captain Ron Shiftless. Ron is a research scientist in physiology."

"Fuck off," Blexit mumbled.

"Fine, then," the general said as he furrowed his brow. "The other two men that are here with us are actually contracted mercenaries from the Brownwater Security Group. Allow me to introduce to you the Balzac twins, Harry and Musty. Both of these soldiers are proficient with a multitude of weapons and are rated to operate multi-engine prop planes.

The Balzac twins nodded and waved at Joe Cephas and Ron before Harry spoke for the first time. "We're all ears, General Sibley. Give us the skinny."

"Harry," General Sibley started, "as you're older than your twin by a minute and thirty seconds, you'll be the pilot of a low-profile twin engine Piper on loan to us from the Texas Fish and Game Commission. The team will fly in low over the border to avoid radar contact with the Mexican civil air control. You'll be landing on a private airstrip at Rancho O'Rear on the outskirts of the town of Santa Sangre and Estado Jalisco. The proprietor of the ranch is a gentleman named, Julio O'Rear."

"O'Rear?" Harry Balzac asked. "That's a gringo name. What's wrong with this picture?"

"If you're a gringo, what does that make me?" Speedy Blexit asked. "Am I a gringo?"

"No, you're a Negro," Joe Cephas answered to needle his new associate.

"Where are you from?" Blexit asked Joe Cephas.

"God's country," Joe Cephas answered.

"You mean Texas?"

"No," Joe Cephas answered. "I mean Arkansas."

"I hate red necks from Arkansas," Blexit said.

"Tough shit," Joe Cephas replied. "Deal with it."

"Enough!" The general demanded. "If you must know, Harry, a lot of Americans who fought in the War with Mexico in the mid 1840s defected and never went home. They established new lives and new families with our next door neighbors across the Rio Grande. Ergo, a gringo place like Rancho O'Rear now exists."

"Where did the derogatory term, gringo, come from anyhow?" Musty Balzac asked. "I don't like it when I'm called a gringo. That term just pisses me off! If somebody calls me a gringo while I'm down in Mexico, I'm just going to shoot their ass on the spot."

"Relax," the general said. "The expression 'gringo' comes from the title of a song that was written by the famous Irish bard named, Robert Burns. Apparently the Irishmen who fought with the Americans in the War with Mexico would sing a little dilly that was popular at the time called, 'Green Grows the Rushes, O!' when they marched into battle. The title of the song was eventually shortened as a vernacular idiom, and allegedly that's where the expression 'gringo' comes from."

"Begging the general's pardon," Joe Cephas interrupted, "but that's just a load of malarkey. First of all, Robert Burns was *not* Irish. He was Scottish. You're likely referring to a *poem* called, 'Green Grows the *Rashes*' which was originally written by Burns in 1783, some 60 years before the War with Mexico. If you're referring to a *song*, then you must be talking about 'Green Grows the *Rushes*, O!', and this is actually an ancient English folk tune that dates all the way back to the 12th Century. The word 'gringo' is likely a bastardization of the word 'griego', which is no doubt a reference to somebody of Grecian origin. I'm glad that I could clear up that rather trivial matter for you gentlemen. After all, the fate of the free world must no doubt reside upon this mundane issue."

The members in the conference room were momentarily stunned by the etymological vignette espoused in detail by Joe Cephas Smoot.

"When in hell did you grow a brain, Hayseed?" Ron Shiftless asked.

"Likely when you were jerking off instead of getting any serious work done." Smoot answered.

Ron's face turned red when the room erupted into laughter.

"Settle down, people!" the general said. "We have a lot of work to do. Your contact in Mexico will be one of our assets on the other the side of the border named Buen Ojo."

"CIA?" Joe Cephas asked.

"No," the general answered. "He's another mercenary from the Brownwater Security Group. Ojo has made arrangements for transportation to get you to the Astilladora de Madera cartel compound on the outskirts of Guadalajara where the rescue will take place. I'm going to pass around dossiers for each of you that have extensive photographs and schematic floor plans of your target. Before we get into the logistics of the operation, let's take a five-minute restroom break. As for Joe Cephas and Speedy Blexit, there's an ice cooler in the hallway with a couple of units of fresh beef blood. Help yourself gentlemen and we'll reconvene on the hour."

Joe Cephas and Speedy elbowed at each other to see who'd get out of the room first to commandeer the ice chest.

"Back off, Hillbilly!" Blexit said. "I was here first!"

"Go ahead, you greedy bastard!" Cephas said. "There's plenty of blood to go around for everybody. Don't be a pig, however."

"I'll just have you know that I will *not* tolerate a cracker like you trying to appropriate any of my highly refined black culture," Blexit said.

"Does that mean I'm not allowed to whistle the fade-out on the song, 'Dock of the Bay,' by Otis Redding? It's always been one of my favorites."

"That's exactly what it means," Blexit answered.

"Fine by me, then," Joe Cephas replied. "That means you can't appropriate any of my white culture, either, if that's the case."

"What do you mean?" Blexit asked. "White people don't have a culture."

"Have you ever used a flush toilet?" Joe Cephas asked. "The existence of such a hydrological sanitary device was first referenced by a *white* Englishman named Sir John Harrington, circa 1596 A.D. Therefore, if you're amenable to not appropriating any *white* culture, I suggest that in the future whenever you need to take a shit, you should first go outside and find the nearest oleander bush to relieve yourself, you godless spear chucker."

"Why am I not surprised that your only reference to white culture has to do with shit?" Blexit asked. "Seems rather fitting to me, I suppose."

As it was past the 5-minute break, it was time for the logistical conference to resume. "We have a lot of things to cover this afternoon," General Sibley said. "Where are the two vampires? They need to be here."

"Joe Cephas and Speedy Blexit are beating the hell out of each other in the hallway," one of the Balzac twins answered. "Can't say who has the upper hand as of yet."

"Swell," Sibley said sarcastically. "I guess this meeting is going to take a lot longer than I originally thought."

⚶

"It's Mono!" Lobo Grande exclaimed when the cartel captain pulled up in a pickup truck on the scene of carnage strewn across the highway on the outskirts of Guadalajara. "What have they done to him, Villanueva? It looks like he's been impaled upon the top of a fence!"

"This must be the work of the vampiro named, Blake Barker!" The driver of the truck said.

"No doubt," Lobo Grande agreed. "I'm going to kill that animal if it's the last thing I ever do. Stop the truck, Villanueva. Get Russian Bear out of the back and have him attend to Mono immediately. Tell the doctor that if Mono dies, then Russian Bear dies. Am I clear?"

"Yes, Lobo," the driver answered as he jumped out of the cab to extricate Russian Bear from the back of the bed of the pickup. "Get out of the truck, and be quick about it. The man stuck on the fence is named, Mono. Get over there and fix him up. Do it now!"

"Fix him up?!" Bear asked. "I can't fix jack diddly shit while I'm handcuffed." The Russian doctor sat placidly in the back of the pickup truck and made a point of not moving a single inch. "Well, I'm waiting!"

Villanueva returned to the cab and dutifully returned with Lobo Grande who had the handcuff keys in his pocket.

"Okay, your hands are now free," Lobo Grande said as he removed the uncomfortable shackles from the doctor's wrists. "Happy now?"

"Ecstatic," Bear answered.

"The driver and I will help hoist Mono free from the steel rod that's jammed through his jaw," Lobo said. "Your job will be to keep him from bleeding to death."

"I'll have you know that if I was working as an emergency room doctor in United States, we would either take a pair of bolt cutters or a carbide tipped circular saw to cut away the rebar at the concrete base. The steel rod stuck through the throat of Mono should *not* be physically extracted outside of the setting of an operating suite."

"The reason being?" Lobo asked.

"Simple," Bear replied. "He could bleed to death if we simply pull him off of the steel shank out here in the middle of nowhere."

"An operating suite is not an option right now," Lobo said. "You have your orders. Don't let him die or otherwise–"

"Yeah," Bear said to cut off the cartel captain. "I get the picture, okay? I'm just telling you that you've been sufficiently warned about a potentially adverse outcome."

Lobo Grande kept Mono's head steady while Villanueva wrapped his arms around his torso to heave the hairy man upward. Lobo had to jostle the head back and forth several times to finally liberate the man's jaw free from the rebar spike. As soon as Mono's head was free, blood gushed forth like a faucet from the inside of his mouth.

"Who did this to you, Mono?" Lobo Grande asked.

"Un Vampiro!" Mono mumbled as he choked on the blood flooding into his oral cavity. "I think it was Blake Barker!"

The Russian doctor had to be "Johnny-on-the-spot" with a thick wad of gauze that was promptly jammed into Mono's mouth in an attempt to apply direct pressure to the gaping wound underneath his tongue.

Bear looked at Lobo with an equal measure of disgust and contempt. "Happy now?"

"Ecstatic," Lobo answered to parrot Bear's prior response. "Get Mono into the truck and we'll drive him to the University Hospital at the San Augustin College of Medicine."

"Shouldn't I just go into Guadalajara by myself and call for an ambulance?" Villanueva asked.

"No!" Lobo answered the driver. "That'll draw too much attention. We're just going to drop him off at the emergency room. I want you to camp out at the hospital, Villanueva. Make sure nothing bad happens to Mono. He's my favorite monkey. Speaking of monkey, I have one on my back. I need to get down to the Yucatan with about a dozen armed men to shut down the coca farm that's being run by the Maya on our behalf. I don't want to do it, but the Mexican Department of Defense is threatening to crawl up my ass and pull out a burrito if I don't get it done right away."

"Am I going on this trip with you, Lobo?" The driver asked.

"Not this time, Villanueva," Lobo answered.

"How about Colonel Placard?" the driver asked. "Supposedly, he's your military advisor. Personally, I think it would be unwise for you to engage in open warfare with the Maya without first devising a plan with the colonel."

"Although the Russian doctor who's standing beside you seems to have recovered quite nicely from the disciplinary measures that we levied upon him in Chihuahua, the same cannot be said for my good friend, the colonel," Lobo regretfully answered.

"Maybe El Tercero was a bit too enthusiastic when he beat the hell out of Placard," the driver said.

"Maybe it's because the colonel is considerably older than Russian Bear," Lobo added. "Maybe it's because of a myriad of different reasons. In any event, Placard is still out of commission. If he is going to be any use to our cartel in the future, I am obligated to let him heal up."

"Well," Villanueva said, "He needs to either heal up or die."

"Let's hope it's the former and not the latter," Lobo said with a nod. "We captured that whore named Lucia Aragon at the Chihuahua cartel compound in Ciudad Camargo. I want you to tell her to keep her panties on and attend to the colonel's injuries. The same goes for Russian Bear."

"You want me to tell Bear to keep his panties on?" Villanueva asked. "I'll bet the Russian is the kind of guy who goes 'commando,' if you catch my drift."

"No, you idiot!" Lobo exclaimed in frustration. "I want you to tell him to take care of the colonel, also. I don't give a shit if Russian Bear wears panties, a bra, or even high heeled sneakers!"

"What about me? Are you sure you don't want me to come with you?" Villanueva asked. "I could be your driver down in the Yucatan, you know."

"Not this time. Queen Lorena has promised to meet me at the airstrip in Peto. I want you to camp out at the hospital and make sure that nothing bad happens to Mono while he's there. I don't want any rival cartel personnel appearing at his bedside to put a bullet in his head."

"That's right," Bear added, "I know exactly what will happen to me if Mono has, shall we say, an untoward outcome for *any* reason."

"The only damned thing you have to worry about is the here and now. Don't let him die on the way to the hospital, 'Dancing Bear,' or otherwise–"

"Yeah, yeah, yeah," Bear answered yet again with a scowl. "I get the picture, okay?"

"I'm sorry to say that all three of you have now totally transformed into vampires," Dr. Blanks said to his clinical subjects in a conference room at the CDC. "However, hope is on the horizon."

"Is that so?" the former hospital phlebotomist from Farmington named Penny Schaeffer asked. "If that's the case, that may be the first good news I've heard since I accidently got a needle stick from Domino Lackey a while back."

"Before I go any further, I have to give credit where credit is due," Dr. Blanks explained to the three patients who were rescued from the Memorial Hospital in New Mexico. "Dr. Kohl and Hoefferle did a magnificent job in getting the vaccine program up and running here at the CDC."

"Do you mean to say you weren't working on a treatment before we got here?" Nurse Raquel Abril asked.

"Well, not exactly," Blanks explained. "Earlier this year, we were spinning our wheels on trying to effect a therapeutic passive immunoglobulin transfer trial to infected animal subjects, but it just turned out to be a big waste of time."

"What went wrong?" the patient Marcus Cruz asked.

"As it turned out, RV–1986 virus is sneaky. It was undergoing genetic drift right under my nose and my team just didn't realize it initially."

"How is this any different from the vaccine that you want to try upon us now?" Marcus Cruz asked. "I was under the distinct impression that a vaccine is utilized as a *prophylaxis* against getting an infection. I didn't know that vaccines could actually *treat* an infection once it has already happened."

"By and large, your observation is correct," Blanks concurred. "However, we're working on a completely new concept. We believe we've developed a *therapeutic* vaccine that will be a bona fide game changer. We hope that it will work in the setting of a patient who has already been infected and gone through the transformation into a human vampire. Using duck eggs as a viral reservoir, our team has engineered a vaccine to attack a specific universal protein found on the outer viral coat. We think it will be effective, regardless of genetic drift. With a combination of antiviral agents in addition to our new vaccine, we've been able to clear the viral particles out of the avian animal model that has been tested to date. Now it's time to try the vaccine on human subjects. Any volunteers? Who wants to go first?"

"The three of us have decided to try the vaccine together at the same time," Penny Schaeffer replied.

"In the end," Nurse Abril mused, "we're all up shit creek together, are we not? Collectively, we'll either sink or swim."

"Is that true?" Dr. Blanks asked.

"I'm sick of consuming animal blood as my solitary source of nutrition," Marcus Cruz said. "I believe my friends feel the same as I do. We're ready, Dr. Blanks."

"That's the spirit!" Blanks said. "We'll get started today. Good luck and God speed, everybody."

⸻⁂⸻

Lobo and a dozen of his thugs landed at the airstrip in Peto for the long drive into the jungle to meet Lorena Pastore and the Maya farm hands at the Fortress Camazotz. There to greet the cartel members was an old school bus painted in camouflage relief that was driven by the Maya warrior named, Joaquin.

"Greetings, Lobo Grande!" Joaquin said with an insincere smile. "I'll have you know that Queen Lorena was quite surprised that you wanted to make a trip down to the Yucatan at this particular time, as we're not due to export any raw coca leaves to you for another two weeks. I hope that you've been pleased with our agricultural efforts. Our coca farmers seem to have worked out our harvesting methodology to a fine science, if I may say so myself."

"Frankly, I've been quite pleased with your production efforts," Lobo answered, "but I have a specific problem with your entire tribe."

"What would that be?" Joaquin asked.

"Your tribe made an unauthorized raid into the neighboring country of Guatemala and kidnapped a man there known as General Carmel," Lobo said. "We understand that the Maya are currently holding him as a prisoner of war."

"Oh, yes indeed!" Joaquin answered. "As a matter of fact, I drove the commandos involved in the assault right on this very bus! From a logistical standpoint, I also helped formulate the plan to capture General Carmel and destroy his coca processing laboratory. I don't know how many of his men that we killed, but we slaughtered a boat load of those bastardos!"

"What?!" Lobo asked. "You were involved in that commando raid?"

"I most certainly was!"

"I should shoot you on the spot," Lobo said. "You people have caused an embarrassing international incident and the Guatemalan government wants revenge."

"Is that so?" Joaquin asked. "It's been said that people in hell want *agua fria*."

"Where's Lorena? She told me that she would meet us at the airstrip when we landed."

"I'm taking you there to meet her now," Joaquin answered. "You've arrived on a very special day. Once we get to Fortress Camazotz, you'll have the pleasure of witnessing the execution of General Carmel."

"Not if my men have anything to say about it!" Lobo boasted.

"Actually, your men aren't going to have anything to say about it," Joaquin replied as he pulled the bus over to the side of a culvert and yanked the hand lever that opened the door on the vehicle. Once done, two dozen heavily armed Maya warriors stormed onto the bus before any of Lobo's foot soldiers had a chance to react.

"I want you to meet my colleagues, Lobo. Say hello to El Dolor and his men," Joaquin said as a pulled out a .38 caliber revolver and pressed it against the temple of the cartel captain. "You'll have to stay on the bus, Lobo Grande, but this is where your men must exit."

"Exit the bus here?" Lobo asked.

"No," Joaquin answered. "They're going to exit the planet here!"

At gun point, the Maya warriors forced Lobo's thug's off the bus and had them stand in the culvert by the side of the road.

"Why is your colleague named 'El Dolor'?" Lobo asked. "Is he a man who is in pain for some reason or another?"

"Quite the contrary," Joaquin replied. "El Dolor is a man who dispenses pain."

No sooner said, El Dolor's men opened fire upon the cartel squad with their automatic weapons and killed each and every one of them. Once done, the Maya warriors took machetes and decapitated the dozen dead foot soldiers previously under Lobo's command.

"By Lord Camazotz and all that is unholy, what have you done?!" Lobo cried out. "This means war!"

"Yeah," El Dolor replied when he climbed aboard the bus. "We kind of figured that out from the get-go. The Maya are ready. In fact, we've been ready for centuries. How about you?"

⚜

"Since you refuse to carry your own weight around here, Colonel Placard, it would appear to me that you need a bit of extra motivation," El Tercero threatened. "I bet you'd never guess that besides Lobo Grande and Martillo Grande, I'm the only man in this cartel with a college education. What do you think of that?"

"Well, whoop-dee-fucking-do for you, ass hole!" Placard answered.

"If it wasn't for you, Colonel Placard, Lobo Grande would surely entrust me with future military logistical planning, I'll have you know."

"Fine by me. Thus far, this particular line of work doesn't particularly agree with me, if you'd like to know the truth," Placard said. "You can take the job from me if you want it that bad, Tercero."

"I just might do that," Tercero said with a sneer.

Colonel Placard was forcefully hauled down to the laundry room in the basement of the compound where his arms were tied to a beam above his head. Even if Placard wanted to use the pistol that he had secretly secured in his under shorts, there was no way that he could reach it. This was unfortunate, as this would have been a perfect opportunity to kill his tormentors and escape from the premises.

"There was a game that I played when I was a kid called, tic-tac-toe. I'll bet that you played this very same game in Los Estados when

285

you were un *mozuelo*, no? I'll be the referee while my two friends, Idioto and Perezoso play this game upon your back. We're going to alter the rules just a bit to make this child's contest a bit more interesting. Idioto, why don't you show the good colonel what you have in your glass jar?"

The man named Idioto was one disagreeable and malodorous individual with a single snaggletooth that had a furry, blackish-green appearance, somewhat reminiscent of a forgotten avocado that had accidently fallen behind a college dorm room mini-refrigerator and subsequently escaped discovery for weeks on end.

The rotten fang in his mandible had advanced stages of deterioration from neglected caries that had grossly eroded the enamel from the edges of what was once a tooth. Idioto held up a glass jar that contained no less than a half dozen, fat, black scorpions. The disheveled thug rattled the jar and agitated the prehistoric arachnids which caused one of the malevolent creepy-crawlers to elevate its stinger above its thorax, much like a medieval warrior held a double-bit battle axe above his head.

"I was once an entomologist before I found out that drug trade was a much more lucrative endeavor," El Tercero said. "Did you know that there are a total of 221 species of *alacran* in Mexico? Despite this large number, less than a dozen species are thought to have a sting that is poisonous enough to be potentially lethal to human beings. There are approximately 50,000 cases of scorpion stings per year in Mexico, and I'll bet that you'd not be surprised to learn that the majority of human fatalities from these vicious little whores occur right here in Estado Jalisco!"

"Why don't you just fucking shoot me and get it over with?" Placard pleaded.

"What would be the fun in that?" El Tercero said. "I want this to be an educational experience for you, Colonel! The black monsters in this jar are particularly nasty. Their scientific name is, *Megacormus segmentatus*. This toothless, filthy cretin standing in front of you is going to use these scorpions as his marker in the tic-tac-toe game."

The borderline edentulous moron called Idioto flared his nostrils as he sat across from the colonel and gently rolled the jar of deadly arachnids in front of Placard's face. It was now time for Perezoso to show the colonel what toys he brought to the fiesta.

"Alright, you lazy bastardo," El Tercero said to the other contestant. "Why don't you introduce the little black and yellow fiends in your jar to Colonel Placard?"

Perezoso slammed a glass jar down upon the table beside the colonel. Inside this particular vessel were six angry wasps that had their wings clipped so they couldn't fly away once the jar lid was opened.

"Well, well, well, what do we have here?" El Tercero asked. "It looks like Perezoso brought a jar containing the ecologically important female Mexican honey wasp. How exciting! The scientific name of this insect happens to be, *Brachygastra mellifica*."

"Do tell," Placard said. "Get on with it, will you?"

"Patience, my dear friend," El Tercero said. "Good things come to those who wait. These are one of the few wasps in the entire world that are known to make honey, much like their cousin, the bee. The *gente* in some parts of Mexico will actually fry these angry creatures up in a pan and then eat them like popcorn! To be honest, I've never eaten a wasp, cricket, or ant, unlike many of my countrymen who do so from time to time."

"Why not?" Placard asked. "I figured an insect like you would have relished the opportunity to cannibalize his own kind if the opportunity had ever arisen."

"Glad to see you still have a little bit of fight left in you, Colonel. I must tell you that this particular wasp has a rather aggressive disposition. Unlike a bee that can only sting once and then die, this little terror can sting over and over and over again! I want to do a little experiment today, Colonel. I'd like to see if you'll be able to discern whether the sting from a wasp, which is an insect, is as painful as a sting from a scorpion, which is an arachnid. Let the games begin!"

El Tercero ripped open the back of Colonel Placard's shirt and proceeded to cut a hash mark upon his back with a pocket knife. Despite the pain, Placard uttered not a sound.

By a flip of a peso, Perezoso was awarded the first move in the macabre game. With a fine pair of long forceps, the thug extracted a wasp from the glass jar and secured it to one of the squares in the hash mark on the colonel's back by impaling the insect through its thorax with a thin gauge needle directly to Placard's skin. This action didn't kill the insect per se, but it certainly pissed it off. The wasp lashed out by stinging the colonel repeatedly. This time, the colonel did indeed scream out in pain.

Now it was time for Idioto to make his move. In a similar fashion, he extracted one of the scorpions from its jar with a fine pair of forceps and secured the poisonous arachnid to Placard's back by impaling the creature with a skinny gauge needle within the confines of one of the squares on the makeshift tic-tac-toe board.

The pain was excruciating once the scorpion began to sting the colonel. Placard felt as if his back was on fire as he emitted high-pitched screams of agony. The colonel's pain did little to deter his tormentors, and the game continued unabated. Once the third scorpion was finally affixed to Placard's back, his screams were finally registered on the upper floor of the cartel compound. Fortunately, Lobo's personal driver named Villanueva came down to investigate what was going on.

Villanueva was charged with the responsibility of making certain that Colonel Placard had recovered from his previous injuries sustained during the attack upon the Chihuahua cartel. When he realized what was going on, it was incumbent upon him to bring the festivities to a swift conclusion. Villanueva grabbed a pail of soapy water from the corner of the washroom and threw it up on Placard's back which immediately neutralized the invertebrate assailants. Villanueva then picked up a wet towel in the laundry room and quickly swept away the wasps and scorpions that were still impaled upon Placard's back. Despite a sudden reprieve from the repetitive intradermal inoculations of potent scorpion neurotoxins and painful insect inflammatory peptides, the colonel nonetheless promptly fainted into a blissful fog of self-engendered, auto-anesthetizing, endorphins.

Villanueva swung the bucket into the face of Perezoso which caused him to collapse into a basket of freshly washed linen destined to be sent back to the bordello. El Tercero was wise enough to back off from the altercation, but the same could not be said for Idioto who picked up the pocket knife from the table top and lunged at Villanueva. Lobo's personal chauffeur would have none of it. He simply pulled out his side arm and squeezed the trigger. Once Villanueva discharged his weapon, Idioto unfortunately lost the only tooth that he had when it was blown out of a new gaping crater the size of ripe mango which had suddenly appeared in the back of his skull.

"I told you fuckers to leave the colonel alone!" Villanueva exclaimed as the now faceless corpse of Idioto fell forward into a bloody heap upon the laundry room floor. "I'm responsible for the colonel's welfare. If I ever see either of you touch him again, I'll kill both of you on the spot. I don't care if you are a lieutenant in this cartel, El Tercero. Go ahead. Test my resolve!"

The madam whore named Lucia Aragon"and 'er old friend, Russian Bear, were called down to the washroom to attend to the colonel's wounds. At least for the time being, it appeared as if Augustus Placard would live to see another day.

"Madam Aragon and Russian Bear, you need to take care of Colonel Placard. If Perezoso or El Tercero cause you any trouble, just let me know," Villanueva said.

"Do you really think that the two of us could stop anybody in this cartel if they decided to come back here and kill Colonel Placard?" Bear asked.

"You can get in touch with me in the front lobby at the University Hospital at the San Augustin College of Medicine."

"What's going on there?" Madam Aragon asked.

"Not that it's any of your business," Villanueva answered, "but my friend, Mono, was attacked by un vampiro. Fortunately, he was not bitten, but his face was impaled upon a rusty shank of rebar along the highway just west of Guadalajara. He's lucky to be alive. When Lobo flew down to the Yucatan to attend to some business, he wanted me to check in on Mono and to make sure that everything was okay."

"Well, is he okay?" Bear asked.

"Too soon to tell. He just had surgery yesterday," Villanueva said as he turned to leave the basement. "The only thing you have to worry about is taking care of the colonel, understand?"

Once Augustus Placard was revived, Russian Bear was compelled to whisper a question to his colleague. "If you still have that damned pistol that Llaves gave you a while back, why didn't you use it? These guys could have killed you!"

"Patience, my dear friend," Augustus Placard said. "Good things come to those who wait. I'll be the first to admit however, that I can't wait much longer!"

⁂

Lorena Pastore beckoned Lobo Grande to kneel beside her while long-awaited justice was finally about to be dispensed to the mass murderer named, General Carmel.

"My people are ready to subject the general to a glorious punishment that truly will be long remembered," Lorena said to Lobo who was bound at the wrists. "All my tribe ever wanted was to live in peace. If Carmel is convicted of his war crimes against the Maya people, I assure you that the general's ultimate demise will make our ancestors proud. Word of what we do today will spread through the jungle like fire ants, and this will act as a significant deterrent to anybody in the future who would mean to do us harm."

"Why must I watch this?" Lobo Grande asked nervously.

"After we dispatch with the general," Lorena explained, "you'll be next. You tried to double cross my people after we were loyal to you. You tried to double cross my people after we made you a lot of money. Like the general, you'll also be punished when you're found guilty of your crimes. As for now, I just want you to relax and enjoy the spectacle that you're about to witness!"

Lobo Grande and the Queen of the Maya waited patiently atop the pyramid adjacent to Fortress Camazotz while her subjects secured General Carmel to a canvas litter and dragged him up the side of the ancient monument. After setting the accused man upon a narrow ledge at Lorena's feet, the warrior named Joaquin emerged and stood behind Lorena while he brandished the ceremonial obsidian blades over either shoulder.

After an ostentatious tribal dance was performed at the base of the pyramid, the Queen of the Maya began to recite by chapter and verse, a litany of all the heinous genocidal barbarity that Carmel and his para-military murderers had perpetrated upon the peaceful Maya during Operation Sofia in the decades long Guatemalan Civil War. One by one, Lorena read aloud the indictments against General Carmel, while her subjects anticipated the expected verdict.

"General Carmel," Lorena asked, "on or about the summer solstice of 1967, did you and your band of soldiers known as, Los Carniceros, attack a Maya village outside of the town of Seibal in Guatemala?"

"Guilty as charged," Carmel answered. "Burned everybody alive. Men, women, and children. We killed them all. I enjoyed it, too!"

"Why did you do such a thing?" the Queen of the Maya asked.

"Are you an idiot?" Carmel asked. "I did it because they were Maya. No other reason."

"General Carmel," Lorena continued, "on or about August 17, 1967, did you and your band of soldiers known as, Los Carniceros, attack a Maya village outside of the town of Las Pozas in Guatemalala?"

"No."

"What?" Lorena scoffed. "There's an eye witness standing at the base of this pyramid. He's the old man watching these proceedings from the second row. I can clearly see him from where I'm now standing. He signed an affidavit that states he saw you on the outskirts of La Pozas when no less than eighteen Maya children were decapitated with a machete. It was done so right in front of their parents! Do you now have the audacity to deny that you were ever involved with this specific war crime?"

"You misunderstood my answer," General Carmel casually replied. "I indeed was there that night. I was the one who killed all those children with a machete. I committed these murders on my own accord, however. You asked me if my soldiers were involved, but Los Carcineros weren't there that particular night. You see, I was selfish. I wanted to have the enjoyment of slaughtering those children all by myself!"

The crowd gasped in astonishment.

"How much longer is this going to take?" Carmel asked. "Exactly how many trivial indictments am I facing? I don't plan on being here all day, you know."

"There are a total of 63 indictments over a 15-year span. You and your men are accused of killing at least 13,815 human beings."

"Is that all?" General Carmel snickered. "I would've guessed that there were a lot more of those filthy Maya dogs that I put down."

With that inflammatory comment, the crowd at the base of the pyramid rushed forward, but was ultimately kept at bay from the object of the communal ire by a dozen armed Maya warriors.

"I suppose we could expedite matters if you would just like to go ahead and confess to all of these charges now," Lorena said.

"Happy to do so," the general said.

"You seem surprisingly content for man who is about to have his beating heart cut out of his open chest with a razor sharp obsidian blade," Lorena curiously observed.

"You'll do no such thing to me," the general chuckled. "I have a bargaining chip."

"Is that so? What would that be?" The Queen of the Maya asked.

"If you promise not to cut my heart out of my chest, I'll give you the names of all the soldiers who served with me on the Los Carniceros extermination squad. Most of them are still alive. I know where they live."

"So, do you think you can cut a plea bargain with the Queen of the Maya?"

"I most certainly do," the general smugly answered.

"El Dolor?" Lorena addressed her favorite Maya warrior. "Please be so kind to go back to my hut inside Fortress Camazotz and recover a pen and a note pad. Bring it back to General Carmel and untie his hands. I'd like to afford this pathetic coward the ignominious opportunity to sell out all of his former colleagues to us."

"Wait, your Highness!" Joaquin protested softly in Lorena's ear. "You simply can't let this man get away with what he's done, even if he gives up the names of everybody who served with him on his Los Carniceros execution gang."

"Fear not, Joaquin," the Queen whispered back. "Rest assured, justice will be served one way or another."

Once El Dolor returned with the notepad and writing implement, General Carmel quickly wrote down the names of nearly thirty of his colleagues who at one time served with him on the Los Carniceros squad of assassins. When finished, he handed the pen and note pad back to the Queen.

"There," Carmel said. "I held up my hand of the bargain."

"I'm also a woman who keeps my word," Lorena answered. The Queen turned to the Maya warriors and instructed them to unbind the general's feet. "Take this convicted criminal to the Cave of Camazotz!"

The crowd went wild.

"Wait!" The general pleaded. "You said you wouldn't cut out my heart!"

"Yes, General Carmel, that's indeed true," Lorena replied, "but I didn't say that I wouldn't have you executed, however!"

The Queen took one of the obsidian knives from the hand of Joaquin as she accompanied the condemned prisoner to the broad mouth of the Cave of Camazotz. While the entire crowd followed her, nobody was paying attention when the cartel captain, Lobo Grande, lagged toward the back of the throng.

Lorena made General Carmel kneel down at the mouth of the Cave. She took the obsidian blade in her possession and swiftly excised the left ear lobe of the condemned man as he cried out in agony. Lorena deftly pitched the severed ear into the maw of the cavern to draw out the horrific crypto-zoonotic executioner that dwelled within.

When the Maya witnessed that General Carmel started to bleed from the side of his head, a great roar erupted from the crowd. That's precisely the moment Lobo Grande made his move. Unseen by his captors, the cartel captain dashed into the brush and fled back through the rainforest to hopefully find the camouflaged jungle bus that was parked adjacent to the outer wall of Fortress Camazotz.

There was much to be done before he could make his escape. He had to find some kind of sharp object to cut the rope that tied his wrists together. In addition, Lobo had to figure out some way to hot wire the bus which was an ancient motorized vehicle he was totally unfamiliar with. Nonetheless, if he wanted to live, it had to be done.

Meanwhile, the crowd of Maya and their Queen started to slowly back away from the mouth of the cave once an intermittent high-pitched chirp could be discerned from the recesses of the deep rent within the Earth's crust. Momentarily, a hideous winged mammal with the mug of a pug, the color of pitch, and the size of a panther slowly emerged from the cavern. It only had back legs that in any way, shape, or form, appeared to be conventional in nature. The biological abomination crudely ambulated in a most ungainly manner, using its folded front wings in a crutch-like fashion to saddle up to the now petrified condemned war lord.

After the monster sniffed at the blood oozing from the general's face, it gently lapped away at the vacant real estate on the left side of the man's head from where a now-missing ear was unceremoniously evicted with extreme prejudice. It seemed as if the terrifying cryptid carnivore wanted to affectionately snuggle intimately with the doomed mass murderer, but nothing could have been further from the truth.

The great bat opened its massive jowls to utter an audible yawn before it grabbed the general by his head. To the great delight of the Maya people, the unmistakable resonance of a skull cracking like a walnut was readily appreciated by all in attendance. The great beast casually ambled back into the Cave of Camazotz with its satiating lunch now in tow, which had been graciously offered gratis by the generous forest dwellers.

Before Lorena realized that Lobo Grande had escaped, the cartel captain had already freed himself from the rope that tied his wrists together, hot-wired the camouflaged jungle bus, and made it safely back to the airfield at Peto where his plane was still waiting for him.

"Lobo got away!" Lorena lamented to El Dolor. "I'm absolutely certain we've not seen the last of this man."

"Relax, Queen Lorena," El Dolor replied. "The Maya warriors will be ready for El Lobo if and when he returns."

"Lobo Grande, to be frank, is a relatively insignificant mosquito," Lorena said. "He's of little concern to me."

"Well, if that is the case," El Dolor asked, "what could any of us be afraid of?"

"Now that Lobo Grande has an understanding of what the Maya are capable of doing," Lorena explained, "he won't underestimate us in the future. What I'm concerned about is if and when he comes back down here, what'll he bring with him?"

Sadly, Lobo Grande had fled the scene before he had witnessed what kind of ungodly creatures reside within the bowels of the earth at the Cave of Camazotz. If he had, he likely would have never planned another return visit to the Yucatan for the rest of his life, irrespective of what kind of army he could possibly muster for a counter attack against the Maya.

12

BROTHERHOOD OF THE DAMNED

"Why does my face look like una *sandia*?" Mono asked the nurse at his bedside.

"You're only a day out from reconstructive oral surgery and you still have a lot of post-operative edema. That's why you require this post-surgical drain embedded in the underside of your jaw. The region underneath your tongue on the floor of your mouth received a substantial traumatic injury. Frankly, I'm amazed that the ear, nose, and throat team was able to put you back together, but we have the best doctors in all of Mexico right here at the University Hospital at the San Augustin College of Medicine."

"That may very well be true," Mono said, "but I better get discharged soon, or otherwise I'm going to leave this place against medical advice whether anybody likes it or not. I have things to do and I can't afford to be out of commission for much longer."

"What's so important that you need to leave the hospital at this very moment?"

"I have to find a dear friend of mine named, Blake Barker."

"I like you, Mono," the nurse said. "You're cute! I shouldn't tell you this, but I know that there's a patient in this hospital named, Blake Barker. For some reason, he's registered at this facility as, 'Señor X.' He's up on the third floor. If he's a friend of yours, you should go up there and visit him."

"Well, it's a small world indeed!" Mono said with a grin. "I believe I'll do just that. I think I might stretch my legs a bit. Before I pay Blake a visit, I'm going down to the hospital lobby. There's a fellow down there named Villanueva who's also an acquaintance of Mr. Barker. Perhaps the three of us could get together for a little impromptu fiesta!"

While Mono meandered down to the first floor to find his colleague, Villanueva, the medical student named Felix paid Blake Barker a visit prior to the initiation of remission induction chemotherapy for the management of the vampiro's acute myelogenous leukemia.

"How're you feeling today, Blake?" Felix asked.

"Stop right there, Felix," Blake replied with a laugh. "Aren't you supposed to refer to me as, 'Señor X'? After all, Dr. Guzman is afraid that there's a bandito around every corner who might eventually find out my true identity!"

"My mistake," Felix said. "Frankly, it is no laughing matter as there are rumors that you're a wanted man by the new Astilladora de Madera cartel that has arisen from the ashes of the old Calle Vampiro gang. Dr. Guzman made be promise that I'd only call you, 'Senior X,' and I promise to do that at all times in the future."

"Relax, Felix," Blake said. "I was just pulling your chain!"

"Let's start from the beginning," Felix said with a chuckle. "How are you feeling today, 'Senior X'? Did you tolerate the trial of solid food that we gave you?"

"I feel terrible!" Blake responded. I tried the low microbial dinner tray last night, but I didn't tolerate it at all. I immediately vomited."

"That's not a good sign," Felix said. "If we had truly cleared all of the RV–1986 virus out of your body, you should've been able able to tolerate a solid meal."

"This morning for breakfast, I decided to go back and resume the consumption of beef and pork blood," Blake explained. "I was at least able to hold that down. Otherwise, it feels as if I have been run over by an old Bronco truck and dragged along the bottom side of the undercarriage. How do my counts look today?"

"Not good," Felix answered. "Your white cell count continues to climb. It's now at 76,000 per cubic millimeter, and you are running 90% blasts in the blood. Your platelet count is only at 18K, but Dr. Guzman wants to hold off on another platelet transfusion until you get the chemotherapy started today. Despite the fact that you've resumed the consumption of beef and pork blood ad lib., it's no longer having any bearing on your red cell production. Your hematocrit is at 22.7%. In all likelihood if you drop any further, you're going to need another packed red blood cell transfusion."

"I figured as much," Blake said. "Even with the blood that I consume by mouth, it's hard to convert any of it into my own new red blood cells. I guess it's a consequence of this damned cancer in my bone marrow."

"That's indeed the case," Felix agreed.

"Spell it out for me, Felix," Blake asked. "What's on the agenda for me this week?"

"Today we'll start what is known as the 7+3 protocol. You'll get three days of an anti-mammalian anthracycline antibiotic called daunorubicin in conjunction with fourteen doses of high-dose cytosine arabinoside given every twelve hours over a seven-day schedule."

"I suspect I'll get worse before I get better," Blake postulated. "I bet this chemotherapy will make me sick."

"As a dog," Felix added for emphasis. "I can't lie to you about that."

"I wouldn't want you to," Blake said with a nod. "If I'm going to be a prisoner here for the better part of a month, be a good lad and take me downstairs to the lobby so I can get one last breath of fresh air before Dr. Guzman starts the chemotherapy today."

"I'd be happy to do that," Felix said as he wheeled Blake down the hallway toward the elevator for a trip out to the front lobby.

Felix wheeled Blake Barker out the front-door exit to allow his patient a brief respite from the dreadful ordeal of having to battle a life-threatening hematological malignancy. As everything in the universe is somehow connected, Felix and Blake had inadvertently paused within ten feet from a fellow hospital patient named Mono who was having a very animated conversation with a fellow cartel thug named, Villanueva. Blake and Felix could not help but listen in on a conversation that was now becoming rather confrontational.

"I'm telling you right now," Mono said, "if Blake Barker is upstairs on the cancer ward, you and I are going to march right up there and blow his brains out!"

"Are you sure that the vampiro who impaled your jaw upon a fence post was Blake Barker?"

"Who else could it have been?" Mono asked. "After all, how many other vampiros are out there walking around?"

"What does he look like?" Villanueva asked.

"I was told that Blake Barker was a gringo. Well, after meeting him face-to-face the other day on the outskirts of Guadalajara, I can tell you that's not the case. Barker is a young, thin, muscular Indian. In fact, he's extraordinarily strong."

"We can't kill this guy," Villanueva said. "Lobo Grande wants him taken alive. He wants him to work for our cartel."

"Not if I have anything to say about it!" Mono countered. "I'm going to kill that vampiro the minute I lay eyes on him!"

Suddenly, Villanueva realized that two interlopers were listening in on a very private conversation.

"Hey! What are you doing there, you damned gringo!" Villanueva glared at Blake Barker. "Have you been listening in on our conversation?"

Blake shrugged his shoulders and said, "I don't speak Spanish. I have no idea what you're saying to me."

"Is that so?" Mono said as he turned to the medical student named, Felix. "Well, this skinny kid with a white medical jacket and a pair of glasses looks like he knows how to speak Spanish! You two better get the fuck out of here right now if you know what's good for you!"

With that, Felix promptly wheeled Blake Barker back up to the oncology ward and returned him to his room. "See?" Felix said. "Those hombres are looking for somebody named Blake Barker. They were looking for you, but clearly they don't know what you look like."

"Sounds like they have me confused with somebody else," Blake said. "Doesn't matter, Felix. We're in trouble!"

⟷

Zachary Hawk found the car keys to the highway patrol car in the pocket of one of the dead Federale officers who was named, Estofado. As he had multiple broken bones, it was a bit of a struggle for Hawk to stuff the dead policeman into the trunk of the patrol car, but the corpse would be needed for sustenance much sooner than later.

When the car key was inserted into the ignition switch, Hawk was pleased to see that there was 3/4th of a tank of fuel, and this would be plenty for him to get to Santa Sangre. As his right wrist was broken as well as his right humerus and tibia, Hawk had to reach around the steering wheel with his left hand in an awkward fashion to turn the engine over. He would only be able to steer the car with his left hand and use his left foot to control the accelerator and brakes. This was a bit of a challenge for him at first, but he quickly got the knack of how to operate the vehicle utilizing only the left lateral aspect of his upper and lower extremities.

"I'm an idiot!" Hawk said aloud to no one in particular when he had already driven ten miles or so away from the site of the violent and bloody melee. "I should have taken the cartel's car instead. I'm going to stick out like a sore thumb driving around in a stolen federal police highway patrol car!"

In short order, Dr. Hawk had found his way to the township of Santa Sange, but it was as if he had driven into a ghost town. The place appeared to be abandoned without sign of life.

"Hello?" Hawk called out. "Is anybody home?" When there was no reply, Hawk pulled up to a gas pump underneath the shade of an awning at a Pemex station. After all, it was time for a snack. Utilizing only his left leg to hop about, Hawk opened the trunk of the highway prowler and pulled out the dead body of Estofado. Employing only his fangs and still-functional left arm and hand, Hawk was able to rip open the chest of the dead policeman which offered the vampiro the opportunity to dine upon a venerable buffet of tasty internal organs.

"You might not be the freshest sushi I've ever sampled, but I must admit," Hawk paused to look at the dead man's name badge on his police uniform, "Officer Estofado, your heart was sweet and tender with overtones of butternut and a dash of sea salt. I'm certain that this organ served you well during your lifetime, and after your death, it has indeed served me well."

Hawk should have spent more time in paying attention to his circumstances than engaging in an epicurean editorial soliloquy. Santa Sangre was nearly abandoned as a consequence to the devastation rendered by the vicious adolescent gang of vampires known as, The Brotherhood. Estado Jalisco was certainly aware of what had transpired in the small town, but despite a dramatic increase in the presence of the Federale, no apprehension of any of the suspects had been made at the time of Hawk's arrival to the now desolate community.

Zachary Hawk cradled his fractured right arm against his abdomen while he extended his splintered left lower extremity upon the concrete drive of the filling station before he leaned back against the front wall of the edifice to take a nap.

Hawk must have been in a deep slumber when a patrol car slowly passed by the scene and witnessed an eviscerated federal officer adjacent to a highway patrol car with its trunk open. Against the front wall of the filing station, there was a satiated vampiro who was blissfully snoring away after he had apparently gorged himself!

It was a macabre scene that was frankly hard to comprehend. Nonetheless, the Federale had managed to gather his courage, withdraw his side arm from its holster, and slowly approach the sleeping predator.

"What have you done, you nasty animal?" The officer loudly declared to awaken Dr. Hawk. "Are you the creature that's wiped out this community? Raise your hands were I can see them!"

Hawk awakened with a jolt and realized that he was in a world of trouble. "I can't raise my right arm," Hawk pleaded. "It's broken!"

"Bull shit!" the patrolman replied.

The federal officer was not about to take any chances with the dangerous creature he had just apprehended, so he discharged his weapon into the abdomen of Zachary Hawk who immediately emanated a cry of pain reminiscent of an amplified and prolonged guttural belch as the vampiro fell to the side. Believing the scene was secure, the federal officer returned to his squad car to report what had happened over the police radio. He never made it.

The gunshot had brought forth the surviving members of the Brotherhood who appeared out of nowhere to pounce upon the doomed federal agent.

Even Celena, who was missing her fangs, enjoyed the meal, although she was sadly reduced to choking down the victim's kidneys by swallowing each bolus whole as she was now afflicted with the inability to properly incise her food to any great extent.

"Have you no table manners?" Isaac asked Celena. "You're enjoying a fine meal. You should learn to slow down and observe the rules of proper etiquette. I'm certain your mother raised you better than this before you decided to eat her. You're acting like a cheap whore. Come to think of it, that's what you are."

Without saying a word, Celena picked up the dead officer's pistol and clocked Isaac in the face with it. As Isaac fell back, she straddled the boy and jammed the barrel of the gun into his mouth. When she cocked the hammer back, Amelia was there to save her little brother from being murdered.

"Enough, Celena," Amelia said as she gently pulled the gun away from her colleague. "You've made your point. As for you, Isaac, the next time you say something stupid like that, I might not be here to save your sorry ass."

"Sorry, Sis," Isaac apologized. "I don't know what gets into me sometimes."

It was now time for the Brotherhood to focus their attention toward the critically wounded Zachary Hawk. "Look!" Jesus proclaimed as he cautiously examined the unresponsive individual. "This guy has fangs. He's a vampiro. He's just like us!"

"He's hurt," Enos said. "Hurt real bad."

"Your house isn't too far from here, Enos," Amelia noted. "Let's haul this vampiro over there. If he's lucky, maybe he'll have a chance to recover."

"If he does," Enos asked, "do you think he'd want to join the Brotherhood?"

From Ciudad Juarez, Birdy Marshall had no trouble crossing back into the United States across the Rio Bravo and then into El Paso, Texas. So far, so good. Nobody bothered to stop her or ask any pesky questions about the old Bronco truck that she had stolen from Dr. Zachary Hawk. She zipped North on Interstate 10 and soon crossed the border into the state of New Mexico.

When she hit Las Cruces, she followed the highway signs that directed her onto Interstate 40 that would ferry her past Albuquerque and back to Santa Fe. Were things about to get dicey? Nope! Her luck held out thus far. If she could only find her way back to Dr. Parker Coxswain, she would tell him that she loved him, and maybe together they would have a chance to escape the dreaded Land of Enchantment and avoid the long arm of Captain Ray Noche and the Vampiro Containment Unit.

After all, what did she really have to worry about? She never got infected with the RV–1986 virus, and as best she could tell, she was never really exposed per se. She was down in Mexico long enough that perhaps the dust had settled and the military force that had been activated by the Night Crawler Public Safety Protocol had already long forgotten about her.

She would soon be able to publish a peer-reviewed article about the vampire skull that was recovered at Chaco Canyon. In fact, the artifact was still in her possession. Once accomplished, it would blow the lid off of the vessel of corruption that kept the entire evidence about human vampirism under wraps. This peculiar infectious illness was apparently part of the human condition that dated back to the days of antiquity. Was it something to be concerned about? Certainly. Was it something to dread as a disease that could possibly cause a pandemic that would potentially end life on the planet Earth as far as we knew it? Highly unlikely.

As best Birdy Marshall could discern, this was a disease process that would wax and wane periodically, but ultimately it always appeared to burn itself out in the end and slip into another dormant phase. The evidence was there. She just had to put it altogether. Besides, once published, she would be famous. This was important not for the sake of some unfulfilled egotistical compulsion or for any potential financial windfall, but for her own personal protection. After all, the more famous a person might be, the more difficult it would be for that person to simply disappear because of a misguided prosecutorial edict from a paranoid progressive government that felt it was compelled to control every facet of human life, irrespective of any untoward happenstance.

Perhaps if left unchecked, such a radically leftist government would force its citizens into a prolonged quarantine and also the lockdown of commerce that would destroy not only the economy, but also the very spirit of the American people. Perish the thought! There could never be any progressive government in the United States that would be so hungry for power that it would actually erode the constitution as we know it and effectively strip away our God given rights for life, liberty, and the pursuit of happiness, now could there? Oh, yes. Yes indeed. Birdy just hoped that she would never live long enough to see something like that happen to her beloved country.

While lost in thought as she approached the Highway 550 intersection in the town of Bernalillo, Birdy suddenly realized she was coming upon a roadblock. It was a roadblock that was waiting for her! As she pulled to a stop, it took only moments before the old Bronco was surrounded by heavily armed men who comprised the Vampiro Containment Unit.

"Keep your hands on the steering wheel!" One soldier commanded. "Don't move! We have the authority to use lethal force if necessary."

The door of the Bronco was suddenly ripped open. Birdy Marshall was pulled out of the front seat of the vehicle and handcuffed before she was brought to a waiting unmarked sedan. Standing outside of the vehicle were two men that she had never met before. One was an obese corporal who was the designated driver and the volunteer executioner.

The other person was a military captain. Captain Ray Noche, to be precise. In the backseat of the sedan was a 17-year-old Navajo teenager who was handcuffed to a barrier of heavy mesh extruded steel that separated the rear compartment of the sedan from the front seat occupants.

"Corporal Nadler," the captain ordered, "put Dr. Marshall in the backseat of the sedan and handcuff her just like you did Domino Lackey. Wow! Is this a great day, or what? These people will no longer be a threat to society after today!"

"Just for the record, I'm not a threat to society," Birdy protested. "Where are you taking me?"

"You'll see soon enough," Noche answered. "Where's Dr. Zachary Hawk? I thought he'd be with you when you tried to sneak back into the United States. Did he go through the transformation as we all had anticipated?"

"I left him down in Mexico," Birdy answered. "When he transformed into a vampiro, he became violent. With my own eyes, I witnessed him kill two Mexican federal police officers and one drug cartel member. He also impaled another cartel member atop a fence post. Frankly, I feared for my own life."

"The Mexican people deserve that," Noche said. "After all, the disease likely originated down there. Did Hawk attack you?" Captain Noche asked.

"He most certainly did," Birdy answered.

"Did he–did he bite you?"

"I don't think so," Birdy replied. "Why were you chasing us?"

"I think you just answered your own question," the captain answered. "Take a look at the Navajo kid who's handcuffed beside you. Do you know him? He was up at Chaco about the time you and Zachary Hawk pilfered the vampire skull at the archaeological dig site."

"I've never seen this person before," Birdy answered while she carefully scrutinized the other prisoner in the backseat of the sedan.

"Don't look at me, you whore!" Domino Lackey spoke for the first time. "I'm the kind of guy who would eat you as soon as look at you. Understand?!"

"Settle down, Domino," Noche said. "Don't make this harder than it has to be. Okay, Nadler, let's get out of here."

As the unmarked sedan barreled off the highway and plowed into the desert past Placitas, Birdy Marshall realized that in short order, she would likely be drawing her last breath. "What are you going to do with us?" Birdy asked.

"I'm going to haul you out into the badlands and Corporal Nadler here is going to take his service pistol and shoot you both in the head," the captain answered in an absolutely emotionless and matter-of-fact manner.

"Are we under martial law?" Birdy asked.

"No," Captain Noche answered, "but we should be, if you want to know my opinion."

"Has the Writ of Habeas Corpus been suspended for some reason?" Birdy asked.

"Not to my knowledge," the captain replied.

"I know about the Night Crawler Public Safety Protocol," Birdy said.

"Well, do you now?" Noche asked.

"Does the Night Crawler Protocol give you an explicit authority that supersedes federal law that would allow you to shoot me?" Birdy asked.

"No," Captain Noche answered, "but *if* the protocol was drafted correctly at the beginning of this outbreak, it should have."

"I don't know who this kid is chained up beside me, but does the Night Crawler Protocol give you the explicit authority to shoot him?"

"No," Captain Noche answered. "You both need to shut the fuck up right about now."

"Then by what authority do you have to kill either of us?" Birdy asked. "Is this a mandate from God? It better be. After all, to my knowledge, He's the only authority that supersedes the Constitution."

"May I ask a question?" Domino Lackey requested.

"No, you may not," the captain replied harshly.

"Good," Lackey said, undeterred. "Thanks for your cooperation. I want to know why you didn't just kill me on the night that you captured me back in Farmington. Why did you have to wait until now? Why did you torture me with those electrical prods?"

"Contact tracing," Noche answered.

"What does that mean?" Domino asked.

"You attacked several people in the Farmington area. We had to figure out who were the people you killed and who were the people you merely infected," the captain explained.

"I already told you that I killed everybody that I attacked except for the four people that you already know about. One was my neighbor, Speedy Blexit. The other was the patient at the Farmington Memorial Hospital that was in an adjacent room next to mine. He was that nice man named, Marcus Cruz. I already explained all of that to you in detail. The other two were also hospital employees named, Penny, and the nurse, Ms. Abril. You didn't have to torture me to get that information!"

"We also needed to know if you had any contact with the lady sitting beside you," the captain answered. "If you two have never met each other up until now, we have no further need with either of you."

"If I knew that you were going to torture me, I would've never surrendered that night. I should have killed every one of you sons of bitches when I had the chance!" Domino exclaimed.

"Enough, already!"

"Go ahead and shoot me then, you bastard!" Lackey exclaimed. "The Hispanic people have had a boot on the back of the neck of the American natives ever since the damned conquistadors came to this territory 450 years ago!"

"Stop the car, Nadler!" the captain ordered. "I'm going to kill these people right now. I can't take any more of this incessant harping coming out of the mouth of the black bitch or from fang boy!"

The car kicked up a cloud of dust when it rumbled to a stop in the middle of the desert, east of Interstate 40. Nadler and Noche quickly got out of the car. Nadler unchained Domino Lackey while Captain Noche simultaneously extracted Birdy Marshall from the backseat of the sedan. That was their first mistake. From a tactical standpoint, each prisoner should have been executed separately. After all, two soldiers overseeing the execution of one prisoner at a time would have been a significantly safer and wiser course of action, but that was not to be.

Although still handcuffed, once Domino Lackey was taken out of the backseat of the sedan, he lunged at Nadler's neck with his bare fangs and quickly ripped out the corpulent corporal's windpipe.

"You're mine now, you chubby fuck!" Domino proclaimed.

Noche was on the opposite side of the vehicle and was initially unable to render assistance to his colleague. He tried to climb across the backseat of the sedan and get through the open door on the driver's side of the car, but Birdy Marshall abated his flank attack by throwing herself on top of the captain and pinning him down to the back seat of the car.

Now that the corpulent Nadler was neutralized, it was time for Domino Lackey to terminate his primary nemesis once and for all. The Navajo teen viciously gnawed away at the occipital skull of Ray Noche until the posterior aspect of his cerebral cortex was exposed. It was now time for Domino Lackey to finish his meal.

When Birdy Marshall realized that the Navajo teen was eating the brain of the military captain while Noche was still very much alive, she recoiled in horror. She recovered the key to the hand cuffs from Noche's jacket, crawled off of the captain, and ran into the desert after she jumped out of the car.

Domino Lackey was filled with rage. After he completely consumed the entire intracranial contents of the misfortunate Captain Noche, he saw that additional potential prey was attempting to escape his grasp. Domino quickly pursued Birdy Marshall, and when he caught up to her, she had already freed herself from the hand cuffs. He knocked her down to the ground and mounted her with the intent of draining her blood.

"You have the key to these cuffs!" Domino bellowed. "Unlock me now!"

Terrified, Birdy complied. Once free from his shackles, Domino swooped down upon Birdy to finish her off. When his fangs were only inches away from the lateral aspect of her neck, Domino Lackey inhaled the essence of his next potential victim. He inhaled the essence of somebody afflicted with the inherited sickle cell trait. Lackey immediately evacuated the bloody contents of his stomach upon the mortified Birdy Marshall.

"You—you smell like shit!" Lackey exclaimed. "You smell like death itself!"

Lackey jumped up and ran back to the sedan that he hoped would eventually convey him to the tall grass at El Malpais where he could hopefully find refuge. Before he climbed into the sedan to flee, he looked over his left shoulder and yelled out to Birdy Marshall a pertinent question. "What in hell is wrong with you, lady?"

"I have the sickle cell trait, you asshole!" Birdy crowed. "You better get out of here if you know what's good for you!" Yet again, Dr. Marshall was saved by a peculiar genetic anomaly that she had always thought to be little more than a family curse.

⸺⸙⸺

When Dr. Blanks arrived at the conference room, he closed the door behind him and sat at the head of the table to face his colleagues, Dr. Hoefferle and Dr. Kohl.

"Status report, gentlemen," Dr. Blanks said. "How goes the battle?"

"Penny Schaeffer and the nurse, Raquel Abril, unfortunately have shown no signs of response to the therapeutic vaccine as of yet. Otherwise, we've got some good news and bad news," Hoefferle replied. What do you want to hear first?"

"I know how this is going to shake out," Blanks said. "First, you're going to get my emotions keyed up with some superficial and trivial matter before you kick me in the balls. Is that about right?"

"You have been around the block a few times," Kohl said. "You know how the game's played. Good news first. Of the three patients we've tried the therapeutic vaccine upon, Marcus Cruz appears to have had a complete response!"

"What?" Blanks asked as he jumped out of his chair. "That's no superficial or trivial matter and it's certainly no kick in the balls!"

"Indeed!" Hoefferle added. "The qualitative viral assay test is now negative. He still has fangs, but otherwise, no other residual clinical evidence of human vampirism. He's producing his own red cells now without an exogenous source of hemoglobin. He's no longer lysing his red cells and he's no longer spilling iron through his urine."

"Looks like we should expect a generous infusion of funds into CDC coffers with a fat new grant from the NIH and Uncle Sam," Kohl added.

"I'm pleased beyond measure," Blanks said. "However, I'm trying to temper my enthusiasm as I have a feeling that you're now about to clobber me over the head with the bad news that I suspect I'm not going to like one bit."

"No, you're not," Kohl said. "Here comes the kick in the balls. Since Mr. Marcus Cruz is no longer a vampiro, he's completely lost his extraordinary regenerative capabilities."

"I guess that's not so bad," Dr. Blanks said. "After all, I surmise that simply means he's going to have a normal projected life expectancy like the rest of us. As long as he doesn't get run over by a bus or accidentally get his arm caught in a powered wood chipper while cleaning up brush in his back yard, life should be a bowl of cherries for him!"

"Not so fast," Hoefferle answered. "You see, while hospitalized out at the Farmington Memorial Hospital, Mr. Cruz was actually about to enter the hospice service for terminal care because of an end-stage cardiomyopathy with resultant congestive heart failure. At the time, Mr. Cruz was dying. He only had a cardiac ejection fraction of about 15% when he was attacked by Domino Lackey. The poor guy was so weak, he couldn't even defend himself when Domino bit him in the neck."

"Well, that's all behind him now, is it not?" Blanks asked.

"Sorry, Boss," Kohl replied. "Once we cleared the virus out of his blood with the therapeutic vaccine, Mr. Cruz reverted back to his pre-infection state. All of the beneficial improvement to his internal organs immediately receded. Sadly, Mr. Cruz is yet again suffering from terminal congestive heart failure!"

"Are you kidding me?!" Blanks asked. "How could this happen?"

"From a clinical standpoint, it's now clear that his superhuman strength and the recovery of his cardiac function were only transient," Kohl emphasized. "His improved physical condition up until now was only a consequence to the active viral infection."

"In the course of life's events," Hoefferle explained, "Mr. Cruz would have been better off if he had never received the vaccine. At least he could have stayed alive by consuming beef and pork blood and keeping a low profile for the rest of his life."

"Now that we cleared the virus out of his body with our new vaccine," Cole added, "Mr. Cruz now has a death sentence."

"Does the patient know about any of this?" Blanks asked as he buried his face in the palms of his hands.

"No," Hoefferle answered. "It's your responsibility to tell him the bad news."

"Why me?" Blanks asked.

"You're the guy who makes the big bucks around here," Kohl said. "Hoefferle and I are just peons!"

"No," Blanks editorialized. "You and Hoefferle are just cowards."

"And you're not?" Kohl asked rhetorically.

"I'll do it," Blanks said, "but you boys have to be in the room and provide back up for me when I tell him the bad news."

Momentarily the three research scientists entered the patient's hospital room where they found Marcus Cruz gasping for air. He was sitting on the side of the bed while his forearms were perched upon a Mayo table. His over-taxed accessory neck and intercostal muscles heaved his fluid-burdened thorax up and down. Sadly, it was a desperate yet ineffectual attempt to move as much air in and out of his lungs as was physically possible. Mr. Cruz appeared cyanotic as his pulmonary tree was actively filling up with his own bodily fluids from a now dying heart in extremis from pump failure.

"I'm drowning!" Mr. Cruz panted. "This is exactly how I felt when I was supposed to enter the hospice program at the Memorial Hospital in Farmington. What's happening to me?"

"Once we cleared the virus out of your blood" Dr. Blanks explained, "your clinical condition reverted to where you were before you got infected from Domino Lackey. I'll have the nurse administer some Lasix and change your oxygen therapy to a 100% non-re-breather mask. That might help you just a bit, but you need to get transferred to the ICU."

"Are you telling me now that I would have been better off if I had just remained a vampire?" Marcus Cruz asked.

"Unfortunately," Dr. Blanks replied, "that's indeed the case. We tried to do a good deed on your behalf, Mr. Cruz."

"I'm painfully aware of that, Dr. Blanks, but you of all people should know the old adage. No good deed goes unpunished, right? Can I at least get back on the cardiac transplant recipient waiting list?" Marcus Cruz asked in a last ditch effort to grasp at any possible hope that sadly would not be forthcoming.

"Because you were infected with the RV-1986 virus," Blanks explained, "you'll no longer be considered a transplant candidate, even after we successfully cleared the virus out of your blood."

"Why not?"

"Transplant protocol patient selection criteria," Blanks elaborated. "Similar protocol criteria exclude individuals afflicted with active malignant disorders. See?"

"Sadly, I do," Marcus said in resignation. "If that's the case, I refuse a transfer to the ICU."

"Does that mean you want to enroll back into the hospice program now?" Kohl asked.

"I do indeed," Marcus Cruz replied. "Can you get them up here this afternoon? In the meantime, for God's sake, see if you can get some of this water out of my lungs so I can at least breathe a bit better. I'm not a fish with gills, you know!"

On the following morning, Hoefferle and Kohl stopped at the nurse's desk to get an updated report about the clinical status of Mr. Marcus Cruz.

"How did he do last night?" Hoefferle asked.

"He must be resting comfortably," the nurse said. "I haven't heard a peep out of him since 4:00 this morning. I know Mr. Cruz was upset because the hospice team wasn't able to pay him a visit yesterday afternoon as they had promised. I guess they got too busy. They left the night supervisor a message that they'd try to come by, and see Mr. Cruz later on this afternoon if he could just hold out until then."

"Let's pay him a visit to see if the therapeutic diuresis measures we employed improved his oxygenation somewhat and relieved his air hunger," Kohl said.

Evidently, the medical management that was utilized had failed miserably. Dr. Kohl and Hoefferle had sadly found that Marcus Cruz had taken the tie from his hospital robe and he hanged himself from the shower curtain rod in his bathroom sometime in the wee hours of the morning...

⁂

"Martillo Grande is here to see you, Lobo," Perezoso explained to the cartel captain.

"Damn!" El Lobo said with considerable concern. "It's just not like the head of the cartel to come by here for a surprise visit. Has he come alone?"

"He brought a contingency of his twelve body guards with him," Perezoso answered.

"He must have a burr up his ass about one thing or another," Lobo said.

"He most certainly does," Perezoso said. "To be frank, he has steam coming out of his ears!"

"I wonder what he's all worked up about," Lobo said. "What do you think?"

"I couldn't imagine," Perezoso said. "I'll bet it has absolutely nothing to do with the fact that you completely neglected the rec-ommendations from Colonel Placard and decided to take on the Chihuahua cartel with a frontal assault that ended up getting our men slaughtered. No, I can't imagine that would have anything to do with it."

"That was just a minor miscalculation on my part," Lobo said. "That couldn't be it. If that's the case, what else could it be that has Martillo upset with me?"

"I couldn't imagine," Perezoso said. "I'll bet that it has absolutely nothing to do with the fact that you got twelve of our best men butchered down in the Yucatan without any of them even having a chance to fire off a shot. No, I can't imagine that would have anything to do with it, either."

"That was just another minor miscalculation on my part," Lobo said defensively. "That couldn't be it. If that's the case, what else could it be that has Martilllo upset with me?"

"I can't imagine," Perezoso said with a smirk. "I'll bet it has absolutely nothing to do with the fact that Colonel Esteban from the Mexican Department of Defense gave you an ultimatum to shut down the Maya coca farm and thus far, you've failed miserably. You've even managed to get poked in the eye with a sharp stick by none other than the lovely and immensely talented Queen Lorena Pastore, from what I understand. You're lucky you came out of the Yucatan with your hide. No, I can't imagine that would have anything to do with it, now that I've come to think about it."

"Well, I guess I'll just have to sit down and have a chat with him and see what's on his mind," Lobo said. "Where's he now?"

"He's waiting for you in the conference room," Perezoso said. "His body guards are positioned right outside."

"Listen to me, amigo," El Lobo said. "Maybe it's time for me to make a move and take over this cartel. How'd you like to be a captain?"

"You'd pick me over Tercero?"

"Tercero tortured Colonel Placard against my orders," Lobo said. "Did you know about that?"

"No," Perezoso lied. "I wasn't there. How did you hear about such a foul deed?"

"Colonel Placard told me all about it. Tercero and his little toadie, Idioto, affixed wasps and scorpions upon the back of Colonel Placard," Lobo explained. "Of course, Idioto is now dead, but apparently there was somebody else that was in on it. Unfortunately,

Placard told me he had never seen the other fellow before. If and when I find out who else was involved with the abuse of such a valuable cartel asset, I just might have to run that person through the wood chipper!"

"That's terrible," Perezoso said to feign concern. In light of El Lobo Grande's threat, it was now imperative that Perezoso had to murder the colonel when nobody else was looking!

"The Colonel got stung so many times that the scorpion neurotoxin has now caused partial paralysis in his lower extremities. Yet again, he'll not be available to help me dispense revenge against the Maya down in the Yucatan. For that reason, Tercero slit his own throat as far as I'm concerned. He'll never have a chance to become a captain in this organization if I have anything to say about it."

"In regards to Martillo Grande, what do you have in mind?" Perezoso asked.

"Round up thirty men," Lobo instructed. "Once I've been in the meeting for five minutes, you'll know what to do."

"Fine by me," Perezoso said, "but do you want me to take any of Martillo's men as prisoners? After all, his body guards are merely mercenaries. They'll likely pledge an allegiance to whatever boss pays them the most money."

"When it comes to the men that follow Martillo Grande," Lobo replied, "I don't think that's the case. I've seen them in action. As best I can tell, they're all willing to lay down their lives for him."

"So be it," Perezoso said. "If that's indeed the case, then they'll lay down lives for him on this very day."

Lobo Grande was well armed with a box of pastries and an urn of hot coffee when he entered the conference room to meet the head of the cartel, Martillo Grande.

"What a wonderful surprise to find you here!" Lobo said. "It has been a long time, Martillo. I trust that you are well. However, I have a question. Did your men actually have to pat me down for concealed weapons? I found that to be rather, well-impolite."

"You know the rules," Martillo said as he pushed the box of pastries away and rudely poured the urn of hot coffee upon the floor. "Nobody talks to The Hammer alone without a pat down."

"I stand corrected," Lobo said as he raised his palms.

"You've failed me miserably, Lobo," Martillo said as he surveyed his captain with disgust. "I had a truce with Tigre Negro and the boys in the Chihuahua cartel. We certainly didn't have overlapping territories. All you managed to do was get a lot of our good men killed and piss off a rival gang that we had no quarrel with. You might have decapitated that organization when you killed Tigre Negro, but most of his organization is still intact."

"Why should you be worried?" Lobo asked. "In the end, we still have many more soldiers and will be just fine."

"I'll be just fine," Martillo answered. "However, you likely won't. I have it on good authority that the remnants of the Guadalajara gang will be coming after you soon."

"Anything else?" Lobo asked.

"I'm aware that Colonel Esteban from the Mexican Department of Defense paid you a visit and specifically ordered you to shut down the Maya operation in the Yucatan. You managed to royally fuck up that operation also, as the twelve men you sent down there got exterminated. Frankly, Lobo, you're totally incompetent and it's time for me to remove you from the leadership role that you have in this organization."

"Well, what do you plan on doing with me?" Lobo asked in a rather nonchalant manner. "Perhaps you'd like nothing better than to run me through the wood chipper."

"As a matter of fact," Martillo said, "that's exactly what I'm going to do to you."

"Before you have me executed," Lobo interjected, "I need to know one thing."

"What might that be?" Martillo asked.

"How old are you?"

"I'm 33 years old now," Martillo answered.

"I thought so," Lobo said with a nod.

"How could my current age have any possible bearing upon the unfortunate circumstances afflicting this pathetic life of yours, Lobo?" Martillo asked. "A life, I might add, that appears to be rapidly entering its final, miserable chapter."

"A lot of important figures in world history died at the age of 33," Lobo observed. "Jesus of Nazareth comes to mind. King Richard II of England and King Charles IV of France were both only 33 when they passed away, just to name a few."

"Do tell."

"Do you enjoy American R & B and early black soul music, Martillo?" Lobo asked.

"Not so much."

"Well, I do," Lobo added. "The most important black singer America ever produced didn't live past the age of 33, either. His name was Sam Cooke. Did you know that he was originally a Gospel singer before he became a pop sensation?"

"Never heard of the guy."

"I'm sorry that you must have lived your life in a cultural vacuum. Be that as it may, Alexander the Great also died young," Lobo noted. "As I've told you before, I'm a big fan of ancient Greek history and culture.

"So, you've said."

"Were you aware that Alexander the Great actually received a formal education from none other than the extraordinary and famous philosopher known as, Aristotle? That's the truth! After conquering most of the known world, Alexander the Great supposedly contracted some serious febrile illness and he died in Babylon during early June of the year 323 B.C. It was just about a month or so before his 33rd year!"

"Yeah. I knew that. What is this, Lobo?" Martillo asked. "A didactic tutorial on Western Civilization, perhaps?"

"It is indeed," Lobo answered. "If there are no other interruptions from the class, I'd like to continue. To this day, historians have wondered if Alexander the Great died in Babylon from an acute infectious disease such as dysentery. Maybe he contracted malaria on his last military campaign to India and he finally succumbed to this illness upon his return to the Middle East. That would make the most sense to me."

"None of this rant makes sense to me," Martillo said. "Get to the point, will you?"

"Patience, Martillo," Lobo pleaded. "The historical records are unclear, as the oldest known biography of Alexander the Great was written by the Greek historian, Cleitarchus. It was thought to have been composed in the late 3rd century BC, apparently long after Alexander's death. In any event, only fragments of that original biography are extant. Who knows the real story? Perhaps the conqueror was ultimately poisoned by a contemporary political rival at the time."

"Maybe his own generals ran him through a wood chipper," Martillo mused.

"Whatever is thought to have been the cause of his premature demise is just speculation now, nothing more and nothing less. If Alexander had lived, he would have eventually set his attention upon the conquest of the Arabian Peninsula, North Africa, and Europe. Truly one of the greatest military minds the world has ever seen, don't you think? Before Alexander expired upon his death bed, his generals asked him who would be the rightful heir to his conquered territories."

"Well, I'm just dying to know," Martillo said. "What was his answer?"

Before Lobo could reply to Martillo's question, the unmistakable sound of automatic gunfire could be heard immediately outside the conference room. Martillo reached for a concealed pistol that he had secured in his waistband, but Lobo was not about to simply play defense. Lobo rapidly procured a trusty 9mm Smith and Wesson that had been secretly hidden away within the confines of the box of tasty pastries that still resided atop the conference table. Although it took considerable restraint of his primal instincts, Lobo refrained from pulling the trigger when he jammed the barrel of his weapon directly against his adversary's forehead.

Once Martillo Grande dropped his weapon and raised his hands above his head, it was all over. The door to the conference room opened and Perezoso and several of Lobo's foot soldiers rushed in to surround the man who was the erstwhile head of the feared Astilladora de Madera drug cartel.

"Perezoso," Lobo asked, "please give me the body count."

"Two of our men are dead," Perezoso answered. "As for Martillo's bodyguards, nine are dead and three are wounded."

"Please take care of my wounded," Martillo pleaded. "They were loyal to me."

"Rest assured, they'll be taken care of, all right," Lobo answered before he turned his head to Perezoso. "Have the men fire up the astilladora!"

"Why are you doing this?" Martillo asked.

"When we run your wounded men through the wood chipper, I want you to hear them scream! It will definitely give you something to think about. Put Martillo in the cell block until I decide what we should do with him," Lobo instructed his men.

"Well, congratulations!" Martillo said. "You got the drop on me. Before you haul me out of here, Professor Lobo, you need to finish your history lesson. When Alexander the Great was asked as to whom should be awarded his vast empire after he died, what was his answer?"

"I'm surprised that you don't know," Lobo replied with a broad smile. "His answer was, 'to the strongest,' Martillo. To the strongest!"

⚕

"You can't leave now!" Dr. Guzman explained to Blake Barker. "You haven't even started the chemotherapy for your leukemia. If you leave now, you won't have access to the antiviral treatment that you're on, and your infection from the RV–1986 virus will likely recur. When it does, it will come back with a vengeance."

"What is the projected life expectancy of a person with acute leukemia who doesn't undergo remission induction chemotherapy?" Blake asked.

"Perhaps about six weeks from the time of the official diagnosis, and that's only if the patient gets blood product support along the way. You're already deep into this, as we've delayed cancer treatment up until now to try and get your viral infection under control."

"I get it," Blake said, "but what am I to do? If I stay here, that hairy monkey fucker and his scary little friend will be up here in no time and then I'll be dead for sure. If I am going to die from this illness, then so be it. I would select a death by natural causes down the road over a bullet to the brain if I had a choice. Besides, if I stay here, those two cartel thugs may very well kill other people on this ward besides me. I couldn't live with that."

"Wherever you go, the cartel will continue to hunt you in all likelihood," Felix said.

"There's only one thing left that I need to do that would make my life complete," Blake explained to the doctor and her medical student.

"What would that be?" Dr. Guzman asked.

"I've got to see my son, Nathan, one last time before I die. I believe that he's being cared for by my friend Miguel Pastore at the Rancho Feliz near Santa Sangre. If I could just tell Nathan goodbye, then I could die in peace."

"Santa Sangre is a long way from here," Dr. Guzman said. "What do you plan on doing? Hitching a ride with some stranger?'

"That wouldn't be particularly practical, I suppose," Blake said.

"I'll loan you my car," Felix said. "I'll sneak you out to the back parking lot. I can get you there down the stairwell without being seen."

"I owe you big-time, Felix!" Blake exclaimed.

"You have no idea, 'Señor X'! Let's go!"

With that, Felix and Blake hurried down the cancer ward corridor and slipped into the stairwell that would lead them to safety. Within moments after their departure, Mono and Villanueva showed up at Blake's now empty hospital room to confront Dr. Guzman.

"Tell me now, Dr. Guzman, what happened to the patient named, Blake Barker?" Mono asked.

"He signed out against medical advice," Dr. Guzman replied.

"Now, why would he do something like that?" Villanueva asked.

"I don't know," Dr. Guzman replied. "You'll have to ask him when you find him."

"Did somebody tip him off that we were coming to pay him a visit?" Mono asked.

"Since I don't know who you are," Dr. Guzman responded, "how could I possibly tell him something to that effect?"

"Where did he say he was going when he left the hospital?" Villanueva asked.

"He didn't tell me anything," Dr. Guzman replied.

"Is that so?" Mono probed as he opened a short canvas bag and pulled out a chrome, 0.45 caliber, classic, 1911 automatic model with custom mother of pearl grips. "I'll have you know, Dr. Guzman, that this is my favorite pistol. I'm absolutely certain it has the fire power to blow one of your legs off with just one round. Let's see if I am right about that!"

"No! Wait!"

It was too late. Mono discharged his weapon and the round shattered Dr. Guzman's right tibia below her kneecap which caused her to crumble.

The gun shot brought a security guard and an orderly running to the room to see what was awry. Sadly, both men were dead the moment they entered the room.

"Let's try this again," Mono said as he turned back to Dr. Guzman who was writhing in agony. "Where did Blake Barker say that he was going?"

"I'll tell you!" Dr. Guzman said as she raised her right hand defensively. "Please don't shoot me again!"

Her plea fell upon deaf ears. The second round emitted from Mono's weapon struck Dr. Guzman above her right wrist, blowing off her hand.

"For the love of God, I'll tell you," Dr. Guzman said as she rapidly tried to make a tourniquet with her belt and apply it to the distal stump of her right arm which was gushing blood profusely. "Well," Villanueva said, "we're all ears. Tell us what we want to know."

From out in the hallway, the medical care team on the oncology unit cowered in fear as they heard Mono's pistol fire one shot after another, again and again, until the magazine was finally exhausted. Before the dust cleared, Mono and Villanueva stepped out of the hospital room and leaned against a wall in the hallway to take a breather.

"Tobacco?" Villanueva asked as he passed a half pack and a lighter to his colleague.

"Don't mind if I do," Mono answered as he lit up a cigarette and blew a smoke ring. "Would have gone a lot easier if the bitch just told us what we wanted to know from the get-go. I burned up an entire magazine on her scrawny ass!"

Just then, an elderly nun approached Mono and gave him a vicious tongue lashing. "What's the matter with you, young man? There's no smoking in here! After all, this is a cancer ward. You better snuff out that cigarette right now if you know what's good for you!"

"Sorry, Sister," Mono apologized sheepishly as he dropped the cigarette upon the floor and extinguished it with the toe of his shoe. "Won't happen again."

Mono and Villanueva strolled to the elevator to casually exit the hospital just as Felix returned from the parking lot after he sent Blake Barker on his way. Felix sprinted to the hospital room previously occupied by the patient, only to discover what all the commotion was about. Beyond the corpse of a hospital orderly and security guard was the horrific site of the bullet-riddled body of his beloved attending physician as she gasped for her last breath.

⸎

The radio speaker loudly snapped just before the voice of the pilot, Harry Balzac, came over the intercom. "Okay, boys and girls, it's time to gear up. ETA at Rancho O'Rear in ten minutes. I repeat, ten minutes."

When the team of commandos was originally issued seating assignments in the twin engine prop plane before takeoff on the rescue mission down to Mexico, the two vampires were purposefully placed a row apart from each other in an unsuccessful effort to keep the two hostile individuals from bickering. Just before the plane was scheduled to land on a dirt airstrip on the outskirts of Santa Sangre, it appeared that another squabble was brewing. It quickly was about to go from brewing to boiling over, and this argument was about to get physical.

"I heard a nasty rumor about you and Dr. Ron Shiftless back in San Antonio," Speedy Blexit said while he tapped the shoulder of Joe Cephas Smoot who was sitting directly in front of him.

"What rumor would that be?" Smoot asked as he whipped his head around, primed for yet another altercation. "It better be a rumor about our intellect and dashing good looks. Otherwise, you just might be in need of some serious dental work when this mission is all over."

"Not even close, you big galoot," Speedy replied.

"Well," Joe Cephas said as he balled both of his hands into fists, "You better have the dangles of a brass monkey if you plan on insulting me once again. I'm getting sick of your crap. Go ahead, dip shit. Whatever it is you feel compelled to say, just say it."

"I heard that when you and Shiftless were under the command of Colonel Placard, you raided the Calle Vampiro cartel compound near Guadalajara and killed everybody there."

"All fact," Joe Cephas said, "no brag."

"That's what I heard, all right," Blexit said. "I also heard that the casualties included women and children. So, tell me, Bumpkin—are you really a baby killer? You must be proud of what you've done. You know, He'll never forgive you for a sin like that."

"Who won't forgive me?" Joe Cephas asked.

"Three letter word. All caps. Begins with a 'G.' Ends with a 'D.' If you're that fucking stupid, Joe Cephas, I'll even spot you the middle vowel!" Speedy harped on as he glared at his adversary with utter contempt.

Well, that was it. Joe Cephas Smoot had been called a lot of things in the past. As he was originally from Arkansas, he had been insulted throughout his entire life by narrow-minded individuals imbued with unspeakable bigotry. Being called a "baby killer" however, turned out to be the straw that broke the bumpkin's back.

In an instant, Joe Cephas had unbuckled his seatbelt and rolled into the backseat to engage in a Battle Royale with his new nemesis, Speedy Blexit. Initially, it appeared that the plane had engaged with some unexpected turbulence just before landing, but it was soon realized by the other three occupants that there was a full-on fist fight occurring in the back row.

"Fuck this noise!" Musty Balzac said. "These guys are going to get us killed!"

Musty and Ron Shiftless pulled their weapons, flew into the backseat, and pressed the barrel of their guns against the temples of Joe Cephas and Speedy.

"I haven't killed anybody yet today," Shiftless said, "but I don't need much of an excuse to spill blood. Knock it off! Next time, Musty and I will pull the trigger."

As Joe Cephas and Speedy settled into a truce and established a 'demilitarized zone' between the seats at the back of the plane, Harry Balzac made a low pass over the dirt air strip at Rancho O'Rear.

"Something's wrong," Harry said over the intercom. "Our colleague from the Brownwater Security Group, Buen Ojo, is supposed to be down there with a truck waiting for us."

"Maybe he's late," his brother Musty said.

"He's never late," Harry replied. "Something's wrong I tell you."

"Put it down just the same," Ron Shiftless said. "We better be on our toes, however."

No sooner had the twin-engine rolled to the end of the dirt airstrip, Colonel Esteban from the Mexican Ministry of Defense suddenly appeared. Esteban boldly stepped out in front of the airplane as soon as the props shuttered to a stop. The colonel was pulling a red utility wagon that looked very much like an oversized version of a child's toy. There was some type of lumpy object in the bed of the utility wagon that was covered with a brown canvas tarp.

"Oh, shit!" Harry exclaimed as he and his brother looked at each other in astonishment.

"It is Colonel Esteban!" Musty cried out.

"Do you know this guy?" Shiftless asked.

"Yeah," Harry said. "We've tangled with this man before. He's dirty."

"How dirty?" Shiftless asked.

"He's on a first name basis with the very devil," Musty answered. "Is that dirty enough for you?"

The plane was suddenly surrounded by half a dozen armed men dressed in uniforms sans any obvious insignias or military branch designations.

"Well, well, well," the colonel shouted at the men he could see sitting in the cockpit. "If it's not my good friends, the Balzac Brothers!"

"How did you know we were coming, Colonel?" Harry asked through the pilot side window that he had opened. "Looks like you caught us with our pants down."

"I'm friends with the proprietor of this ranch, Julio O'Rear. He sold you boys out. So sad. By the way, I have a friend of yours in the back of this wagon. He was known as, Buen Ojo. He had a really nice camera with a huge telephoto lens. For some reason, he was taking pictures of me, and I didn't like that one bit," Colonel Esteban said as he pulled the tarp away from the bed of the utility wagon.

In the back of the wagon, the Balzac Brothers were mortified to see that their former colleague from the Brownwater Security Group was very much naked and very much dead. It must have been an exceedingly painful and undignified demise, as the corpse of Buen Ojo was propped up upon his elbows and knees and his signature spy camera was jammed deep into his rectal vault.

"I asked your friend not to take anymore pictures of me," Colonel Esteban said with a laugh, "and to make sure that he complied with my request, I jammed his fancy camera and telescopic lens up his *culo*. He screamed in agony, just like you boys are about to do! Tell me something, Harry. Do you think that I would be able to fit the barrel of a FAL rifle up your ass before I pull the trigger?"

"Don't shoot," Harry said. "We're coming out."

"No weapons, Harry, or we *will* shoot," Colonel Esteban shouted out to the occupants inside the plane. "Now, get down from there."

"I'm sorry, boys," Harry said as he turned to his colleagues behind him in the aircraft. "I guess it's all over."

"I never took you to be a pussy, Harry," Blexit said with more than just a hint of disappointment in his voice. "After all, there are two human vampires standing right here. You've got me and also this crazy-ass Saltine sitting in front of me. You boys just need to sit tight. Joe Cephas and I will go down there and clean this mess up. This should only take about a minute or so. Are you ready, Joe?"

"I'll take the port site of the plane," Joe Cephas said, "and you can take the starboard side. Deal?"

"Sounds like a plan," Blexit said.

"Do you want me to break out a couple of bags of beef blood for you boys when you get back?" Ron asked. "You guys might be somewhat hungry after you've had a bit of aerobic activity."

"If it's all the same to you, Ron," Joe Cephas said, "Speedy and I will just eat the guys that are down there once we finish them off."

After Joe Cephas and Speedy climbed down the ladder to leave the plane, they placed their hands above their heads as they feigned cooperation with their captors. As the Balzac Brothers and Ron Shiftless watched through the portals on the plane, they were absolutely mesmerized when Joe Cephas and Speedy went to work. It was all over in a matter of seconds.

When Colonel Esteban realized that his team of soldiers had been annihilated, he turned and ran toward a Jeep that was parked on the end of the runway. He jumped into the vehicle and fired up the engine in an attempt to escape.

Musty jumped out of the plane and gave a truncated yet very specific order to Blexit.

"Speedy!" Musty shouted. "Stop that bastard!"

"Don't you worry none. I'll go urban gangster on his sorry ass!" Speedy replied as he pulled off his shirt that was soaked in the blood of three of Esteban's henchmen. Before running after the Jeep, Speedy suddenly broke into a suave shuffle dance. "I'll just strip down to my grimy wife beater that's covered with chitlin' grease, and then I'll break out my inner angry Negro when I catch up to that fucker. Dude won't know whether to shit or go blind when I roll up on him!"

"Well, quit flapping your gums and just go do it!" Harry said.

"Go with him, Joe, in case he needs any help," Ron called out. "We can't afford to let this guy get away!"

"I'm on it!" Joe Cephas said as he took off in a dead sprint.

Colonel Esteban was just about to pull away when Speedy Blexit intercepted the Jeep. The human vampire threw himself into the cab of the vehicle and pitched Colonel Esteban into the waiting arms of Joe Cephas Smoot who was running along the right side of the military car.

"Leaving so soon?" Joe Cephas asked as he pinned the corrupt military official down to the ground. "Let's go up to the Hacienda. My friends and I would like to have a little chat with you and perhaps also the proprietor of this ranch if he's anywhere to be found."

⸻ ❦ ⸻

"How are you feeling today, Dr. Hawk?" Amelia asked. "Are your broken bones starting to heal up yet?"

"Why, hello," Zachary Hawk answered as he awakened upon a living room sofa. "I guess I've been out of it for a while."

"Going on two days now to be precise," Amelia answered.

"Two days?" Hawk asked and astonishment. "This is not good. If I don't feed soon, I'm going to starve to death!"

"Well," Amelia explained, "you're in luck. There'll be a feeding later today and it'll be in your honor!"

"So, you're planning on providing me a fresh meal? To what do I owe this honor?" Hawk asked.

"We're going over to visit the parish priest for dinner," Amelia said. "I'll explain the details to you later."

"Thanks for saving my bacon back there at the service station," Hawk said. "By the way, how do you know my name?"

"We rifled your wallet," Amelia said. "Let me introduce you to the Brotherhood. My name is Amelia and the petulant whore standing behind me is Celena. She's taken a liking to you, but be advised of one important matter."

"I'm all ears," Hawk said.

"She lost her fangs!"

"Pity," Hawk said as he turned to Celena. "Does that mean you'll just be relegated to sucking on your meals?"

"Amongst other things," Celena interjected with a wink.

"The boy to my left is my brother, Isaac," Amelia continued, "and behind him is Jesus. The guy standing in the doorway is, Enos. This is his house."

"Thanks for letting me stay at your house, Enos," Hawk said. "I guess I should be polite and thank your parents, also."

"That won't be necessary," Enos said. "After all, my friends and I ate them!"

"Wow!" Hawk exclaimed. "You guys really are hard-core."

"You never answered my question," Amelia said. "How are you feeling today?"

"Besides being hungry," Hawk said, "I'm feeling pretty good! I had several broken bones but as best I can tell, I believe they've already healed. Of a greater concern is the fact that I was gut-shot by that police officer who tried to kill me."

"You already passed the lead slug in your waste," Jesus said.

"The bullet wound in your belly has already closed up," Isaac added. "Happened over night, as a matter of fact!"

"Looks like I owe you kids big-time," Hawk said. "If you guys hadn't appeared when you did, the next bullet from that guy's gun would've ended up in my brain!"

"Just glad that we could be of service to you in your time of need," Amelia said. "We have an important question to ask you, however."

"Feel free to ask," Hawk said. "What is it?"

"Would you consider joining our organization?"

"I would indeed," Hawk replied, "if only the current members would perhaps consider one humble petition."

"What would that be?" Amelia asked.

"Amelia, you referred to your organization as simply, the 'Brotherhood,' is that right?" Hawk asked.

"Correct."

"That's it? Just the Brotherhood?" Hawk asked for clarity. "In light of how you guys attacked that police officer who blew a bullet hole right through my transverse colon, that moniker alone is totally insufficient as far as I'm concerned. Your group deserves a new name that more accurately reflects your mission statement. Your group deserves a new name that will enhance brand recognition and also improve your market share in this highly competitive new world of bipedal humanoid vampirism! I'm talking about establishing a well-heeled, upper class clientele that goes above and beyond the blue-collar, rural rubes upon whom you now prey upon."

"Sign me up!" Jesus pleaded.

"It's time for you to set aside your Paleolithic, pedestrian, cannibalistic proclivities," Hawk ranted. "It's time for you to learn how to consume your fellow Homo sapiens with abundant grace, and if I may dare say so, a refined, genteel etiquette with a touch of panache!"

"I don't know what you just said," Amelia confessed, "but I'm so excited right now, I could just pee my pantaloons!"

"Back off, Amelia!" Celena warned. "I already claimed Hawk for my own. I'll fight you for him if I have to!"

"That's the spirit!" Hawk enthusiastically proclaimed as if he were the reincarnation of the Pied Piper. "You guys should be called the Brotherhood of, oh—I don't know, of something *important*, I guess."

"Such as?" Amelia asked.

"I've got it!" Hawk said as he flashed his pearly fangs and extended his arms with an evangelical fervor. "I bestow upon all of you a befitting and glorious title! May mere mortals behold and bow in reverential homage to the newly sanctioned and soon to be internationally renowned, '*Brotherhood of the Bat*!'"

13

NO EVIDENCE OF MEASURABLE DISEASE

Joe Cephas Smoot and Speedy Blexit gleefully dragged Colonel Esteban by his ankles toward the beautiful, white, sprawling hacienda which was the focal point of Rancho O'Rear. En route, the two vampires passed a row of what appeared to be squalid living quarters. Each "apartment" was little more than 150 square feet in size and poorly constructed of scrap wood, likely salvaged from truck pallets.

Some of the makeshift roofs were palm thatch, but the majority were constructed from mangled galvanized sheets of ill-fitting corrugated steel planks. Within the confines of about half of the living quarters were malnourished children and haggard women who were likely decades younger than their projected age.

"What the fuck am I my looking at here, Joe?" Blexit asked.

"Hired help, I presume," Joe replied.

"What's wrong with this picture?" Blexit continued to press his colleague for an explanation of the human misery that he was witnessing.

"You've not been to Mexico before, have you, Speedy?"

"First time for everything," Speedy answered. "It's strange. In all the years that I lived in New Mexico, it never occurred to me to make a trip across the border."

"There's no middleclass here," Joe Cephas explained. "90% of the GNP is controlled by 10% of the population."

"So, this is what—slavery? As an angry black man, I just can't abide by slavery!"

"Well, if it is not slavery," Joe Cephas postulated, "it's something that must be akin to it."

"Not right!" Speedy said, "Especially when I see the hacienda on the hill that the rancher lives in."

"Take a look, Speedy," Joe Cephas cautioned. "There's another big rock on the trail in front of us."

"I see it!"

"Let's be certain that we've got the Colonel lined up correctly this time," Joe Cephas advised.

Joe and Speedy made sure that the large obstruction in the trail first injured the colonel with a blast to his groin followed by a blow to the back of his head as they dragged him over the large rock.

"Much better this time!" Speedy said. "We make a good team here."

"Indeed, we do," Joe Cephas said as the two vampires dragged the colonel through the front door of the grand home where the rest of the rescue team was waiting for them.

"Look what the bats dragged in!" Ron Shiftless said. "Glad you could join us, Colonel Esteban."

"Who's the redheaded bastard you have tied up to the chandelier?" Speedy asked.

"Forgive my manners," Harry said. "I'd like to introduce you boys to Julio O'Rear. His family has been at this ranch for generations. He lives here in this enormous home all by himself now. Can you imagine that?"

"Don't you get lonely once in a while?" Musty asked.

"If I do, I just force myself upon one of the bitches that lives down at the bottom of the hill," O'Rear casually replied.

"That's nice," Shiftless said. "I say we should just shoot this fucker now and be done with it."

"That is not a bad idea," Harry said. "After all, he's the guy that sold us out to Colonel Esteban. He's the guy who got our colleague from Brownwater, Buen Ojo, murdered."

"Why did you do it?" Musty asked.

"Nothing personal," O'Rear answered. "Just business. How can I make it up to you?"

"What kind of vehicles do you have at our disposal?" Shiftless asked.

"Chevy Suburban," O'Rear answered. "It'll fit all of you."

"You don't understand," Harry added. "We're taking every car that you have!"

"Wait!" O'Rear said. "That is not fair!"

With that, Musty pulled out his side arm and began to viciously pummel Julio O'Rear in the head until his face was bloodied.

"I'm sorry," Musty said. "I must be troubled by a build-up of pesky cerumen in my canals. I should probably see an audiologist for a good ear flush once I get state side. I didn't hear what you said to me on the first go around."

"I–I also have a Ford F-150," O'Rear muttered in an attempt to avoid another beating. "With that and Colonel Esteban's Jeep, that will give you a total of three vehicles. I hope that'll suffice."

"Wait!" Colonel Esteban protested. "Let's be reasonable about this. Do you also have to take my Jeep?"

"Damn! I guess the colonel wasn't paying attention to current events," Harry said as the commando team turned upon Esteban and brutally kicked him repeatedly in the face and groin.

"Enough!" Speedy said. "Joe and I will likely need to tank up before we forge on to Guadalajara. It would appear that our meals have been sufficiently tenderized by now, thank you very much."

"I have just one question to ask you, Señor O'Rear," Joe Cephas said. "I'd like to know why you live in such a splendid house while your ranch hands are forced to live in abject squalor. If the Humane Society ever paid this place a visit, those nasty shacks wouldn't even be acceptable as living quarters for a barnyard animal destined for slaughter!"

"I try to live by the teachings of Jesus," O'Rear answered smugly.

"What did you say?" Speedy asked as he furrowed his brow.

"Matthew 22:11. New Testament. You need to read it some time," O'Rear said. "You just might learn how the world really works."

Joe and Speedy stopped in their tracks and looked at each other with their jaws now wide agape.

"Blasphemer!" Speedy said. "Would you like the honors, Joe Cephas?"

"I'll gladly defer to your preference," Joe answered. "I'd be honored if you take Señor O'Rear to a back room. As for me, I'd be happy to finish off Colonel Esteban if that's okay with everybody else."

"Fine by us," Harry said. "Just make it snappy."

"I have one request for you, Ron," Joe Cephas said. "I want you to go down to the bottom of the hill and invite all of those poor bastards living in those nasty-ass shacks to move into this nice, beautiful, hacienda. In a few minutes, the owner of this establishment will not only be vacating the premises, but he'll be vacating life as he knows it!"

"I'd be happy to do it, Joe," Ron said as he walked out the front door.

Musty and Harry Balzac propped their feet upon the dining room table and lit up a couple of choice 52 ring, hand-rolled cigars that had been appropriated from a humidor in the living room. As they listened to the terminal screams emanating from the back rooms of the hacienda where Speedy and Joe Cephas elected to dine in privacy, an unanswered question demanded resolution.

"Hey, Bro?" Musty asked.

"Yeah?"

"What was the passage from Scripture that got Joe and Speedy all bent out of shape?"

"Matthew 22:11," Harry answered.

"Well, what is it?"

"The poor will always be with you," Harry replied.

"Are you kidding me?!"

"No shit," Harry said. "Crack open the Good Book if you dare to doubt the veracity of the factual data that's deeply embedded within my vast and generally flawless memory banks, you agnostic knave."

"I'd hate to interrupt Speedy if he's in the middle of a feeding frenzy," Musty said, "but I'm just going to have to go back there and shoot that redheaded son of a bitch myself!"

Miguel Pastore certainly had good reason to be suspicious. His ward, Nathan, was indeed up to no good. Nathan would often profess that he was going over to nearby Rancho O'Rear to play with the numerous children previously sired by the ranch hands that lived there. Miguel certainly had his doubts about the veracity of what young Nathan would tell him, however. On more than one occasion, he could see that Nathan was walking home from the West which was the location of Santa Sangre, and not from the East which was the location of the sprawling O'Rear complex.

"Uncle Miguel?" Nathan petitioned. "I've been invited to play in a baseball game with the farm kids at Rancho O'Rear today."

"You know Estado Jalisco has placed this area under quarantine," Miguel explained. "I think it would be smart if you stayed home for now."

"You're the only vampiro that I know, Uncle Miguel," Nathan lied. "If there are any other vampires around here, they're in Santa Sangre. There certainly hasn't been any trouble here or at Rancho O'Rear that I know of."

"Okay," Miguel relented, "but I want you back in 2 hours."

With that, Nathan scampered off. After Nathan left Rancho Feliz, Miguel was approached by Mayordomo. "You seem troubled, Miguel."

"Do you remember what it was like to be a kid?" Miguel asked.

"I most certainly do," Mayordomo replied.

"Do you remember how you behaved when you tried to fool your parents with a mischievous deception?"

"I most certainly do."

"I remember lying to my parents to keep them in the dark about a premeditated plan I once hatched to sneak away from the house and get into trouble with some bad kids in my neighborhood," Miguel recalled. "Do you think Nathan is acting like that now?"

"I most certainly do."

"If you want to know what I think," Miguel concluded, "Nathan has no intention of going over to Rancho O'Rear. He's going down to Santa Sangre, and this time I'm going to follow him!"

"Please be careful, Señor Pastore."

At the time, Miguel had no idea that those were the very last words that he would ever hear from his faithful Mayordomo. Miguel followed Nathan down the road that led to Santa Sangre, but lagged about 50 yards behind so the young boy had no idea that he was being followed by the man he considered to be his uncle. Once in town, Miguel was surprised to see Nathan enter the rectory at the Church of Our Lady of Perpetual Motion.

With all that had gone on at Santa Sangre, there was only one priest left in the rectory, and that was Padre "Garrapa the Groper." Miguel was ignorant of the rumors that had previously circulated about the community that Padre Garrapa was a flaming sexual deviant. Miguel erroneously believed that young Nathan perhaps was simply seeking spiritual guidance. Nonetheless, this was a situation that warranted careful scrutiny.

When Nathan entered the rectory, Miguel quietly followed, but he elected to secretly wait in the lobby while the young boy paid the priest a visit. Once upstairs, Nathan met the members of the newly ordained Brotherhood of the Bat who were waiting for him in the hallway, along with two adults that he had never met before.

"Nathan, we would like to introduce you to a new member of our organization. His name is Zachary Hawk, and he's going to help us today." Amelia whispered. "The other man is named, El Lobo. He wants to evaluate the quality of our work. He might want to hire us if *we* do a good job today. Now, if *you* do a good job today, maybe we'll invite you to join our group someday when you get older."

"I'd like that!" Nathan exclaimed.

"What do you want me to do?" Nathan asked.

"It is quite simple," Isaac said. "Just knock on the door and tell Padre Garrapa that you're all alone and frightened. Tell him that you heard that he's a man who really loves kids, and that you need affection and attention. After he lets you in, we'll do the rest!"

Nathan followed his instructions and knocked upon the door. Momentarily, a voice called out. "Who is it?"

"Hello, Padre Garrapa, it is me, Nathan."

"Is anybody out there with you?" The priest asked. "There's been a lot of trouble going on in Santa Sangre, and I've heard that two boys you know named Isaac and Jesus are behind it all. Those kids are not happy with me for one reason or another, and I'm trying to avoid them."

"I'm here alone, Padre," Nathan lied. "I'm scared and I'm lonely, and I just need somebody to give me a hug."

"Well," Padre Garrapa said, "you've come to the right place little boy!"

With that, the door to the priest's quarters swung wide open. Nathan was quickly pushed aside, and the members of the Brotherhood swarmed into the room like a colony of bats. The priest screamed, but what happened next was so swift and savage that Lobo Grande actually had to step back out into the hallway to catch his breath.

"By the love of Lord Camazotz," Lobo said, "that was the greatest spectacle of barbarity that I've ever witnessed! You children are hired!"

The adolescent members of the Brotherhood cheered with delight when Lobo Grande strolled back into the room and kicked about the few shards of bone and scraps of flesh that were left on the floor.

"I also want you to come work for my organization, Dr. Hawk," Lobo said as he looked toward the newest member of the bloody Brotherhood. "These children are going to need adult supervision from time to time, and I think you're the man who could offer them the sadistic guidance that they'll need in the future."

"I'd be honored to work for you in that capacity," Hawk said. "After all, now that I've gone through the transformation into becoming un vampiro, I'll never be going home again. Now that I've tasted human blood, I don't want to ever stop!"

When Miguel heard a high-pitched scream of agony come from the upper dormitory of the rectory, he ran up the stairwell to see what happened.

"Nathan, are you okay?"

"Oh, no!" Lobo said as he pulled out his side arm. "Another vampiro! Surround him, children, and don't let him move! Are you by chance a man named, Blake Barker?"

"No," Miguel said, "but he's a friend of mine. I don't know if he's still alive however, as he was taken captive by the Calle Vampiro cartel a while back."

"Oh," Lobo said as he took aim at Miguel, "I can assure you that he's very much alive. He's brought a lot of grief to my organization. He recently killed several of my soldiers and seriously injured one of my best men named, Mono."

When Lobo uttered that last comment, Zachary Hawk looked away and tried to appear inconspicuous, as he was the individual who was guilty of Lobo's harsh accusations.

"What's going on here? Nathan, are you okay?" Miguel asked.

"I'm fine, Uncle Miguel," Nathan said before he turned to El Lobo. "Please don't hurt him!"

"You look familiar to me," Lobo said to Miguel as he pulled Nathan aside. "What's your name?"

"I'm Miguel Pastore."

"I see a strong resemblance with somebody I know named, Lorena Pastore," Lobo noted. "She's called, the Queen of the Maya."

"Well," Miguel answered, "she should look like me. After all, she's my sister."

"So, you're the brother of Lorena Pastore?!" Hawk exclaimed.

"Who might you be?" Miguel asked.

"My name is Zachary Hawk. My cousin, Dr. Horatio Cloud, came down here to Mexico to find your sister."

"I know all about it," Miguel said. "Dr. Cloud was also a friend of mine. He went down to the Yucatan to find Lorena, but never returned."

"Wait a minute," Nathan interjected as he pulled on the sleeve of El Lobo. "You mentioned the name, Blake Barker. My name is Nathan Barker. Do you know my daddy, Blake Barker?"

"Praise Lord Camazotz!" Lobo exclaimed. "This just keeps getting better all the time! Do you ever get the feeling that everything in the universe is connected somehow?"

⚊⚋⚊

"Let me introduce you to your new cell mates," Tercero said to Miguel and Nathan as he and Perezoso guided them to a locked room. As Miguel was a dangerous vampiro, the barrel of a 12-gauge shotgun was held against the back of the head of young Nathan the entire time to ensure that the transfer of the new prisoners to the Astilladora de Madera cartel compound detention center would be made without a hitch.

"The pathetic Mexicano who looks like he just lost his puppy used to be the leader of this cartel. Now he's just another hombre waiting to meet the unholy Lord Camazotz in a pit of hell fire," Tercero laughed.

"Allow me to be the first to welcome you to this most unhappy little group of the damned that I like to refer to as the Brotherhood of the Condemned. My name is, Martillo Grande. What are your names?"

"I'm Miguel Pastore and this young fellow is Nathan Barker."

"Nathan Barker?" Russian Bear interrupted. "I knew your father, Blake!"

"The furry eyebrow that looks like a caterpillar who just spoke to you is our doctor, Ilya Putinov," Tercero explained. "Everybody calls him, Russian Bear."

"Wait! You knew my father?" Nathan asked.

Russian Bear and Miguel both instinctively pressed their index fingers against the lips of Nathan in a simultaneous fashion to petition the child to remain silent at that perilous juncture.

"Please allow me to finish this mandatory formal introduction," Tercero sarcastically continued. "The older man on the cot is a United States Army colonel named, Augustus Placard. His legs are weak and he has a hard time walking. Apparently he was stung by one or more black scorpions. The neurotoxins from the nasty little creatures seem to have caused a partial lower extremity paralysis. Isn't that right, Colonel?"

"Fuck off, Tercero," Placard replied with his eyes closed, not realizing the child, Nathan, was his new cell mate.

"Shame on you, Colonel!" Perezoso exclaimed. "There's a child present! It would seem to me that you need another lesson in proper manners."

With that, Perezoso and Tercero began to pummel the Colonel with their fists. As Placard was too weak to fight off the assailants, all he could do was assume a fetal position upon the cot. The colonel covered his head and neck region with his arms in a futile attempt to protect himself from another vicious beating that was sadly becoming a rote, bi-daily ritual.

"As soon as Lobo Grande goes down to the Yucatan with the young little blood-sucking monkeys that he brought into our organization," Tercero said, "I'm going to have you shredded in the wood chipper. Sooner or later, I'll be forever done with you, Colonel!"

Upon the departure of Tercero and Perezoso, Nathan pleaded for details from Russian Bear about what this stranger had known about his father, Blake.

"How did you know my daddy?" Nathan asked.

"Blake and I were both prisoners with the Calle Vampiro cartel.

He and I became good friends. In fact, he was like a brother to me. He's one of the most decent human beings I've ever known," Bear explained.

"Is he, well—is he still alive?" Nathan hopefully asked.

"Honestly, I just don't know," the Russian doctor answered. "He was badly hurt when I last saw him. Nonetheless, Lobo Grande and his band of thugs talk about Blake all the time. They're convinced that he's still alive and causing trouble."

"If there's smoke, there's fire," Miguel said.

"One can only hope," Russian Bear said as he turned his attention to Miguel. "In order for you two to be in this hell hole,

Lobo Grande must have a good reason or another to lock you up as prisoners."

"Leverage," Miguel succinctly answered.

"How so?"

"You see," Miguel explained, "I asked Lobo Grande the same question. He believes that Nathan is a valuable commodity. His presence here will eventually flush out Blake Barker and force him to surrender to the cartel."

"Yeah," Bear said. "I get that. But what about you?"

"Lobo Grande has a beef with my sister, Lorena, who's hiding out down in the Yucatan. Tomorrow, Lobo is going down there with a group of young vampiros to try and exterminate the Maya who were once working on his behalf. I have no doubt that I'm going down there as a hostage to try and convince Lorena to surrender to him."

"Well," Bear asked, "does your sister still love you?"

"That remains to be seen," Miguel answered.

"I heard that your sister is considered by many to be the Queen of the Maya," Russian Bear noted. "Do you think if Lobo Grande held you at gunpoint, your sister would surrender the Maya to him on your behalf?"

"I seriously doubt it," Miguel confidently answered. "When I go down to the Yucatan with Lobo Grande tomorrow, it will likely be a one-way trip. That's why I need to ask you a great favor. If you once considered Blake Barker to be like a brother to you, I want you to promise me that you'll try and take care of his son, Nathan, once I'm gone."

"You can bank on that," Bear said. "You didn't even have to ask."

⚬⟨⟨⟨ ∫ ⟩⟩⟩⚬

On the following day, two vans arrived at the compound to ferry Lobo Grande, Zachary Hawk, Miguel, and the entire Brotherhood of the Bat to the airport in Guadalajara for their scheduled chartered

343

trip down to the Yucatan. It was time to eliminate Lorena Pastore and her pesky Maya tribe once and for all.

"I don't know if this is such a good idea, Lobo," Tercero complained. "After all, it's been quite some time since you've heard from Colonel Esteban about the Maya problem. Perhaps he forgot all about it."

"The fact that Colonel Esteban is not answering his calls matters not to me at this time," Lobo said. "Besides, he's not the man that we need to keep happy, anyhow. The order to eliminate Lorena Pastore and the Maya came directly from the Department of Defense. If we don't get this job done now, they'll be coming after us next."

"Are you bringing down enough fire power to get the job done right this time?" Tercero asked. "Maybe I should come down with you."

"Don't think for a moment that I'm not wise to you, Tercero," Lobo Grande said. "Now that Martello Grande is my prisoner, you now happen to be one step closer to becoming the head of this organization. How do I know that you haven't planned a little accident for me down in the Yucatan?"

"Have I not been loyal to you?" the henchman asked.

"Frankly, no," Lobo answered. "Every time I come down to check on the clinical progress of Colonel Placard, it seems to me that he's acquired serious new medical problems. You wouldn't know anything about that, now would you?"

"I can't help it if el bastardo is clumsy and he falls down a lot," Tercero said.

"The very minute that I find out that you've been the one responsible for his injuries," Lobo threatened, "it will be the very minute that I'll turn you into fertilizer, amigo. As for fire power, I'm following the guidelines established by the ancient Maya. They utilized teams of assassins that were comprised two vampiro and four humans per team. If that worked for the Maya, it'll work for me."

After Zachary Hawk entered the first van, four cartel thugs brought out Miguel from his holding cell. "I am surprised you don't have me bound and gagged," Miguel said. "Yo soy un vampiro, and one that happens to be extraordinarily pissed off. Aren't you afraid of me, Lobo? After all, you should be!"

"I own you, Miguel, and I know beyond a shadow of a doubt that you won't get out of line," Lobo replied with an inflection of indifference.

"Are you certain of that?"

"I am, indeed," Lobo smugly answered. "After all, one word from me and young Nathan will get sent through the wood chipper. Now shut up and get in the van."

After Miguel and several additional foot soldiers entered the second van, the Brotherhood of the Bat finally arrived, eager to go on their first assigned mission. "Wait one moment," Lobo said as he pulled Celena aside. "What's wrong with you?"

"I feel fine, Lobo," Celena answered. "I'm ready to go to work."

"Is that so?" Lobo asked. "When the Brotherhood attacked and killed the priest, all you did was lap up the blood from the floor like you were a dog. Open your mouth. Let me see your teeth."

Celena complied with Lobo's request. When the cartel leader realized that Celena was missing her canine incisors which had been previously ripped out of her mouth by the deranged Sister Cabeza de Bala, Lobo became furious. "What good are you to me if you don't have any incisors? You're supposed to be a warrior! You're not coming on this mission."

"Don't do this to me," Celena pleaded. "I want to work for the cartel!"

"Okay, then. If you want to work for us, it'll be in the whore house!" Lobo barked out a new order to Tercero in anger. "Have Perezoso get this bitch out of here! Tell him to take her to Madam Lucia Aragon."

"I'll do it," Tercero said with unbridled lust.

"No, you won't." Lobo said. "Have Perezoso do it. For some reason, Madam Aragon is afraid of you. As for the rest of us, it's time to go."

"These Maya might be a lot tougher than you think," Tercero warned as he forcefully pulled Celena away. "If you don't want me to go with you, why don't you at least call down Mono and Villanueva?"

"No," Lobo answered. "They're on a mission on my behalf. Now that Mono is out of the hospital, he and Villanueva are actively tracking down the vampiro named Blake Barker as we speak."

"Well, it's your call," Tercero said with a shrug. "Who do you want to assign to be your replacement as the boss of this cartel, just in case you don't come back?"

"To the strongest, Tercero," Lobo answered. "To the strongest!"

❧

Once in the van that was slated to take the Brotherhood to the airport in Guadalajara for their chartered flight down South to wage war against the Maya, the young vampires naturally gravitated towards Zachary Hawk.

"I'm nervous about flying," Enos said. "None of us have ever been on an airplane before. Would it be okay if I sat beside you when we fly out, Dr. Hawk?"

"Why sure, Enos," Hawk replied. "That would be fine."

"I like you, Dr. Hawk," Enos said. "Would you mind if I called you Uncle Hawk?"

"That would be fine, I suppose," Hawk replied.

"Great!" Enos beamed. "We could be, well—we could be a family!"

"If it is all the same to you," Hawk interjected, "I don't think that would be a good idea."

"Why not?"

"Didn't all the vampires in the Brotherhood of the Bat eat all of their own family members?"

"Oh, yeah," Enos said. "I forgot about that."

"Well," Zachary Hawk replied with pursed lips, "I haven't!"

❧

Domino Lackey found refuge in a lava tube amongst the tall grass in the Malpais, south of Fort Wingate. Although the lava cave was intermittently occupied by a transient cloud of free-tail bats, the high-frequency eco-location chirps that emanated from the peculiar flying mammals were, for some reason, an irresistible siren call to the troubled adolescent vampiro.

Knowing that Joseph would come looking for him one day, Domino had the wherewithal to establish a series of signature off-trail rock cairns at fifty yard intervals that the elder would be able to follow into the wilderness. Domino elected to use the symbol of the bat which was an asymmetrical diamond, fashioned on each occasion from twelve flat stones.

For many Navajo, the bat was believed to be a spiritual liaison between man and the Creator. One might hope that the bat at times could offer wisdom and guidance in the night for those who were literally or perhaps figuratively lost. For Domino however, the symbol of the bat was little more than a specter of pending death.

As he warmed his hands by a small fire of aromatic pinion scrub, Domino became rather alarmed when his hyper-acute hearing registered the unmistakable report of soft footprints slowly crunching through a thin blanket of new fallen snow near the mouth of the lava tube.

"Who goes there? Identify yourself now!"

"Yá'át'ééh!" Elder Joseph called out the commonplace Navajo greeting. "Don't be alarmed Domino. It's just me."

"Elder Joseph?" Domino asked. "Did you come alone?"

"I have indeed," Joseph said. "I'm glad I was able to find you, son. You're a pretty clever trail blazer. It was a good idea to leave a trail of rock cairns shaped in the symbol of the bat. How did you ever get so smart?"

"Why, you taught me, Elder. You were a great instructor," Domino said. "I hope you're proud of your star pupil."

"Sadly, not anymore," Joseph replied. "You've left nothing but a pile of dead bodies and a mountain of broken hearts in your wake. I assume that you were the party responsible for the two dead soldiers that were recently found by the authorities east of Placitas."

"So, you've come to judge me?" Domino asked. "Is that it?"

"Just in this life," Elder Joseph answered, "but not the next. That will be up to the Great Spirit and Creator of all things."

"When it's your turn to meet the Creator," Domino asked, "are you going to ask forgiveness for your own culpability in making me what I am?"

"What are you talking about?" Joseph asked. "You're almost eighteen years old! You're responsible for your own sins, now. You and nobody else."

"Did you not send me to the plateau north of Chaco?" Domino asked. "Did you not ask me to look for historical Anasazi artifacts on behalf of the tribe? For what purpose? Just so we could hawk more trinkets to the white man underneath the portico of the Governor's Palace at the Santa Fe Plaza? If so, that's pathetic. That's all on your head, Elder Joseph!"

"Perhaps," Joseph replied, "but how does that have any bearing on the crimes you've committed?"

"I did what you asked of me," Domino sadly noted. "Because of you, I found the skull of an ancient vampiro. Because of you, I excavated that particular artifact. Because of you, I impaled my hand on a sharp fang that was still firmly embedded in that skull bone. Because of you, I got infected with the virus that causes human vampirism. Because of you, I am now what I am!"

The indictment that Domino proclaimed rang true, and Elder Joseph bowed his head in guilt and shame.

"I was hoping somehow when you came to find me that you'd be the key to my redemption and perhaps even my salvation," Domino sadly reflected. "Unfortunately, that apparently will not be the case. I have an idea, however, Elder Joseph. If it's true that the Creator will be the judge of all mankind after this life is over, then maybe he should judge us both right here, right now, and at the very same time!"

"Perhaps you're right," The elder solemnly replied with a nod.

Domino bared his incisors and lunged at Joseph, but the elder was ready with a twelve inch obsidian blade. Before the misguided teen could sink his fangs into the elder, Joseph thrust the blade deep into the young man's gaping, voracious maw. The knife pierced through Domino's posterior pharynx and cleaved his upper cervical spine. The vampiro was dead before he hit the ground.

After Joseph decapitated Domino, he dragged the headless torso over the now raging camp fire, and he added additional wood fuel to create a somber and all-consumptive funeral pyre. Joseph prayed before he buried Domino's head in an adjacent, yet separate location.

Once done, Joseph completely disrobed and began a long and lonely hike to the Sandstone Bluff vista point. The temperatures atop the summit that night were expected to drop far below zero degrees. The temperatures atop the summit that night were expected to drop far below the point that any human could possibly survive without wearing a stitch of clothing.

⸺ formform ⸻

"Have you told Raquel Abril or Penny Schaeffer the good news?" Dr. Blanks asked.

"Not yet," Dr. Hoefferle replied. "As you're the director of the CDC research program on the RV-1986 virus, Dr. Kohl and I wanted you to be there to give them the report. After all, it's your honor, Seth."

"Surely they must be anticipating good news," Dr. Blanks said.

"They're completely asymptomatic, and a qualitative titer assay can't detect any disease by our current laboratory technology," Kohl said. "The only peculiar phenomena are the canine incisor fangs that are still embedded in their maxillary bones."

"Do you anticipate that their fangs might turn out to be a deleterious social stigmata for either of them?" Blanks asked.

"I don't think so," Hoefferle replied. "Penny told me she plans on getting her fangs filed down by a cosmetic dentist someday, but the nurse, Raquel, says she wants to keep them as a 'souvenir' if you can believe that!"

"What?!" Blanks asked with incredulity. "You can't be serious. For what reason, pray tell?"

"In a pinch, she said that she could use her fangs to pry open a bottle of beer if she ever decides to go back out on a summer vacation camping trip. In addition, she states that she's not been particularly successful in pair bonding in her former life. By her account, she admits that her prior boyfriends have not always been on their best behavior. In the future, a set of fangs might prove to be a powerful deterrent to unwelcomed amorous advances!" Dr. Kohl explained.

"Let's go tell them the good news!" Blanks said with a hearty laugh. "Where are they now?"

"The orderly brought them to the conference room," Hoefferle said. "They're waiting for us now."

When the scientists entered the conference room, the two patients were already suspicious that something was afoot. "Is there anybody in this room who wants to hear some good news?" Dr. Blanks asked.

Penny and Raquel beamed with excitement. "We are all ears, Dr. Blanks!" Penny said. "What's going on?"

"I'm happy to report that you ladies are in remission," Blanks stated.

"Does that mean we're cured?" Raquel asked.

"For the time being," Dr. Kohl said, "it means that there's no evidence of measurable disease."

"I understand that," Raquel said, "but does that mean we're cured?"

"Frankly, it's too soon to tell if that's indeed the case," Blank said. "We just don't know if this disease of human vampirism may ever come back to haunt you someday in the future."

"Does this mean that we'll be able to come off the oral anti-viral medication that we're taking in addition to the vaccine that we previously received?"

The three scientists looked at each other and shrugged their shoulders. They simply didn't have an answer to that question.

"We just don't know," Hoefferle said. "Our recommendation is that for the time being you stay on your current regimen of anti-viral treatment."

"Well," Penny asked, "for how long?"

"We just don't know," Kohl replied.

"Where do we go from here?" Raquel asked. "The life I once had is now long gone. I know Penny feels the same way. What does the future hold for us?"

"You're talking to a man that always has a 'Plan B'," Dr. Blanks said.

"What would that be?" Penny asked.

"Dr. Hoefferle and Kohl would like to offer their expertise to become your agents in a lucrative business proposition. There's a German pharmaceutical firm called, Leben Kur, that I'd like to tell you about. This company was working to develop cosmetic and medicinal products with a human vampire until just recently, but for one reason or another, this vampire's services are no longer available. Now that you ladies are in remission with no evidence of measurable disease, the Leben Kur firm would like to offer you a fat contract to develop future therapeutics from your post-remission serum."

"So, Dr. Hoefferle and Kohl are willing to become our representative agents in this endeavor?" Raquel asked.

"Absolutely!" Dr. Blanks replied as Kohl and Hoefferle smiled and nodded their heads. "They can handle all the marketing and contract negotiations. After all, they know how much you're potentially worth on the open market. I'm absolutely certain that they'd be willing to cut you the same kind of great deal that the famous talent agent, Colonel Parker, once offered Elvis Presley!"

❦

Several foot soldiers searched all over the compound to locate Tercero, but it was Perezoso who finally found him in the electronic shack that held the short wave.

"I'm surprised to see you in here. What are you doing in the radio room, Tercero? You know that this place is off limits for everybody except for Lobo Grande and some of his few select captains, and you sure as hell aren't one of them. Lobo specifically told you to stay out of here." Perezoso warned.

"You need to mind your own affairs," Tercero answered. "Why are you bothering me? I happen to be conducting important business."

"Be that as it may, we have a problem, Tercero," Perezoso explained. "The new whore that I took over to Madam Aragon refuses to work. What did you expect her to do?"

"Now that El Lobo and his coven of baby bats have flown down to the Yucatan, there's a new sheriff in town," Tercero boasted. "It's time for me to clean up some of this mess that Lobo left behind. I asked the teenage vampira, Celena, to physically service Martillo Grande and Colonel Placard before I ran them through the wood chipper today. It was the least that I could do. I wouldn't want anybody to ever accuse me of being an unreasonable or cruel leader now that I've taken over this cartel. It looks like Celena is going to meet the same fate as Martillo and the colonel, if she refuses to follow my orders."

"Perhaps my mental faculties are a bit cloudy from the line of coca that I just snorted up my *nariz*," Perezoso mused. "For a moment there, I could have sworn that you just said that you're now the leader of this cartel. So, who died and who ordained you to become the new Pope?"

"Don't be an idiot," Tercero said. "If you don't want me to run you through the chipper like the others, you better fall in line. What makes you think that Lobo is ever going to come back from the Yucatan?"

"What have you done, you jack ass?" Perezoso asked. "Who were you talking to on the short wave when I found you hiding in here?"

"You're beginning to try my patience," Tercero cautioned. "Go get El Chistoso and his brother, Bromisto. I want you three to go over to the cell block and drag out Colonel Placard and Martillo and take them to the wood chipper. Bring Russian Bear, also. We're going to make this a fiesta grande. At gun point, I want you to force the Bear to run his friend, Colonel Placard, through the chipper. It'll break his spirit once and for all, and he'll never forgive himself for what we're about to force him to do! Don't forget to bring along that brat, Nathan Barker."

"What are your plans for that little bastard?" Perezoso asked.

"I want you to set him in front of the chipper exhaust chute when Russian Bear runs the colonel through the grinder. It's time for Blake Barker's baby boy to get baptized in blood!"

"Praise and honor to the evil Lord Camazotz!" Perezoso exclaimed. "I was wrong about you, Tercero. It appears to me that you do indeed have the makings of a great cartel leader after all! What are you going to do while Chistoso, Bromisto, and I round up the colonel and Martillo Grande?"

"First, I need to finish my business here in the radio room. Then it'll be time for me to pay a visit to Madam Aragon," Tercero answered. "I'm going to force her to hand over the new little whore, Celena, to my custody. If this young vampira doesn't have a hot twat ready to trot before it'll rot, then the cartel has no need for her around here."

⸺◈⸺

"I know that you miss Cletus Barker, Queen Lorena. We all do," El Dolor said, "but you just have to snap out of it!"

"Well, you've got my attention, El Dolor," Lorena said with a sigh. "What's the big emergency that you wanted to talk to me about?"

"It looks like it's going down tomorrow," El Dolor said.

"How do you know?"

"Joaquin took a call on the shortwave from somebody at the cartel compound. Lobo's coming down here to the Yucatan with a dangerous force this time," El Dolor cautioned. "The warning we received is that Lobo still has active orders directly from the Department of Defense to exterminate us once and for all because of what we did to the Guatemalan war criminal who called himself, General Carmel."

"Damn! Who's this person from Lobo's cartel that calls us on the radio from time to time?" Lorena asked. "Do you think we can believe this mysterious messenger?"

"Although he's never given us his name, he does appear to be trustworthy," El Dolor opined. "After all, it was the same guy who gave us a warning when El Lobo came down with his henchman the last time around. I have no idea who the caller is, but maybe he's got an axe to grind against El Lobo Grande. After all, who doesn't?"

"What are we going to be up against this time?" Lorena asked.

"Lobo fashions himself to be an amateur historian, and this time he's taken a page from our own Maya culture," Dolor replied.

"How so?"

"Classic Maya rectangle assassin teams. Two teams. Six individuals per team. Four humans, two vampires per team. Here's the kicker: the vampiros on the hit teams are adolescents!"

"You can't be serious!"

"They're also sending in two additional adult vampiros, no doubt as reserve backup."

"Okay, El Dolor, you better get Joaquin over here," the Queen of the Maya ordered. "We have our work cut out for us, and then some. The first order of business is to take a large burlap tarp and cover the cenote at the base of the pyramid. After that, sprinkle the tarp with leaves and foliage to camouflage the entire site."

"To what end?" El Dolor asked.

"One never knows when a fall trap might come in handy..."

※

The moment Madam Aragon realized that Tercero was at the entryway to the whore house, she tried to slam the door in his face. "What do you want with me, you filthy animal?" Madam Aragon cried out in anguish. "Do you plan on raping me again with the electric cattle prod? I'm still injured from the last time that you had your way with me!"

Tercero forced the door open and punched Madam Aragon in the mouth with a closed fist. "I'll take you any time that I want," Tercero said, "but as for now I'm here for Celena!"

"What do you want with Celena?" Madam Aragon asked as she raised her arms defensively to ward off another blow. "What has she done?"

"That's the wrong question to ask," Tercero replied. "It's more of a matter as to what she has *not* done. I gave her an important order before she was brought over here that she needs to sexually service Colonel Placard and Martillo Grande today. I don't know what the problem might be, but Perezoso informed me she refuses to perform what should be a relatively simple task for her."

"She's new here," Madam Aragon said in defense of her new, young prostitute. "Let her warm up to the idea."

"Warm up to the idea, eh?" Tercero asked. "Celena's so-called nasty friend, Amelia, told me that Celena used to pick up a peso here and there on the side."

"What are you talking about?"

"That little vampira reputedly offered sex to the boys out at the high school in exchange for money," Tercero elaborated. "As best I can tell, she's way beyond warm. In fact, she's hot!"

"Why on earth do you want her to service Colonel Placard and Martillo Grande?" Madam Aragon asked. "After all, they're your prisoners. It's not like this cartel to offer any favors to its political enemies."

"I'm going to introduce them both to the Astilladora Attitude Adjustment Program today," Tercero answered. "I at least want those two men to die with a dowser in their trousers!"

"No! Please don't!" Madam Aragon pleaded. "Martillo Grande and I had relations when I worked for the Calle Vampiro cartel. To be frank, I'm rather fond of him and I'd hate to see you run him through the wood chipper. What's the matter with you, Tercero? Are you that evil?"

"I'll show you how evil I am," Tercero said with a smirk. "If at one time you and Martillo were lovers, I'm going to force you to watch what will happen to him!"

The two cartel thugs, Chistoso and Bromisto, each put a dog collar and leash around the neck of Nathan Barker and secured him in front of the exhaust chute of the wood chipper to ensure that the young boy would be drenched in the blood of the prisoners that were to be sacrificed to the bat god, Camazotz, on that fateful day.

Tercero supervised the proceedings and ordered Perezoso to have Russian Bear man the throttle of the chipper machine at gun point. After all, his friend, Colonel Placard was slated to be the first victim reduced to mere scraps of sinew and tissue.

"Line the prisoners up in the order that we're going to run them through the wood chipper," Tercero ordered. "After Colonel Placard, put Martillo Grande in the second position, and we'll save the little vampira for last!"

"If you want to survive this day, Russian Bear, you'll do as I say," Perezoso threatened. "I'll assist Chistoso and his brother to load the Colonel feet first into the spinning blades of the chipper. Once we get the Colonel's legs into the intake chute, throttle up the device."

"Wait! Before you force me to murder my good friend," Russian Bear petitioned, "at least let me have an opportunity to say one last word to him."

"You have our permission," Tercero replied as he pulled Madam Aragon close, "but you must say adios to the colonel from the throttle switch as you'll not be allowed to leave your post until the ceremony is over. If you do a good job today, you might have an opportunity to become the permanent executioner for our organization!"

"Fair enough," Bear said as he leaned over the control panel of the wood chipper to address Augustus Placard.

"Colonel, if you still have that gift that the jail keeper, Llaves, gave you a while back, I think it would be a good time to introduce it to all of our friends here," Bear said. "Although this might not be the one-on-one opportunity you've long waited for as El Lobo Grande is now down in the Yucatan, it would seem to me you are not going to have another chance."

"So it would seem," the colonel replied.

"If you have a gift, Colonel Placard, you need to share it with Chistoso and me," Bromisto said with an eager look of anticipation.

"I have a treat for you, Bromisto," Placard said as he discreetly put his right hand down the front of his pants to retrieve the longhidden revolver that Llaves had once given him. "Eat this!"

The bullet that was discharged from Placard's pistol struck the thug just above the bridge of his nose and this afforded Martillo

Grande the opportunity to grab the man's FAL long rifle and put it to good use before Bromisto even hit the ground.

Tercero recoiled when Madam Aragon clawed at his eyes. The self-ordained cartel boss sprinted away from the scene to recruit reinforcements while dodging a volley of automatic weapon fire. As Madam Aragon instinctively tackled Nathan and covered him with her body to keep him from harm's way, Martillo Grande and Placard turned their weapons upon Chistoso, killing the foot soldier where he stood.

Reflexively, Parezoso throttled Celena by the neck with his left hand and held his automatic weapon against her face with his right hand.

"Let me go," Perezoso demanded, "or I'll finish off this little whore right here and right now. Drop your guns! Do it, damn you!"

Placard and Martillo dropped their weapons, but Perezoso underestimated the resolve of his adversary. Although Celena had lost her canine incisors, she was still una vampira, and this meant she was still immensely strong. She pushed the barrel of his weapon away from her face and issued a punishing head-butt upon the forehead of Perezoso, stunning the villain. As if she was a worldclass power-lifter, Celena hoisted Perezoso into the air above her head and proceeded to jam him feet first into the running wood chipper. Once done, Russian Bear hit the throttle!

Perezoso clutched his FAL rifle as the spinning blades of the chipper compelled him to enter the bowels of the mechanical beast on a one-way trip. Once the shredder had reached Perezoso's pelvis, his rifle had jammed the machine, and the thug was now trapped, despite the fact that the lower half of his body had already been reduced to steak tartare.

Placard and his crew were completely oblivious to the screams that emanated from Perezoso as they planned their avenue of escape. "Tercero will be back in no time and he'll be bringing an entire army with him," Placard said. "I'll hold them off as long as I can, but the rest of you have to get out of here! If you split up, that will reduce the risk of you getting caught and dragged back here."

"I know where the motor pool is and where they keep the keys to the various vehicles that are over there," Madam Aragon said. "What should we do?"

"You and Martillo Grande need to get away in one of the cars. I recommend you drive West. As for you, Russian Bear, Nathan Barker is now your responsibility. Take one of the vehicles and get to the American consulate in Mexico City. As you are both American citizens, maybe Uncle Sam can get you safely out of this damned country. Take Celena with you. She's already shown her value as a brave warrior, and she might be able to get you out of trouble if you get caught somewhere along the way. Go! You don't have much time."

"You saved my life, Colonel Placard," Martillo Grande rightly noted. "I'll never forget what you've done for me today."

"Do me a favor, Martillo," Placard asked as he gathered up the scattered munitions for what would likely be a last stand.

"If I can, I will," Martillo said. "Just name it."

"I might somehow crawl out of this situation alive and still breathing when it's all over," Placard said. "After all, if the truth be told, I've been in tougher spots in the past."

"You're a mean old bastard and your violent reputation precedes you," Martillo noted. "Anything's possible, I suppose."

"By chance, if you and I ever pass each other on a dark and lonely street some night in the distant future," Placard wryly petitioned as he shook Martillo's hand, "let's just pretend that we've never met."

<hr>

"Am I seeing a ghost, or is Blake Barker actually alive and well?" Mayordomo asked as he opened the front door of the Rancho Feliz hacienda to find out who had come for an unexpected visit.

"Well," Blake Barker answered, "I'm indeed alive, but my health is far from well, Mayordomo."

"What's wrong with you?"

"If the truth be told, I'm dying," Blake answered with a shrug and pursed lips.

"Based on your appearance," Mayordomo said, "I'd venture that you now have cancer of the blood. I've been on this earth for many years and most of the vampiros I've met eventually died from this kind of illness. Please come in, Señor Blake, and relax on the couch."

"Gracias, no." Blake answered. "Just let me sit here and rest on the front porch for a bit."

"When was the last time that you had an opportunity to take in sustenance?"

"I haven't eaten in three days," Blake answered. "If this leukemia doesn't kill me, I'll simply die from starvation. Maybe in the scheme of life's events, that would be a blessing after all."

"Don't talk that way," Mayordomo said. "I'll have the kitchen staff prepare you a cocktail of beef blood. Where have you been, Señor Barker? Everybody assumed that you were no longer amongst the land of the living after you foolishly marched off to wage your own personal war against the Calle cartel."

"I've been receiving medical care at the University Hospital at the San Augustin College of Medicine in Guadalajara," Blake explained. "I would have called to tell you folks that fact, but you don't even have a phone at this damned ranch. I was about to undergo chemo-therapy treatment for my leukemia, but two thugs from a new cartel found out that I was there, so I fled. I tried to save the hospital staff at that institution from being slaughtered. Frankly, I don't know the outcome of what happened there upon my departure. I hope trouble hasn't followed me here, but it's imperative that I see my son Nathan before I die. Where is he, Mayordomo? Where's my good friend, Miguel?"

"Neither of them is here at the ranch," Mayordomo explained. "They went into Santa Sangre to conduct some business but they never returned."

"Well, if that's the case, I need to dust myself off and find them in Santa Sangre," Blake stated.

"That won't happen," Mayordomo explained. "There was a recent outbreak of human vampirism in the community that the local officials weren't able to get under control. Estado Jalisco asked for help from the Mexican government and the town is now under federal jurisdiction. Soldiers are crawling all over the place. You're un vampiro, Señor Barker. If you show up at Santa Sangre in your current condition, you'll be killed on the spot. Frankly, you're just too weak to defend yourself."

Just then, the ranchera named La Ardilla and her two boys approached the front porch. "Looks like trouble is coming our way, Mayordomo," La Ardilla said. "*El puesto de observar* spotted two armed men coming down the dirt road."

"You know what to do," Mayordomo said. "When you're finished, bring the bodies to our guest, Blake Barker. I don't want him to starve to death."

La Ardilla and the boys casually walked down the dirt road to intercept Mono and Villanueva who were in hot pursuit of the vampire named, Blake Barker. From his seat on the front porch, Mayordomo slowly nodded his head in approval as he witnessed automatic gunfire reduce the vehicle driven by two cartel thugs into useless scrap metal.

La Ardilla's team quickly pulled the two bodies from the wrecked vehicle. There was little of anything left of Villanueva, but Mono was still breathing at that time. La Ardilla opened the trunk of the car to see if there was anything of value, and she found a jumper cable that could be readily utilized to ferry Mono into the compound.

Mono still had a hole at the base of his mandible from the time that Zachary Hawk had impaled him upon a fence post, so La Ardilla rammed the end of the jumper cable through the wound and threaded the heavy copper wire through the man's jaw as if he was little more than a fish trapped on a hook. Once done, La Ardilla directed her two boys to drag Mono's still writhing body into the compound.

Upon Mono's arrival to the front porch, La Ardilla flipped the end of the jumper cable over the top of a portico cross beam, and she then instructed the boys to pull on the end of the cable until Mono was suspended in the air. While Mono tried to pull at the cable that was now threaded through his jaw, his legs proceeded to make a repetitive circular motion as if he were merely a man riding a cruiser bicycle in a public park on a Sunday afternoon.

When La Ardilla instructed the boys to secure the end of the battery cable to the porch railing, Mono quickly became a piñata and he was subjected to merciless beatings with a tire iron until he was no longer moving.

"Señor Barker?" Mayordomo asked. "I know you're famished. Please take your fill."

There was no reply.

"Señor Barker?" Mayordomo asked again as Blake Barker was no longer responding.

"Señor Barker?" Mayordomo asked again as Blake Barker was no longer breathing...

Colonel Placard was down to his last magazine of rounds for the FAL rifle in his possession. Thus far, he was able to thwart any attempt that Tercero's men had made to out-flank him. He was safely ensconced behind a shallow berm adjacent to the wood chipper, but his place of refuge would become his own tomb once the cartel foot soldiers had him surrounded.

Placard couldn't believe his own eyes when he saw a Chevy Suburban and a Ford pickup truck smash through the front gate of the compound with guns blazing through every window and every portal. The cavalry had arrived!

The colonel readily recognized Joe Cephas who barrel-rolled out of the back of the pickup truck, but he had no idea of the identity of the black man who accompanied him on the mission. A new colleague, no doubt, but one who was obviously a skilled and seasoned warrior. Joe Cephas and his associate blasted through the ranks of the enemy like a bowler rolling a 300 game!

"I'll be damned!" Placard said when he recognized that the driver of the pickup was his sometimes friend and sometimes enemy, Dr. Ron Shiftless. Ron steered the pickup with his right hand while he reached through the driver's side window of the truck and braced an automatic weapon against the front fender. Ron plowed through his adversaries, running over and crushing numerous cartel members. It appeared that nothing was going to stop Dr. Shiftless until somebody lobbed a live grenade into the cab of the truck as it sped by.

The explosion was deafening, as the roof of the truck's cab was blown skyward. The pickup truck slowly rolled to a stop while flames engulfed what was left of the vehicle.

"It's Ron!" Joe Cephas cried out as he tried to run toward the burning wreck.

"Stop Joe!" Speedy Blexit said as he tackled his new friend while bullet strikes merrily danced in the dirt around them. "It's too late! He's gone!"

The Suburban made a bee-line for Colonel Placard. Musty provided cover fire through the open window on the passenger side while his brother, Harry, jumped out of the cab and grabbed Colonel Parker.

"Hello, Colonel! You don't know us, but were private contractors from the Brownwater Security Group here to rescue you. Harry and Musty Balzac!"

"I don't give a shit about your personal hygienic problems," Placard replied, "just get me the fuck out of here!"

"There's a plane waiting for us at Rancho O'Rear, East of Santa Sangre," Harry answered. "Just relax, Colonel. We'll have you back in the land of the free and the home of the brave in no time."

"Are there any more prisoners in this compound that we need to bail out of here?" Musty called out.

"No! I'm it!" Placard exclaimed. "Everybody else got out! Let's roll."

Once Placard was secured inside the Suburban, Harry threw the vehicle in reverse and negotiated a U-turn before heading toward the exit gate at break-neck speed.

"Wait!" Placard pleaded. "What about Joe Cephas and his friend?"

"Don't sweat it," Musty said as his brother Harry hit the accelerator even harder. "They'll catch up!"

Musty's words rang true when Joe Cephas Smoot and Speedy Blexit caught up to the rear of the Suburban and jumped upon the back bumper while grabbing the top luggage rails on the roof of the vehicle. "See?" Harry asked as the Suburban sped West on Mexican Highway 15. "I swear to God, those boys could out run a Cheetah!"

⚜

Back at the cartel compound, one of the thugs heard screaming from the direction of the wood chipper while Tercero surveyed the scene to take account of the casualties of war.

"It's Perezoso!" One of the foot soldiers called out. "The lower half of his body has been run through the wood chipper, but he's still alive! It looks like the blades got jammed!"

"I'm coming to help," Tercero replied as he ran toward the wood chipper. When Tercero looked down the intake chute, he realized that Perezoso was missing his entire body distal to his navel! A direct crush injury to the lower half of his body apparently kept Perezoso from immediately bleeding to death.

"Get me out of here!" Perezoso pleaded. "My rifle jammed up the machine, and that's the only thing that spared me when I got thrown into this damned meat grinder. Please hurry! The pain is unbearable!"

"Did you happen to hear where the rescue team was taking Colonel Placard?"

"I sure did," Perezoso said. "When they loaded Placard into the Suburban one of the fellows said that there was a plane waiting for them at Rancho O'Rear, East of Santa Sangre."

"That information's very helpful!" Tercero said. "Now, let's get this done. I'm going to restart the device. I'll then hit the drive gear forward and backward until we free the rifle from the blades. After that, we'll be finished in no time."

Tercero restarted the engine on the wood chipper and carefully goosed the drive train front and back repeatedly while his men pulled against the barrel of the FAL rifle that had fouled the spinning blades.

"The gun's free!" One of the cartel members finally exclaimed as he held up the damaged weapon into the air once it had been recovered.

"Good!" Tercero said. "Get every available man over to the motor pool. Let's saddle up and head to Rancho O'Rear. We have to stop Colonel Placard from escaping. If he makes it back to the United States and the authorities there are informed as to what we're doing here, we won't be in business for much longer."

"What about me?" Perezoso asked. "The gun's free now. You need to take care of me!"

"You're absolutely right!" Tercero said as he throttled up the machine to full power and ran what little remained of his colleague through the wood chipper. "Goodbye, Perezoso!"

After Perezoso was liberated from his burdens in life, Tercero turned his head toward his remaining foot soldiers. "Don't forget to take this wood chipper with us. I need some of you boys to hook it up to the back of one of the pickup trucks. We're going to need it later today!"

⸎

"Why are you slowing down?" Musty asked his brother. "You're down to 40 miles per hour now. At this rate, those bastards back at the cartel will eventually catch up to us!"

"I'm going to pull over to the side of the road and let Joe Cephas and Speedy get back inside the Suburban. Make sure you get them fully weaponized. I'm not going to be able to go any faster than about 40 miles per hour or so. We've dropped our oil pressure down to 15 PSI. I think we must have taken a round into the crankcase. If I push it any harder, we'll scour the main bearings and then the block will seize up on us. Besides, how could those ass bags back at the compound have any idea where we're headed?"

"This is Mexico," Placard said. "For this being a shit-hole, third world country, you'd be surprised at how fast information travels through what I call the 'tamale telegraph' around here!"

Once Joe Cephas and Speedy were back inside the vehicle, Harry slowly resumed their westbound journey. "I'm devastated that Ron didn't make it," Joe Cephas said. "He was one self-serving and cynical son of a bitch, but for some reason he was starting to grow on me."

"I knew the guy for years," Placard said. "Half the time I wanted to hug him, and half the time I wanted to throttle him! He was just that kind of guy. Yeah, I'll miss him, too."

Rancho O'Rear was in sight, but unfortunately by now, Tercero and his band of cut throats were less than a hundred yards out from the Suburban, and they were closing fast!

"Looks like we're going to have to shoot our way out of this mess," Harry said. "Speedy? I want you and Joe to chuck a few live rounds at those jokers that are behind us, and try to keep them from fucking us in our tail pipe."

"On it!" With that, Joe and Speedy simply crawled into the luggage compartment of the Suburban and shot out the back window. Speedy took aim at the lead car and held down the trigger until the windshield was splattered with gray matter, causing the trailing cartel car to crash into the lead vehicle from the rear.

"Two down," Speedy said, "but there's still more of them than there are of us!"

"What's the count?" Placard called back to the two vampires.

"There are four vehicles that are still hot on our trail," Joe Cephas replied. "I'm guessing a total of four or so men in each car."

"Keep track of your ammo count," Placard instructed. "A good soldier always knows how many arrows are left in the quiver."

"Too late for that!" Speedy exclaimed. "I'm out!"

"How about you, Joe?" Musty asked.

"Half a magazine," Joe Cephas answered.

"How many more can you take out if that's the case?" Harry asked.

"None," Joe Cephas answered. "I'm saving the rest of the ammo for all of my friends that are riding in this Suburban with me. I'll put a bullet into everybody in here before I'd let those bastards have a chance to run any one of us through that goddamned wood chipper!"

"We can run a lot faster than those boys are driving behind us," Speedy said. "I think it's time we even up the odds just a bit more, Joe."

"Good call," Joe said. "I'll take the car on the right, and why don't you get the one on the left." With that, both of the vampires jumped out of the back of the Suburban and attacked the cars directly behind them.

"Stop!" Placard said. "Whatever you're thinking, it's not going to work!"

Placard's concerns were unfounded. Joe sprinted back to the driver's side of the vehicle that he was planning to disable. He smashed out the windshield, crawled inside, and started to gnaw upon the face of the driver while the other terrified occupants simply opened their car doors and jumped out of the vehicle in abject terror.

Meanwhile, Speedy tested the door handle on the car that he was going to attack, but the door was locked. Nonetheless, Speedy effortlessly kept pace with the cartel vehicle. With a circular motion of his left hand, Speedy requested the driver to roll down his window. Needless to say, the driver was somewhat reluctant to comply with that unusual request.

A rider in the rear seat however, rolled down his back window and aimed the barrel of his gun at Speedy. The vampire grabbed the man's arm and simply ripped the entire extremity out of its socket and cast the disarticulated limb into the weeds on the side of the road way.

"Damn! I should have kept that guy's gun," Speedy said. "I bet it would've come in handy down the road. Oh, well–I guess I'll have to do things the hard way."

Speedy smashed the driver side window and stuck his head through the gaping hole to address the driver. "Hi! My name's Speedy! What's yours?"

The terrified driver began to curse at the vampiro while keeping his hands on the vehicle's steering wheel. "Chinga! Chinga! Chinga!"

"I'm not sure what that means," Speedy said, "but I bet it translates to 'brunch'!" Speedy stuck his fangs into the driver's neck while all the other passengers jumped out of the vehicle and sacrificed themselves to the pavement below.

The landing strip at Rancho O'Rear was now only yards away, but something strange had occurred. Surrounding the twin engine aircraft were approximately a hundred armed men lead by none other than Martillo Grande who was obviously protecting the plane. When Joe and Speedy realized what was about to occur, they both abandoned the vehicles that they had just commandeered and ran to the side of the tarmac to get out of harm's way.

Martillo ordered hundreds of rounds of lead projectiles to be extruded through barrels of his men's automatic weapons. Short work was soon made of the rest of Tercero's crew, affording Martillo's foot soldiers the opportunity to ensure that everybody was dead. Miraculously, Tercero somehow survived the ambush, although he was seriously wounded.

Madam Aragon stepped forth from the throng of foot soldiers and gave Colonel Placard a hug before she took him by the arm and led him directly to Martillo Grande.

"Martillo!" Placard exclaimed. "How on earth did you find us?"

"This is Mexico," Martillo said. "For this being a shit-hole, third world country, you'd be surprised at how fast information travels through what I call the 'tamale telegraph' around here!"

Two of Martillo's men dragged Tercero out of one of the bullet-riddled vehicles and propped him up on his knees at the feet of the cartel leader.

"So," Tercero observed, "the glorious Martillo Grande has resumed control of the cartel yet again. How did this happen?"

"It was destiny that the cartel would again come back to me one day," Martillo replied.

"Why to you?" Tercero asked.

"To the strongest, amigo," Martillo answered. "To the strongest."

Two individuals unhitched the wood chipper and brought it forth before the key in the ignition was turned to the "on" position to start the motor.

"I'd honestly like to give you the grand opportunity to run Tercero through the astilladora de madera while he's still alive, Colonel Placard, but I already promised that I'd give that particular honor to Madam Aragon."

"Although disappointed, I totally understand," Placard said. "Looks like everybody's got an issue or two with this guy."

"If there's nothing else, Colonel Placard," Martillo concluded, "I think that now would be a good time for you and your men to make a hasty retreat back to Los Estados Unidos while you all still have a chance to leave."

"You don't have to ask us twice," Placard said. When he looked over his shoulder, the colonel realized that everybody else was on the plane and Harry Balzac was already firing up the twin-engine craft.

"By chance, if you and I ever pass each other on a dark and lonely street some night in the distant future," Martillo Grande wryly petitioned as he shook Colonel Placard's hand one last time, "let's just pretend that we've never met."

⁂

Deep in the heart of the Yucatan jungle, Lobo was the last to get off the plane after it rolled to a stop on a private dirt airstrip that had just been cut with a bulldozer and a grader that very morning. "Well, so far so good," Lobo said. "It seems to me nobody knew that we were coming this time. I think it's highly likely that we're going to catch Lorena Pastore and her Maya warriors taking a nap by the time we roll into Fortress Camazotz."

"Not so fast," Zachary Hawk said. "Have you forgotten about the battle of Okinawa? After all, you consider yourself to be an amateur historian and you should well know what happened to the American Marines when they attacked that island South of Japan during World War II."

"The difference is that the Japanese knew the Americans were coming, and they remained hidden in the hills to draw the Marines into a killing zone. This is a completely different situation. The Maya have no idea that we're here! This will be a sneak attack. This situation is much more akin to the Japanese attack upon Pearl Harbor than the American attack on Okinawa, or any of the other islands during the Pacific Theater of Operations, for that matter."

"Hope you're right about that."

"Of course I'm right," Lobo said. "After all, I'm the boss!"

"Famous last words," Zachary softly whispered to himself.

"I'm sorry," Lobo said. "Did you just say something?"

"I said that I'm sure that you're correct about this matter, Lobo," Hawk lied. "We've got about a mile hike or more to get to the Fortress Camazotz. I've assembled the two teams of assassins, and for safety measures, I believe it would be smart if each of the teams socially distance about fifteen meters apart. That would deter somebody getting the drop on us."

"Good idea," Lobo said. "It's also time to get the handcuffs on Miguel Pastore and a leash around his neck, just in case he decides to run off into the forest. The first order of business is to go to the fields where the coca plants are being harvested. The crops must be destroyed and burned, or otherwise the Mexican Army will come to our cartel compound to pay us a very unpleasant visit."

After a long hike, Lobo and his team found the coca fields, but oddly enough there were no farmers to be found or evidence of any security at the site. After the foot soldiers and the Brotherhood of the Bat left the fields in a smoldering ruin, Lobo finally muttered the obvious question on everybody's mind. "Where in hell is everybody? What happened to the Maya?"

"Welcome to the Battle of Okinawa," Dr. Hawk answered as he looked at the cartel leader directly in his eyes. "I'm warning you, Lobo. The Maya are setting us up for an ambush."

"Enough!" Lobo answered. "If you keep putting a scare in the others, you'll regret it before the day is over. On to Fortress Camazotz!"

Upon the arrival of Lobo's team to Fortress Camazotz, Lorena was placidly waiting for the invaders at the entry gates.

"What took you so long, Lobo?" Lorena asked. "I've been waiting for you. I see you brought my brother, Miguel, as a hostage. Do you really think that will have any bearing on any of the decisions that I make today?"

"If you love your brother," Lobo answered, "it will."

"What do you want from me and my people?" Lorena asked.

"It's not what I want, Queen Lorena," Lobo explained. "It's what the Mexican government wants. You caused an international incident when you and your warriors crossed the border into Guatemala and kidnapped General Carmel and brought him back to the Yucatan to have him executed here. You pissed off the Guatemalan government. Now they're breathing down the neck of the Mexican government. To avoid open warfare between Mexico and Guatemala, you must turn over all of the warriors that went on the raiding party that captured the general. If you simply do that, I'll let you and the rest of the Maya live alone and in peace."

"General Carmel was a war criminal," Lorena said. "He admitted as much, and had no regrets. During the Guatemalan Civil War, he and his cut throats murdered more than 13,000 Maya civilians. When we executed General Carmel, justice was finally served."

"I just don't give a shit," Lobo said. "Turn over the men that were on the raiding party, or otherwise blood will freely flow today."

"Don't give him anything!" Miguel said before the butt of a rifle struck him in the back of his head to discourage further petitions.

"Even if I wanted to give you the names of the Maya warriors who comprised that raiding party that kidnapped General Carmel, it won't do you any good. Look around. There's nobody here. The people have scattered into the forest and abandoned Fortress Camazotz once and for all. I'm all alone here, now."

"Let's see if I can loosen your tongue," Lobo said. "Dr. Hawk, do you have anything you'd like to ask this woman before we take this matter to the next level?"

"My name is Zachary Hawk. My cousin, Horacio Cloud, came down to the Yucatan to find you. What happened to him?"

"I don't recognize the name," Lorena lied as her eyes glanced up to look at the sky.

"She's not telling the truth!" Hawk said to Lobo. "It's time for blood to be shed!"

"I agree!" Lobo said. "Dr. Hawk, please escort Miguel Pastore to the top of the pyramid. It's time for Lorena to see what I'm capable of doing."

Within a few minutes, Lobo, Zachary, and Miguel Pastore had scaled the pyramid on the outskirts of the fortress. Ready to accept his fate, Miguel closed his eyes and remained stoically motionless beside the other vampire, Dr. Hawk. Lobo Grande circled behind the two men while he brandished an obsidian blade that was clearly an ancient Maya artifact.

Without saying a word, Lobo Grande thrust the knife into the right flank of Zachary Hawk, piercing his kidney. It was a mortal wound from which Hawk would not recover.

"Don't think for a minute that I didn't figure out who you are!" Lobo exclaimed. "All this while, I thought it was a vampiro named Blake Barker who was tormenting my cartel. It was you all along, wasn't it? I met Blake Barker's son, and he's a gringo. I spoke to Mono before he got out of the hospital and he told me that the vampiro that attacked him was un indio, not a gringo. You're a vampiro and un indio, aren't you? Admit it to me now, and your death will be swift. Are you the vampiro that killed Jirafa and the two highway patrol officers that were on my payroll?"

"Yes!" Hawk exclaimed.

"Are you the one who seriously injured my best man, Mono?" Lobo pressed for further details. "What else have you done?"

"Yes! You might as well accuse me of killing Santa Claus and the Easter Bunny!" Hawk answered as he gasped for air while he exsanguinated. "It was me! Finish me off, and make it quick!"

"I lied," Lobo said. "I'll finish you off, but this won't be quick."

When the members of the Brotherhood witnessed Lobo Grande extract the beating heart from the thoracic cavity of Zachary Hawk, they went into full attack mode.

"Uncle Hawk!" Enos cried. "No! I'm going to kill you, Lobo!"

Enos was the spear tip in the charge up the pyramid while the other three members of the Brotherhood followed close behind. Lobo's men made sure that the leader of the cartel would be protected at all cost. Gunfire erupted that quickly brought down Amelia, her brother, and Jesus.

Although Enos was seriously wounded, he was undeterred. Miguel stepped aside to allow Enos to have a clear path to El Lobo. Miguel was bound hand and foot at the time, or otherwise he would have finished off Lobo Grande by himself.

Enos lunged at the cartel leader, but the obsidian knife was plunged deep into the vampire's left eye, and subsequently thrust all the way to the hilt. Once Enos fell, he was quickly dispatched with a swift decapitation.

"So, these little ingrates have turned on me?" Lobo said to his foot soldiers. "Drag these baby bats out into the forest and bash their brains out! Be quick about it!"

Eight of Lobo's foot soldiers tied ropes around the necks of Amelia, Isaac, and Jesus and dragged them deep into the jungle where they were to be executed. Waiting for them however were El Dolor, Joaquin, and the Maya warriors who were able to quickly dispatch with the cartel thugs without firing a shot.

"We should kill these children now," Joaquin said. It's the strict policy of the Maya that each and every vampiro should be immediately exterminated."

"Not this time," El Dolor replied. "Queen Lorena has a plan for these children. I want you men to tie each of these vampires to the trunk of a stout tree and then guard them carefully. Bring pig blood to them. It will help expedite their recovery."

"Wait!" Joaquin exclaimed. "What's this all about?"

"Queen Lorena will explain it to you soon enough," El Dolor said. "In the meantime, you need to come with me to the Cave of Camazotz, Joaquin. Better bring the two catch poles that we use when we have to capture and put down rabid dogs from time to time."

"Are we were going after rabid dogs?" Joaquin asked.

"What we're going to catch today might very well carry rabies, but they're certainly *not* dogs," El Dolor explained.

Back at the pyramid, Lobo Grande was facing a dilemma. Clearly, Lorena would be willing to sacrifice her brother to protect the Maya people. Clearly Lorena would be willing to sacrifice herself to protect the Maya people. What to do? Perhaps if she was soiled, she would be forced to live in shame. It was the one avenue that Lobo Grande had not explored.

"Miguel, I want you to sit at the bottom of the pyramid and watch what I'm going to do to your sister, Lorena."

"Leave her alone, Lobo," Miguel pleaded. "Give me a chance to talk to her and I'll extract the information that you're looking for."

"Too late for that," Lobo said as he disrobed. "Tell me, Lorena, would you like me to be on top of you or behind you?"

Lorena stood a few yards beyond the base of the pyramid while she also disrobed in an effort to entice El Lobo to fulfill his wanton lust.

"What makes you think that I wouldn't want to be on top of you?" Lorena asked flirtatiously as she lifted her breasts with both hands and engaged in an erotic, serpent-like, choreiform dance.

It was all that El Lobo could bear. He ran down the pyramid, and when he was only inches away from reaching Lorena, he stepped directly upon the foliage covered tarp that had hidden the mouth of the cenote.

As Lobo fell deep into the cavern, Lorena quickly redressed before she recovered the obsidian knife that the cartel leader had left on top of his pile of clothing on the lower tier of the pyramid. Lorena picked up the blade and deeply cut the palm of her left hand to allow blood to pour down into the cenote.

As Lorena's blood splattered upon the sheer walls of the seemingly bottomless pit, El Dolor and Joaquin appeared at the edge of the forest walking two of the giant carnivorous bats that had been recovered from the Cave of Camazotz. Each bat was held in check with the six foot long catch pole that had a looped noose at the end. Both men approached Lorena for an executive conference.

"Is this really necessary?" El Dolor wondered. "Maybe the fall killed him."

Just then, a faint voice could be heard from the bottom of the shaft. "Help! I'm hurt! Lorena, what have you done to me? Get me out of here!"

"Does that answer your question?" Lorena asked with a wicked smile. "Allow the great creatures to smell the blood on the walls of the cenote, and then release them from the catch poles."

El Dolor and Joaquin followed the orders from their queen. After the great bats were allowed to sniff around the mouth of the cenote, they were freed from their catch poles. One of the great creatures began to crawl down the wall of the pit to investigate what was at the bottom of the shaft, but surprisingly one of the great beasts turned upon Lorena as it smelled the blood that oozed from the palm of her left hand.

The animal opened its mouth and was about to devour the Queen of the Maya. Although Miguel's feet were tied at his ankles, he was still able to leap forward from the base of the pyramid to tackle the creature. Sadly, Miguel's hands were also still bound together which prevented him from defending himself. The great bat grabbed Miguel by the face and proceeded to slowly climb down the wall of the cenote to the bottom of the shaft.

"No, Miguel!" Lorena cried out, but it was too late. The screams from the two men were heard from the bottom of the pit before the Maya villagers appeared from the jungle and quickly placed enormous tree trunks across the mouth of the cenote to make certain that nothing escaped.

Lorena quickly composed herself. After all, she was now royalty. "Take me to the surviving members of the Brotherhood of the Bat. I have a specific mission for those children."

Joaquin and El Dolor brought Lorena into the jungle where the three vampires were securely tied to tree trunks. "My people will nurse you back to health," Lorena explained, "but when you recover, you'll be working for me. I have a mission for you, and if you want to live, you'll do as I say."

Lorena pulled out the piece of paper that had been given to her by the late General Carmel before he was executed. "I have a list of names on this sheet of paper. It also includes the addresses where they live. They're all in Guatemala, and they were members of a group of assassins that worked for a very evil man named General Carmel, who now happens to be dead. These men were known as, Los Carcineros. They participated in the genocide of thousands of the Maya people. Once you have healed from your gunshot wounds, which you assuredly will, you'll go down into Guatemala and kill each and every one of the sons of bitches. Joaquin and El Dolor will now be in charge of your Brotherhood. Is everyone agreeable to this order?"

The three vampires agreed without hesitation.

Joaquin took Lorena aside for a private conversation. "Do you think this is a good idea? After all, it has long been the policy of the Maya people to exterminate any vampires that we encounter."

"I want you and El Dolor to lead these children into battle," Lorena explained. "Once each and every member of Los Carcineros has been killed, I'll then have you and your men decapitate these children, burn their bodies, and bury their heads in a separate location in the jungle."

"Should we resume the cultivation of coca plants?" El Dolor asked. "After all, this was a very profitable business for us."

"No," Lorena answered. "Let all of the fields remain fallow for now. It's time for us to get out of the illegal drug business once and for all and tackle a new economic venture."

"What do you have in mind?" El Dolor asked.

"Eco-tourism" Lorena exclaimed. "We'll turn Fortress Camazotz into a rustic resort. Liberal Democrats from the United States, amongst other white idiots who drive Volvos, wear Birkenstock shoes, and are perpetually filled with self-loathing, environmental guilt, will pay a fortune to come here. I tell you now, we'll make a killing out here in the middle of nowhere!"

"Are you sure about this?" Joaquin asked.

"Indeed," Lorena answered. "After all, not only am I the Queen of the Maya, *Yo soy una gran bruja.*"

⚬⟞⟊⟐⟊⟝⚬

"That was close," Celena said to Russian Bear, "but I don't think that guy saw us."

"Are you certain that the man we passed at the corner was a member of the cartel?" Bear asked as he and his two young companions sped toward the American consulate in the heart of Mexico City.

"I'd stake my life on it," Celena said.

"How can you be so certain?" Bear asked.

"After the Brotherhood killed Father Garrapa, the man we just now passed on the road was the very same person who drove us in a big van all the way back to the cartel compound once we left Santa Sangre."

"Well, he might not have recognized the passengers in this vehicle," Bear said, "but if he did see this car, he might have realized that it was one of the vehicles that had been stolen from the cartel motor pool. Stay sharp and keep your eyes peeled wide open."

"Don't talk like that," Nathan said. "You're starting to scare me, Uncle Bear. I don't want those bad guys to find us!"

"There is only one thing that you can do, Nathan," Russian Bear said as he parked the car a few blocks from the consulate.

"What's that?" Nathan asked.

"Be brave, my little friend," Bear instructed. "Be brave."

The three travelers plowed out of the parked car and briskly walked toward the American consulate in an attempt to get safe passage to the United States, but something caught Celena's eye that had alarmed her. "Something's wrong, Uncle Bear!"

"What is it, Celena?"

"The same car passed us twice," Celena explained. "Each time, the car slowed down and the two passengers took a long look at us!"

"Turn right at this alleyway that we're coming up upon," Bear instructed, "and let's see if we can find our way to the American consulate down a side street."

By then, it was too late. The car in question passed again for a third time, and on this occasion, the vehicle pulled over the curb and blocked the three travelers from turning down the alleyway. The driver and passenger jumped out of the car and rushed at Russian Bear and his two young companions. Each of the assailants was armed with a pistol, but fortunately, they would turn out to be no match for Celena.

Nathan cowered while Russian Bear struggled with the driver. As the Bear was a large and imposing man, he was able to grab the assailant's right arm that held the pistol. With a supreme effort, the Russian doctor forced the pistol to point directly skyward. A technical stalemate was achieved when Bear pinned his adversary's body against the side of the car.

Unbeknownst to Russian Bear, Celena had already dispatched the first assailant by crushing his windpipe with a furious blow to his throat. As the man that she had tussled with fell to his knees gasping for air, Celena turned her attention to the thug who was battling with the Russian.

Leaping upon the roof of the car, Celena extracted the pistol that the cartel henchman clutched. Although she had never fired a weapon before, she had the wherewithal to pull back the hammer of the pistol before she pulled the trigger that sent a hot smoking round through the crown of the man's head.

People who are walking along the street averted their eyes as if there was nothing to be seen. While Celena grabbed the two dead assailants and easily pulled them into the alleyway, Russian Bear and Nathan got into the car and pulled it off the sidewalk to park it in a proper fashion in an attempt to avoid further public scrutiny.

Bear and Nathan sat patiently while Celena quickly dined on the two dead assailants in the vacant alley. Although she lacked incisor canines, Celena had the strength to simply rip open the chest and abdominal cavity of each of the dead cartel members to consume their hearts and livers. When finished, Celena calmly crawled into the backseat of the car with a demeanor that was surprisingly calm, cool, and collected.

"Nice work, Celena!" Bear proclaimed.

"I don't think so!" Nathan professed. "You're a mess! You're not a very tidy eater, if you want my opinion. You've got blood all over yourself. That's just disgusting."

"Is that so?" Celena asked as she wiped the blood from her face and hands upon the back of Nathan's shirt.

"If you do that again," Nathan boldly proclaimed, "I'll box your ears!"

"Any time, you little pip squeak!" Celena laughed. "Where to now, Uncle Bear? Are you still going to try and get us to the consulate?"

"I don't think that would be a good idea right now," Bear said. "After what happened just now, there's a good chance that we'll all get apprehended."

"Well, where do we go from here?" Nathan asked. "Why don't you just drive all the way back to the United States and take us with you?"

"As I'm not your legal guardian," Russian Bear explained, "I'd never be allowed to bring you across the border."

"Why don't you just hire a human smuggler?" Celena asked. "There must be ten or twenty million illegal aliens from Mexico living in the United States. How do you think they got there?"

"That would never work in our situation," Bear answered.

"Well, why not?"

"Human smuggling, just like the illegal, cross-border, under age, sex-traffic business is predominantly controlled by the cartels."

"What's the problem?"

"You just escaped from that kind of life, Celena. If we get double-crossed by a coyote, I'd be dead, and you and Nathan would end up as sex slaves," Bear explained. "Is that worth the risk?"

"I suppose not," Celena reluctantly concluded.

"Cartel coyotes are *exactly* the kind of people we're trying to avoid. Don't worry, kids," Bear assuredly replied as he started the engine and slowly steered the car away from the curb. "We'll think of something. Yeah, that's the ticket. We'll think of something..."

"Wow!" J.D. Brewster said. "That's quite a story. I'm glad you lived to tell about it. Someday, you should think about writing a book about what you've been through, but you should try to peddle it as a work of fiction. After all, nobody's ever going to believe something like that could've really happened to you."

"I don't think I could ever write a book about what happened to me," Birdy said.

"Well, why not?"

"I hate to read a book that has an open ending. I want to know exactly what happens to all of the characters in the story. There are people that moved in and out of my life throughout this whole ordeal, and to this day, I don't know their ultimate fate. After all,

Elder Joseph has disappeared as well as the teenage Navajo vampire that tried to kill me. I'm not even going to speculate what happened to Dr. Zachary Hawk after his life went off the rails."

"This is where you and I will disagree," Brewster said. "Mystery and uncertainty are part of life. The only important character that had any existential bearing on your personal story was Captain Noche who was the head of the Vampiro Containment Unit, and he's dead. Parker told me that this guy went rogue and took it upon himself to murder anybody infected with, or even exposed to, the virus that causes human vampirism. Even that doesn't matter now, because Noche's long gone, is he not?"

"Perhaps you're right."

"Of course I'm right!" Brewster crowed. "Besides, a clever author will likely leave hints here and there about the fate of any important characters that were left out on the clothes line and flapping about in the proverbial breeze."

"You think so?"

"I know so. It just takes an intelligent reader to find the clues. In any event, I'm just sorry that you never had an opportunity to disperse your brother's ashes upon the beach at Galveston. Booker would've appreciated that."

"Well, I certainly hope he's happy that his earthly remains ended up in Mexico. By the way, did you tell Parker that I was coming?" Birdy asked Dr. J.D. Brewster as she gave him a big hug.

"Oh, hell no!" Brewster answered. "I most certainly did not!"

"What?! Why not?"

"I figured by now that you would've realized that Parker Coxswain is an absolute turd and that you've already squandered a considerable amount of unrequited love on an individual who's not particularly worthy of your valuable time or affection. If that's indeed the case," Brewster explained, "then this would be a good opportunity for me to make my move on you. I can see it now, Dr. Marshall. As the old saying goes, I'm 'in like Flynn.' Tell me now, Baby Bird, if I have any kind of chance here!"

Birdy Marshall furrowed her brow and laughed as she playfully slapped Brewster in the middle of his sternum with the palm of her right hand. "Slow down, cowboy! I thought you would've found somebody to love on your own accord by now."

"Been busy."

"Humans are social creatures and we're hard-wired to pair-bond. Having a mate is what makes us complete as spiritual beings. Life is short."

"So, I've heard. Let's wrap things up so we can get you back to see Dr. Coxswain," Brewster said. "After all, he seems to be rather fond of you."

"Where is he now?" Birdy asked.

"He's giving a lecture on anatomy and physiology to the freshman medical school class right down the hallway," Brewster explained. "Come with me and I'll take you there."

Brewster escorted Dr. Birdy Marshall to the first floor lecture hall auditorium. "He's likely standing at the podium. Peek through the door window and lightly tap on the glass, Birdy," Brewster suggested. "Maybe you can get his attention."

Birdy cupped her hands over her face to shield her eyes from the glare of the overhead fluorescent lights imbedded in the hallway ceiling as she peered through the window.

"Well," Brewster asked, "did he see you?"

The enormous smile on Birdy's face told Dr. Brewster everything he needed to know.

THE END

COMPLETE GLOSSARY OF MEDICAL TERMS

VAMPIRO, VOLS. 1, 2, AND 3

anterolateral: Referring to the position found in front of and to the side of a subject.

blast: An immature cell that is a precursor to a more mature subset.

choreiform gyrations: A writhing, snakelike motion.

cloacal aperture: The exit site of the combined rectal, vaginal, urinary tract repository found among lower vertebrate lifeforms such as birds and reptiles.

Coomb's test: A clinical laboratory test to evaluate the presence of pathologic antibodies against circulating erythrocytes. A positive test by either direct or indirect methods confirms an immune hemolytic disease process.

coprophagic arthropod: An insect whose dietary requirements include (either partially or exclusively) the feces of other organisms. A nasty bug that eats shit.

creatinine: A nitrogenous waste product cleared by the kidneys. A rising creatinine level in the serum is consistent with renal dysfunction.

diener: A mortuary assistant.

ectoderm: One of the three primary embryonic tissue planes that constitute the outer layer of cells in embryonic development.

endoderm: One of the three primary embryonic tissue planes that constitute the inner layer of cells in embryonic development.

enteral: Referring to the gastrointestinal/digestive system.

erythroblast: An immature bone-marrow-dwelling precursor to a circulating red blood cell.

erythrocyte: A circulating red blood cell.

haptoglobin: An alpha-2 globulin in serum whose concentration is inversely proportional to the severity of active hemolysis.

hematocrit: A measurement in percentage of what proportion of the blood is actually made up of red blood cells.

hemithorax: One side of the chest cavity.

hemoglobin: The oxygen-carrying molecule found within red blood cells.

hemolysis: The clinical presentation of the pathological rupture of circulating red blood cells by either an immune or nonimmune process.

hemosiderin: A storage form of iron. An increase of this substance in the urine documented by clinical laboratory assay is found during episodes of active hemolysis.

heterozygous: The clinical state of having different genetic alleles within a chromosomal profile.

homozygous: The clinical state of having the same (matched) genetic alleles within a chromosomal profile.

hypoxia: A pathological clinical state where there is a low concentration of tissue oxygen.

icteric sclerae: A visible yellowish discoloration noted in the white part of the eyeball as a consequence of a rising serum bilirubin level.

inflammatory mitogenic cytokines: A biological or chemical substance that has the ability to induce cellular division, generally in reference to the induction of an immune response.

immunohistochemistry: Referring to a pathology service technique that selectively utilizes various immune markers to help ascertain the nature or characteristics of tissues that are being analyzed.

immunologically nude mice: A subset of rodents that lack an intact immune system.

indirect bilirubin: A by-product of hemoglobin degradation that is elevated in the serum in the setting of pathological hemolysis.

interphalangeal joint: A joint found between the digits of a finger or toe.

jaundice: A yellowish discoloration of the skin as a consequence of elevated serum bilirubin levels, often noted as a consequence of hepatic dysfunction or extraordinarily severe hemolysis.

LDH: Lactate dehydrogenase. A chemical marker that may be found elevated in the serum during a pathological hemolytic event.

Loop of Henle: A nephron component distal to the proximal convoluted tubule.

MCHC: Mean corpuscular hemoglobin concentration, which is an assay to determine the hemoglobin within the confines of circulating erythrocytes.

mediastinum: The center of the thorax where the heart and great vessels dwell.

mesoderm: One of the three primary embryonic tissue planes that constitute the middle layer of cells in embryonic development.

micturition: Urination.

Neisseria gonorrhoeae: A specific bacterium responsible for the infectious sexually transmitted disease known as gonorrhea.

nephron: One of many microscopic filtration units found in the kidney.

parenteral: Beyond the realm of the gastrointestinal tract, usually as a reference to nutritional support administered through an intravenous route.

phlebotomy: The therapeutic removal of a specified amount of circulating blood.

porphyria cutanea tarda: A metabolism disorder of a hemoglobin substructure.

priapism: A pathological unrelenting penile erection often seen as a complication of sickle cell disease.

protozoan parasite: A eukaryotic single-cell infectious organism.

pruritic vesicle: A skin blister with associated itching.

quadriplegia: A paralytic condition that involves both the upper and lower extremities.

reticulocyte: A new red blood cell that just entered circulation from the bone marrow.

sternocleidomastoid: A muscle in the anterolateral position on either side of the neck.

supraclavicular: The region of the body located above the thorax and collarbone.

trypanosome: A eukaryotic single-cell organism that is often parasitic.

COMPLETE GLOSSARY OF SPANISH WORDS AND MEXICAN SLANG EXPRESSIONS

VAMPIRO, VOLS. 1, 2, AND 3

a la ver, gatos y ratones: Literal translation, "to see cats and rats." A clever play on words, as "a la verga," translates into English as "into the cock (penis)."

abuelito: Little grandfather.

Adelante, Comandante: Later, commander. This is similar to the expression "See you later, alligator."

adios: goodbye

agua fria: Cold water.

agua preciosa: Precious water.

ahora: Now.

alacran: Scorpion.

albahaca: Basil herb; often used in huevo limpia ceremonies.

amarillo gusano de maguey: Yellow maguey worm (caterpillar).

amarillo: Yellow.

americanos: Americans.

amigo: Friend.

Ardilla: Squirrel.

arrachera: A reference to carne arrachera, which is a relatively inexpensive cut of beefsteak.

arroz, frijoles, y un delicioso pod de chile caliente en ocasiones: Rice, beans, and a delicious hot chile pod on occasion.

astilladora de madera: Wood chipper.

Avenida de los Muertos: Avenue of the Dead. **Azteca:** Aztec.

bambino: Baby.

bandito: Bandit.

barrio: Hispanic neighborhood.

bastardo: Bastard.

basura: Trash.

blanco: White.

bolillo: A bread roll.

Bromisto: Joker

bruja: Witch or sorceress.

Buen Ojo: Good Eye.

Buena Comida: Good Food.

buena suerte, senor: Good luck, sir.

Buenas noches, Tio Pepe. Buenas noches, mi amigo viejo: Good night, Uncle Pepe. Good night, my old friend.

Cabeza de Bala: Bullet Head.

cabrito: Kid. Young goat

cabron: Goat. An insult.

caldo de res: Beef soup.

Calle Vampiro: Vampire Street; the name of a fictitious Mexican drug cartel.

cálmate: calm

capitan nuevo: New captain.

cara de temptacion, querpo de repentamiento: An old saying that translates as "the face of temptation, the body of repentance."

casa: House.

cerdo viejo: old pig

cerrado: Closed.

cerveza fria: Cold beer.

chema: Brother.

chilongo: A derogatory word for a resident of Mexico City.

chingar no: Fuck no.

Chino: Chinese.

chispas: Sparks.

chiste: Joke.

chistoso: Clown.

chones: Underwear.

chupacabra: A goat sucker; a mythical bloodsucking monstrous hairless canid, supposedly dwelling in Latin America, Texas, and other regions of the US Southwest.

cinco minutos, mas o menos: Five minutes, more or less.

ciudad: city

cocina: Kitchen.

Cojo Gato: Cat Fucker.

cojones: Boxes. Slang word for testicles.

comadreja: Weasle.

con crema: with cream

corazon: Heart.

criadillas: Crickets.

cucaracha: Roach.

cuerpo: Body or corpse.

culo: Ass

curandera: Folk healer.

coyote: In addition to referring to a wild, dog-like canid, the word is also a slang term for a human smuggler.

desayuno: Breakfast.

desierta: Desert

Diablo: The Devil.

dinero: Money.

Dios mio: My God.

drogas: Drugs (illicit).

El Codo: A frugal man. This is a derogatory slang word for a resident of Monterrey, Mexico.

El Diablo: The Devil.

El Gato: The Cat.

El Gran Brujo: The Grand Wizard.

El Grifo: The Gryphon.

El Mago: The Magician.

El Martillo Grande: The Big Hammer

El Mayo: The Maya.

El Primero: The First (in command).

El Punto: The tip of a knife, or a point.

El Sapo: The Toad.

El Segundo: The Second (in command).

El Submarino Amarillo: The Yellow Submarine.

El Tor: A nickname for the leader of the Calle Vampiro drug cartel. El Tor is a deadly strain of bacteria that causes the infectious disease cholera.

El Toro Grande: The Big Bull.

en la tierra de los ciegos, el que tiene un ojo es rey: In the land of the blind, he who has one eye is king.

en tu calaca: In your skull.

entre menos burros, mas elotes: An old saying that translates as "the fewer donkeys, the more corn for everyone else to share."

eres Indio nativo, verdad: You are a native Indian, true.

eres Tejano, verdad: You are a Texan, true.

eres un cerdo: You're a pig.

eres un gran hero: you are a grand hero

esclavas: Slaves.

eres feliz americano: you are a happy American

eres un serpiente de pantalon: you are a trouser snake

ese: A slang word that roughly translates as "dude."

Esquela de la Publica: Public School.

Estado de Coahuila: The state of Coahuila. One of the thirty-one federated states in the country of Mexico.

Estado de Jalisco: The state of Jalisco. One of the thirty-one federated states in the country of Mexico.

estas listo?: Are you ready?

Estofado: Stew

Estoy aqui: I am here.

estrago: Damage.

exactamente: Exactly.

federale: Federal. An abbreviation for the Mexican national police or policeman

fiesta: Party.

frijoles refritos: Refried beans.

futbol: Soccer.

gato hembra: pussy cat

gente: People.

gracias, señor: Thank you, sir.

gran bruja: great witch

gringo: Slang word meaning a male Anglo individual.

guayabera: A stylish short-sleeved man's dress shirt.

guedo: A derogatory slang word for a male Anglo.

gusano rojo: Red worm (caterpillar).

hacienda: A grand estate.

hasta la vista, jefe: Until we see each other again, chief.

higado: liver organ

hipopotamo: Hippopotamus.

hola: Hello.

hombre: Man.

hombre simpatico: A likable man.

hora: Hour

Hormiga: Ant.

Idioto: Idiot.

huevo limpia: A chicken egg used in a spiritual cleansing ceremony.

huitlachoche: a bitter yet edible corn fungus

Japones: Japanese.

jefe: Chief.

Jesus salva: Jesus saves.

Jirafa: Giraffe.

joto: A derogatory slang word for a gay male.

jovencito: A small male child.

la bruja de la desierta: desert witch

la cucaracha: cockroach. An alternate meaning is a derogatory, yet accurate slang expression which describes a liberal democrat from a "blue state."

La Frontera: The Frontier.

La Mordita: The Bite. This term reflects the deeply entrenched political corruption throughout Mexico.

la pequeña gato hembra: vulgar slang for female vulva

la rana pequeña: the little frog

La Ranchera: A female ranch hand.

La Reina del Bosque: Queen of the Forest

La Reina Mexicana: Mexican Queen

ligado: Liver.

lima: Lime.

listo: ready

llaves: Keys.

llevar a este vampiro y decapitarlo: Take this vampire and decapitate him.

Lobo Grande: Big Wolf

lo siento, senor: I am sorry, sir.

Los Dorados: Warriors who served with Pancho Villa during the Mexican Revolution.

Los Estados Unidos de America: The United States of America.

Los Estados Unidos de Mexico: The United States of Mexico.

los huevos amarillos: The yellow eggs.

los papeles correctos: The correct papers.

madera: Wood.

madre: Mother.

maldito torpe: A clumsy oaf.

malinchismo: sad or melancholy

maloliente: Malodorous.

mano-a-mano: Hand-to-hand.

mañana: Tomorrow.

mas jamon por este par de juevos: Too much ham for these eggs.

mayordomo: The manager of a hacienda.

Maya: A pre-Columbian Mesoamerican civilization that lived predominantly in the Yucatan region of Mexico.

Mexicanos: Mexicans.

mescal: A distilled alcoholic beverage made from any type of agave plant found in Mexico. Mescal is a spirit that is thought by many not to be as refined as tequila.

mija: Term of endearment. A conjugate word from "mi hija," meaning "my daughter."

mijo: Term of endearment. A conjugate word from "mi hijo," meaning "my son."

mineros: Miners.

minuto: Minute.

mira: Look.

mojado: A derogatory term for any illegal alien.

momento: moment

Mono: Monkey.

mozuelo: Youngster.

muchachos: Boys.

mucho: Much.

mujeres: Women

murcielago: A flying mammal commonly known as a bat.

muy deliciosa: Very delicious.

nalgas: Buttocks; ass end.

nariz: Nose.

niño: a small boy.

no cages donde comes: Don't shit where you eat.

no quiero más problemas: I don't want more problems

no se: I don't know.

noches: Night.

Novia de Christo: The Bride of Christ. A term referring to the Catholic Church.

ojos amarillos: Yellow eyes.

orale cabron: Pay attention, you goat.

Oso Negro: Black Bear.

Padre: Father

Paloma de la Noche: Dove of the Night.

pan dulce: Sweet bread.

para sangre caliente: For hot blood.

parasito: Parasite.

Parilla Tejas: Texas Grill.

pendejo, donde come no se caga: Dumbass, you don't eat where you shit.

Pequena Rana: Little Frog.

perro: Dog.

pez muerto: Dead fish.

Pharmacia del Norte: Pharmacy of the North.

pinche gringo salado policia: Damned salty Anglo policeman.

Pirata: Pirate.

pito: Gun.

pobrecito: poor little thing

policia local de Juarez: Local police of Juarez.

Primero: The First. In the context of this novel, the first in command.

puerta: Door.

puesto de observar: Look-out

puntas: tips- a culinary reference to brisket beef tips

punto: The point of a knife.

puta: A derogatory slang word for a prostitute.

que desdichado: how sad

que huele: That stinks.

que magnifico: How magnificent.

que onda, carnal: What's happening, bro.

que padre: The literal translation is "what father." This is a Mexican expletive similar to the American expression "cool, daddy-o."

que pasa: what's happening

quesadilla: An open-face grilled flour tortilla covered with cheese, among other food items.

queso fundido: Grilled cheese.

queso menonita: A white cheese originating from the Mennonite settlers in Chihuahua.

quete: A slang word for pistol.

quien es mas malo: Who is the baddest.

quinceanera: a debutante party held in honor of a Latina who has reached her fifteenth birthday.

Rancho Feliz: Happy Ranch.

raton: Rodent.

Ratoncito Perez: Perez, the little rat. Hispanic version of the tooth fairy.

Redencion y salvacion: Redemption and salvation

regalo especial: Special gift.

Reina de Bosque: Queen of the Forest.

Reina de los elefantes: Queen of the Elephants.

Rio Bravo: Brave River; alternate name for the Rio Grande that separates Texas from Mexico.

Rosquilla: Donut

routa: Route or pathway.

salados: Salty.

sandia: Watermelon

Sangre de Indios: Indian blood. This is a specific type of obsidian volcanic glass.

sangre impia: Unholy blood.

Santa Sangre: Sacred Blood.

Segundo: The Second. In the context of this novel, the second in command.

Señor: Mister.

Señor Stewart, eres un gran heroe: Mr. Stewart, you are a great hero.

serpiente de pantalon: Trouser snake.

Siete Leguas: A prized brand of tequila.

¡Silencio, saco mentiroso de caca! ¿Por qué sigues tratando de proteger a este vampiro?: Silence, you sack of shit! Why are you protecting this vampire?

simpatico: Agreeable or likable.

sin fuerte: Without strength.

soldados: Soldiers.

Soldado Primero: First Soldier

Soldado Segundo: Second Soldier

sopapilla: Fried bread.

te aye watchto: I'll be seeing you.

te gusta mota: Would you like some marijuana.

Tejanos: Texans.

Tejas: Texas.

tequila viejo con lima: aged tequila with lime

Tercero: The Third. In the context of this novel, the third in command.

tia: Aunt.

Tiburon: Shark.

tiempo: Time.

Tio Chico: A brand of carbonated water.

tio: Uncle.

tonel de pollo: Chicken coop.

toques: A parlor game where participants receive dangerous electrical shocks.

torta: A sandwich served on a bolillo bread roll with meat, vegetables, or avocado.

tu eres el vampiro con el nombre Morales: You are the vampire with the name Morales.

un corazon de cerdo: Pig heart.

un crudo pinche guey: A jerk with a hangover.

un gato grande: a big cat

un momento, por favor: One moment, please.

una pista fria: Slang for a cold beer.

va chinga un gato, gringo, mientras que la miedra tu abuela: Go fuck a cat, white boy, while I'm fucking your grandmother.

va chingar mi abuela: vulgar invitation to have sex with a grandmother

vampiro: Vampire.

verdad: True.

viejo: Old.

voltios: Volts.

y: and.

y un barril grande: And a big barrel.

y un desierto delicioso: And a delicious dessert.

Yo soy indio: I am Indian

Yo soy mas malo, pendejo: I am the baddest, you dumbass.

Yo soy una gran bruja: I am a great witch.

Zopelotes: Vultures.

zorillo: Skunk.

PRAISE FOR THE VAMPIRO SERIES

"I was thrilled to see that Dr. Hill was able to resurrect many of the beloved characters that he first introduced to the public in his masterpiece The DNR Trilogy. This new work of fiction is a story that I wanted never to end. I'm grateful that Thomas Cavaretta pressed Dr. Hill to get on board with this project."

— S. Carol Maple, LPN. Casa Grande, Arizona

"Stunning in its scope and depth, this is not like any work of fiction that I have ever read related to the subject of human vampirism. At times, I found that Dr. Hill's soaring command of written English to be no less than breathtaking."

— Kelli Terrell, Tucson, Arizona

"Although certainly not a sequel to the triumphant DNR Trilogy in the truest sense of the word, this new work of fiction, Vampiro, certainly continues to espouse the mystical theme that everything in the universe is connected somehow."

— Vicky Atkinson, RN, Kona, Hawaii

"This is not a novel that one can casually read, as it is an intense and disturbing work of fiction. It's all here: the evidence, the history, the legends, and the truth. ... At some point, you will invariably ask yourself, "Am I really beginning to believe?"

—J. C. Sullivan, Tucson, Arizona

"Thomas Cavaretta's deep and reverential insight into the Hispanic culture of the American Southwest has bestowed upon this amazing work of fiction an undeniable patina of authenticity."

— C. Darter, Tucson, Arizona

"Dr. Hill's scientific rationale for the possibility of human vampirism is certainly compelling. Just as important, the authors are able to successfully portray the perpetual human quest for salvation, even amid the darkest hour just before dawn."

— Wynn Madden, Tucson, Arizona

"If one were to scrutinize the lore of human vampirism dating all the way back to the fifteenth century, one would find that it has generally consisted of little more than a ghastly folk tale about some desperate individual who rendered his immortal soul to the devil. Well, what if vampirism were actually a bona fide, horizontally transmissible illness? Hill and Cavaretta have certainly made a strong argument that such an infectious disease process is not only feasible but also possible. Frankly, I find that terrifying."

—Judy Kahler, RN, Kona, Hawaii

www.ingramcontent.com/pod-product-compliance
Lightning Source LLC
Chambersburg PA
CBHW070821020826
48982CB00014B/148